UNSPOKEN SECRETS

LYNETTE MATHER

Outskirts Press, Inc.
Denver, Colorado

TFIC
12/11
CL

Outskirts Press, Inc.
http://www.outskirtspress.com

ISBN: 978-1-4327-8057-9

Outskirts Press and the "OP" logo are trademarks belonging to Outskirts Press, Inc.

PRINTED IN THE UNITED STATES OF AMERICA

Dedication

First and foremost, I'd like to dedicate this book to my husband, Jimmy, who never gave up on me, and who gave me the courage to keep writing when I couldn't find the words to put on paper. He's my rock, my love and my life. Thank you for everything you've done to make this book a reality. I love you for so many reasons, and I thank you for the dedication that you've always had in regards to reading and re-reading, editing and re-editing and for being one of the greatest men I've ever known. Thanks for holding my hand when I thought that I was going to fall and for making me try again. This book wouldn't have been possible without you. Thank you from the bottom of my heart for everything you've done. I love you.

To my children: Jessica, Kevin and Deven, for being my inspiration in life which led to this book, and the reason I wrote it. I love you so much.

To my step-children: Molly, Amanda and Jenna, for letting me be a part of your life, I'm thankful for it.

To my grandbabies: Nathan Thor, Journey Rose, and Baby B, for making me smile. All of you are so precious I couldn't imagine my life without you.

To my dad: Thank you for always being there for me. You've been there for me in more ways than I can count, and you've always been a great influence in my life, and someone I can talk to about anything. Thanks for everything, dad.

To my mom: Who passed away in 1989. She was killed by drunk drivers, and I miss her every day. I wish she were here to read my book, but I know she's smiling down on me from heaven.

To my step-mom, Lynn: Whose love and encouragement has always meant a great deal to me.

To my sisters: Lisa and Chris, who pushed me to get published and love the way I write. Thanks for your support and for always being there to talk, oh, and for always making me laugh so hard that I can't catch my breath. I love you both.

To my little brother, Norm: Who has always has the ability to make me laugh, and who is a big part of my life. I love you.

To my extended family: Thanks, I love all of you.

To my bosses: Karen, Gerry and Jeff, who believes in family first, and is always there to listen when I need to talk. Thanks Jeff for reading, and giving me your honest opinion on what I write.

To my co-workers: Sherry P, Kenny, Benny, Shannon, and Lindsay who encouraged me to pursue my books, and who make me laugh when I'm feeling down.

To all of you that I work with: thanks for being my second family.

To my closest friends: Terese, Donna, Crissy, Sherry Lord, Karen S., and all my other friends, thanks for letting me in your life, and giving me support in everything I do. You're always there for me. Its friends like you who deserve the best in life. I love all of you.

To Phil and Christine, who are wonderful people, and thanks for believing in me.

To a couple of special teachers: Chris Drews, and Patrick Foley, for reading this book and believing in me, thank you so much.

PRELUDE

The day started out much like any other day in Kimmy Washington's life, except for the dark swirl of mist that she discovered outside her bedroom window this morning when she awoke. Being the brave teen that she is, she opened the window and watched the dark mist slowly enter her room, where it drifted over to her bedroom door, opened it, and slowly made its way down the hall to her parent's bedroom. Kimmy followed it, and slipped into her parent's room, undetected, she hoped, because if her mother ever found out Kimmy was in her room without permission she would be grounded until she turned eighteen. In Kimmy's calculation that was five years away, so she made sure she stayed as quiet as possible, as she watched the mist travel over to a wall. The mist removed a mirror and Kimmy noticed a dark blue circle.

Somehow, the mist opened the circle and Kimmy saw a key, which immediately illuminated the entire room. Kimmy watched in fascination and horror as the mist placed the key in her hand. She studied it for a moment not knowing what any of it meant, and when she heard the stairs creak, she knew her mother was coming. Kimmy slowly opened her parent's bedroom door saw the hallway was clear, and walked quickly to her room. Once she closed her bedroom door, she watched the mist travel back over to her window, and float outside. She raced over to it, but the mist was gone, it had completely vanished. When she placed the key in her pocket she felt her heart beating as if it were in a race against time. She took a few deep breaths, trying to calm down, and wondered again what just happened. Why was the strange mist outside her window? What was the key to, and why did the mist give it to her? What was she suppose to do with it now?

She got up off the bed, grabbed her cell phone and called her best friend Bobby Martin. When he didn't answer, she walked into her closet, and that's when the door slammed shut, and a warrior looking man that Kimmy had once seen in her history book at school, appeared.

"Who are you?" Kimmy demanded her blue eyes ablaze with anger.

"I am Onebuyo, and you are Kimmy?" He crinkled his nose.

"Yeah that's right I am. Got a problem with that?" Kimmy folded her arms.

The warrior shrugged. "No, it's just not a very strong name."

"Says who?" Kimmy asked.

"Says everyone that I know." The warrior watched her with his penetrating blue eyes, and Kimmy noticed how his long, dark hair touched the collar of his shirt.

"Who are you, and why are you in my bedroom?" Kimmy raised her voice.

"I'm Onebuyo, and I come with news about your life."

"What news, and how do you know about my Life?"

"I know all there is to know about you. So hush so I can relay the message I was sent here to deliver."

"How do you know me, and you better talk fast because I'm giving you three seconds before I scream."

"That's a human trait, huh? The screaming?" the warrior asked.

"I guess, now hurry up," Kimmy said, as her heart raced once again.

The warrior watched her before he spoke, "your spirit is strong, but you do have a hard time listening."

"Oh, I listen when it's important. So get on with it."

"Okay, but try not to interrupt."

When Kimmy remained quiet the warrior continued, "Today you will meet your best friend Bobby Martin at the fountain. Today is the day you will tell him about the dark swirl that was outside your window. The one you let into the house without permission. The one who went into your parent's room, and invaded their privacy. The mist that gave you the key, you were not supposed to know about, yet. Once you're finished telling him about the dark mist, you will tell him about the dreams you've been having about your grandmother. Once this is complete you shall tell him about your friend, Camille. After this is done, be prepared for your life to change forever. After today things will never be the same again. Keep your eyes opened for the dangers that await you at every turn. Be advised that some of the new people you meet you can trust. The others you can't. Your journey will be difficult, but the first seal of your fate was broken when you let the mist into this house, the second, when you accepted the key. Now the rest will unfold as quickly as your heart is racing. Do you understand?"

Kimmy stared at him as she chewed her bottom lip. "No, none of this makes any sense."

"It will." The warrior nodded as if he were agreeing with what he had just said.

"But it doesn't, so why don't you leave the way you came in?"

As Kimmy watched, the warrior faded, and before she knew it, he was gone. She glanced around her walk in closet, and realized she was alone, so she reached in her pocket, felt the key nestled there, and grabbed her cell phone. The sooner she got a hold of Bobby the better.

CHAPTER ONE

"Will you tell him today?" Camille asked Kimmy as she sat on the edge of the fountain in downtown Plymouth, waiting for her best friend Bobby Martin to arrive.

"I don't know what to do. I mean I want to tell him, but I don't know if I will today."

Camille tapped her foot. "Oh, you have to tell him, if you don't who knows what's going to happen. Besides, if you don't tell him, I will."

Kimmy laughed. "You can't tell him, and I need to think about how I'm going to tell Bobby about what's going on."

"Why can't I tell him?" Camille asked.

"Because you know the rules, and you know you're not allowed to tell him. Camille we were both told the rules this morning."

"Yeah but…just this once. Please, oh please. Maybe if I tried really hard I'd be able to talk to Bobby. "

"It doesn't matter how hard you try, it's not going to work. Now we were both told that the world that you come from forbids fairies to talk to humans, and the last time I checked Bobby was human."

"But I can talk to you."

"Yeah, but you've always been able to talk to me."

"Well will you at least let me try to talk to Bobby?"

"No." Kimmy smiled when she spotted Bobby walking across the park.

"Please, Kimmy."

"Camille, I said no. Now be a good fairy and leave this to me."

Camille moaned, "but you're so boring."

"No, I'm not."

"Yes, you are."

"Oh my goodness, no I'm not Camille."

"Yes you are. You never do anything wrong. Well at least not yet."

"What's that supposed to mean?"

Camille smiled. "It means that Bobby's got a secret. Bobby's got a secret."

"What kind of secret?" Kimmy asked.

"The kind that's going to make your life exciting and I can't wait. Like I said you're boring, and I'm tired of yawning over it."

"Ha ha, that's very funny Camille."

"Who's Camille? Bobby asked sitting next to Kimmy.

"No one," Kimmy sighed.

"So do you talk to yourself often?' He smiled.

"I wasn't talking to myself."

"So who's Camille, and where did she go?"

"It's a long story."

Bobby grabbed Kimmy's hand. "Good thing I've got all day."

Camille fluttered her bright green wings and Kimmy watched the white sparkle of stardust swirl around her. "Oh, hurry up Kimmy and tell him."

"He's going to think I've lost my mind, Camille."

"I already think that." Bobby laughed. "You're talking to yourself again."

"I'm not talking to myself. I'm talking to Camille."

"Yeah, so you've said, but I can't see her, so you must be talking to yourself."

Kimmy sighed, as Camille giggled. "I'm glad you think this is funny, Camille."

"I don't think it's funny. I'm just excited that you finally get to tell him what's going on."

"Well, where do I start?" Kimmy asked Camille.

"Tell him what happened this morning."

"Fine." Kimmy turned to look at Bobby.

"Are you ready for this?"

"Yeah, I'm ready to hear what's going on with you."

"Okay, when I woke up this morning, I went to my window and parted the curtains. I saw a dark swirl outside my window."

"What kind of dark swirl?"

"I don't know. But anyways, I watched a white mist come out of the center of it, and without thinking, I opened my window."

"What, you're right, you are crazy?"

"Yeah. I know. Anyway, the white swirl traveled over to my bedroom door, opened it, and went to my parent's room."

"What did you do?"

"I followed it."

"Oh my gosh, what happened?"

"The white mist went over to the wall in their room and moved a mirror. Behind the mirror there was a small dark blue circle on the wall. The mist opened it, and I saw a key that illuminated the entire room and before I knew it the mist had put it in my hand."

"Wow. Are you serious?"

Kimmy nodded, reached in her pocket, and handed him the key.

"Did you get caught?"

"No. Thank goodness. When the mist put the key in my hand, I heard the stairs creak, and ran to my room, before my mother caught me."

"So what's this key to?" Kimmy watched Bobby jiggled it in his hand.

"I haven't figured it out yet. I know it's not to my bedroom door. I tried it, but it didn't work."

"That's weird."

"I know."

"So now what are you going to do?"

Kimmy shrugged. "I don't know. I keep having these dreams about my grandmother, and she keeps telling me that I need to find a book."

"What book?"

"I don't know. I've been having these dreams for months now, and it's always the same thing. I see an old building, and in it my mother is screaming at me to be a good girl, my grandmother is telling me to find a book, and that's when the ghost arrives. The ghost walks back and forth in front of the window in the old building."

"Okay, then what happens?"

"I usually wake up. So this morning, my mom took me down here so she could prance around. You know how my mom loves attention."

"Yep."

"Anyway, when we went back to the house earlier this morning, I had this eerie feeling when we pulled up in the driveway. I don't know why, but I glanced up at the attic window and I saw the ghost that's always in my dreams."

"What? Are you sure?"

"Oh, I'm sure."

"What do you think it means, Kimmy?"

"I think it means I need to sneak up in the attic to find the book my grandmother is so adamant about me finding. The only problem is my mother keeps the attic locked."

"Hey, maybe this is the key?" Bobby studied it for a moment, before Kimmy shook her head.

"I doubt it. Nothing in life is that easy."

"I know, but you should try it and see if it unlocks the attic door."

"I will. The hard part is going to be sneaking up there without getting caught."

"I know. If that happens, I'm not sure what your mother will do to you."

"Me either, but I've got to do it. If it is the key, I can find out why my grandmother is haunting my dreams."

"Yeah, but I don't want your mother to catch you."

"Me either." Kimmy looked at him. "But I've got to take the chance. Something is going on and I know the book would answer some questions. At least I think it might."

"This whole thing is weird."

"I know. How do you think I feel?"

"Confused."

"Yeah."

"So when are you going to tell me about Camille?"

Kimmy smiled at Bobby. "I guess I'll tell you now, since you already think I'm crazy."

"Yeah pretty much, so keep talking, and let me decide how crazy I think you are. Right now you're only kind of crazy."

"Ha ha, very funny."

Camille fluttered her wings. "Oh, I knew I liked him, Kimmy. He is such a nice, decent boy, so tell him now. You've already kept me waiting longer than you should have. I mean you could have started this whole conversation about me, and not the stupid mist you saw this morning."

"I had to start there, Camille. This whole thing wouldn't have sounded right if I would have started with you."

"Oh, yes, it would have. At least it would have started out exciting. For a minute there I thought for sure I was going to start yawning again."

"Okay, Camille. I get that you think my life is one big bore."

"You can say that again. I mean I don't remember a time in your life when you've ever gotten into trouble."

"Yeah, and I'd like to keep it that way," Kimmy snapped.

"Okay, so obviously Camille is still here." Bobby smiled.

"Yeah, she is."

"So tell me about her."

"Okay. Well, it all started when I was about three. I remember seeing Camille for the first time. I thought it was cool to have her to play with, and little did I know at the time that she was a fairy."

"A what?" Bobby asked.

"You heard me. A fairy."

"You mean like colorful wings and a pretty face, and all that?"

"Oh, Kimmy, he's so smart. He nailed it. I do have a pretty face, and my wings are colorful. Tell him how gorgeous my gown is. Tell him how it has swirls of pink running through it. Don't forget to tell him how beautiful my hair is."

"Camille, please. Well you let me talk without interrupting?"

"Oh, I'm trying, but I get this way when people talk about me. Don't forget the part about how funny I am."

"Camille I'd tell him everything, and get done much faster if you'd stop talking."

"Okay then, hurry up."

Kimmy bit her lower lip. "Where was I?"

"The part about the fairy."

"Yeah, she is beautiful and funny and I guess I was a lucky kid to have had her around, even though I didn't understand why."

"So she's been around your whole life and you never told me?" Bobby looked hurt.

"I couldn't tell you. I remember wanting to tell you, but I couldn't."

"Why?"

"I was sworn to secrecy, and at the time I didn't realize it. But this morning everything changed."

"You mean with the mist and all?"

"I mean with all of it. I'm obviously allowed now to tell you about Camille, and the book my grandmother wants me to find."

"Yeah, but none of it makes sense to me. Why is there a fairy in your life?"

"I don't know. All I can tell you is that this morning I went in my closet to get dressed and that's when Camille and a guy named Onebuyo appeared. Onebuyo told me that it's time. Whatever that means, and he said that I needed to tell you about Camille and the dreams I've been having. He also said that we've got a lot of work to do, and that time was of the essence or something like that."

"So who is Onebuyo?"

"I don't know. He looked like a warrior or something that I saw once in my history book."

"Man, this whole thing is confusing me."

"You? Try to be me. I've spent my life thinking that I was lucky to have Camille, and now all this other stuff happened. I'd trade places with you in a second because I don't know what's going on. All I know is that Onebuyo wanted me to tell only you about Camille and my grandmother. Now I need to swear you to secrecy, just like I had to do for so many years."

"You know I'd never say anything, especially when you ask me not too."

"I for one believe him, Kimmy," Camille shouted.

"Camille, do you have to shout? You scared me."

"Oh, sorry, I just wanted you to know that I trust him."

"Yeah, I trust him too. He's been my best friend since I've been born."

"I wish I could hear Camille. It would make this whole thing much easier to believe."

Kimmy looked at Bobby annoyed. "Well I don't know why you

can't hear her. I thought for sure you'd be able to once I told you what happened. But you don't need to make me feel bad."

"I didn't mean too. It's just that I'm trying to understand everything that's going on, and everything you've told me, and it's a lot."

"Don't you think I know that? I know it's a lot, which is why I should have kept it to myself."

Bobby grabbed Kimmy's hand. "Listen, I'm sorry for what I said. I didn't mean to upset you." Bobby smiled. "Now it's time for us to meet Dave and Manning at Taco Bell."

"Oh, that's right." Kimmy stood.

"Not so fast," Camille said. "Ask him about his secret."

"Okay. So Bobby, Camille said you had a secret."

Bobby smirked. "Really?"

"Yeah, really."

"That's weird."

"Bobby, do you have a secret?"

"No, now let's go meet our friends. I'm starving."

"He's lying to you, but you'll find out soon enough."

"What's Camille saying now?"

"That you're lying to me, but I'll find out soon enough."

"Whatever," Bobby said.

Once Kimmy and Bobby walked in Taco Bell they saw their two friends already sitting at the table, and Kimmy and Bobby ordered their food before they joined them.

"What's up?" Manning asked.

"Not much, just hanging out," Bobby answered.

"And of course the two of you are always hanging out," Dave said, nodding toward Kimmy.

Kimmy smiled. "Of course we are always hanging out. That's what you do when you've got a best friend, Dave. You'll learn that maybe one day when you have a best friend."

Dave glared at Kimmy. "I have best friends, Kimmy. The difference is I don't need to be with them all the time."

"Oh, he's lying, Kimmy. He doesn't have best friends because he runs his mouth when he needs to keep it closed," Camille said.

Kimmy didn't answer her because Dave and Manning couldn't find out about Camille.

"Did you hear me? I said he doesn't have best friends."

Kimmy stood. "I've got to use the ladies room." She walked away, went in the bathroom, and turned around. "Where are you, Camille?"

"Look up."

Kimmy looked up and Camille was flying around near the ceiling.

"What are you doing way up there?"

"I'm keeping my distance. I know when you're mad at me, and right now I get the feeling that I said something annoying, so I'm staying up here until I know."

"Yes, you said something annoying. Dave and Manning aren't suppose to know about you, so I would appreciate it if you would keep quiet when their around. I can't have you whispering in my ear things that I can't answer when I'm with them."

Camille twitched here tiny nose, like she always did when she was upset. "Okay, okay. I was only trying to help. I'll just keep my lips together until you're alone."

"Camille, I didn't mean to hurt your feelings. It's just that all of this has happened so fast, I don't know how to handle it."

"What do you mean? I've been around forever."

Kimmy sighed. "I know. Just forget it. Now let's get back out there."

When Kimmy approached the table she knew something was wrong. She could tell by the expression on Bobby's face.

"Oh, Kimmy, glad you're back." Dave laughed. "So tell me do you know about the treasure chest Bobby found?"

"What? No," Kimmy answered.

"Well, sit down, and listen. Bobby is telling us that this morning he went into an abandon building on Mill Street to check it out and he found a treasure chest buried in the corner under some wood, and now he wants us to go with him and see the treasure he found."

"It's true, Kimmy," Bobby said.

"See I told you he had a secret," Camille shouted, making Kimmy jump. "Oh sorry, I forgot I'm not allowed to talk when you're with your friends."

"Why didn't you tell me?" Kimmy looked hurt for a moment.

"Because I wanted to tell all of you at one time."

Kimmy nodded, as she sipped her drink.

"So, let me tell you what Bobby said," Dave winked.

"You already did. Is it true, Bobby? Did you really go into an old, deserted warehouse, and find an old chest buried under some wood in the corner filled with treasure?

"Yes, I did," Bobby answered.

"And now you want us to go with you to see the treasure you found?" Kimmy stopped talking long enough to swallow the lump that had risen in her throat.

"Yeah Kimmy, I do."

"Wait a second," Dave blurted. "Bobby we all know you're not that brave. Face it. You'd never go in an empty warehouse, alone."

"Dave, stop it," Kimmy scolded.

"Stop it," Dave mocked her. "You know it's true. He's not the type who would wander into an empty warehouse, especially alone."

Kimmy rolled her eyes at him in annoyance.

"Face it, Kimmy, Bobby would never go in a deserted warehouse. He's not brave enough."

Kimmy glared at Dave, and was just about to speak, but Bobby beat her to it.

"Believe what you want Dave, but it's true, and you're right most of the time I wouldn't go into an empty warehouse alone, but today I did, and if you don't believe me, I'll show it to you."

"Give me a break. Is this a trick or something?" their other friend Manning asked.

"Just forget it." Bobby looked at them.

Dave snickered. "Don't get mad, Bobby. You've got to understand that we're freshman now, and we don't believe in that sort of thing anymore."

Bobby shrugged. "Fine, don't believe me, but when I'm rich and famous, I don't want to hear about it."

"You won't." Manning laughed.

Kimmy watched the scene unfold, and felt sorry for Bobby. Dave and Manning always picked on him and it wasn't fair. Ever since they were young, Bobby was always the brunt of their jokes. She imagined it was because Bobby was such a nice guy. He was more mature then most boys his age and she knew that was the reason Dave and Manning taunted him. Bobby was also honest with his feelings, and told people the truth whether they wanted to hear it or not. Those two traits were just some of the reasons Bobby was Kimmy's best friend. She could talk to him about almost anything and he was always there to listen. At times, she knew it bothered Bobby when she told him about certain things going on in her life, but she did it anyway.

She glanced over at the three boys, stood, and went over to Bobby on the other side of the table. She playfully punched him in the arm. "If you found treasure, I want to see it," her voice cracked with emotion thinking about the legend her Grandmother Culver had told her when she was eight. "Besides, how fair would it be if you were rich, and I wasn't? Girls like money a lot. I'm willing to go with you Bobby."

Bobby smiled, stood, and looked at his other two friends who laughed.

"You two run along. Go find the treasure. We'll be at the roller rink later if you want to catch up." Dave teased.

"Okay, fine. Have it your way. But if what Bobby's telling us is the truth, you'll both lose." Kimmy was upset and it wasn't lost on any of them.

"We'll take our chances." Manning laughed again.

Bobby turned to look at Kimmy. "You ready then."

"Yeah, Bobby I am. I've always wanted to find treasure. So, Bobby Martin led the way to my richness." Kimmy felt her heart flutter with the thought of finding treasure, and she smiled at Bobby remembering how the two of them use to draw treasure maps for the field that was down the street from their houses when they were younger. She also recalled how the two of them would dig through the field pretending to search for the hidden treasure.

"I hope you don't mind walking," Bobby stated. "But it's not too far away from here."

"Bobby, why would you say that? We walk all the time because we're not old enough to drive yet." Kimmy grabbed her drink off the table, took Bobby's arm, as Dave and Manning continued to laugh, and the two of them left Taco Bell.

Once they started walking, Kimmy glanced at Bobby. "I'm sorry about what happened with Dave and Manning."

"They're just jerks!" Camille shouted.

"Camille, we know they're jerks."

Bobby smiled. "Don't worry about Dave and Manning. I'm use to them treating me that way."

"Yeah, but still," Kimmy paused. "I bet if I looked up jerk in the dictionary, Dave's picture would be right there next to the word."

Bobby chuckled. "That's a good one, but like I said don't worry about it."

"But I do. Dave always picks on you, and he makes me so mad."

"He shouldn't. He's been doing it forever."

"I know, and that's only because he gets away with it. But someday he'll be taught a lesson. My mom always tells me you can't treat people differently than you want to be treated, or it'll eventually come back and bite you."

Bobby chuckled again. "Don't let him ruin your day. He's not worth it. Besides, I'm over it. I know what I told them is the truth, and that's all I need to know."

Kimmy nodded, and fell quiet. She knew Bobby wouldn't talk about Dave and Manning anymore.

"Ask him why he didn't tell you when the two of you were sitting at the fountain. It would've saved him a lot of grief from the Taco Bell Jerks."

"What's she saying now?" Bobby asked.

"She wanted me to ask you why you didn't tell me when we were sitting at the fountain."

"I already told you that I wanted to tell all of you together."

"That's a lame excuse. He knows how mean Dave is, so why didn't he save himself the grief and just tell you?" Camille asked.

"Camille, I don't know."

"Well, find out."

"Camille wants to know why you'd tell them, when all Dave does is bring you grief."

"I thought because we were freshman he'd of grown up some."

"Oh, he should've known better, Kimmy. It'll take Dave a long time to grow up."

"I think he knows that now, Camille. How far is the warehouse?"

"I don't know. Several blocks at least."

"So how did you find the treasure?" Kimmy asked.

"Well earlier today I felt like taking a walk. You know how I am. I love to walk around, especially in the summer. Anyway, as I was walking down Mill Street I saw these abandoned warehouses and decided today would be a good day to investigate. I don't know why I wanted to see what was in them. Maybe because it's so hot out here, and I thought the warehouses would be cooler. So it's where I ended up."

Kimmy squinted against the sun, as she glanced up at him, and they both stopped. "How did you find the treasure though?"

"Well, I went into the biggest warehouse first, through a broken window at the back of the building. I got to tell you it was really dark when I went in, and dusty. I could tell that it was old and hadn't been used for quite a few years. Anyway, I saw a bunch of wood in the corner, and I saw something glittering. So, I crossed the warehouse, and started pulling the wood off the stack. This is going to sound weird, but I felt like something was coaxing me to do it."

"Yeah, you're right that's weird." She giggled. "So continue."

"Well, as I reached the bottom, I saw the old, wooden treasure chest."

"Oh my gosh, you must've been surprised."

"That's putting it lightly. At first, I told myself to leave it alone, and get out of the warehouse. But curiosity won and I opened it."

"What'd you see?"

"Treasure."

"No kidding." Kimmy laughed. "I know that silly. What kind of treasure?"

"Every kind you could ever want. There were different colored jewels and coins."

"Oh my gosh, this is so exciting. I can't wait. So after you saw the jewels and coins what did you do."

"I closed the lid, and met you at the fountain."

"That's it."

"Yeah, that's it. What did you expect me to say?"

"I expected you to say something besides that."

"Well, sorry to disappoint you. But that's all I did. Now if you don't mind can we start walking again? I want to hurry. I don't want anyone else to find it."

"Tell me how much treasure there is," Kimmy's blue eyes sparkled with excitement.

Bobby shrugged. "Enough that we couldn't carry all of it without help."

"Really. So you're not just making it up."

"No. I'm not making it up."

"So when you found the treasure were you scared?"

"Not exactly. At first, I thought I was dreaming. Like I said, the chest is full of all different kinds of jewels. Every color anyone could ever want."

"That's cool. I can't wait to see it."

Bobby cleared his throat, "Listen, before we get there, I got to tell you something." Kimmy looked up at Bobby and noticed how broad his shoulder had become. Gone was the baby fat that she remembered. Now he stood beside her pure muscle. Kimmy knew it was because of the different sports he played, and she had often wondered how he could keep up with everything and still manage to get good grades. She herself was on the dance team, and cheerleading squad.

The two of them had grown up together, along with Dave, Manning, Renee and Shelby. For as long as Kimmy could remember, they had always been friends. The six of them were inseparable their mother's were, too. Despite the arguments they had sometimes, nothing stopped them from being friends. Not even Dave's ill temper manner.

Kimmy thought about Dave again, and the arguments she had with him. Their personalities went together like bologna and peanut butter, and out of the group, he was her least favorite.

Bobby suddenly waved his hand in front of her face, making her thoughts rush back to reality. "I'm sorry Bobby, what were you saying?"

"I was saying when I opened the lid on the chest I picked up a red jewel and saw something weird."

"Something weird? Like what?" Kimmy stared down the street.

"I saw these things inside the jewel that weren't normal looking. Not like we are anyway."

"You lost me. What'd you mean?"

"Yeah he lost me too. If you ask me you're the weird looking ones. Not any of us."

"Camille, what's that supposed to mean?"

"What did she say?" Bobby asked.

"She said that we're the weird looking ones."

"You're correct, Kimmy. That's exactly what I said."

"Okay, Camille I heard you now please be quiet so Bobby can tell me about the jewels."

Bobby sighed, "When I picked up the jewel like I said, these things appeared."

"What things? Do you mean things that are alive? Like people or something?"

"I guess you could say their people but they looked different."

"What'd you mean?"

"Just what I said. Look, you'll see when we get there."

Okay," Kimmy paused. "Could you at least tell me what the things were doing?"

"At first they were sitting around a camp fire. Then all of a sudden I think they knew I was watching because all at once they turned their squinted eyes and stared at me."

"Oh my gosh, what'd you do?"

"I stared at them. I was shocked because I wasn't expecting to see anything inside the jewel, and finally I put it back in the treasure chest."

"I don't blame you. I would've done the same thing."

"Oh, no, the two of you are so dramatic. I know what those people look like and I happen to believe they're all gorgeous."

"Camille, please," Kimmy said, "will you let Bobby finish without interrupting?"

"I can't help it. It's the way I was raised. What do you call it, Kimmy? Oh yeah, I was blessed with the gift to gab."

"So I've noticed, but right now Camille I wish you'd stop."

"Fine, tell Bobby to continue, and once you reach the warehouse don't ask me for help, because I won't give it to you."

"Good," Kimmy answered. "Please continue Bobby."

Bobby nodded. "Trust me, they didn't look friendly."

"Do you think it's safe for us to go in there?"

"I don't know, but we've got to. I don't want someone to find it. If that happens we might miss our chance to be rich." He chuckled.

"You got a good point there."

"I know."

"I'm telling you Kimmy, do not go in the warehouse," Camille said.

"Why, Camille?"

"Because you're not supposed to do this, I just know nothing good is going to come from you two venturing into that dirty warehouse."

"Camille, please. Bobby and I are old enough to make our decisions. So we're going in the warehouse and you can't stop us."

"Why is she so upset?" Bobby asked.

"I don't know, let me ask," Kimmy said.

"I heard him, Kimmy and I'm upset because if you go in the warehouse, I can't go with you."

"Why can't you go with us, Camille? You go everywhere else with me, so why is this any different?"

"Because it is, and I'm telling you Kimmy, not to go in the warehouse. I think something bad is going to happen."

"It's a warehouse, Camille. Nothing bad is going to happen."

"Tell her that I'll protect you," Bobby said.

"Oh, he thinks he'll be able to protect you, but he won't be able too. So just save me the sore head I'm sure to get if the two of you don't listen."

"Camille, it's called a headache."

"Yeah, so you've told me, but I call it a sore head."

"Why is she so upset?" Bobby asked.

Kimmy shrugged. "I don't know, but she said she'll get a sore head if we go in there and not listen to her."

"Tell her we're sorry, but we've got to go in there. We don't have a choice."

Camille folded her arms, and tapped her foot. "Tell him I heard what he said, and the two of you are going to be sorry."

"Camille said that we're going to be sorry."

"Tell her it'll be alright."

"No it won't. You two need to listen. It won't be alright. No my body is tingling, and I'm going to disappear."

"What do you mean?"

"Just what I said, good-bye for now, Kimmy."

"What did she say?"

"She said goodbye."

"What, why?"

"Because we weren't listening to her about the warehouse."

"But we've got to go in there."

"I know."

They fell silent until Kimmy asked, "What'd they look like?"

"The people in the jewel?"

"Yeah."

"Little men."

"Little men? Like dwarfs or something?"

"Kind of, but not really. Look, it's too hard to describe them. But I will say I've never seen anything like them. Not around here anyway."

"Did it scare you?"

"Yeah. But don't go telling Manning or Dave what I said. They already think I'm a wimp and I don't want either one to have any more ammo against me. Face it, when it comes down to me, Dave and Manning I rank last for bravery. Sometimes I wonder if anything scares those two."

"Oh I'm sure there's plenty that scares them, but they'd never admit it, and what you tell me stays between us. I would never do that to you. Besides, you know I don't get along with Dave. I think he can be the biggest jerk. I also think Manning just goes along with him so that Dave will leave him alone. But to tell you the truth, I think they pick on you because you'll say when something isn't right."

"What'd you mean?"

"I mean that Elise and I were talking yesterday on the phone about all three of you, and we both agreed that you keep it real. You know, that just because you're a guy, you still admit when you're scared, or when people do things that aren't cool you'll refuse to go along with it. You don't care what people think. That's cool. So, anyways, Elise and I think you're brave for standing up to other kids about what's right or wrong."

Bobby smiled. "I don't know what to say."

"You don't have to say anything, silly. I just wanted you to know how we feel. Oh by the way, Elsie and I both think Manning and Dave are the real wimps. Neither of them have the courage you have. I mean if you think about it they always have to be tough and they never admit when something's wrong, or if they're freaked right out of their skin."

"So what're you saying?" Bobby's green eyes pierced hers.

"I'm saying don't change Bobby Martin. You're doing a fine job."

"Thanks, Kimmy."

"No problem. I do have another question though."

"Okay."

"If you found treasure why didn't you bring a jewel back with you? I'm only asking because if you would have done that, you could've shown Dave and Manning. I bet then they would've believed you."

He shrugged. "You're right. But I never thought about doing that. I mean the treasure doesn't belong to me, and everything happened so fast, and when I saw those weird looking things inside the jewel I threw it back in the chest, slammed the lid and got out of there."

"Yeah, I would've done the same thing." Kimmy shivered as she stared down the street, which was deserted. She felt the heat from the hot sun beating on her back, and was grateful when she saw the abandon warehouse. "Is that it?" She pointed at the chipped dark, blue building and cracked cement parking lot.

"Yeah, that's it. Come on." Bobby held his hand out and she took it.

When they reached the warehouse door, Bobby stopped. "Are you ready?"

"Yes. I can't wait."

"Okay, but before I crawl through the window again to unlock the door, I've got to tell you one more thing."

"Okay, what?" Kimmy stared at him.

"When I saw those weird things they said something to me that didn't make any sense."

"Like what?"

"They said that one of my good friends is a witch."

"What? Who?"

"They didn't tell me that."

"Are you sure that's what they said?"

"Yeah, I'm positive. All the little creatures were chanting it."

Kimmy shivered, again, despite the heat of the day. The whole situation was scaring her. "Oh great. I feel better now. Thanks for sharing that with me."

"Sorry, I just thought I should let you know. Do you still want to go in?"

"Of course I do. I want to find out what's going on."

"Me too." Bobby pulled himself up with ease, and slid through the window. A few seconds later Kimmy watched the door being pushed open and soon she joined Bobby inside. Both of them waited a moment until their eyes adjusted to the dimmer light of the warehouse.

"It definitely feels better in here," Kimmy stated.

"Yeah, its cooler that's for sure. Come on, the treasure is over there." Bobby pointed to the corner at the far end of the huge room, and Kimmy heard the echo of his voice in the big, empty warehouse. "Let me close the door first." He grunted, as he pushed the heavy door shut, which echoed as it closed.

"It's kind of creepy in here," Kimmy whispered.

"I know. I still can't believe I came in here."

"I can. You're braver then you think."

"Thanks. I've always liked that one thing about you. You're very sweet. I don't think there's a mean bone inside your body. Unless Dave's around." He laughed. "Now, come on." Bobby grabbed her hand and pulled her across the warehouse.

After Bobby took all the wood off the treasure chest, they both knelt down. He slowly lifted the heavy lid and it moaned as it came open.

Kimmy's breathe caught in her throat.

"Oh my gosh it's real. Look at all the beautiful jewels." She stared into the array of colors that were glittering and winking.

She reached out to touch a jewel. "Be careful Kimmy."

"I will." She picked up the big, blue gemstone. "Oh my gosh. It's so pretty." She laid the stone in the palm of her hand, and Bobby reached over and touched it. Then he picked up the red ruby that he had held earlier when he saw the little men.

When he saw the same vision, he looked at Kimmy, and saw confusion on her face. "What's wrong?"

"I don't know. I keep seeing knights on horses." Kimmy told him with her eyes closed.

"What?" Bobby put his red gemstone back in the treasure chest. "Let me see that?"

Kimmy placed the stone in his hand, and instantly Bobby saw the knights on the horses running through startling green fields.

He dropped the stone back in the chest.

"Did you see them?" Kimmy wanted to know.

"Yeah, I saw them. Now I want you to see these strange little creatures." He picked up the red stone, and put it in Kimmy's trembling hand.

"What are they?" she asked staring at the little people, sitting around a campfire, dressed in rags, with big shoes that curled at the top.

"I don't know, but this whole thing is weird, huh?"

"Yeah, it is, and I want to know what these stones are and why people are trapped in them."

"Yeah, me too." Bobby took the stone Kimmy was holding and put it back in the treasure chest.

"What color do you want next?" Kimmy asked him.

"I don't know. Which one do you want?"

"The green one, I guess. It reminds me of your eyes. But before I pick it up let's hold hands."

"Okay." Bobby held his hand out as he picked up the stone. When they felt the vibration, both of them knew they were in trouble, and then all went dark.

When Kimmy opened her eyes, she saw Bobby sitting next to her at a long table, before a huge fire. Foreign music was playing and as the two of them looked around, they were frightened.

"Where are we?" Kimmy whispered.

"I don't know," Bobby kept his voice low. "What kind of creatures are those."

"I don't know, I never seen anything like it before." Kimmy looked at the creatures gathered around the table. They looked like dwarfs, but they weren't. The things had long necks like an ostrich. Their eyes slanted upward, and each had a turquoise jewel at their temple.

"What kind of creatures are they?" Kimmy whispered.

"Heck if I know."

"What's this stuff on our plate?" Kimmy asked.

"I don't know, but don't eat it."

"I'm not." Kimmy starred at the sparrow's head lying raw on her plate. The bird's dead eyes were vacantly staring.

When the two of them heard the trumpet, they turned their attention to the head of the table, and watched a huge creature walk in, then take a seat.

"Okay, I've had enough, Bobby. Get us out of here right now."

"I don't know how. I don't know where we are or how we got here."

"Then figure something out. I mean have you noticed the thing at the head of the table. It looks like a pig's head on a human's body, not my idea of a fun afternoon. Besides, it's drooling all over the table, and I feel like I'm going to be sick."

"Okay, what would you like me to do?"

"Silence!" The roar of the pig man stopped all activity in the room. His eyes looked like those of an eagle, which stared directly at Bobby and Kimmy. "Who are these creatures?"

When no one answered, he roared, "Why are there creatures at my table? Both creatures that dare join me for dinner as ugly as they are should be thrown to the floor. They're to take their meal like the other animals around here."

"Excuse me," Kimmy blurted, before Bobby could stop her. "Did you just say that my friend and I are ugly, and we should be shown to the floor?"

"Kimmy be quiet."

"To the floor with you!" The pig man yelled.

When one of the dwarfish looking creatures grabbed their arms, they both struggled, but the little people were stronger and threw both of them to the floor where they landed with a thud.

Kimmy glared at Bobby. "Get me out of here. I don't care how you have to do it, but figure it out. I don't want to be here anymore."

"I know. Now start crawling toward the door, right there." Bobby nodded toward the door that was next to them and watched as Kimmy started inching her way.

"Now go." Bobby told her forcefully, and as soon as Kimmy got out the door, Bobby followed.

Once they were outside, they heard the pig man yelling, "After them."

The two of them took off running, and never looked back.

When they finally stopped running, confident they had lost the creatures, Kimmy fell to her knees in the grass exhausted, and breathing heavy. "I don't know where we are, but I want to go home," her voice was choppy.

"Me too. Whatever happened isn't cool. But I don't know how to get us back." Bobby sat next to her, and the two of them looked around.

They were in the middle of a brilliant green field, filled with wild flowers that neither had seen before. Both shielded their eyes against the brilliance of the colors, which instantly made their eyes burn and water. Through blurred vision, they noticed the field they were in was surrounded by weirdly looking twisted trees. The bark was violet blue, and the leaves were crimson.

"These are the strangest trees I've ever seen," Kimmy stated.

"Yeah, I know. If they're trees."

"Sure they are. What else could they be?"

"I don't know, but right now nothing's going to fool me."

"The colors from the wild flowers are hurting my eyes."

"Mine too." Bobby lifted his hand shielded his eyes and saw a reflection of something glitter brightly. "Did you see that?"

"See what?"

"Did you see that flicker over there?"

"No, the only things I see are all the bright colors that are burning my eyes."

"Look over there." Bobby pointed.

Kimmy squinted hard. "Yeah, I see it. What is it?"

"I don't know. It's almost like someone is using an object to reflect the sun."

"Should we go find out what's going on?"

"No way. We stay here. We don't know whose over there, and after what happened back there, I'm not in the spying mood."

"What're we going to do?" Kimmy asked sadly.

"I don't know yet."

"Where do you think we are?"

"Kimmy, I have no clue."

"Well personally, I think the jewels had something to do with it."

"You think. I know they did. Our life was normal until a couple hours ago."

When the flicker of light became stronger, Bobby stood and pulled Kimmy to her feet. "Let's walk. I want to know what's around here. There's got to be somewhere better to hide until we can figure out what to do, and how we're going to get home."

"Yeah, I agree. Look, the flash is coming closer. I don't want whatever it is to catch up with us."

"I know. Now let's walk faster and talk about what we're going to do." Bobby pulled Kimmy through the field into the trees, and finally their eyes felt better.

"I've never seen colors so bright before. Now I just want to go home, Bobby. I don't like it here."

"Me either. But try to stay focused, okay? We're not going to get home any quicker by complaining about it. You know."

"I know."

"Now look over there through the trees. Do you see how thick the bark is?"

"Yeah, I see."

"Good, that's where we're going."

"Okay, but keep your eyes open. I don't want anything popping out at us."

"It won't. But if it does, we'll deal with it. Now, hold my hand tightly and don't let go no matter what happens, okay?"

"I won't." Kimmy squeezed his hand.

The two of them ventured deeper into the thick, twisted forest, and neither one noticed the little sprinkle of stardust dancing behind them.

CHAPTER TWO

"She is here amongst us, but she is not alone," one of the pixie dust angels told the queen of the woods.

"And?" the queen demanded.

"She is with some boy. Both look strange, if you ask me."

"Strange, how?" the queen asked.

"Strange. You know they don't look as we do."

"How do they look?" The queen turned and looked at the pixie angel with her purple eye that sat in the middle of her forehead.

"I don't know. They have things like the little people in Vanduesa."

"What things might you be referring to?" the queen's voice rose impatiently.

"You know those things that the little people get around with."

The queen laughed, revealing yellowing teeth. "Oh, the things the little people in Vanduesa refer to as legs."

"That's it." The pixie angel did an excited flip, and then nodded her head.

"What else?"

"They have those weird eyes, like the little people, one on either side of their orb. As a matter of making this conversation smaller, they're just like the little people, but much bigger."

"Much bigger, how?" The queen stared at the pixie angel flying in front of her, fluttering its colorful wings.

"I don't know. I guess if I had to say, why yes, they're tall like the trees."

"That tall?"

"Well, maybe a tad bit shorter, but not much."

"So both are tall like the trees, you say?"

"Yes, Queen."

"Both have everything the little people do on their vessels?"

"Yes, Queen, they do. However, you know the little people call their vessels, bodies."

"Yes, so I've heard. I've also heard they call their orbs, heads." The queen tapped one of her tentacles. "Do these tree people fly?"

"Not that I've witnessed."

"So they have no powers?" The queen glared at the pixie angel.

"I don't know, Queen."

"Is that the best you can do, Rozello?"

"Queen?"

"I asked if that was the best information you could bring to me. You've disturbed my feeding over nothing of importance." The queen jumped on the wall, agitated, as the pixie angel stared, then flew over to her.

"Rozello, tell me again how the tree giants look like the little people?"

"I told you. They've got the same resemblance to the little people. The difference is they're tall as trees."

"That will be all for now." The queen lifted her tentacle off the wall, and shoed the pixie angel away.

"But Queen, what should we do? Those tree like people will take over."

"Nonsense. Now, leave me alone. I must compute what you've told me."

"Don't take too long computing. The creatures of the woods have already communicated that these tree people will surely take over our world."

"That's complete and utter nonsense. Now leave me. I've got a lot to compute, and I don't need your pixie dust irritating my nose."

"Very well." The pixie angel fluttered her wings, then, disappeared.

Once the pixie angel was out of sight, the queen crawled over to her sword, pulled it out of the sheath, rubbed it twice, and Vixbit materialized.

"Yes, Queen. What is it?" Vixbit asked, annoyed.

"There's talk of giant creatures in the woods."

"Yes, Queen, that's true."

The queen laughed, irritated. "You're a spy for me, Vixbit. I should've heard this from you. Not Rozello, an angel pixie."

"I was busy gathering information to bring to you, my dearest Queen." Vixbit bowed its tiny head.

"Very well, then speak." The queen looked at him with her purple eye.

"They're giants in the woods. One male, one female, but I don't know where they came from yet," Vixbit told her from the blade of the sword where he landed. His huge dark eyes filled most of his face, as he rubbed his tiny legs together.

"You are by far the best spy I have, Vixbit. Why would you not know where these giants come from?" The queen was impatient.

"They just entered the woods, Queen. I'm gathering information on them. When you summoned me, I had landed on the female creatures arm, and was privy to the conversation she was having with the creature boy."

"What did you hear?" The queen squeezed Vixbit with her tentacle.

"So far, they don't know where they are. They think they're lost," Vixbit moaned.

"You know who she is!" The queen threw Vixbit across the room. "You know what she wants! So gather your army, and stop them!"

"Yes, Queen."

"Do it now, and don't come back until you finished the job."

"Yes, Queen."

"Vixbit, you're small enough to find out much. Stay close to the giants, then when the time is right, I want you to destroy them."

"Yes, Queen. But if I guessing right, isn't the girl a witch?"

"Yes, you imbecile, she is."

"Is she a high, powerful witch?" Vixbit asked, nervously.

"Yes, which is why you must gather your armies, then, destroy her."

"But what if she uses her power?"

"Vixbit! You should worry about me using my power. If I must do that, not only will you die, but the entire army of the woods as well. Now be gone. Seek and destroy, then, come back with a report. If you don't..." She snapped her tentacle hard against the wall, crumbling it.

"Yes, Queen." Vixbit told her, and then he vanished.

"Do you see the cave over there?" Kimmy pointed.

"Yeah, but it looks blocked by something." Bobby stared at the opening of the cave, tucked between trees. The cave looked as if it was made of rock, and Bobby was puzzled because the rock was the same violet blue as the tree bark. The opening of the cave was etched in gold and shimmered, from the distance it was hard to tell by what. As the two of them approached the cave, they saw the opening was filled with a white, liquid substance that flowed into the black dirt, turning it a milky brown. "Come on, let's go over and check it out. It if looks safe we can hide in it until we figure out what to do."

"Okay."

When Bobby and Kimmy reached the cave, they noticed the white substance started to flow harder.

"Do you think someone lives here?" Kimmy asked.

"Hard to say. Right now, I don't care. I'd rather take my chances inside there, then out here. Now come on."

The two of them ran through the white milky curtain of the cave, felt the coolness of whatever it was drench them, and made their shoes sticky. Once they were in the cave it was dry and the dirt was black as night. They both looked around and saw nothing.

They sat down on the ground, and Kimmy leaned against the wall as she pushed her wet, clingy hair out of her face. "I just want to go home."

"Listen Kimmy, do you still have the yellow and blue jewel?"

"I don't know. So much has happened I wouldn't be surprised if I dropped it."

"Check your pockets."

Kimmy stood, checked the pockets of her jeans, and pulled out both jewels.

"Good. Now let's hold hands, and see if it'll be enough to get us home," Bobby said.

"Okay." Kimmy laid the jewels in one hand and held Bobby's with the other. Both of them focused on going home. When nothing happened, Bobby opened his eyes.

"Maybe we need my green jewel too."

Bobby placed the green jewel in Kimmy's palm with the other ones, but nothing happened.

Okay, I guess we need to think of something else. Apparently it's not working."

"Do you realize how upset our parents are going to be when we're not home in time for dinner? I'm going to be grounded forever. My mother will make sure of it."

"Yep. I know."

"How can we let them know?"

"We can't, Kimmy, we're stuck and I'm sorry that I involved you with all of this. It's my fault."

"No it's not. I agreed to do everything with you. Come on. Don't beat yourself up over it. Hey Bobby, do you think our phones work?"

"I doubt it."

They both pulled out their phones and noticed they were searching for service.

"Great," Kimmy mumbled.

When the two of them heard the foreign music right outside the cave, they swung their eyes to look through the sheer white foam. On the other side, they saw the pig man from the dining hall in which they had escaped.

Bobby put his finger to his lips indicating to be quiet.

"I know you creatures are in there. I can smell you all the way out here!"

Kimmy continued to stare at Bobby, until she heard the loud roar.

"The pig man found us," Kimmy whispered, "and he's not happy. Do you think he's going to try to come in here?"

"I don't know what that thing is going to do," Bobby's voice was soft.

"Come out here, right now!" The pig man yelled into the cave.

When neither one responded they watched in horror as the pig man stepped through the white foam.

Moments later, the pig man's eagle eyes landed upon the two of them. His teeth shown brilliant in the dimness of the cave and Kimmy thought they resembled alligator teeth. "You," he pointed at Kimmy, "are the ugliest creature, who talks too much, so you shall die first. Besides, I know you're a coward."

The creature lifted his finger toward Kimmy, and both watched in fascination and horror as yellow fog rolled out of it.

"Do something," Kimmy whispered, barley able to find her voice.

"I don't know what to do," Bobby whispered back.

"Get up!" The pig man yelled.

"No!" Kimmy yelled back at him.

"I said get up right now, or you'll be sorry."

"No. I'm not getting up. If you want me, you'll have to come and get me!" Kimmy stayed where she was as they both watched the yellow fog traveling toward them.

"Who are you and what do you want?" Bobby finally asked.

The creature before them laughed and it sounded like the laugh of a hyena. "I said get up, you creature." He pointed again at Kimmy, who cringed but stayed where she was.

Finally, the creature shrugged. "Fine, have it your way." He sucked in his breath, and then blew the yellow fog toward them.

"Cover your nose and mouth with your hand Kimmy. Don't breathe it in," Bobby told her.

As she did, the creature took another step.

"You're both foolish creatures. Covering your nose and mouth won't stop the power of the spell I just cast!" The cave trembled.

"Listen to me," Bobby lifted his hand to get the words out. "As soon as I say go, get up and try to run past him."

"What? Are you crazy? Have you lost your mind? He fills the entire entrance, so how are we going to get past him?" Kimmy wanted to know.

"I don't know. You got a better idea," Bobby challenged.

"No, I don't."

"Then on the count of two, get up and make a run for it, ready?"

"Yes, I guess. But it better work because if he catches us it won't be good."

"I know."

"Enough!" The pig man yelled again rattling the cave more. "Get up!" Again, he pointed toward Kimmy as the yellow fog engulfed them.

Both of them felt a tingle throughout their bodies, and struggled to hold their eyes opened. Kimmy reached her hand back bracing it on the wall and lifted to her feet, as Bobby did the same.

At the same time they both tried to run, and ended up falling face first into the dirt, and all went dark.

Zuella the good pixie angel watched TriZad as he stood over the two children in the cave. She knew she had to do something quick in order to save them. As she searched her memory for the right remedy, she watched TriZad collecting the scraps of woods thrown about the cave. He stacked them neatly in a pile, and Zuella knew he intended to build a fire, and eat them.

Zuella watched intently as she conjured up one of her favorite spells to cast upon him. When she felt the spell was ready to be discharged from her tiny wings, she flew invisibly over to where he was and released it. Within moments, TriZad fell to the ground with a loud thud, and Zuella flew over to where the children were laying lifeless. She blew a tiny breath on Kimmy's face first, and watched her squirm, then did the same thing to Bobby. Within seconds, both children opened their eyes, and slowly stood, trying to regain their sense of balance.

Kimmy's voice was hoarse, "what happened."

"I don't know," Bobby told her as his voice shook.

Both of them noticed TriZad was out cold on the ground and saw the pile of wood.

"Looks like he was going to build a fire," Bobby nodded at the woodpile.

Kimmy shivered. "Yeah, it does. I wonder what he was going to cook."

"I don't even want to think about it."

"Me either."

"Come on, Kimmy. I think we should get out of here while we can."

They both glanced at TriZad and knew they had to get away from him. Even in sleep, he looked evil.

"Kimmy can you hear me?" a soft voice whispered.

Kimmy looked at Bobby. "What was that?" she whispered.

"I don't know."

"Kimmy, can you hear me?" the voice asked.

"Yes, I can hear you," Kimmy answered.

"Good, now you need to listen."

"Who are you?"

"I can't tell you that. Not yet anyways."

"Okay, then where are you?" Kimmy's eyes darted around the cave.

"Right in front of you," the voice answered.

"I don't see you."

"That's because I'm invisible. I was given the power to be."

"What's your name?" Kimmy asked.

"The name's Zuella."

"Zuella?"

"Yeah, Zuella. What's wrong? Don't you like my name?"

"I like your name. I just don't know what's going on, and why you're invisible."

"I'm invisible because my mother gave me the power to be. Now hush girl, you talk too much, and there's a lot to be said."

"Where are we?" Bobby demanded.

"I was getting to that. You're in Walby, the land of the queen."

"Where's Walby?" Kimmy asked.

"Far away from the world you came from."

"How far? Like how many miles?" Kimmy wanted to know.

"Dear child with the mouth full of questions, too far. There are many miles between you and the place you call home."

"Just tell us where we are, so Bobby and I can start walking."

"Listen, child. Whining won't get you home. You can't walk you're much too far away for that nonsense."

"I don't understand," Kimmy said.

"Kimmy, you're light years away from home."

"But I don't understand, and how come you know my name?"

"It's not for you to understand. Right now, all you need to know is that you're both in danger. You're both stuck in Walby, the queen's part of the country. I don't know how you managed to end up somewhere so dangerous either. TriZad is one of the meanest people in the lands, and you've managed to get his attention as well. I swear kids today don't pay any attention to where they're going. Then have the nerve to complain when they finally figure out where they've ended up."

"Would you stop talking in riddles and putting us down, and just tell me how to get back home," Kimmy demanded. "And you never told me how you know my name."

"I can't tell you, either. But you'll have the answers, eventually."

"I have another question," Kimmy blurted.

"Surprise. Go ahead."

"Are we here because we found the treasure?"

"Ah, now you're getting on the right track. You're wanted here, my child. Yes, that's right. Don't look so surprised. This was all planned out by some very special people, but I can't tell you whom."

"Can you tell me why they had to bring Bobby into it?"

"He brought himself into it. The special people, who need you here, knew that you and Bobby have always been best friends. The people who planned it knew it would be perfect for the two of you to travel to the world you are now in."

"Why?" Kimmy asked. "Why did they think it'd be perfect to drag Bobby into all this?"

"They didn't drag Bobby anywhere. He was a willing participant. Besides, ever since you've been little you and Bobby have always done everything together."

"So, what does that have to do with it?"

"Everything," the voice told her.

"What's the name of the world we're in?" Kimmy asked, again.

"I've already told you, Walby. You need to listen and stop asking so many questions. When you keep asking the questions you do, it wastes not only my time, but yours as well. Do your friends tell you the same thing?"

"Not really."

"Well, bravo to those brave souls then. You've asked more questions in this short time frame then anyone that I know in this world."

"Then this world is boring," Kimmy, said, "as far as me and Bobby being best friends, how do you know that?"

"Because we know everything there is to know about you, even more then you know about yourself."

"I doubt it." Kimmy was annoyed and confused all at the same time.

"I don't," the voice was crisp.

When both Kimmy and Bobby fell silent, the invisible thing laughed. "Ah, finally I draw silence out of the talkative humans. That's what they call you, right?"

"Yes," Kimmy snapped.

"Settle down child. The truth is never easy once you're confronted with it. It's what you do after you learn the truth that counts."

"You still haven't answered my question. Why are we here?"

"That's for you to figure out. Now, if I were the two of you, I'd find somewhere else to hide. You don't want Kixmox to find you in his cave, or TriZad to wake up."

"Who's Kixmox?" Bobby asked.

"The son warrior of the lions."

"You've got to be kidding. Kixmox is a lion?" Kimmy asked astonished.

"Not just any lion or the lion you may have seen at your zoo. Kixmox is the lion of the woods. If he catches you, he'll make you pay by torturing you. Once that's finished he will take you to the queen."

"What's the queen's name?" Kimmy wanted to know.

"Watesa."

Kimmy felt an odd surge of nostalgia over hearing the name, but didn't know why.

"What will she do if she finds us?" Bobby asked.

"Kill you. Now get up, and search for somewhere safer to hide. Kixmox is on his way. If he catches you here you'll be dinner."

"Can you take us somewhere else?" Kimmy asked.

"No. I'm sorry I can't. This is all I can do for you. The rest you've got to figure out on your own."

"Wait!" Kimmy felt panic rise in her throat.

"What is it?" the invisible thing sounded annoyed.

"Our parents will worry when we don't come home."

"Then you better hurry up and find the answers? Sitting around feeling sorry isn't going to help. Now get up before Kixmox finds you and go search for answers."

"Where do we start?" Kimmy asked, standing.

"Start with the truth, Kimmy. If you start there it'll lead you forth," The invisible voice was fading.

"Please don't go."

"I've got too. Now be strong. Go forth and find what you're looking for and what you're needed to do."

"We will."

"Good."

Kimmy felt something brush against her hand and lifted it. Her hand was glowing yellow.

"What the heck is going on Zuella?"

When Zuella didn't answer, she looked at Bobby. "Let's go, Kimmy. You heard what Zuella said. I don't want to be here when that lion comes, or the pig man wakes up." He held out his hand, and Kimmy took it. Together they left the cave and started running again.

CHAPTER THREE

Kimmy and Bobby ran so fast that neither one saw the small body of water until they splashed right through it.

"Great, just great," Kimmy mumbled.

"What the heck happened?" Bobby looked down at his wet clothes.

"Obviously we ran right through water."

The two of them looked around, but neither one could see the water.

"Where did it go?" Kimmy asked spinning around.

"I don't know."

"It was real, right," Kimmy asked.

"Yeah, it was. Look at your jeans."

Kimmy looked down, her jeans were soaked right along with her shoes. "This should be comfortable, huh?"

"Yeah, can't wait to try to run again with wet shoes."

"So, where did the water go?" Kimmy looked around.

"I have no idea. This whole place is freaky if you ask me."

"Yeah it is. Look down at the ground."

When Bobby looked, he watched the black ground bubbling. It reminded him of charcoal, and he didn't want to be dinner. Everything about the land looked contorted. The violet blue tree branches with their gold leaves were low to the ground. The brilliant colors were hurting their eyes, and black ground bubbled, and popped.

"We need to hurry. I don't like the way this place looks."

"Me either. It looks like the ground is trying to swallow us. Where did that invisible person tell us we were?"

"Walby, the land of the queen."

"Well, I'd say the queen has some weird things happening around here."

"I think she knows that. She's probably behind everything bad that's happened to us."

"How do you figure? I doubt she even knows we're here." Kimmy stomped her wet shoe on the ground, and heard it squish.

"Oh, she knows. Anyways, which way do you want to go now?" Bobby stared past Kimmy's head.

"What'd you mean? We're trapped in the woods, it not like there's a path or anything."

"Yes there is. Turn around."

When Kimmy turned, she saw two paths. One was etched in silver the other one gold. "Where did those come from?"

"I don't know. They weren't there a few minutes ago. Now which one do you want to take?"

"I don't care. It doesn't really matter, does it?"

"No, I guess you're right. It doesn't."

"Alright then, you pick the path Bobby. I don't want to make the wrong choice."

"Psss, Kimmy. You need to choose a path. Kixmox is coming quickly through the woods. He's following your scent, which is why you ran through the water. It was put there to help throw him off your trail. Now you must hurry."

"Let's take the silver path," Kimmy blurted.

The two of them grabbed hands, and started running again.

Their shoes felt heavy and slowed them down.

They finally stopped, when they saw two more paths, but this time they were different colors. One path was blue the other was orange.

"Isn't this special?" Kimmy asked Bobby.

"Yeah, real special."

"Pick one Bobby. I picked last time."

"Let's take the orange path."

"Hurry Kimmy, Kixmox is catching up with you."

The two took off again, and Kimmy yelled, "Why can't we see Kixmox coming?"

"Because Kimmy," Zuella answered, "sometimes he can be invisible like I am. Now hurry, run faster."

"We can't. Our clothes are wet, and our shoes are heavy. It's slowing us down."

"Well then, don't dwell on the things that don't feel right, push ahead. Come on, you can do it." Zuella cheered.

As they ran, Kimmy felt like she was going to pass out.

"Have we lost Kixmox?" Bobby asked.

"Almost. Now keep going, don't stop no matter what," Zuella's voice was rushed.

"Easy for you to say, you're not the one running."

"I know, but I am flying right along with you. No easy feat for wings as small as mine."

"Stop, right this instance!" Someone yelled. Both of them stopped where they were, and noticed a tall woman with flowing blonde hair wearing a red gown.

She floated proudly before them, before floating over to where they had stopped.

"What's your name child?" she asked Kimmy.

When Kimmy didn't answer, she felt a light tap on her cheek.

"Ouch, what was that for?" Kimmy yelled.

"I asked you your name child, now speak," the woman scolded her.

Again, when Kimmy didn't answer, she felt a harder slap on her cheek.

"Would you stop hitting me?"

"Hitting you? I've not touched you child," the woman said.

"I'm not talking to you," Kimmy snapped.

"Okay then." The woman turned. "What's your name young man?"

Bobby stared at her but didn't answer, and he felt something bite his ear.

"Ouch, that hurt."

"Then tell her your name," Zuella scolded.

"No."

When he felt a stronger bite, he screamed in pain, and then shouted his name.

"There that's better." The woman smiled. "So your name is Bobby. What is your friend's name?" The woman nodded toward Kimmy.

"Her name's Kimmy."

"Are those human names?"

"Of course. Why did you ask that?" Bobby looked confused.

"Because both your names are those of the humans. All humans have strange names."

"Says who?" Bobby asked.

"Says everyone in this world."

"Let me guess. This is Walby world, right?" Bobby was sarcastic.

"Wrong." The woman looked down her nose at him. "You just left Walby, and crossed over into Parona. Can't you tell?"

"I really wasn't paying that much attention. So, we're in Parona and no longer in Walby," Bobby asked.

"That's right."

"So will Kixmox come to this part of the world?" Kimmy finally asked.

"He could, but he doesn't very often. Kixmox doesn't get along well here," she informed them.

"Why not?" Bobby asked.

"Because he's a beast who works for the queen. We have our own workers here, who work for me. I'm in charge of this part of our world."

"So let me get this straight." Bobby stopped her. "You're in charge of Parona, and the queen is in charge of Walby, right?"

"That's right."

"So how do we get back to earth?" Kimmy demanded.

"Not so fast my child. There's much to do here. I know who sent for you, but I mustn't tell you. It would not sit right if I did that, and I'm not one who looks for trouble. Now come along children, you both must be starving, and in need of dry, clean clothes. Now follow me." She looked at both of them, and then she began floating in the direction she wanted them to follow.

"Where do you think she's taking us?" Kimmy asked.

"Hopefully to a bus station or something so we can get out of here." Bobby smirked.

He watched Kimmy smile. "I wish."

Bobby reached over and took her hand. "Remember no matter what happens you hold tightly to my hand, okay?

"Okay."

"I don't care what anyone else tells you, do not let go," Bobby whispered.

"I won't, I promise."

The woman continued to lead them over the land, and Bobby and Kimmy noticed right away that the trees in Panora were different then the ones in the land of Walby. In fact, everything was different.

The ground where the green grass should have been was a beautiful purple, the sidewalks were gold etched in red, and the bark of the trees were multicolored. The leaves here were silver with tiny flecks of red. As Kimmy stared, she realized the trees held all the colors of the rainbow. The best part was none of these colors hurt their eyes.

The house they approached was baby blue with white shutters, the sidewalk was a brilliant gold etched in silver and so was the long porch that surrounded the house. Kimmy felt as if she was finally home. A feeling that took her by surprise.

Once Bobby and Kimmy were seated in the round, weird looking dining hall, they were served strange looking food. They both noticed none of the food resembled any of the food on earth.

"Excuse me," Kimmy blurted. "What's your name?"

"Firey," the woman stated.

"Okay. So, Firey, can we go to Taco Bell or McDonald's?" Kimmy asked.

"What are those?" Firey asked.

"You don't know what Taco Bell and McDonald's are?"

"No. I'm afraid not."

"They're fast food restaurants." Kimmy smiled.

"Well I've never heard of it. Now eat your food. It's good for you."

"But I can't. It looks awful and too weird looking to put in my mouth."

"No it doesn't, now eat." Firey scolded.

Kimmy looked at her plate, and winced. The food on it resembled a rainbow. Much like everything else, she had seen this far. There were purple long things that didn't look appealing, and the meat once again looked raw.

"Now eat." The woman's voice was firm, as she looked down her nose toward the two of them.

Kimmy and Bobby finally gave in, and dug into their food. They were both surprised to find it quiet good. Even though neither one tried the raw meat.

Once they finished, they changed their clothes, not knowing how this strange woman would have extra clothes for them, but they really didn't care.

Then the woman led them into a colorful room, filled with multi colored furniture, and told them to sit and rest. Kimmy thought all the colors in the room made it look too busy, but she sat down anyway when she realized how exhausted she was.

Once they were settled, Kimmy put her head on Bobby's shoulder, and closed her eyes. Before she knew it, she was fast asleep.

As Bobby watched her, he felt his eyes go heavy, reached over, took Kimmy's hand and he too fell asleep.

When Kimmy woke up, she jumped out of her bed, looked around, and ran to the hall. "Mom!" she yelled.

"Yeah, down here in the kitchen."

Kimmy took off down the steps, ran across the kitchen, and then flung herself in her mother's arms.

"Goodness Kimmy, why are you shaking?" her mother asked. "Could it be because you never listen to me when I tell you not to do something?"

"No, it's because I had the worst dream you could possibly imagine."

"Do you want to talk about it?" Her mother watched her.

"Yeah, I guess."

"Come on. Let's sit down at the table." Her mother led her over to a chair.

"It all started out when Bobby and I found a treasure, and I touched this green stone, and the two of us ended up in this weird, strange world. At first, we're at this long table. Then this pig headed man walked in, sat down, and then ordered that Bobby and

I be thrown to the floor, to take our meal with the other creatures. That's when Bobby told me to crawl out the door of the place we were in, so I did, and he followed. As we ran, I remember we ended up in Walby, and this queen named Watesa, ran that part of the world. So, Bobby and I were running because we had that king of the lions chasing us. His name was Kixmox. The invisible thing that came was helping us, but we never saw who it was because as I said it was invisible. Then we ended up in Parona, where this beautiful woman took us to this quiet comfortable place, feed us this strange looking food, and gave us dry clothes, because Bobby and I had run through this water that we never saw, and it soaked our clothes. Then I put my head on Bobby's shoulder, and fell asleep. When I woke up, I was back home." Kimmy smiled.

Her mother reached over, and grabbed Kimmy's hand. "If you never listened to me before, you must do so now and stay away from the queen, Kimmy, she'll hurt you, and you must stay far away from the warrior lion. Promise me." Her mother squeezed her hand. "Say it."

"I promise, Mom."

Her mother handed her an old book. "This is for you. I should have given it to you a long time ago, but I was hoping this would never happen. But it has and now it's your turn to learn of the things I've kept from you."

"What do you mean, Mom?"

"Just what I said, Kimmy. There's much to say and they've only given me a little time to tell you everything."

"Mom, you're scaring me."

"Be still my child, and let me speak."

Kimmy stopped talking.

"Very well. When you wake up it'll be important to know what your given name is. Now you know that your name on Earth is Kimmy. But your given name is Charisma, but its spelled Karisma."

"Mom, I don't understand what any of this means."

"Just listen to me carefully. Hold onto the book I just gave you. Read it when time allows, and remember your given name is Karisma, which means to charm and allure."

Mom, where are you going? Why are you fading?"

"I must go home now, Kimmy. You're wanted here, and now you must stay. They've taken you. I knew someday it would happen. I just wasn't expecting this to be the day, but I should have. You did everything I cautioned you not to do, so now you're on your own. I can't help you anymore. The only other thing I can tell you is to be brave." Kimmy watched as her mother started to fade. "Remember, everything I did to you was done so that I could protect you from what's happening right now. I'm sorry if I was harsh. I just never wanted them to get you."

"Mom, wait. Don't go. Mom, please don't go. Take me with you."

Bobby watched Kimmy shake her head back and forth, as she talked in her sleep.

He gently reached over and woke her. When Kimmy looked around, she was still in the weird, strange world she had just spoken to her mother about, and she noticed she was still holding the book her mother had given her.

"Where am I?" Kimmy asked, but already knew the answer.

"Oh, we're still where we were when you fell asleep. What's with the book your holding?" Bobby asked.

"Be still and silent my children. All will be explained in good time," Firey said, as she stood next to them wearing a long, deep blue gown.

"What's your name again?" Kimmy asked.

"My name is Firey," she answered.

Kimmy continued to look at her.

"What is it child?" the woman asked.

"Do you know my mother?" Kimmy whispered.

Firey nodded her head. "Yes, I know her."

"How?"

"I just do."

"If you know her then what's her name?" Kimmy stood.

"Her name is Rain."

Kimmy stared at her confused. "I don't understand."

"Child, you don't always need to understand."

"Yes, I do. I just had a dream that I was home with my mom. I told her everything that happened to me, and she insisted I come back here. She even gave me this book, and told me to read it when the time allows." Kimmy's eyes swelled with tears. "Now that's why I need to understand. I also need someone to tell me where Camille went, and why she's no longer with me."

Bobby stood and threw his arm around her shoulder. "It's not worth getting all upset over, Kimmy. I'm sure we'll find out why we're here soon enough."

Kimmy sniffed. "I know, but I feel bad that I brought you into this."

"Excuse me. As I recall I'm the one who talked you into following me to the hidden treasure I found."

"Yeah, you did. But obviously, they had it all planned out that way. Face it, they wanted us here. Now we're stuck because obviously we can't go home."

"I don't mind. I figure if you're here, that I should be too. Someone's got to look out for you."

"Well I'm glad the two of us are together. It could be worse. I could be stuck here with Dave." She winced at the thought.

"Yeah, we all know he's your favorite."

"Ha. Yeah, I like him just about as much as I like taking tests at school that I forgot to study for."

Bobby wiped her tears, and smiled.

"Come children that's enough tears, and talk. We've much to do. I heard the rumor as you humans call it that Kixmox is going to be paying us a visit very soon."

"But I thought you said he's not allowed here," Bobby said.

"Ah, I did. But he may travel the lands when the stars are aligned just so."

"So when are the stars going to be aligned?" Kimmy asked.

"Soon, children, very soon, now come. We've much to do in a short time span."

Bobby and Kimmy followed her, and Firey started talking, "What is your given name, my child?" she asked Kimmy.

"Kimmy."

"No, listen what I'm asking you. What is your given name?" she asked again.

"Why?"

"Because it's an important part of who you are that's why."

"I don't see how it's important. Everyone calls me Kimmy."

"I know, but you need to speak your given name, and then I'll explain to you why your hands are glowing yellow, and why you're here." Firey looked at Kimmy's hands.

"My given name is, Charisma, with a K."

"That's right, it is. Do you know why your mother switched the first letter to a K? I mean we all know how Charisma is spelled, but do you know why your mother changed it."

"No."

"Ah, so that is your first lesson. Do you know what your name means, my child?"

"Yes," she answered, looking at Bobby.

"What does it mean?" Firey asked.

"My mother told me my name means to charm and allure."

"Very good. Your mother's always been very bright." Firey smiled at Kimmy.

"So tell me why my hands are glowing yellow."

"I will, but not yet. You've much to learn."

"I don't understand what this is all about?" Bobby blurted.

"You will, Bobby. Now let me ask you, do you know your given name?"

"Yeah, it's Bobby."

"To the humans it is. But do you know what your given name is?"

"I just told you, it's Bobby."

"No it isn't. Your mother just chose to call you that in the human world. Much like Kimmy's mother did. Has she told you of your heritage Bobby Martin?"

"No, she hasn't."

Firey lifted her finger and pointed. "It doesn't surprise me. Your mother was the one always denying what we all are."

"I'm sorry, but I'm confused. How do you know our mother's, and why haven't they told us about you?"

"Because the law of this land forbids them from talking until their granted permission from the highest power to do so," she paused. "By the time this is done, you'll be even more confused then you are now. So let it go."

"Let it go? No way. Tell me what my given name is," Bobby demanded.

"If I tell you, will you believe me?"

Bobby looked at Kimmy who slightly nodded her head.

"Yes, Firey, I'll believe you."

"Very well, come sit around the fire, and I shall tell you about your given name." Firey led them into a beautiful room with colorful furniture and rugs in all shades of blue.

She titled her head, indicating they should sit on the rugs thrown on the floor. "Sit, both of you."

When Bobby and Kimmy were situated, Firey blew the smoke

coming out of the fire and sat back, and watched.

At first, Bobby and Kimmy were alarmed when they watched the smoke form a cloud, and both of them saw their mothers. When the two women smiled at their children, Bobby and Kimmy smiled back.

"Listen to your mothers my children. They've much to tell in a little span of time."

Bobby watched as his mother sat up straighter on the cloud, floating in front of him. "Bobby your given name is Boulder. It means my son that you're as strong as the rocks, as powerful as the mountains and as bold as an eagle."

"I don't understand, Mom."

"I know, but you will."

"No, I won't. I mean look I still don't get it."

"It isn't for you to get. You see you were born into a very special family. One with great…"

"Windy, you must stop now," Firey told Bobby's mother. "Too much too soon, is no good."

"You're right," Windy agreed with Firey.

"I know." Firey smiled at all of them. "That lesson is obviously one that I must teach your children."

Then Firey turned to Rain. "Your turn."

"Kimmy your given name is Charisma, but with a K."

"Why?"

"Why what?" Her mother looked at her confused.

"Why did you change the first letter to a K?"

"Because you're full of charm with the power to allure, I changed the first letter to a K because it is the letter of the city you were born too."

"Mom, you know I was born on earth."

"Yes, you were. But on the day you were born…"

"That's quite enough," Firey told Rain.

"Okay." Rain smiled at her daughter. "Remember the power of your given name Kimmy and you'll do well."

Both of the kids watched as the smoky cloud started drifting away from them, and slowly disappeared.

They looked at Firey.

"That was really weird, and you've got a lot of explaining to do," Kimmy said.

"You're right, so let's get started shall we?"

CHAPTER FOUR

As Manning and Dave arrived at the roller rink neither one saw Kimmy or Bobby.

"Do you think they'll show?" Manning asked.

"Hope so, but I don't know."

"Do you really think that they snuck in the old building?" Manning asked lacing up his skates.

"No way. I think Bobby was just trying to lure Kimmy away." Dave winked, then, laughed.

"Seriously, you can't really think that. If he wanted to lure Kimmy away, he would've never invited us to eat lunch with them, or told us that strange story."

Dave shrugged. "Come on Manning, most people have to dive for treasure, or something like that." Dave finished with his skates, leaned back, and waited for Manning.

"But what if it was true?"

"Then I guess we find out when Kimmy and Bobby show. Until then, it's just a giant question mark, isn't it?"

"Yeah." Manning stood. "Let's go skate."

When Dave and Manning saw Renee and Shelby, two of their other friends on the other side of the roller rink they skated over to them.

"Did you just get here?" Manning asked them.

"Yeah," Renee told him. "We were hoping Kimmy would already be here, but it doesn't look like she is."

"Yeah, for real," Shelby agreed. "She told us this morning on the phone, she was coming up here tonight."

"Well, hate to break it to you, but she's not here yet," Dave told them as the four of them exited the rink, and stopped so they could talk.

"Where is Kimmy, do you know?" Renee asked the boys.

Manning laughed. "She took off with Bobby right after lunch."

"What's so funny? Where'd they go?" Renee wanted to know.

Dave looked at both girls. "Neither one of you would believe it if we told you."

"Try us." Shelby glanced at him with her stormy gray eyes.

"Yeah, tell us what's going on," Renee demanded.

Dave shrugged. "Okay, you asked for it. Bobby found a treasure chest in an abandoned warehouse on Mill Street and wanted all of us to go with him to see it. Truth is, Manning and me didn't believe him so Kimmy and Bobby took off. Now we don't know where they are. They left after the four of us had lunch at Taco Bell, and we haven't seen them since."

"Very funny," Renee's voice was snide.

"Yeah, I wasn't expecting that one," Shelby admitted. "Why would you lie to us?"

"Look, the two of them took off like I said, to look inside this old building for treasure," Dave said.

"They did," Manning agreed.

"Okay, whatever. If she took off with Bobby after lunch to go into an old building, shouldn't they be back by now?" Shelby looked worried and upset at the same time.

"Not really. Manning and I figured Bobby was just trying to get Kimmy alone for a while."

"Why? They're not dating," Shelby said.

"Who cares, gosh, I'm tired of talking about it. This is what I think is going on. Kimmy and Bobby lost track of time, or maybe Bobby asked Kimmy to be his girl, and they don't want company." Dave smiled.

"I doubt it, and even if Bobby asked Kimmy to be his girl, they're not like that. They would have called and told us," Renee stated.

"Yeah, she's right," Shelby agreed, as she swung her head, her long blonde hair tumbled down her back.

"Did you at least call Bobby on his phone?" Renee asked.

"No. Now can we go skate? I'm telling you that Manning and I know for a fact that Bobby likes Kimmy. I'm not worried about them because they're probably off somewhere talking and having a good time, which is what we should be doing. Now come on." Dave looked at them.

"Oh that's good. Two of our friends are missing, and you want to skate?" Renee was upset.

"Yeah, that's right I do. They're fine, besides, Kimmy's not one of my favorite people." Dave skated away, and left Manning standing there.

He looked at both girls. "Well we all know that he doesn't get along with Kimmy, but he's probably right, you know. I think we should go skate and see if they show. Let's give it an hour. If they're not here by then, we'll call them on their phones."

"No way. I'm not waiting."Renee took out her phone and called Kimmy, when it went right to voice mail she left a message. "Something isn't right, but I can't put my finger on it, yet." Renee flipped her dark hair over her shoulder. "Come on, let's go skate, but I'm telling you, Manning that if anything happened, I'd hate to be you and Dave. Our parent's are going to be mighty upset with the two of you. First, for not calling them and letting them know that Kimmy and Bobby aren't here when their supposed to be, and because you let them go into an old deserted building by themselves. What kind of a friend does that, huh?" Renee took off and skated fast around the rink, listening to the music.

Finally, Shelby and Manning caught up to her."Don't be mad," Manning said.

"Don't be mad. Is that the best you can do? Come on, Manning, two of our friends have disappeared and all you can say is don't be mad? Do me a favor and, go away," Renee told him.

"Renee, don't be mad at me. I'm begging you," Manning continued to plead with her.

Renee said nothing. The whole story didn't make any sense to her, and finally she knew she needed to call Bobby's mother, then Kimmy's house, and would do so once she reached the other side of the rink.

Dave saw his friends, and noticed a bright, blue circle form around all of them as they skated.

He wondered if anyone else on the rink had noticed the eerie blue light that surrounded them, and as he looked around at the other kids skating, he realized they were oblivious to it.

Dave sped up, and tried to catch the three of them to ask about the blue circle, but by the time he got to the other side of the rink, they had disappeared.

Dave looked around the rink, frantic, but couldn't see them anywhere.

He exited the rink, skated through it, searching, but he couldn't find his friends.

He skated to the boy's bathroom. "Manning, are you in here!"

No one answered. He waited outside the girl's bathroom knowing he couldn't go in. When he saw a group of girls skating over to it, he waited. When they reached the door, he stopped them. "Wanna do me a favor?" Dave asked the group.

"What?" a cute blonde girl smiled at him.

"When you go in there will you ask if there's a Renee or Shelby?"

"Why?" The girl stared at him with big, blue eyes.

"Because I'm trying to find my friends, and I can't very well go in there, right?"

The girl giggled. "I don't think that'd be a good idea."

"So you'll do it."

"I guess." The girl skated into the bathroom, and moments later she emerged. "Sorry, if anyone in there is Renee or Shelby they're denying it."

"Great." Dave ranked his hand through his dark hair. "Listen, you didn't happen to see the blue light on the rink a few moments ago, did you?"

"What blue light?" the girl looked at him.

"You know the blue light that appeared out of nowhere, and took my friends. Now I can't find them anywhere."

"Okay. That's just not right. Are you telling me a blue light made your friends disappear? Listen to what you're saying."

"I know what I'm saying. Just forget it," he said and skated away. He searched the entire rink and they were nowhere to be found.

He stopped by the front desk and asked if anyone had seen the three of them leave, and the girl behind the counter told him, they didn't. Now as he thought about what he saw, he wondered why no one had seen them disappear.

He thought about leaving, but didn't want to chance missing Kimmy and Bobby if they showed up. He wished that if they were coming, they'd hurry. He needed to tell someone what just happened.

He skated over to the D.J. booth.

"Yeah, what can I play for you?" the D.J. yelled.

"Nothing. I was wondering if you saw the strange blue light on the rink a few minutes ago!" Dave had to scream the music was too loud.

"What strange blue light?"

You know the light that surrounded my friends. The one that made them disappear."

"Sorry, kid. I didn't see the light." The D.J. gave him a strange look.

"Whatever." Dave skated back onto the rink, letting his eyes wander around all the kids skating, but he didn't see his friends.

He continued to skate, and he saw another circle, this time red moving toward him on the rink. He tried to avoid running into it, but it didn't work, and soon Dave felt like he was falling.

When Manning, Shelby and Renee realized they were suddenly in the middle of a field, surrounded in brilliant colors, they all waited a moment, trying to recollect what happened.

Manning finally looked at the girls. "Where are your shoes?" he asked when he noticed they were barefoot.

"The same place as yours, obviously." Shelby nodded toward his feet.

"Where are we?" Renee asked.

"Who knows?" Manning sat up.

They heard a loud sound and Manning lay back down next to his friends, as they all covered their heads with their arms.

When they heard a deep moan, Manning opened one eye, and saw Dave lying next to him.

"So you made it, too?" Manning asked, watching Dave jump up then he spun around and glared.

"Thank goodness I found you guys," Dave said, "why did you take off like that, huh?"

Manning shrugged. "I don't know."

"What happened?" Dave asked.

"Dave, we know as much as you do," Shelby snapped standing.

"Where are my shoes?" Dave looked confused as he stared at his bare feet.

"The same place as the rest of ours." Renee stood.

When the four of them heard the horse hooves barreling toward them, they looked at each other and took off running.

———— ⟨⟨◉⟩⟩ ————

Watesa the queen sat watching the four giants running through the field, and smiled.

Soon they would enter the woods, be captured and become prisoners, trapped in the land of Walby. She would see to it that they were locked in the dungeon far beneath their world, pitched in darkness where it was cold and damp. They would not make it as far as the other two giant people did.

She pulled out her sword, rubbed twice and Vixbit appeared. "Yes, Queen."

"More giant people have just entered the woods. Find them, and bring them to me, alive."

"But my Queen there's no way. The whisper of the forest suggests that they yield magic in their bones. If what they say is true, it'll be the end of my life."

"Silence!" Watesa glared at Vixbit. "If what you say is true, then we must take them as prisoners now."

"But my Queen you don't understand. This is a job for Kixmox, not me. I'm a spy, not a warrior."

Watesa held up her tentacle, and looked at it; saw the four giant people still running, then, saw the knights on the horses.

She immediately picked up her sword, swung it three times, and Kixmox appeared.

"What is it?" Kixmox asked annoyed.

"They're more giant people in the woods. Find them and bring them to me," Watesa demanded.

"If I must bring them to you then when shall I eat?" Kixmox growled.

"Later. When you've earned it. Now go." She waved her tentacle. "Be gone."

Vixbit watched as Kixmox disappeared.

"Now you." Watesa turned to stare at him with her purple eye. "Go to the giants find out who they are, then report back to me."

"Yes, my Queen."

"Now be gone." Watesa lifted her tentacle, and Vixbit disappeared.

The horses ran closer to the four of them, and Shelby stopped. She was out of breath, and tired of running.

"What're you doing?" Manning asked her.

"I can't breathe, so I needed to stop."

"Is it your asthma?" Manning looked at her, and realized Dave and Renee were still running.

"Yeah."

"Do you have your inhaler?"

Shelby nodded, reached in her pocket, took it out, and dispensed it. "I'm sorry Manning. We're going to be caught."

"Don't worry. I'd rather be with you, than know you're alone with them." Manning stared at the knights that stopped before them. Both of the knights looked powerful and strong sitting high on their horses.

"You are in Walby on the land ruled by, Watesa," one of the knights with long, jet black hair and summer blue eyes told them.

"Yeah, so?" Manning shrugged.

"What does yeah so, mean?" the knight looked at him quizzically.

"It means we don't care," Shelby said.

The knight threw his head back and laughed a rich, deep sound. "You'll care when she takes you prisoner."

"She can't," Shelby answered, "the worse she can do is call the cops on us for trespassing."

"Cops, you say? What is that?" the knight asked.

"You can't be serious?" Manning asked. "Everyone knows who the cops are."

"Cops? What are those?" the second knight asked, as his long, blond hair blew in the wind.

"You know, like when you do something wrong. The police, cops, same thing."

"I don't know what you're saying." The knight shook his head confused. "You come with us. Kixmox is on his way."

"Who's Kixmox?" Shelby asked.

When they heard the roar, both looked at the knight, as he held out his hand to Shelby, and another knight held out their hand to Manning. "That's Kixmox."

Neither one argued, as the roar grew louder. They grabbed the knights' hands, and were flung behind them on the horses bareback.

"Wait!" Shelby yelled. "We've got two more friends running through the woods."

"They're on their own. We can't enter the woods to save them now. The invisible shield will not allow it," the knight said, as the horse flew over the field carrying them further away from their friends.

Dave and Renee heard the roar of something getting louder, and Dave finally looked over his shoulder. "Where did Manning and Shelby go?" he asked Renee, still running.

"What'd you mean? They're right behind us."

"No they're not."

"What?"

When Dave saw Renee try to stop, he grabbed her arm. "There's no stopping right now. Whatever that roaring is, it's coming closer to where we are. Now keep running," his voice was harsher then he intended, but Renee kept going.

"Hey, Dave, over here."

"Who said that?" Dave asked Renee.

"I don't know. I'm not stopping to find out either," Renee answered.

"Hey Dave, you deaf? I said over here," Dave heard the voice again, but ignored it, and continued hanging onto Renee's arm.

When they heard the roar again, Dave looked behind them, and saw the lion.

"Renee, we're in trouble."

"Don't tell me that."

"Well, we are. There's a lion chasing us."

"A what?" Renee panicked.

"A lion."

"No way."

"Yes, way."

"What should we do?" Renee glanced over.

"Keep running."

"What if it catches us?"

"Then we're dinner."

"Dave, are you ignorant?" Both of them heard someone ask. Dave pulled Renee to him, and the two of them stopped running.

"Who's calling my name?" Dave yelled, and saw the lion closing the distance between them.

"I am." Dave watched the little man step out from behind a violet blue tree in the woods.

"Who are you?" Dave looked down at the little creature with the white hair, oversized reading glasses, and big, curly shoes.

"I'm Tibbs," he told Dave, then, raised his hand. Dave and Renee watched as the lion froze in mid stride.

"How'd you do that?" Dave asked.

"Magic."

"Yeah, whatever. What'd you want?"

"You've a sharp tongue, huh?" Tibbs watched him.

"What'd you mean?"

"You've a sharp tongue. A thank you would be good."

"For what?"

"For not letting you be dinner, as you called it."

"Thanks." Dave was embarrassed. "How'd you know I said that?"

"Magic. Now you must hurry. The lion has three minutes until it comes again. Now follow me up this tree. You'll be safe there."

"I can't climb that tree," Renee said. "I don't have shoes."

"Bah, you don't need shoes, watch me." He scaled the tree quicker than their eyes could travel. "See." He smiled from far up in the tree.

"Yeah, we see." Dave looked at Renee. "I'll hoist you up, and you grab the branch. It's the only way."

Renee went to put her foot in his hands, and instantly she and Dave were at the top of the weird looking tree, staring down at the hungry lion at the bottom.

"Now let's go," Tibbs told them.

"How are we going to go anywhere? We're stuck in this tree." Renee noticed the crimson leaves, and violet blue branches, and thought it was strange and beautiful all at the same time.

"Close your eyes, both of you," Tibbs said, jumping up.

When the two of them closed their eyes, they felt their feet leave the tree.

"Do not open your eyes until I say. If you do, you'll fall," Tibbs said.

Neither Renee nor Dave opened their eyes. Not because they believed the little man called Tibbs, but now, they had no other choice.

CHAPTER FIVE

Kimmy and Bobby stared at Firey confused over what happened with their mother's.

They both noticed she was still smiling gently at them.

"When are you going to start talking?" Kimmy demanded.

"In a little while. You see my children, you've much to learn."

"We know that, but what about our life on earth?" Kimmy asked.

"Be still my child. You won't miss earth that much in time. Soon it will all become a distant memory for you, much like this world did, when you were taken from it."

"I don't understand any of this," Kimmy pouted.

"It isn't what you understand, Karisma. It's what you do with what you find out here in this world that counts."

"But why are we in this world?" Bobby asked.

"Boulder, you must not be that way. Both of you must clear your mind. Forget earth, or you'll fail in your task."

"How can we forget, huh?" Kimmy asked. "All our friends are there, our families, our schools. Not to mention our lives."

"I know you're upset my children, but you must stop it," Firey said, "There's much to do. Now if you're ready we'll continue. If not, I shall leave the two of you to think about what you need to focus on. The choice is yours." Firey stood.

"Fine. Let's get on with it," Kimmy said.

"Very well. But first, you must rest. You're minds are foggy."

"I don't want to rest. I don't want to do anything, but figure out how to get back to earth," Kimmy snapped at Firey.

When they watched Firey tilt her head to one side, they watched her face cloud with anger, then, she smiled, looked at the two of them, and waved her hand.

Kimmy and Bobby watched as she disappeared, leaving behind a fine mist of smoke.

"Where did she go?" Kimmy was alarmed.

"I don't know." Bobby yawned.

"I'm tired, Bobby," Kimmy said.

He reached over, threw his arm around her shoulder, and she laid her head down. He leaned his own head back against the sofa, and soon the two of them were asleep.

Firey flew through the forest, and stopped suddenly when she saw what Camille, Kimmy's fairy had told her.

She moved silently through the trees, and her eyes came to rest on two of the other children. They were as beautiful as the others, and she knew that soon they would join her. But not yet. Not until the moment presented itself.

Firey silently snuck up on Tibbs, tapped his shoulder, and watched him jump, as she laughed.

Tibbs swung around, watching Firey materialize in front of him.

"I hate when you do that, Firey." Tibbs shook his head.

"I'm sorry." Firey smiled. "You did well today, Tibbs. These are the other two children that our world needs."

Tibbs nodded. "I figured they were. They're different creatures, aren't they?"

"Different because they're from earth." Firey watched Dave and Renee then glanced at Tibbs. "You mustn't let them out of your eye sight."

"I won't. I haven't yet, but I'm telling you, they're both unruly."

"I know which is part of who they are. Please Tibbs; watch carefully, they're many dangers now."

"I know, Firey. I feel it."

Firey blew smoke toward Renee and Dave, and watched them close their eyes. "They'll sleep now, and as for me, I'm going to venture out." Firey smiled at her friend.

Tibbs nodded. "Be quick about it, I feel the queen approaching."

"Then I surely must get back to the other children." Firey panicked and Tibbs watched her go up in smoke.

When Manning and Shelby finally felt their horses stop, they were grateful.

"Can we get down now?" Shelby asked the knight.

"No. Stay," the knight answered.

"Why?" Shelby argued.

"Because we feel the queen, she is moving through the land. It is not good. She shall search, and destroy," the knight answered.

"Search and destroy what?" Manning asked.

"Silence!" the knight carrying Manning yelled.

The knights stared through the darkness, which had fallen on the land, and then they looked at one another, nodded and took off riding.

"Where are we going now?" Shelby complained.

"Be silent, you foolish child. If the queen hears you, she'll come."

"Then what will happen?" Shelby asked.

"Then you'll be her prisoner. She'll never let you go."

Shelby didn't respond. Right now, she wasn't taken the chance. If what the knight told her was true, she didn't want the queen to find her and Manning.

"When can Manning and I go home?" Shelby whispered.

The knight stopped his horse, turned to look at her, then reached out, placed his hand over her mouth, stared in her eyes, and Shelby fell asleep.

Then knight took off again barreling over the land.

"Hey what'd you do that for?" Manning yelled.

The knight in front of Manning, stopped his horse, swung around, spit in his face, and Bobby felt his world go dark. Then the knight continued riding.

When the queen landed just outside Kixmox cave, she stood at the entrance. "Kixmox come out here this instance."

"What is it now, Watesa?" Kixmox asked.

"You fool, who dares to rest when I've given you an order to capture the giant people in the woods." A beam of light came out of her purple eye, stinging Kixmox, making him cry out.

"What do you want?" Kixmox asked once he recovered from the sting.

"I want the giants. Yet, you dare to sleep?" She challenged.

"Yes, I dare to sleep. I'm weak, but don't know the cause."

"The cause you imbecile, is the giants. They're taking your powers, and you must take them back at once. If you don't Kixmox, you'll be ruined. Then who will guard this land?"

"I don't know who?"

"I will summons, Dagg. Then turn the job over to him."

"You wouldn't become a traitor," Kixmox said.

"Oh wouldn't I?" She snapped her tentacle, crumbling part of the cave.

Kixmox stared. "Very well, what would you have me do?"

"What I told you. Find the giants. All of them, and destroy them. If you don't find them, and destroy them, I'll summons Dagg."

Kixmox growled, took one more look at the queen, and then started his search.

As Kixmox ran over the land, he yelled out for Vixbit.

"What is it?" Vixbit demanded appearing on Kixmox nose.

"You must fly to the tree up here on your left. Fly up until you see the children, and find some way to lure them down to me," Kixmox snapped.

"How am I going to do that? Huh? I'm but a mere fly. The only recognition I ever get is a swat from most. Face it, Kixmox; I'm nothing more than a spy."

"Kixmox over here," he heard a voice say.

"What was that, Vixbit?"

"I don't know. I was ready to ask the same thing."

"Kixmox, if you want the children come here," the voice whispered.

"Come where?" Kixmox demanded drooling from his mouth because he felt so weak.

"Over here, behind the tree."

Kixmox ran to the tree, realized too late it was a trap, felt his legs caught in the rope, and soon he was hanging upside down.

When he heard the giggle, he wasn't pleased. "Release me now. If the queen finds out what you've done, she'll come. Then she'll kill you."

"She'll never find me," the voice told him, giggling again.

"Vixbit are you still with me?"

"Yes, Kixmox."

"Then do something. Release me now."

"I can't Kixmox."

"What do you mean you can't, Vixbit?"

"I can't. There's tiny ropes attached to me, and I can't move either."

"Then chew through them."

"It won't work," the voice told him. "You can't chew the rope of the invisible."

"Who are you?" Kixmox asked.

"The name's Tomkin, at your service." Kixmox heard the giggle again.

"Tomkin, you say?"

"Very good Kixmox, you're not as stupid as I've heard you to be," the voice told him giggling again.

"Tomkin, if you release me and Vixbit, then every wish shall be yours for the asking."

"Oh, but that's where you're wrong. Every wish is already mine for the taking. Sorry, you lose," Kixmox heard the voice slowly fade away.

"Wait!" Kixmox yelled, hanging upside down.

When no one answered, Kixmox growled. "Vixbit find a way to get me out of here, or you shall die a painful death."

When Vixbit didn't answer, Kixmox realized he was alone.

Kimmy yawned, stretched, then opened her eyes, and realized Bobby was still sleeping. She quietly lifted his arm from around her, walked to one of the glass windows, and stared into the darken night.

Something flickered right outside the window, making Kimmy turn, and then she walked to the door, opened it, let herself out, and walked to the area of the flicker.

"What're you doing out here, Kimmy?"

Kimmy spun around, but saw no one.

"I asked you a question, which needs an answer," the voice told her.

"I...I saw something flicker, so I came out to investigate," she said.

"Do you always do what you're told not to do?" the voice asked.

"No, not always."

"So why did you leave the safety of the house!" the voice yelled at her.

"I told you!" Kimmy yelled back.

"So it's true. You're the child from the planet you call earth, aren't you?"

"Yes." She was irritated.

"That's why you don't listen."

"No, that's not why. I just want to find out where I am, and how to get home. I don't like it here."

"Ah, but it isn't up to you."

"Who are you anyway?"

"My name's Redilla."

"Redilla? Where are you from?"

"I'm from here, the land of Parona."

"Who are you?" Kimmy asked.

"I told you child. I'm Redilla."

"I know that. But why can't I see you?"

"I'm invisible to the naked eye."

"What does that mean? Do I need special glasses to see you or something?"

"No. You need special powers. Only then will I be revealed."

"Then I guess I'll never see you."

"That would largely depend on you."

"I don't understand."

"I know, its quiet common, and 'understand,' must be one of your favorite words." Redilla giggled.

"Why do you say that?"

"Because Child, since you've arrived here, you've said the word 'understand', at least twenty times."

"So what? I like that word."

"Obviously."

"What's your point?"

"My point, as you call it, is not to understand, but to know what is."

"You've completely lost me now."

"Okay, okay. You were summoned here, and your mother gave permission for you to return…"

"Redilla enough!" Firey yelled.

"Sorry, Firey."

"You should be. You know the rules, yet you open your mouth anyway. Camille will not like it, and neither do I."

"You know Camille? Where is she?" Kimmy asked.

"Never mind, Karisma, enough has been said, now into the dwelling you must go."

"Dwelling? You mean house?" Kimmy was confused.

"House?" Firey looked at her. "Get in the structure. You're not safe out here."

"Why?" Kimmy asked.

"You ask way too many questions," Firey answered.

"I know she does, and she uses that word 'understand' all the time," Redilla said.

"Yes, she does."

"I think she likes that word a lot," Redilla said.

"I believe she does, but now we must go Redilla. Something is moving about the land, and it's not friendly."

Firey grabbed Kimmy by the arm, pulled her to the dwelling, and slammed the door. "Don't ever leave the dwelling without letting me know!"

"You weren't here, so how was I supposed to let you know."

"If I'm not here, it means don't wander." Firey glared at her.

"Why? I don't..."

"Don't say it. You will learn soon enough if you'd only open your mind to what's going on."

"I don't want to open my mind, Firey. I just want to go home."

"That's not possible. The time is upon us, and now no one leaves and no one comes through."

"What does that mean?" Kimmy asked.

"It means, for now, you can't leave to go home to earth, and no one from earth is allowed to come here. All portholes are now closed. You're stuck in this new world, and you better adjust quickly if you want to survive."

"Fine!" Kimmy opened the door to the room Bobby was sleeping in, and slammed the door behind her.

Firey watched and knew Kimmy would be just fine. Her spirit was strong, an ingredient all the children needed for the fight that lied ahead.

CHAPTER SIX

Bobby opened his eyes when he heard the door slam, and saw Kimmy standing by it with her arms folded across her chest. "What's wrong?" he whispered.

"Nothing, besides the fact that I went for a walk, met some creature by the name of Redilla, and we were having a perfectly good conversation about why we're here, when Firey showed up out of nowhere, and yelled at both of us."

"Maybe Firey was worried about you wandering off alone."

"Oh, no, not you too. I'm sick of people worrying. Everyone acts like I'm not old enough to take care of myself."

"I think you're taking it the wrong way." Bobby stood. "Kimmy we're in a strange place with weird things going on. I don't think it's safe for either of us to wander off, especially alone."

"I don't care, Bobby Martin. Gosh, sometimes I just need a little space to get my thoughts and feelings together. A lot has happened in a short period of time."

"No, really? Kimmy you act as if you're the only one affected by what's happened, but you're not. I'm not thrilled about being here either, but there's obviously nothing we can do."

Kimmy looked at him. "I know, you're right, I'm sorry."

"Stop. You don't have to say that to me. You and I are friends. I just want you to know it's bothering me too."

"You're so nice, Bobby."

"Thanks."

"Oh my gosh." Kimmy stared at him.

"What?"

"I was just thinking your birthday is in two days, and we're stuck here. Are you bummed out?"

"A little. I mean this is not the ideal place to celebrate a fifteenth birthday, but I'm sure I'll get over it."

"Yeah, you don't have a choice."

"Yeah, neither do you. You're birthday is one week away Kimmy, and then you'll finally be fourteen. I hope we're back on earth by then."

"Well if not, it's no big deal. Like you said, I'll just have to deal with it."

Bobby walked over to Kimmy, brushed the hair back from her face, and stared in her eyes. "We're going to be alright. I promise you. I won't let anything happen."

Kimmy nodded. "I trust you Bobby, I always have. Ever since we were little, I've always felt like I had nothing to worry about if you were with me."

"Good. You keep that feeling close to you. I don't know what's going to happen while were here, but I won't leave you, as long as I can help it."

Kimmy kissed his cheek. "Thanks."

"You're welcome now let's try to get some sleep. I've got a feeling tomorrow's going to be busy." He led her back to the sofa, put his arm around her, and the two of them watched the fine mist of smoke bellowing toward them, and soon fell asleep.

When Manning opened his eyes, he realized it was morning, and he and Shelby were in a cave.

He sat up to look around, and saw the two knights. When he

saw Shelby open her eyes, he watched her look around, and she too sat up.

"Who are you?" Shelby demanded.

The knight she had ridden with looked at her. "I am Zambler, and he's Juniper." The knight continued to stare.

"Are we your hostages?"

"What does hostage's mean?" Zambler asked.

"You know, have you kidnapped us for a ransom, or are you going to shoot us or what?"

"You humans talk in a weird way."

"Just answer the question." Shelby eyed him.

"I don't know how to answer what you've asked. So let me say what happened last night was part of our job."

"Yeah, right. Now I want you to listen, Zam..."

"Excuse me," Zambler interrupted. "My given name is Zambler, not Zam."

"Okay, Zam, as I was saying, our parents will double the money you want for us, if you'll return us alive."

"Your talk confuses me." Zambler looked at Juniper who nodded.

"All I'm saying is..."

"What is your given name?" Zambler cut Shelby off again.

"My name's Shelby. He's Manning."

"Are those your given names?" Juniper asked, crinkling his nose in disdain.

"Yes, those are our given names, as you call it," Manning told them.

"You are almost a man." Zambler looked at him.

"I guess." Manning shrugged. "My birthday's ten days away, then I'll be fifteen."

"Yeah, my birthday's tomorrow. I'll be fourteen." Shelby volunteered.

"That explains it," Juniper said.

"Explains what?" Shelby asked.

"Why you're here."

"No it doesn't, so start talking," Shelby demanded.

Juniper shrugged. "Okay you see, it's time for the two of you..."

"Juniper don't you dare!" all of them heard the female voice.

They watched as a beautiful woman with long blonde hair, wearing a blue long dress approach the cave.

"Enough," the woman told the knights. "I told everyone the rules, but yet your tongues get the best of each of you, every time." She glared at Zambler. "You know better than to let Juniper talk freely with his tongue, and you should've tried to silence him."

Then the woman turned her gray eyes to stare at Shelby and Manning. "You're both beautiful. Never have I seen such beauty in so many children. I should've expected no less." She stared. "My name is Firey."

"I'm Shelby."

"I'm Manning."

"It's a pleasure. Are you children comfortable?"

"No, not really. I hate camping and having to sleep on the hard ground. My back's killing me," Shelby complained.

Firey smiled. "Soon you will touch your head to the softest pillows and sleep. But for now, there's much to do. Zambler and Juniper are good men. They'll take care of you, until I come again. Good bye children." Firey smiled, and Shelby and Manning watched as she disappeared.

"Where did she go?" Shelby asked.

"She has much to do and so do you. Now get up and follow us," Zambler said, as he and Juniper stood.

"Where are we going?" Shelby asked.

"Going? We're going nowhere, but outside. Your time is here."

"Our time, for what?" Manning asked.

"Come, you shall find out."

As Shelby and Manning followed the knights out of the cave, neither one knew what was going on, but they would soon enough.

Firey landed high in the tree, and saw the two children still sleeping, so she turned her attention toward Tibbs. "How did it go last night?"

"It was quiet. The only real mishap was when Kixmox tried to climb the tree. He became tied in the rope that Tomkin had set as a trap. Why even Vixbit was tied up too. I had to chuckle when I saw what happened."

Firey smiled. "You've all done well. Now it's time to wake the children." Firey blew orange dust from her hand, and watched it swirl around the children's heads.

Dave sat up, rubbed his eyes, and stared at Firey. "Who are you?" he whispered.

Renee stirred next to him, and he helped her sit up. "Yeah, who are you?" she wrinkled her nose, as she waited.

"My name is Firey. What are your names?"

"I'm Dave, and she's Renee."

"Those are handsome names then."

"I guess." Dave didn't know what else to say.

"It's a fine day children with much to do. Now get up, and let Tibbs do his job."

"Where are we?" Renee asked.

"You are in Panora."

"Where's that?" Dave asked.

"Far away from earth."

"Yeah, like how far, and what do you want with us?"

"It's far enough that you can't travel back on foot, and what we want with you, you'll both find out soon enough. Now up with you. Both of you have a busy day."

"What're we doing? Today's my birthday," Renee said.

"I know," Firey answered. "Why today your fourteen, aren't you?"

Renee smiled. "Yes, that's right."

"So it's a fine day for celebrating with Tibbs." Firey clapped her hands. "I so love celebrating. Don't you?"

"Yeah," Renee answered.

"How did you sleep children?"

"Fine," Dave answered. "Look if we could go home today that would be great. I'm sure since its Renee's birthday; she would love to see her family."

"Absolutely not, young man, there's excessively too much to do. Now your birthday is in three days, and in the next ten, all of you shall have a birthday. So, it's indeed a fine day. Now, I must go. I too am very busy. Soon my children I'll come back for you. Until then, be good to Tibbs he's a good man. Good bye till next time." Firey smiled warmly, waved her hand in front of her, and was gone.

"Where did she go?" Renee asked.

"She left," Tibbs answered. "Now get up children, we must start our day. There's much too do. Follow me." He jumped from the tree.

"That little man is nuts if he thinks we're following. Shoot, I'm not jumping out of this tree," Dave told Renee.

"Me either." Renee and Dave continued to sit, until they saw Tibbs again.

"Did you children not hear me? I said follow me." Tibbs stood staring at the two unruly humans, tapping his curly shoe.

"We won't follow you, Tibbs. For one thing we can't fly, and for the other it's Renee's birthday."

"Yeah, so?" Tibbs answered impatiently.

"That means she gets to do what she wants," Dave said.

"Oh, maybe down there on the planet you both so fondly call Earth, but in Panora she needs to listen and learn. There's much to do. Are you going to follow me?" Tibbs tapped his foot again.

"No," Dave answered. "We're not going to follow you. We don't know who you are, or what's going on. Until we do, we'll stay right here."

"Oh, no you won't." Tibbs flung his finger in front of him, and Dave and Renee saw the yellow spark fly out of his fingertips, and they were instantly on their feet.

"Now follow me." He chuckled.

As he watched the children join him he jumped, blew in Dave's ear, and Dave felt his feet leave the tree, and noticed he was billowing softly to the ground.

When he looked up, he watched Renee doing the same, and soon she stood next to him.

"Now are you children finally ready?" Tibbs glared at them.

"Not so fast," a female voice told him. Tibbs knew they were in trouble, when he turned and Watesa was standing there.

"What'd you want?" Tibbs asked. "Why are you in Panora? You're not welcomed here. You know the rules."

"Tibbs, rules are meant to be twisted," the queen said, as she turned her purple eye and stared at the two children. "You're to come with me." She insisted, and before Dave or Renee could say anything, Watesa wrapped her tentacle around them, and they all disappeared.

Tibbs stared at where the children had been, and he heard some-one laugh. When he turned around, he saw Kixmox. "What're you doing here?" Tibbs asked lifting his hand, and flinging blue dust toward him.

"I'm here for you, Tibbs. You're breakfast for me."

Tibbs watched as the blue dust hit Kixmox, and he froze. Tibbs scurried up the tree quickly, and jumped, into another, and did that all the way to Firey's place.

Once he arrived, he noticed that she too was alone. He jumped out of the tree startling Firey.

"Where are the children?" Tibbs asked her.

Firey looked at him. "I came back here this morning and they were gone."

"Mine are gone, too. But I know what happened. Watesa tricked me. She waited until I thought the area around our base was safe. When I brought the children to ground level she was there. She wrapped her tentacle around them and now they're gone."

When they saw the two knights riding up on their horses alone, they all knew they were in trouble.

Watesa had taken the children, and now they were all on their own.

As Kimmy opened her eyes for the second time that day, she realized it was very dark, and she couldn't see.

She looked down towards her feet, and watched her hands glow a bright yellow. She lifted them, and she sat up. She felt something crawling over her face, and screamed.

"Kimmy, is that you?" she heard Bobby's voice.

"Yes, Bobby, where are you?"

"I don't know. I can't see anything."

"Me either. Wherever we are, it's not friendly. Something was just crawling over my face."

"Where are you Kimmy?"

"I don't know."

"Then how am I going to find you?"

"Can you see my hands? They're glowing yellow."

"I see nothing but darkness."

Once Bobby told her that she started to crawl, feeling around with her other hand, until it touched a damp wall.

"I think we're trapped Bobby. Me in one room, you in another."

"Great. Just great. So much for Firey keeping us safe, huh?"

"Yeah. I never trusted her much anyway."

"So what should we do?" Bobby asked.

"I guess were trapped for now, until someone tells us what's going on. Or someone finds us."

Suddenly the two of them heard a commotion, it sounded like the ceiling of the rooms they were in was collapsing.

"Bobby what's going on?"

When he didn't answer, she repeated herself, and then she felt something drop on top of her.

She cried out in pain and heard the familiar voice. "Oh my gosh, Shelby?" Kimmy questioned.

"Kimmy?" Shelby sounded just as shocked.

The two girls reached out in the dark, and managed to hug. "What're you doing here?" Kimmy asked.

"I was going to ask you the same thing." Shelby giggled, happy to have found her friend.

"Bobby?" Kimmy yelled.

When he still didn't answer, Shelby grabbed her hand, and then squeezed it. "Bobby's here too? So is Manning."

"Are you kidding me?"

"I wish I was. Renee and I were skating last night, when we ran into Dave and Manning. Then I don't know what happened. The next thing I knew we were in the middle of a field, and then knights came after us, and lifted us up and took us to a cave. When we woke up this morning we met some woman who said her name was Firey. After she left, this gross looking thing appeared. She instantly wrapped Manning and me in her tentacle, now here we are."

"Oh my gosh. I wish I knew what was going on," Kimmy said, "Bobby, can you hear me?"

"Yeah, Kimmy. I can hear you now."

"Thank goodness, what happened?"

"Manning fell on me and it sort of knocked me out."

"Are you okay? Is he with you?" Kimmy asked.

"Yeah."

When the four of them heard the same noise again, they all

covered their heads with their arms, and Kimmy felt something fall on her again.

"Ouch, what did I just fall on?" she heard Renee's voice.

"Oh my gosh, Renee, it's Kimmy."

"Kimmy. Thank goodness. I can't believe I found you. Last night Shelby and I were so worried about you and Bobby. Is he here too?"

"Yeah, he's here, but now we're separated. I think he's in the room next to us with Manning."

"And Dave," Bobby said.

"Now we're all together, but the problem is we have no idea where we are, or how to get out of here," Kimmy voice sounded sad against the darkness of the room.

"Well at least we've got each another now. Whoever did this to us will pay, big time. I hope they're ready for it!" Dave yelled.

When they heard the laughter of the female voice, none of them moved. They all waited quietly to see what would happen.

When the laugher slowly faded, Kimmy held up her yellow hands. "Let's explore around here and find the doors." She told Shelby and Renee.

"What're you doing, Kimmy?" Bobby asked softly.

"We're going to explore this room or whatever it is we're in, and try to find the door."

"It's too dark. You'll never find it." Manning was serious.

"Maybe we will. My hands are glowing a strange yellow, and I'm hoping it'll be enough light so we'll be able to see the door. If we can, we'll plan our escape somehow." Kimmy touched the wall where she was sitting, then decided she needed to do something, to escape before all of them ended up getting hurt, or worse.

CHAPTER SEVEN

I found something," Kimmy's voice was excited in the darkness of the room she and her friends were trapped in.

"What'd you find?" Bobby asked.

"Bars of some sort," Kimmy answered.

"What'd you mean," Dave asked.

"You know, like the bars they use in prison."

"Great. How're we going to break out of here," Manning asked.

"Wait a minute," Shelby blurted. "The first thing, we need to figure out is why we're here. How did you and Bobby end up here in the first place?"

"It's a long story," Kimmy sighed in the darkness.

"All we've got is time," Renee said.

"Yeah, we've got plenty of that," Manning agreed.

"It's got everything to do with the treasure I told Dave and Manning about," Bobby said.

"So it was real?" Dave was astonished.

"Yeah, Dave, it was," Kimmy answered.

"But that doesn't explain how we got here," Shelby complained.

"I think it does. What kind of treasure did you find?" Renee asked.

"The kind most people only dream of finding," Kimmy said,

"close your eyes and imagine a treasure chest filled with glittery gem stones of every color. There were necklaces, earrings, and bracelets too."

"Oh that sounds too good to be true," Shelby said.

"Yeah, that's what I thought," Kimmy answered.

"Keep talking, and forget the frills right now," Dave snapped. "Let's get to the meat."

"What'd you mean?" Kimmy asked.

"The meat, Kimmy, skip all the little details and tell us what happened. The rest, you girls can talk about later."

"I was getting to the meat, Dave," Kimmy snapped.

"I'll tell them, Kimmy," Bobby said. "Before we got to the abandoned building where the chest was, Kimmy and I looked at the red colored jewel, and we saw these little men, with curly shoes, staring at us. We didn't know who they were. Next the jewel showed us knights on horses, galloping through a field, and then we ended up at a table…"

"Silence!" a female voice yell.

"What'd you want with us?" Dave yelled back.

"You'll find the answer soon enough, you sharp tongued boy. Now, I'm going to tell all of you a mid afternoon story, and hopefully all you dimwits will fall asleep," the voice said.

"Plug your ears, don't listen," Kimmy whispered.

All of them plugged their ears, as Watesa started talking, but it didn't take long for the queen to realize they weren't paying attention. "That's it. Do you hear me? If you children chose not to listen to me, then I shall cast a different spell upon all of you. This one will be a spell of obedience. Anything I say, you shall do. If you go against me, you shall suffer the worst punishment."

"We won't listen to you!" Shelby shouted, then she started singing, and the rest joined in, drowning out the queen's voice.

When they heard the snap of electricity and felt the cool breeze, they knew the queen had left.

Once she was gone, all of them scurried to the bars at the front of their cells to talk to one another.

"Listen, Kimmy, I want you to take out the jewels that you still have. Then I want all of us to hold hands. See if you can reach my hand Kimmy," Bobby said.

She reached her hand out of the bars, and Bobby grabbed it. "Now everyone join hands and let's ask the jewel to get us out of here. On the count of three, we will say let us go back home."

"Okay," they all agreed.

"Ready? One, two, three."

As all of them asked the jewel, they felt a low rumble coming from the floor. The vibration tipped them sideways, forcing them to let go of one another's hands.

As they lay separated, the vibrations keep shaking the floor, until finally it faded.

"That didn't work," Dave said, "we're still here."

"Obviously, it must have a different power," Kimmy whispered. "Hold on. I just remembered something. When Bobby and I held the green jewel, it was the last one we touched, before we ended up in this strange world."

"You're right, Kimmy," Bobby agreed. "Let's try that jewel." When nothing happened, Bobby sighed. "Well, that's great, now what?"

"Bobby, remember when we saw our mothers last night?" Kimmy asked him.

"Yeah."

"Remember what they said about our given names?" she whispered.

"Yeah."

"Well, your mother said you were as strong as the mountains, didn't she? I mean she said something like that."

"Yeah, she did." Bobby encouraged her to keep talking.

"So if you're as strong as the mountains, could you use that strength to break through the bars?"

"I don't think so. I mean last time I checked, I was human with no special powers."

"You're right," they heard Kimmy sigh.

"What're you talking about anyway?" Shelby wanted to know.

"Last night, our mothers appeared on a cloud of smoke when we were with Firey. My mother told me my given name was Charisma, but spelled with a K, instead of a C."

"Okay, I don't follow you. That's weird," Dave said.

"Listen, will you?" Bobby snapped at him.

"Okay, I'm all ears," Dave snapped back.

"Anyway, Bobby's mother told him his given name was Boulder."

"Well if he's a boulder, then he better do something, like you said to get us out of here." Renee giggled.

"I know. My name only means that I can charm people. But Bobby's obviously means something more," Kimmy said.

"Wow. I wonder if we've got names like you have. That would be cool. I'd want to be invisible, so we could get out of here, catch a ride, and get back home," Manning told them.

"Yeah, that would be cool," Shelby said.

"Oh, it's your birthday Renee. Happy Birthday," Kimmy said, and the rest told her the same.

"Yeah, it sucks to be stuck here on your birthday, but if we don't figure out how to escape soon, we'll all be celebrating our birthdays in this dark prison," Kimmy whispered.

"What else did your mother's say?" Renee asked.

"They told us to be strong and learn," Bobby answered.

"A lot of good that does us now," Shelby complained. "I mean how are we supposed to do that when we're stuck here?"

"I don't know, but let's try to do something," Bobby said, "come on, let's join hands again, and ask the jewel one more time to get us out of here. You never know what'll happen if we don't give up."

Firey looked at Tibbs, Zambler, and Juniper. "Let's go to the chamber. This is something we need to talk to the high power about." She stood, and led the men to the secret chamber, hidden behind a revolving wall.

As they entered the room, it lit up in brilliant colors, and the orb sat snugly in the center of the room, glowing purple.

Firey approached the orb, laid her hands on it, and felt it pulse. "The power is here," she told them. "Oh great power, one on high, show us the children and do not lie."

All of them stared at the orb and watched it change to orange. As the men gathered around, they saw the children in the darkened rooms holding hands with one another.

"Watesa definitely has them in her dungeon," Zambler said.

"Yes, she does, and she knows we can't cross the barrier," Firey sighed.

"You're right, we can't," Tibbs said, "but Camille can."

"Camille is but a fairy. What could she possibly do?"

"She can take word to the unruly humans about how to escape," Tibbs answered.

"We could even send in Redilla, and Tomkin. They'll know what to do," Juniper said.

When the orb turned yellow, Firey smiled. "The orb agrees with both of you. Good. That's what we shall do. Tibbs summon the pixie angel and fairy."

"What's that noise?" Kimmy asked when she heard the tapping.

"I don't know. As long as it's not that ugly creature that took us, I don't really care," Shelby sighed.

"Bobby, did you hear that noise?" Kimmy asked him.

"Yeah, I heard it. It sounds like two different things are tapping against something, listen."

"Yeah, you're right. I wish I knew…"

"Kimmy, over here," Kimmy heard the familiar voice tell her.

"Who's calling me?"

"Redilla."

"Redilla, from last night?" Kimmy asked excited.

"Yeah, that's right. Redilla, from last night."

"Where are you?" Kimmy asked, as she felt her friends move closer to where she was.

"Who are you talking too, and who is Redilla?" Shelby asked.

"I don't know who Redilla is, but I talked to her last night when I snuck out of Firey's house. Where are you Redilla?"

When all the girls saw the fine blue mist floating around the room, Kimmy went over to it.

"That's better. I must talk quickly and softly. So pay attention to what you're going to hear."

"We will." Kimmy said.

"Watesa has captured you and your friends. Now it's time to trust your own powers. Use your hands, Kimmy. There's magic there. Now, come closer so that I can whisper in your ear."

Kimmy moved closer, listen intently and nodded. "I think I can do it, Redilla. But once we're free, will someone be waiting to get us out of the land of Walby?"

"Someone, yes. But stay clear of Kixmox, and Vixbit. Kixmox is the lion that has chased you, and Vixbit is merely a fly, but with strange, powerful magic. Do not let either charm you. Look the other way. If Kixmox tries to lure you, use your fingers to cast the magic."

"Got it," Kimmy told Redilla.

"Now there's someone else here to speak to the rest of you girls. Kimmy knows her. Her name is Camille. She's the highest power of our kind. Listen with an open heart, Shelby and Renee and you'll learn much."

They watched the blue light fade away, and a white stardust soon replaced it. "My name's Camille. I'm the highest power; now gather around you human souls."

"Oh my gosh, Camille, I didn't think I'd ever see you again, and why do you sound all grown up?" Kimmy asked.

"What'd mean, Kimmy?"

"I mean you sound different. Where's the fairy I grew up with?"

"Oh, she's still on earth. You see, when I became your fairy I had to act as if I were around your age. Now that I'm here I must act differently. I have a huge job here Kimmy, and now I must ask that you treat me as one of the highest powers of this land."

"Who are you?" Shelby asked.

"We've no time for that now. Perhaps later, now gather close so that I may whisper the magic directly to your ears."

All three of the girls did as she asked, and when she finished, the white light disappeared.

"What's going on over there?" Dave asked.

"Be quiet," Shelby said, "we've got something to do."

When the boys watched a bright red glow in the corner of the room, their eyes grew big as they stared. Then they saw a little man floating. "Come here all of you."

When the three boys gathered around, the little man put his hands on his hips. "I need one ear at a time. I'll start with Bobby's."

Bobby leaned forward, and then the little man whispered in his ear, then in Manning's, and Dave's.

Once he was finished, he looked at them sternly. "Do you understand what to do?"

"Yeah." Manning swallowed hard, and couldn't believe what the little man had told him.

"Good. Now I'm leaving, the rest is up to you humans." The little man started fading, when Bobby called out for it to wait.

"What is it?" the little man asked.

"What's your name?" Bobby asked.

"Tomkin," the little man told them and was gone.

Soon all the kids were at the front of their rooms at the bars.

"So all of you know what you're supposed to do right?" Bobby asked.

"Yes," they answered him.

"So on the count of three, we start, okay?" Bobby said, "One, two, three."

"Wait," Kimmy interrupted, "do we do it all at once?"

"Yes," Bobby answered.

"But won't that make a lot of noise?" Shelby asked.

"Yeah, but let's just do what we were told," Manning answered.

"Okay, fine," Kimmy said.

"Ready?" Bobby asked again.

"Yeah," Kimmy sighed.

"Okay, one, two, three."

All of them did exactly what they were told, and soon the bars lifted, and the six of them ran out of the rooms, up the steep stairs, and stopped when they came to the big steel doors.

"Let's do the exact same thing," Bobby said.

They joined hands, and Bobby asked them if they were ready.

"Yeah, we're ready," Manning answered.

"Okay, one two, three."

They did the same thing and the doors swung open.

"Let's go," Bobby said, as they took off running.

"They're the carpets Redilla told us about." Kimmy pointed.

"Jump on," Bobby said, and they all sat on the carpets, which lay on the ground.

When none of them moved, they looked at one another. "What's going on Bobby?" Dave asked.

"I don't know," Bobby answered.

"Are you sure these are the right ones?" Shelby asked.

"Gee, Shelby, I think so. There aren't any other carpets around here, are there?" Dave questioned.

"None that I see," Shelby answered.

"Wait a second. Let's move them all closer together, so we can hold hands," Kimmy said.

The six of them picked up the carpets and laid them next to one another. Then they heard the growl.

"Where do you think you're going?" Kixmox asked them, drooling.

"Out of here," Dave told Kixmox, as all of them joined hands.

When nothing happened, they stared at the lion remembering what Redilla had told them.

Kimmy looked around, and saw it. She stood, and looked at her friends. "These aren't it, but I think I've figured it out. Now let's go."

"Not so fast," Kixmox growled. "You shall not pass me, and live to talk about it. That will not be allowed in the kingdom of Walby."

"He's right," the kids saw Vixbit yelling at them from Kixmox back.

"Who's going to stop us?" Shelby laughed. "You?" she asked Vixbit.

"I may be small you varmint, but stop you I shall," Vixbit shouted, "If I fail, then Watesa won't."

"Come on," Dave said.

"Wait." Kimmy lifted her yellow glowing hand and pointed at Kixmox and Vixbit. Her friends watched in awe as yellow sparks flew from her finger, making the lion and fly freeze where they were.

"That was cool," Manning offered.

"Yeah it was." Kimmy smiled. "Now let's go."

The six of them ran around Kixmox and Vixbit, following Kimmy to a tree.

They watched her scale it quickly, and then she started to toss various colored jewels to her friends. She grabbed the last jewel, climbed down to her friends where they all held hands. Kimmy heard the strange words escape her lips, and soon she realized her and her friends were flying.

"Do not let go of one another," Kimmy said.

"We won't," Renee answered.

"Thank goodness you figured it out, Kimmy." Shelby smiled. "Even though I have no idea what you said."

"Yeah, I don't know what I said either." She smiled.

"Who cares? The important thing is you got us out of there, Kimmy. Man. I can't believe we fell for the old carpet trick," Manning said, and they all laughed.

When they felt themselves descending from the air, they saw Firey, Tibbs, Zambler and Juniper waiting for them on the ground. Each was smiling.

Once they landed, Firey looked at them. "Get in the dwelling, right now, all of you. We've much to do."

CHAPTER EIGHT

They all gathered in the colorful room where Kimmy and Bobby had spent the night. Once they were situated, Firey began talking, "what happened was a close comfort call." She paced. "What we need to do is get down to some serious business. I need all of you human children to pay attention from now on."

"You act like it was our fault that ugly creature took us." Dave stretched his legs as he stared at her.

"I'm acting no such way."

"Yes, you are. Because of what you said, you're blaming us," Shelby told her.

"No she's not." Bobby was calm. "Now let's stop arguing, and let Firey tell us what we need to know."

After they all settled down, Firey looked at Shelby. "I'll start with you. Do you know what your given name is?"

"Yes, I'm Shelby."

"That's your earth name. You're given name is entirely different."

"Then I've got no idea what you're talking about."

"Then I shall tell you." Firey looked at her, and watched Shelby nod for her to continue. "Your given name is Sunburst."

"I don't understand." Shelby looked at Firey. "What does it mean, and how do you know?"

"I know your mother." Firey smiled.

"You're lying. If you know her, what's her name?"

"Which name? Your mother happens to have two names, one on earth and one for here."

"Okay," Shelby sounded unsure for a moment. "I'm listening."

"Her earth name is Violet. Her name in this world is Volcano."

"You're lying, absolutely lying to me," Shelby told her.

"I am not lying. It's the truth."

"She's right," Zambler told her. "I know your mother as well."

"How could you know my mother when she lives on earth?"

"I know her from when she used to live here," Zambler said.

"I don't believe you."

Silence." Firey held her hand up, and all of them watched the fine mist of smoke bellow out, then it floated over to Shelby, where she saw not only her mother, but Dave's, Manning's and Renee's.

"Shelby it's time you knew the truth. Your given name is Sunburst. Just like Firey said it was," Shelby's mom told her smiling. "Your given name means you're beautiful enough to smitten people, yet you can be angry enough to burn them as well. Use your power carefully, make wise choices, and you'll do well in this life," Shelby's mom told her and disappeared.

Then Firey looked at Manning. "Your given name is Mountain. You're strong enough to stop the evil, yet will let others so worthy pass."

"Yeah, so what does it mean?" Manning asked frustrated.

"Listen to Firey," Manning's mother told him gently.

"Your mother's given name here in this world is Tornado. On earth she's known as Tully."

Manning looked at his mother who nodded. "Learn from Firey, Mountain, and you'll do well," his mother told him, then faded from sight.

"Next is Dave. Your given name is Dagger."

He looked at his mother who nodded. "You're as edgy as a sword, and your tongue is as sharp. Tread lightly my son, you carry dangerous power that can help, and hurt."

"Dave, your mother's given name here is Hurricane. On earth it's Helen."

Dave watched his mother nod, smile, and then disappeared.

"Next is Renee. Your given name is Raven. You have the power to soar to heights beyond what is reasonable."

Firey watched her smile, as she looked at her mom who nodded. "You are beautiful, and the world will see this as you venture on the journey soaring before you," Renee's mother said.

Firey stared at Renee. "Your mother's name here in this world is Wings. On earth, she is known as Waynoka. "

Renee's mother nodded, and then she was gone.

The smoke that once held the woman slowly dispersed.

"What does this all mean?" Renee asked gently.

"It means children; you're all here to learn of your heritage, and the Great War between good and evil which is coming."

"So, why us?" Dave asked shrugging his shoulders.

"Because each of you we're born here," Firey told them.

"In Panora?" Kimmy asked.

"No. Kimmy you were born in the town of Karma."

"Oh."

"Bobby you were born in the town of Busha."

"Dave you were born in the town of Danvel."

"Manning you was born in the town of Mella."

"Shelby you were born in the town of Selhorn."

"Renee you were born in the town of Ramo."

"I get it now," Renee whispered.

"Get what?" Manning asked.

"All of our names, the ones here, and on earth, all start with the first letter of the town we were born in."

"Bravo child. You're catching on." Firey smiled, then, clapped her hands joyfully.

"If we were all born in different towns, how come we know one another on earth?" Shelby asked.

"Because our mother's are friends," Bobby told them logically. "Obviously their friend's in both worlds."

"Is that why all our birthdays are so close together?" Shelby blurted out shocked.

"Yes. You were all born within ten days of the other. It makes all of you very powerful, very lucky, but not without dues that have to be paid to the world you're from." Firey looked at all of them.

"I'm lost." Bobby shrugged his shoulders.

"Look kids, what Firey's telling you is called history." Tibbs tapped his foot in annoyance. "Let's show some respect, shall we?"

"We thought we were." Dave glared at him.

"If you were, you would let her finish talking, and stop inter-rupting," Tibbs told them impatiently.

"Okay, fine." Dave crossed his arms, and stared at Firey.

"I'm going to tell you now, why you're here. A long time ago, back when your grandmother's lived here, before they went to live on earth, strange, magical things happened in this land that you've been brought too. You see each of your mother's have been given very special powers. The beauty of it is, each of you children have powers of magic, unlike those of your mother's or grandmother's. This makes all of you unique."

"But why now?" Dave blurted.

"Why now, what?" Firey asked.

"Why did all of you wait till now?"

"I was getting to that." Firey looked at him.

"Oh sorry. Continue."

"So glad she has your permission," Tibbs said.

"You know Tibbs; I think Dave just wants to understand what's going on." Renee was gentle.

"Ah, but I look at him as unruly, and ungrateful for the gifts he has. He should never interrupt when Firey's speaking."

"Yeah, and I'm sure he wouldn't, if this was school. You know like back on our planet earth," Shelby told him.

"That's an excellent idea. Let's call this school, as you said Sunburst. Then you'll be forced to keep your tongues quiet, so Firey can teach you." Tibbs folded his arms once again, and tapped his foot. "I know back when I was just a mere boy, had I spoken out, and interrupted the way all of you keep doing, my mother would have cast the spell of silence upon my lips."

Kimmy giggled. "I bet she would've Tibbs. Come on now lighten up. We're only trying to understand what we're doing here."

"I completely understand that Karisma. But time is of the essence. Now, all of you close your lips, or I'll indeed put a spell of silence on all of you, and don't think for one second I won't do just that." Tibbs tapped his foot so hard; all of them felt the floor shake.

Firey smiled at her old friend, then at the children. "Are we ready to continue then?"

When she saw them nod, she looked at each of them, and then took a deep breath. "Okay, let me explain right away what you're doing here. Then I'll explain what's expected from each of you. Maybe if I tell you your purpose here, and why you were summoned, you won't be so quick to interrupt my speech."

None of the children said a word, and for a moment, Firey wondered if Tibbs had indeed cast his spell of silence on them, but she knew he hadn't.

"In our world, children come of age when..." She paused, held her finger up, and then pointed at each of them. "The girls are turning fourteen, and the boys are turning fifteen."

"Why?" Manning asked.

"Oh great one sentence later, and you're back to interrupting again." Tibbs glared at him.

"Sorry. I'm confused," Manning told Tibbs. "In our world on earth, none of us come into our own, as you called it, until we turn eighteen. That's when the people on earth think we're mature enough to make our own decisions. Even though that's the only thing, we're really allowed to do. At least until later."

"Yeah, Manning's right." Shelby agreed.

"Well, it's different here. By the time girls are fourteen, and boys fifteen, we feel they should be mature enough to listen and learn. But none of you children can keep quiet long enough to let either one take place." Then Tibbs swung his eyes to Firey. "Obviously, we've been mistaken about this bunch of unruly humans," Tibbs told her as he tapped his foot again.

"You're right, Tibbs," Zambler said, "I think the next one who interrupts Firey, will become Watesa's prisoner for good. Because she'll come for all these humans to stop what they're about to learn, and if Firey isn't given the chance to teach them, and Watesa shows up, they'll all be powerless against her. Then it'll be back to the dungeon with all of them." Zambler pulled his eyes from Tibbs to stare at the children. "If that happens, we remain on the outside. Only twice are we allowed to send the magic of the pixie angels, and fairies to help you escape from evil. We've use one of those already. So if you're fond of the dungeon, keep interrupting." Zambler let his words hang in the air, as Shelby stared at him.

She thought he looked different without his helmet. His blonde hair touched the collar of his shirt, and his blue eyes, were enough to captivate. His body was strong, and he was the perfect picture of a warrior.

When everyone waited in silence, Firey cleared her throat, looked at the children's grim expressions over what they just heard, and then, continued. "Now like I've been trying to say, when children are of this world, they're taught differently then you earthlings.

They know from a young age what's expected of them, through their heritage, so by the time they turn the age, all of you will be turning, and the age Renee turned today, they're ready for the challenges of this world, and for the powers they were born into." Firey paused, shocked to realize none of the children interrupted. "The task before you is a long one, and we must teach, and then train each of you about the powers of your own heritage. Then, when the time comes, you will fight the Great War between good and evil with your mother's at your side. Do not let them down. They have high expectations, and I will not fail in pleasing them. First, I must tell you that everything you've learned on earth shall be forgotten. As of now, each of you will act mature, and leave the foolishness and pettiness of earth and childhood behind you. In this world, there's no room for error. Every move must be precise, and the magic bestowed upon you must be used correctly. Now before I go much further, I want to explain why Bobby and Kimmy were chosen to come to this world first. I'll then explain about the treasure chest they indeed found, and why your earthly names shall no longer be used here in this world. I'd advise each of you to think fondly of your given names, for that's how all of you shall be addressed while you inhabit this world." Firey paused, picked up a cauldron, took a sip of the black liquid, put it down, and the children watched Firey's eyes change from gray, to black.

"First, Kimmy and Bobby, now shall be called, Karisma and Boulder." She directed her eyes toward the two of them. "You were chosen to arrive first because Boulder has the gentle spirit, and Karisma doesn't. The highest powers of this world feel it's a good balance between right and wrong. Boulder's convictions along the lines of good and evil are made clear by what he lives by. Karisma, is bold, daring, and needs the balance of Boulder to keep her from straying too far off track. She relies on Boulder's strength to teach her the goodness in life; however she would never willingly admit it.

Your powers are great Bobby, because of your heritage, and as your name suggests you're as strong as rocks, as powerful as the mountains, and as bold as an eagle. What this means is you're power is unmatched by most, challenged by only a few."

"I'm confused." Bobby sighed.

"Listen child," Juniper said, and nodded for Firey to continue.

"Boulder, your heritage spans to the greatest of knights. These bold and daring creatures keep our world safe, our land free, our world peaceful, and now you'll be given the opportunity to see for yourself. Because of your heritage, I've selected Juniper, who is your cousin to train you. The first lesson of magic will come from me. I'm of the highest power of this land, besides Watesa, I have no rival. After I teach you your first lesson, then Juniper shall teach you the rest, along with your other guide Onebuyo. They're your guides in this world, and in training together, the three of you will eventually be unstoppable on the land. Boulder you were born to the land of Busha. You shall travel there to learn of your roots; however this travel will take place as you sleep tonight. Only in your dreams will you ever touch the land where you were created. To actually go there in human form, would give away to the town of Busha who you really are, and that my child would be too much for any of them to bare. Your human form is ordinary and will not do, yet. Not until you're fully trained are you allowed in your waking state of mind to travel to Busha. For now it'll be in your dreams, where Juniper and Onebuyo will come, and guide you through the times of peril ahead. Be prepared Boulder for the things you'll see will devastate you, thus make you stronger. Your powers will prevail, if you let them. Open your mind Boulder, for the first lesson will be unleashing your magic."

When Firey stopped, all the children stared at her, and she read the fear in most of their eyes, over what they heard. However, the only eyes free of fear were those of Kimmy's and Dave's.

"Next I'll talk to Karisma." She turned her blackened eyes to look at her. "You too were born to a family full of richness and power. The power you bestow is tenfold because of whom your Grandmother Culver was. She was more powerful then I." Firey watched Kimmy open her mouth, and then she snapped it shut, knowing not to interrupt. "Your grandmother Culver told you something on the day she passed into the other world. She's in the highest world now, even as I speak, she watches. Your training is paramount to this land, for in the end Karisma, you too will sit on the highest throne, with no rival to the powers you shall have. Some of which will have to wait until your birthday chimes. It'll be on this day; the world you're in shall stop for the first second of your birthday. It's long overdue. You'll have two trainers, the first will be Zuella, and she will teach you certain powers, which will be yours. You do remember Zuella?" She looked at Kimmy.

"Yes, I remember. When I first got here, she spoke to me, but I never saw her. She said that she was invisible because of the powers bestowed by her mother."

"That's correct."

"Now it's your turn to have the special powers. Your second trainer will be Redilla. From now on, you shall be referred to as Karisma the power to charm, and allure. Remember you're beautiful, and the magic in your fingers and that in your heart will work well, if you train hard, and listen. You shall not be permitted to visit the town of Karma, which you were born too, until you're ready. Once the training is over then you shall go into your town as one of power. People will bow to you, as you take your place at the throne. You will then wear the crown your grandmother Culver wore, and the powers she held shall be transferred to you." Firey watched Kimmy's eyes swell with tears. "Do not cry over your loss Karisma. Grandma Culver wouldn't want you to do that."

Kimmy nodded, wiped her tears with her hand, and stared at

Firey. "I'm finished with you for now, Karisma." Firey turned to stare at Manning.

"It's your turn."

"I'm listening." Manning sat up straight.

"You're of course the next power. You're given name is Mountain. It's powerful in its own right. You are strong Manning, but in the midst of your power and energy, you will recognize the weak and the ones not as fortunate as yourself, and you shall let them pass through you. However, be warned that evil will try to pass your mountain, and to let this happen will be a grave error. You must stay alert and look for the ways of magic that seems too good to be true. Evil walks this land my children, and it is your job to conquer it. Evil will challenge each of you, in your own right, but with the careful balance we are all confident that you shall do what's expected, with little or no harm to those you'll very soon protect. Mountain, you were given the magic of illusion, and in time will learn how to transform yourself into a mountain, as strong as the most majestic kind, but don't let this power led you astray. Evil waits with its ugly head for you to come into to your own. The enemy is going to try to stop this, but you shall prevail, if you train hard, and learn all you can. The town of Mella, which you're from, will not let you in, if you try to visit. Right now, some unforeseen force blocks it, and until you unravel the mystery of it, you will not be permitted to enter. You'll train with the highest powers of your heritage, and that will be three different sources. The first trainer is Tibbs, the second is, Grubbs. The third is Zambler. All are men of honor, and indisputable magic. Learn well, and this world shall prevail. Only when your training is complete, will the evil surrounding the town you're from, fall. If you attempt to enter it before you unlock the magic, evil will rain down on this entire world. Be strong Manning you've a lot on your shoulders."

"Gee, thanks. Nothing like pressure, huh?" He looked at Firey, then at his friends.

"You can do it," Firey said, nodding her head. "I have faith in you."

"Next we shall talk about Shelby's powers. Who will now be known as Sunburst." She turned her eyes to stare at her. "You are amongst the high powers too. Your power is very rare, and it is to be treated as such. You will not be permitted to enter your town of Selhorn, until you are completely trained. It would be much too dangerous for you to attempt it. You'll discover during your training that you've got the ability to charm, yet control the weather, and burn those who seek to destroy. It'll benefit you to know, who the enemy is Sunburst. Remember, you never use your powers, until you're fully trained to identify what is good, and that which is evil. You come, like the rest with a long history of power, some of which you've never seen, but always wished to have. I know what's in all your hearts. The powers you each have been given, were always there, yet untouched because none of you knew how to use them. Your powers Sunburst, will burn the evil from the world, but be warned many will come with what you humans look upon as pure of heart, but don't be fooled. Evil walks this land in disguise, and it will be up to your trained eye to spot, seek then destroy. You'll have three trainers, to develop your magic. The first one being Mylano, the second one is Tekio, the third is the most high. He is known as Tubillo, the God of flight. None have been revealed to you children, yet. They are the highest powers, between the sun and the moon. Sunburst, you'll train with some of the grandest magic we know, but it's your heritage to do so. Do you have any questions?" Firey asked her.

Shelby shook her head. "Not right now."

"Very good. Next, we talk about Dave. You are the highest power of your heritage. You bestow magic so rare, that most will doubt your power. You've the ability to transform into the sharpest Dagger known to man and beast. It is through this unbelievable power that you'll learn the difference between evil and goodness. Your heritage encompasses much, and the temper you were born with must be controlled. As well as your sharp tongue. You'll be trained to use your words carefully, your power used only in dire time of need. You will be rich in jewels, and many enemies will seek to destroy, and take the powers you bestow. Yours will not be without sacrifice. Your town Danvel is sealed, until you're fully trained. Only then will you be permitted to enter. You shall have two trainers of great power. The first will be Tomkin, the second will be, Zambo. Both are to be honored and respected. Treat them well Dagger. Do you have any questions?" Firey asked.

"No." Dave simply shrugged his shoulders.

"Next is Renee. Raven your powers are those that will speak volumes. You have the power to fly, and in doing so, shall make an excellent spy for the land. Your powers come from the birds of great spirits, and ones who should be respected. Your powers will not end with flying. You'll have the ability to change color, and to be any bird of your choosing. It will be through this that you may escape this world's evilness, when it rears its ugly head. Don't abuse the power to fly, or warp from one bird to another. Your magic will be in your talons, which can lift others in need to great heights, and carry them to safety, or with those talons, you'll have the power and ability to damage the bodies of those considered in this world to be evil. Use your talons well, and we will rid this land of the evil as it breathes on our homeland. Your town, Ramo, is not sealed. For in your heritage too many have the gift of flight. It would be impossible to seal your town. However, you will not gain entrance to your town or the throne, which awaits you, until you've proven your valor. You must prove to your heritage you deserve the gift of wings, the talons to carry or destroy, and the other magic, which will be revealed to you by your three trainers. The first one is Laurine, the second is

Wrenny, and the third is, Crowey." Firey clapped her hands. "There now, we shall get started indeed. I'll teach all of you your first lesson, and then I shall turn you over to the higher powers of your heritage. First, we shall nourish our vessels, and celebrate what we've learned. Then we shall have cruno, which is what you humans call cake. For we have a birthday today, and that means Renee's entitled to all her magic at once. The rest of you shall gain yours like I said earlier, when the first chime of the clock rings out on your birthday."

Firey walked to the door, then, opened it. "Come children, it's this way to our celebration."

CHAPTER NINE

As the children gathered in the kitchen, they stared at the cake, Firey was ushering into the room. It was beautiful. The six-tier cake, depicting various colors, held the children in awe, and as Firey set the cake on the table, she smiled. "Now I present to each of you, your birthday cake. I'm sorry children to squeeze your cruno all together, but I must be logical in saying that we will not be together for much longer. Once your training starts, all of you will be separated for a time. It has to be this way children, in order to prepare you for what lies ahead. Please, let's now sit down, and nourish our vessels, then we shall sing the celebration song, both ways. The first in that human way, the second is our world's way. Now, let's enjoy the food."

"The training and celebration has begun?" Watesa asked Vixbit.

"Yes, Queen," he whispered.

"You imbecile. I should've known the second those varmints had escaped the dungeon. However, you chose not to report it, until it was too late. Now, they're safe with more magic then I can handle. What do you suggest you stupid fool?"

"I suggest that I go back, listen, and then report back to you. Maybe then we can make a plan."

"Maybe then we can make a plan," Watesa mimicked Vixbit.

"This is what we shall do. You go back, listen, and take the trap with you. Set it up, and rage the spell upon it. That way the first one who attempts to leave for training will be caught, and will never be heard from again."

"Is it safe for me to cast spells in the land of Panora?" Vixbit asked nervously.

"Yes, you imbecile. Now do it!" Watesa yelled so loudly it rumbled and echoed around the room, "I'm in charge! You do what you're told, or you die. Now get!" She snapped her tentacle, just missing Vixbit, as he disappeared from sight.

Next, she rubbed her sword, and Kixmox appeared. "Go to the land of Panora, wait till dark, and then eat the first child who tries to leave Firey's dwelling."

"But you know we're not allowed to enter. Not now. The magic is crackling through the air, and now the Great War will start. The lightening is streaking the sky with wondrous colors, and I'm not going to do it," Kixmox told her.

"You're not going to do it?" Watesa stared at the lion. "Did I hear you correctly?"

"Yes, Queen."

"Very well, then I shall feed you to the first animal that comes along. I'm leaving now to summons Dagg, to take over. Your pitiful services are no longer needed in the land of Walby."

"Fine, I'll go."

"Good. Leave right now," Watesa said flinging her tentacle as Kixmox disappeared.

The children sat back stuffed, and started singing Happy Birthday. Once they finished, all of them blew out the many candles, then, stared at Firey.

"It appears to be our turn to sing our rendition of the birthday song. Shall we?" She looked at Zambler, Juniper, and Tibbs.

When they all nodded, they began. "This is the day of your special magic, which will seep into your bones; we celebrate this happy day, even though you're far from home. May your days be bright, the presents all right, and the love in your life be true, may you never go hungry, or lose your way, this day belongs to you. May your magic stay bright, yet last your whole life, may the cruno taste really good, as you celebrate, and eat your cake, and may all your dreams come true."

When none of the children spoke, Firey clapped her hands joyfully. "Did you like our rendition of the song?"

"Yes, very much," Karisma told them smiling. "It was very nice, and had much more creativity then the one we sing every year."

"Thank you Karisma." Firey smiled. "Now, for your gifts." She clapped her hands, then, each one had a small gift before them. "Boulder." Firey tilted her head indicating he open his first.

Boulder opened it, then, took out the medallion, which was shaped like a rock. "It's great," he told Firey.

"It's the medallion in which holds some of your magic, Boulder. Wear it proudly, guide it wisely, and let no other hand touch it," Firey said.

"I won't. Thank you." Boulder slipped it around his neck.

"Karisma you're next." Firey smiled.

When she opened her tiny gift, she stared into the beautiful blue sapphire ring.

"Put it on the finger of love, and use it to charm all creatures. Guide it tightly, do by it rightly, and your powers will never be lost," Firey said.

Karisma smiled. "It's lovely, and I'll cherish it always," Karisma slipped it on her finger.

Next, she nodded toward Manning. As he ripped the paper off his small gift, Firey smiled. His was a medallion with a mountain etched in the center. "Be brave my mountain, don't judge in haste, be watchful of others, and have good taste." Firey smiled, clapped her hands. "I love that one," she told all of them.

"Sunburst." Firey nodded. As she opened hers, she stared. Encased with tiny yellow stones, Sunburst stared at the bracelet.

"The jewels you wear will shield the sun, from letting the enemies come undone. The sun must shine, we must prevail, find your magic, it's hidden right there." Firey laughed. "This is such fun."

Then she nodded at Dave. He ripped his opened, and found a knife.

"Be proud my Dagger, and hold it close, don't let your tongue hurt the ones you love most. Hold it close, and you will see, the power of magic it has indeed." Firey laughed again, and then wrinkled her nose. "I love all these, don't you?" she asked, as everyone nodded.

"Now Raven."

Renee opened hers, and stared at the necklace laced in various jewels, with three pictures of birds in the center.

"Take flight my dear one, and you shall find your wings await you this time. Hold steady and fast, and you shall see, the powerful magic that's meant to be." Firey watched Renee smile.

"Thank you, I shall treasure it always."

"Now children our time together is finished. It's time for me to hand you over to your guides. Remember, listen and learn. This world is counting on all of you. First, I'll give you all a minute to be together, so that you may say so long to your friends for now. Don't be sad, this is a happy moment in time that's going to change your lives for the better. Once you start your training, you may increase in your age span. Don't be alarmed. It is only temporary, while you are of this world. Once you are released, and go home, one day, you will be the same age as you were when you came here. Nothing will be lost, but much will be gained. Now I shall leave you to say so long to your friends." Firey clapped her hands and she, Zambler, Tibbs and Juniper disappeared.

"I'm not liking this part," Renee said.

"Me either," Kimmy whispered.

"But it might be fun to be on our own." Shelby tried to cheer them.

"Fun?" Bobby asked. "It would be better if we we're together."

"Yeah, but we've got things to do." Dave smiled as he held his knife.

"Maybe it won't be too bad," Manning sighed.

"Yeah, and you're dreaming. Face it we've never spent time away from each other ever since we were babies." Kimmy reminded them.

"The only separation we've ever had is a few days at best, and even then we talk to each other on the phone all the time, but we'll get through it." Bobby looked at them.

"We knew it couldn't last forever," Dave said.

"You're right, but none of us thought something like this would separate us." Renee looked at them.

"I think it'll make us stronger, maybe." Shelby tried to encourage her friends.

"Stronger how? We won't have each other, and that's what we're used to," Manning blurted.

Then they all saw the smoke, which bellowed under the door, and drifted toward them, where it swirled around their bodies, and they all disappeared.

Bobby realized he was standing on a bunch of rocks, as he looked around and saw no one. When he heard the lion roar, he knew Kixmox was coming.

Again, he looked around, saw a large boulder, and ran behind it.

"What're you hiding from?" the voice asked.

"I heard Kixmox," Bobby blurted although he had no idea who he was talking too. He spun around, but again saw nothing.

"Do you think he won't check behind this big rock?" the voice asked.

Bobby shrugged. "I never thought about it, to tell you the truth."

"Obviously," the voice scolded.

"Who are you, and what do you want?" Bobby asked frustrated. "If you haven't noticed I'm trying to be quiet and hide. Now if you'd be so kind as to stop talking until that lion goes away, I'd appreciate it."

"I can't do it. Listen Boulder; somehow, you were separated from Juniper and Onebuyo. They asked me to find you and bring you back."

Bobby saw the faint white light glowing next to his head. "Who are you?"

"I'm Camille. The fairy Kimmy told you about, and thank goodness you can hear me now. My job now is to watch over all of you, while you're on your mission to train. Now please take my white spark into your hand, so that we can leave this area, and I can deliver you safely to Juniper and Onebuyo."

"How do I know I can trust you?" Bobby asked suspiciously, then, heard the lion roar much closer. "How do I know you're Camille?"

"Because I helped you and Kimmy escape the dungeon today, and I was at Taco Bell with you and that mean kid called Dave. Oh believe me, you can trust me," Camille said

"Fine." He reached out grabbed the white light, and soon he was flying through the night.

When Kimmy landed on the soft grass, she stood, dusted off her jeans, and then looked around. "Is anyone here?" she yelled.

"Over hear, Karisma."

"Redilla, is that you?"

"The one and only. Now come on."

"But I can't see where you are," Kimmy said.

"Follow the red and yellow lights. That's where we are."

As Kimmy started walking, she trained her eyes on the lights, feeling excitement run through her veins. She couldn't wait to learn magic.

"We're so glad you could make it." The yellow light twinkled at her.

"Me too, but I think we'll do better if you were real people. You know like I am?"

"We will be, but for now you must hurry, and clasp us in your hands. We must take you far away, from where you ended up. You're in the land of Walby."

"Oh, no, how did I get here?" Kimmy asked scared.

"Watesa side stepped the magic Firey used to send all of you where you need to be. Now hurry, I feel the danger coming."

Kimmy reached out took both the red and yellow lights in the palm of her hand, and felt her feet leave the ground.

"Do not open your hands no matter what," Redilla said.

"I won't," Kimmy answered.

"Don't look down either. We think Watesa cast some spell on the ground. If you look at it, the three of us will fall, and then we will be captured."

"Don't worry, I won't look down. I was trapped there once already, and I've got no desire to be trapped again."

"Then, let's fly like the wind," Redilla said, "hold on tight, Karisma, it's windy up here."

Kimmy felt the wind slap her face, and closed her eyes.

"You must keep your eyes opened Karisma. We can't see."

"I'm sorry." Kimmy opened her eyes again, and watched as they flew through the night.

When Manning landed, he felt his back scrap against something sharp, and cringed.

When he turned around, he noticed he had scraped down the side of a tree.

His back stung, as he looked around. He saw no one.

"So that went well, huh?" Manning heard someone ask.

"I guess." He shrugged. "My back's scratched up."

"Well, by the time Watesa's done with you, you'll have more than just a scratched back."

"Who are you?" Manning felt panicked.

"The name is Vixbit."

"Where are you?"

"If you look down, you'll see me on your arm."

As Manning looked, he saw what appeared to be an oversized fly, with huge eyes, little fangs, and larger wings. "What do you want?"

"I don't want anything. However, Watesa wants you."

"So if she wants me, where is she?" Manning asked rubbing the medallion around his neck.

"She's not here, you stupid human. She sent me."

"Did she now? Well, I'm sorry to tell you this but she'll have to send someone bigger than you to capture me."

"No she won't. I may be tiny, but work the magic I shall."

Manning watched the little fly like creature; stand on its tiny hind legs. Then Manning picked up his hand to swat his arm, but Vixbit was faster and landed on his nose.

"Listen, you oversized human. You're coming with me."

"No, I'm not." Manning swatted his own nose.

"Yes you are. Now it's time for you to sleep," Vixbit said, from the top of Manning's head where he landed. Instantly, Manning felt his eyes close, and his world went dark.

When Shelby landed, she realized with a sinking heart that something was terribly wrong. As she stared at the darkened castle, she knew where she had ended up.

"This way with you." She heard the familiar lion roar.

As she spun around, Kixmox was standing there.

"What'd you want?" she asked.

"I want to eat you for dinner. But, you landed too close to Watesa's castle for me to do that. I guess the magic Vixbit used really worked this time. Now the queen of Walby will be pleased."

"I don't plan to stay here." Shelby touched her bracelet.

Kixmox laughed. "You've no magic to save you. You've not learned it yet. So boo hoo, you're staying here."

Then Shelby watched the red dust floating toward her, and soon she was sleeping.

Dave landed in the field with a thud. Then he stood, and let his eyes roam over the land.

"Zambo, Tomkin are you here?" he yelled.

When no one answered, Dave decided to walk around, and noticed a large ugly creature standing a few feet away. He blinked his eyes, to make sure it was real, and saw the thing was still there.

"You've got a big mouth, that's going to get you in trouble," the thing said.

"So." Dave shrugged. "It hasn't yet."

"But the day will come when your sharp tongue will land you in a world of hurt." The thing looked at Dave with his tiny red eyes.

"So? When it happens, I'll deal with it."

"Well, the day has arrived. So now how are you going deal with it?" the thing asked sarcastically.

Dave noticed it was three times his size, and resembled a Dinosaur. Its front claws were curled, as it sat on its hind legs. "I'm going to pretend you're not here, and then you're going to let me pass."

The thing laughed so hard it shook the ground. "I don't think that'll be possible. I work for the queen, you've landed in Walby, so now…" The thing licked its mouth with its thick tongue. "It makes you fair game."

"My people will come, and you'll be overthrown," Dave said, pulling his knife.

The thing continued to laugh, as the ground shook uncontrollably. "Your people are no match for the magic of Walby. You're nothing more than a kid from the planet earth, and by the sharpness of your tongue, you need to learn a lesson."

"Oh you're scaring me now." Dave held the knife out in front of him, trying to stand, as the ground shook.

"Who are you anyway?" Dave asked.

"The names, Dagg. I work for the queen. She told me that if I found one of you humans on her land, I could do one of two things."

"So?"

"So? I'll tell you what she said."

"Whatever. I'm really not interested in anything that ugly, old bat told you."

"Enough!" the dinosaur roared at him, spewing spit in his face. For a moment, Dave wanted to throw up, but he didn't.

When the thing finally stopped roaring, Dave realized his entire face was covered with mucus.

He swiped at it, clearing it away from his eyes, nose, and mouth. "Move out of my way, or I'll slice you."

"You'll slice me with that tiny knife? I don't think it'll work. And unfortunately you've yet to learn the magic to become your given name of Dagger."

"So?" Dave continued to hold the knife, as he stared at the thing.

"So? That means you're a human, with no powers. It means that I can put a spell on you, and eat you for dinner. It means that you're useless to Panora, and Your Queen Firey."

"Firey's a queen?" Dave asked confused. He didn't remember her telling any of them that.

"Yes, you imbecile. She's the highest power in Panora; she is the queen most high. The problem is your tongue is sharp, your mouth moves fasts, and your ears don't hear. That's creating a lot of problems for you right now."

"So? You got a point, make it?" Dave demanded.

"The point, as you call it, is that right now, you've got nobody willing to save you. Even as we speak, people from your land know where you are, and look around you Dagger, ah, they're not here."

"Maybe they're coming."

"You stupid boy. They're not coming because you're not worth saving. Look at you standing before the great Dagg, with a pitiful knife in your hands. Your eyes are filled with vengeance; yet, you don't use it to your advantage. So you see this is the end for you. By the time Watesa's finished, you'll be given two choices. The first will be to switch your good power to evil. If you do this, you will be in charge of the land around the castle of Walby."

"Never," Dave said.

"Then the second choice will be death. Unless of course she decides to have mercy on your sorry human soul. If she does, you'll remain her prisoner for all eternity."

"Listen, Dagwood, I've got friends on the good side of this world that I won't leave. So take your evil, and shove it."

"Very well." Dagg blew in Dave's face, then, his world went black.

When Renee opened her eyes, she felt her head pound, reached her hand up to her neck, felt her necklace, and then sighed deeply. She closed her eyes again briefly trying to stop her head from pounding, and then she opened them.

She sat up, and saw a strange, wondrous bird standing before her.

"Come Raven, you've much too learn. We must move quickly, there's danger on the land. You magic awaits, and so do your wings."

"Who are you?" Raven asked.

"My name's Wrenny. Now you must climb on my back, so we can take flight."

"Okay." Raven crawled on.

"Your headache will subside, in four, three, two, one…"

"Wow, how did you do that? That was quicker then Motrin." Renee laughed.

"Magic, my dear, sweet Raven. Now hang on tight, we must meet with two elders of our town to discuss the capture of your friends."

"The what?" Renee felt her heart flip in her chest.

"Some of your friends ended up in Walby. But never fear the elders are here. They'll guide us in the direction we need to go."

"But how did that happen?" Renee whispered.

"There must've been a magic trap placed upon you earthly children. Then when Firey transported all of you, to meet your guides, some of her magic failed." Wrenny landed high in a tree, and as Renee jumped off her back, Wrenny led her to the oversized birdhouse where two elders were waiting.

As Renee looked at them, they appeared to be humans with giant multi-colored wings.

"Sit," one of the elders told her.

Renee sat on a lump of twigs and grass.

"There appears to be problems in Walby," the second elder said with its scratchy voice.

Renee nodded.

"We must save the children who are lost," the first elder spoke.

"What're your names?" Renee asked.

"I'm Crowey," the first elder answered.

"I'm Flam," the second elder said. "We know you're Raven the one who will be the highest power amongst us soon. However, you still need to be trained in the ways of your magic, and you need to learn how to use your wings."

"I don't have wings, yet," Raven said.

"Yes, you do," Crowey answered.

Raven reached over, felt the wings on her back, and smiled. "Does this mean I can fly?"

"Not yet, but soon. Now we must figure out how to save your friends from danger," Flam said.

"Why can't we go to Panora? Firey will know what to do."

"Nonsense. We're much too far to do that. Besides, evil magic wraps the land of Panora right now."

"How did that happen?" Raven asked concerned. "I thought Firey was the most high on her land."

"She is Raven. But the magic thrown on the traps, which were set on the evil side, cast a spell over the land of Panora. Which is how your friends ended up in Walby on the queen's land."

"I don't understand. Is Firey okay?" Raven asked.

"We don't know. The only thing our magic will let us see is Firey's lost in the supercharged fog."

"Is she at her dwelling?" Raven asked using this new world's terminology.

"No. She's lost in the fog near the woods of Walby."

Raven stood with a determined look on her face. "Then let's get started shall we?"

CHAPTER TEN

Bobby landed with Camille still in his hand, and he saw Juniper and Onebuyo waiting for him.

"Sorry I'm late," Bobby said, as he looked at them.

"Yeah, so are we. We carry news from the land of Panora," Onebuyo told him.

"What'd you mean?" Bobby asked.

"We carry news that the land of Panora's in trouble. Firey has been taken prisoner of the supercharged fog, and many of your friends never made it to their guides," Juniper answered.

"What? How did that happen?" Bobby asked.

"Apparently there was magic used from the evil side. When all you human's were transported to your guides, Firey's magic was overridden by the evil spell that had been cast. Some of you merely landed in the wrong place. Easy remedy. But your other friends, some of which, never made it to their guides, are now trapped in Walby. Watesa has them. It's been confirmed." Juniper looked at Bobby.

"What can we do?" Bobby asked.

"We can plan, and teach you the basics of your magic quickly. You'll have to fight if we travel there. Even as we speak of this, the others guides have already made contact with the two of us." Juniper nodded toward Onebuyo.

"What did they say?"

"The news is bleak. They said that Dave, as you call him, and Shelby, and Manning, never made it to their guides. They've all been captured. Now Firey is being held in the supercharged fog, which means her magic is useless."

Bobby touched his medallion, and then looked at the knights. "Let's get started then. Tell me exactly what I've got to learn to help, and then let's go."

"We must send word first," Onebuyo said.

Bobby nodded.

"I shall go forth in doing so now." Onebuyo walked away.

"Whatever shall we do?" Camille now appeared, and Bobby saw her for the first time. She was tiny, and her entire being was pure white, and she had the brightest green wings Bobby had ever seen. She was beautiful.

"You shall stay, Camille?" Juniper asked her.

"I shall stay until Firey is free to control her land once again."

Juniper nodded. "Let's get started then."

As Kimmy landed softly on the plush hillside, she opened her hands and watched the red and yellow lights dance before her.

When she saw two women appear, she couldn't stop staring at their sheer beauty.

The first one bowed, and her long, black hair glistened. "I am Zuella."

"Wow, you're beautiful." Kimmy said.

When the second woman appeared, she also bowed with her long flowing red hair. "I'm Redilla."

"I can't believe how beautiful you both are," Kimmy said.

"As are you, child." Zuella stared at her with her dark eyes.

"She'll learn eventually what beauty she holds," Redilla told Zuella, and then looked at Kimmy with her green eyes.

"We've news coming in," Zuella said.

"What kind of news? How do you know?" Kimmy asked in awe, as she watched the two women stretch their arms straight out toward the sky.

Then Kimmy saw the sparks travel the length of their bodies, and she held her breath knowing what was happening to them, had to hurt.

Both women's bodies were glowing blue, and vibrating. Their eyes rolled to the back of their heads, and Kimmy thought they were going to die.

Finally, the sparks stopped, and the two women looked sadly at Kimmy.

"We've received word that all is not well in Panora," Redilla told Kimmy.

"What'd you mean?"

"The news we've received talked of an evil curse that has taken over the land of Panora," Zuella told her.

"Well can't Firey stop it? She's powerful like that, right?"

"Yes, Karisma. But unfortunately the evil has gotten her as well," Redilla said.

"What'd you mean?" Kimmy panicked.

"Just what we've said, the evil has gotten Firey. She's trapped in the supercharged fog, in the woods, and Watesa the Queen of Walby is responsible."

"What should we do?" Kimmy asked.

"There's more news, Karisma. This next bout you mustn't take to heart," Zuella answered.

"What is it?" Kimmy whispered, fearing the worse.

"Some of your friends never made it to their guides. They fell through the evil magic cast upon them."

"What'd you mean they never made it? Where are they?" Kimmy asked.

"They've been taken prisoners. They belong to Watesa now."

"No they don't. Tell me what we need to do to free them."

"You love your friends deeply?" Redilla asked concerned.

"Yes, I love them. We grew up together. Tell me what I need to do to save them." Kimmy stomped her foot. "I'll do whatever it takes."

"It's not that easy. You first must learn how to use your magic. At least some of it. If you go without the powers bestowed upon you, then you'll become a prisoner as well," Zuella said.

"Then teach me what I must know. Let's stop wasting time. I've got to get to my friends."

"We know." Redilla smiled gently.

"Which friends didn't make it?" Kimmy asked.

"We're unsure of that. But we do know three of them are being held as prisoners as we speak. The fourth is our queen of Panora. We must save her first from the supercharged fog, or she'll be lost forever. "

"Then let's get started," Kimmy said.

"First, you must listen, Karisma. When we go to rescue our queen Firey, you mustn't forget your magic, or the ways you cast the spells. The magic that's holding Firey can only be broken with magic that is more powerful. If you fail, Firey will die," Redilla said. "So you must concentrate, learn, and remember every step to the magic we are going to teach you."

"Okay. I promise I won't forget."

"It's paramount, not only for Firey's safety, but also for you and your friend's safety as well."

Kimmy nodded, as she looked at the ring nestled on her finger. "Let's do it."

Raven was concentrating, trying to flap her wings, as her guides taught her too. But when nothing happened, Crowey stared at her. "We haven't any more time to keep going over this. Instead of dwelling on the fate of your friends, and what's going to happen to Firey, you must focus. Concentrate all your energies, Raven. Much as you did as a child when you played make believe. Only this time, instead of pretending, I want you to think with all the conviction that you can, and it'll make your wings flutter enough for you to fly."

"Okay." Raven shut her eyes, concentrating.

"Remember Raven, they're lives at stake on this day. Now you must hurry, or we'll be forced to leave you behind," Flam said.

As Raven concentrated, she felt the soft flutter at first, and for a moment, it scared her. Then she felt her feet leave the security of the tree. She opened her eyes, looked down, and saw the ground below her.

Then, she circled back, landed, put her hands on her hips, and smiled. "I did it. Now let's work on some magic," Raven said.

"Not so fast," Crowey answered. "There's one more thing we must teach you."

"What's that?" Raven asked dreading what they were going to say.

"We need to teach you, real fast, how to make your talons magical. Remember what Firey told you about them?"

"Yes, that I'll learn how to carry, and how to destroy."

"That's good. Now, we shall teach you both. You'll need your talons when we rescue your friends. Now listen very carefully," Flam said, putting his wing around her.

"Karisma, you must listen. You've the ability to charm. You've the ability to disguise, now that we've taught you both, try it." Zuella encouraged.

"I don't know how to charm the two of you." Kimmy pouted.

"Try," Redilla said.

"Okay, fine. I want to be able to train with Bobby," Kimmy said, staring in their eyes. When Redilla and Zuella saw the spark of light flicker in Kimmy's blue eyes, they knew she had mastered the spell.

"Very well done," Redilla said.

"Indeed," Zuella agreed.

"Hold on. If my magic worked why aren't you charmed?" Kimmy asked confused.

"For now we're of higher power then you, and we can throw up our invisible shield to protect us from your spells. Thus, it helps us teach each other new methods of magic," Zuella answered.

"Okay."

"Karisma, now try the disguise," Zuella advised.

"Alright." Kimmy closed her eyes, and pictured a horse. When she opened her eyes, she realized she had four legs. Then she trotted around.

"Very good, Karisma. You're but the best student ever. You learn quickly, and the others will indeed be proud. Now change back, we've indeed a long trip back to Panora, and we feel the others almost ready to leave on the quest."

Kimmy concentrated on being herself again, and when she opened her eyes, she was. "That was very cool." She hugged them both. "Thank you."

"You're welcome, now let's be gone."

As Bobby stood before the two knights, he held a heavy sword.

"Now the trick is when you swing your sword, chant of the powers we taught you."

Bobby swung the sword as he chanted, and instantly, the sword turned gold, and the color ran up his arms through his body, until he felt himself growing.

When Juniper laughed, Bobby stared. "You've done well, Boulder. Look at your feet."

When Bobby looked, he realized he had turned himself into a boulder.

"Listen carefully, do not forget your magic, in the land of Panora, or Walby. Since we've got to gather all the powers of the world to free Firey, it's very important you carry what you've been taught with you."

"I understand," Bobby answered.

"Very well, now change back to human form, so we can leave."

Bobby concentrated, and felt the crack of his outer shell split down the middle returning back to his human body.

"Nice." Onebuyo slapped him on the back. "Now let's go."

The three of them jumped on the horses, and rode, while Camille flew, then all of them traveled like wild fire toward Panora.

Manning, Dave and Shelby all ended up in the same cold, dark room that held them captive earlier.

"Do you still have the gifts Firey gave us?" Shelby asked the two boys.

"I've got mine," Manning answered.

"Yeah, me too. For all the good it did," Dave sighed.

"What'd you mean?" Shelby asked.

"I mean, I pulled the knife, threatened Dagg with it, and he snickered. Made me feel like a fool. I wish Firey would've explained how to use it, before she sent me off." Dave sounded upset.

"Listen to me," Shelby said, "she didn't teach any of us how to use them, but if you remember the little chants she said once the gifts were opened, I wonder if we said them out loud, while holding on to the object, if it would spark the magic inside."

"We could try, if I can remember what she told me." Dave complained.

"Oh my gosh, you better. I mean all of us should be paying attention to what's going on around here, and all of us should be trying to stay positive about what the outcome's going to be. Don't you think?" Shelby asked.

"You're right, Shelby, we should. It's just right now, we're tired, and we've had a bad day, and I don't know if I can remember what she told me either," Manning blurted.

"Well if you can't, then I suppose you'll both make Watesa very happy when she comes to this dungeon to get us. Now I don't know about you, but she doesn't look friendly, and I'm not going to sit here doing nothing. I refuse to feel like, oh pitiful me, save me from the dungeon, when you both know we've got the special gifts that Firey gave us. Now come on, let's try to remember what she told us when we opened them, and see if we can't get out of this prison."

"I'm in," Dave said.

"Yeah, me too," Manning agreed.

"Who goes first?" Dave asked.

"I guess Manning should. He's the one whose given name is Mountain. I mean if he could turn into one, then we could climb on him into the land of Panora. Then he could shake off anyone he doesn't want on his Mountain," Shelby said.

"Yeah, but you've got the power to charm, and burn Shelby. Maybe you should go first." Dave was serious.

"Yeah, and Dave you can warp yourself into a sword, right? Maybe if you did that we could pick the lock on the bars, than break free," Manning said.

"Okay, so we're all useful. Who wants to try to go first?" Shelby asked.

"I will." Manning stood, and chanted the words that Firey spoke, as he held his medallion. When nothing happened, he sat down, then, Dave stood.

He too chanted the words Firey spoke, and when he felt the quick vibration run through his body, he looked down, and then realized he was floating.

"Oh my gosh, you did it," Shelby whispered, "You're a magnificent sword."

"No, he's not a sword silly," Manning said, "he's a dagger."

"Same difference." Shelby shrugged. "Dave can you float between the bars, and try to pick the lock?"

"I can try, but if I can't float maybe you could carry me over there."

"Just try," Shelby encouraged.

When Manning and Shelby watched him float over to the bars, they wanted to cheer, but didn't.

Both ran to the bars, watched him work his magic, and then they heard the click, and realized the cell door was opened.

"That's cool," Manning said.

When the deep vibration scared all of them, Dave floated back in the cell, toward the back of the room to hide. He knew someone was coming down the steps, and didn't want whoever it was, to discover the three of them practicing magic.

When Manning and Shelby saw Kixmox standing on the other side of the cell, he growled, paced, and then looked at them. "Watesa asked me to check on you human things. I see that two of you are still here, where's the other one? The one with the sharp tongue?" Kixmox looked in the cell.

"He's sleeping back there." Manning pointed toward the back of the cell.

"Where? I don't see him." Kixmox was just about to unlock the cell door, when Dave walked up, yawning and stretching. "What's going on?" He asked innocently.

"Just making sure, we've captured three of you humans, and wanted to make sure all three of you were still here." Kixmox growled, backing away from the cell door.

"Let me see, one." Dave touched his head. "Two." Dave touched Manning's head, "and three." Dave touched Shelby on the head.

"Yep, all three of us are here," Dave answered.

"Someday Dave, as your earthly friends call you, we're having at it. One on one and I bet I can guess who's going to win."

"Yeah, I know I'll win Kixmox, but that's what you get when lion meets Dagger, huh?" Dave laughed.

"That's enough. I think I'll doctor the report that Watesa gets now. I'm going to tell her to come visit the three of you for herself. Then I dare you to use that sharp tongue when she stands before you, Dagger. She'll rip your tongue out of your mouth, and then eat it quicker then you'll ever know what happened," Kixmox told them, and then the three of them watched him disappear.

They waited only a few moments, and then they pushed the cell bars back, slipped up the steps, into the field in the front of the castle, then into the woods.

Once they felt they were a safe distance away, they stopped.

"I'm going to try my magic now." Shelby placed her hand over her bracelet and chanted.

Soon Manning and Dave shielded their eyes, as the entire woods lit up like mid afternoon.

As they watched Shelby, she turned into a ball of fire, and began rolling through the woods.

Both Dave and Manning had to run fast just to keep up with her.

When they watched her roll into the fog, just outside the woods, they watched the ball of fire disappear.

"Where did she go?" Manning asked.

"I don't know, but we've got to find her," Dave said.

CHAPTER ELEVEN

Firey looked around, and realized she had fallen into a vicious trap. Right now, there was no way out. For her, this defeat was the ultimate betrayal of her powers. She knew she should have paid more attention to what was going on, but she wanted to spend as much time with the children before they left her as she could. Now as she sat on the cold ground, she wondered if any people from her land knew she was trapped, and if so, were they coming to rescue her?

Every bit of magic she tried to get herself free was of no use. Right now, she was as powerless as she had been when she first arrived.

When a burst of light caught her eye, she stood, hopeful that it was Shelby, but she knew better. In her mind, she knew which children Watesa had taken prisoner.

As she watched the ball of fire bounce toward her, she could not pull her eyes away from the burning sight.

For a moment, she thought the fireball was going to smash directly into her, but she knew it wouldn't be allowed.

Watesa would waylay the sunburst that was rolling through her land.

As Firey stared, she was shocked to realize the fireball had stopped inches from the supercharged fog where she was being held captive.

When the fireball twitched, Firey smiled, and knew a rare and powerful person was controlling it.

If any humans just learning the craft of magic were controlling it, Firey knew the ball and its light would have already extinguished itself.

As the ball lifted, it bounced against the fog surrounding Firey, and finally she smiled. She had no idea who the fireball belonged too, but silently applauded it for its bravery.

Obviously, whoever it was had forgotten that not one single spell of magic could free her. It would take the entire magic of the good side of the land for that.

Finally, the fireball rolled back the way it came, and with a heavy heart, Firey sat back down on the cold ground to wait.

When Dave and Manning saw the fireball rolling back towards them, both jumped behind a tree, and watched the ball of flame stop fairly close to where they were.

Then they watched it crackle and smoke, and then Shelby stood there with a smile on her face.

"I found Firey. I tried to break through the fog holding her captive, but it didn't work. Come on, she's over here." Shelby was excited.

"We've got to be careful," Manning said.

"I know, but our queen is stuck. Now hurry, let's find a way to get her out."

As the three of them approached, they saw Firey standing there, as if nothing was around her.

"What's the problem?" Dave asked staring at Firey as she sat on the ground.

"I don't know. Something's holding her there," Shelby answered. "I told you I tried to break through whatever it was, but I just couldn't do it."

"I don't think you're powerful enough yet," Manning said.

"Yeah, but you know that the people on the good side of the land are," Shelby answered.

"So how do we get in touch with them?" Dave asked. "Last time I checked we were just plain humans with no special powers."

"You know that's about to change," Shelby scolded.

"Yeah, we saw that, bouncing fireball." Dave smiled.

"Let's walk over to Fircy, and see what we can find out," Manning suggested.

"Okay, let's go," Shelby agreed.

"Wait. What if it's a trap?" Dave asked.

"What'd you mean?" Shelby looked at him.

"A trap. What if Watesa's watching? That's all we need. I don't think the answer to rescuing her, requires being foolish, do you?" Dave asked.

"I guess not," Shelby answered. "I just don't know what to do to save her."

"None of us do." Manning shook his head. "I've got a question for you Shelby. Earlier you called Firey our queen. I don't remember her ever telling us she was, so what made you say that?"

Shelby looked confused for a moment. "I didn't realize I called her our queen."

"Well you did." Dave threw his arm around her. "Come on let's go see if we can find anything out from Firey, even if it's from a distance. I don't want any of us getting too close. It'll do us no good to be captured again."

As the three of them stood behind a tree, close to where Firey was, they heard the commotion.

It sounded like a million horses were headed right for them, making them duck further behind the big tree.

"What'd you think it is?" Shelby whispered.

"I'm not sure. It sounds like an army, if you want the truth," Manning answered.

"Yeah, but what I want to know is whose army is it?" Dave looked at them, put his finger to his lips, and they all waited.

When Watesa entered the dungeon, she saw the empty cell, and felt her temper sizzle.

As she reached over, she grabbed the bars of the cell, and slammed it so hard; they went sailing into the back wall.

Then she took out her sword, rubbed it, and Vixbit appeared. "Where are they?" she screamed.

"I don't know. Kixmox said they were still down here. Shouldn't you be asking him?"

Watesa glared at Vixbit, swung her sword, and Kixmox appeared. "You stupid piece of an excuse for a lion! Where are my prisoners?"

Kixmox looked in the damaged, empty cell, then at Watesa. "I don't know. When I came down to check on them, they were all right there."

"Does it look like they're there anymore?" her voice was so loud the entire dungeon shook.

"No."

"So where are they?" she screamed.

"I don't know. You're the one with the power. You're the one who can see things. Not me. You're asking impossible questions, and I don't have the answers," Kixmox said.

When she threw her tentacle toward him, she smacked his body across the room, where he crashed into the wall, and slid to the floor.

Vixbit watched, and knew his queen was livid. But until she dismissed him, he couldn't leave. His power wouldn't let him.

Finally, she swung her eyes to Vixbit. "Find Dagg. I need to speak with him. After you've done that, find Rozello, Fipple, Tupelo, and X-eyes. Send them to me. If you fail in doing what I've asked, you're finished in the land of Walby." She stared at Vixbit, and then nodded. "Remove that stupid piece of flesh from my dungeon. Kixmox no longer works here," she told Vixbit, and then she snapped her tentacle, and was gone.

As Rain, Windy, Tulley, Helen, Wynonia, and Violet sat together at Rain's house, they watched through there crystal jewels, and they were shocked to realize the world of Panora, and their children's life were all at stake.

"Now ladies, you know what we've got to do. We must stand, introduce ourselves, say our earth name if their different, then speak our child's name out loud for any of this to work," Rain said, "so I shall go first."

She stood. "My earth name is Rain. My given name is Rain. I'm the mother of Kimmy." Then she nodded.

"My earth name is Wendy. My given name is Windy. I'm the mother of Bobby."

"My earth name is Helen. My given name is Hurricane. I'm the mother of Manning."

The next woman stood. "My earth name is Tulley. My given name is Tornado. I'm the mother of Dave."

"My earth name is Violet. My given name is Volcano. I'm the mother of Shelby."

"My earth name is Wynonia. My given name is Wings. I'm the mother of Renee."

"Very good. Now let's discuss what's going on." Rain looked at them.

"What should we do?" Violet stood, looked at her friends, and waited.

"We wait until we get word that the people from the good land of Panora need our help. Trust me when I say that it looks bleak, but if it is, they shall contact the six of us to help," Rain said.

"Are you not upset Rain over what's happening?" Windy, Bobby's mom asked.

"Of course I'm upset. But we all know the rules of our heritage. We have to wait until were contacted. To go through the porthole without permission would be disastrous, and everyone here knows it. The only reason all of us are upset this time more than the previous time is because all our children have been taken to learn of their magic." Rain stood.

"Well I'm worried about all of them, but especially Manning. We all know he's strong willed," Helen Manning's mother Blurted.

Dave's mother Tulley laughed. "Not one of those children is more strong willed then my son Dave." She shook her head. "If anyone's going to break the tradition he will. So we need to keep our spirit eye upon that child, or he could endanger all the rest."

"You're right," Windy agreed. "But all of our children could ruin what's going on in Panora, if they don't pay attention, and do what their told."

"I think we need to have a little more faith in our children," Wynonia said.

"Yeah, easy for you to say. I think your daughter Renee is the sweetest child," Violet answered. "I mean even my daughter Shelby has her moments."

"They all do. That's what makes them unique." Helen smiled. "If you think about it, they've all inherited a part of each of us. I know Manning has inherited a lot from me."

All of them laughed. Then they watched Rain's blue eyes cloud over. "Someone from the other side's trying to contact us." She pulled her eyes away from Panora long enough to look at her friends. "Shall we?" Rain asked, as they lit the blue candles that formed a circle on the dining room table, then each sat, and held hands.

As the six women listened to the message, the words were powerful causing each of them to tip back in the chairs.

When the message was over, each woman had a blue streak on her left arm from elbow to pointer finger.

"Does everyone understand the message?" Rain asked standing up from the floor where they had all been thrown.

When she watched her friend's nodded, and then each blew out a candle, as they chanted, still holding hands, and then they all disappeared.

Firey heard the stampede, and shielded herself against the army, which was approaching.

She knew that by the sound of the hooves, it was the enemy. As she turned, she saw Shelby, Manning, and Dave by a tree, a few feet away, and waved her hand as if to shoe them away from the area.

All three of the children continued to stand were they were, even though now, Firey felt frantic, and waved her arm erratically.

Finally, she stopped when she realized they were not going to leave her.

"I think she wants us to leave," Shelby said.

"Too bad, she's trapped in there, and I'm not leaving," Manning answered. "Besides if we were trapped she'd never leave us. I mean earlier she sent in her Pixie angel and her fairy to work their magic, and that's the only way we managed to get out of the dungeon. Now we owe her."

"You're right, so stand ready." Dave pulled out his knife, rubbed the blade, and soon turned into a dagger.

Shelby touched her bracelet, chanted the words she heard Firey use when she presented her with that gift, and soon she turned into a fireball.

Manning watched his friends, then lifted his medallion into his hand, chanted the words he thought Firey had used when she gave it to him, and soon he felt one of the worse pains. He felt his body growing, enlarging to unmanageable proportions, and he knew he was turning into a mountain.

As Watesa's army descended upon Firey, the people of the good land felt the vibration from it, and push to get there.

They knew that Shelby, Manning and Dave were already there, and that the three of them would be forced to protect Firey from the evil. But they weren't strong enough in their power yet.

The only one strong enough to hold their magic, and their power was Renee. Because she had celebrated her fourteenth birthday, all her powers were her own.

As Karisma landed, she opened her hands, and released the yellow and red lights, then she imagined being a dinosaur, big enough to fight the army that was coming, and soon she heard herself roar.

When Watesa's army arrived, Kimmy noticed that many of the good people of the land of Panora, were also showing up.

Kimmy watched as everyone warped into magical beings. Then the fight started, and Kimmy stomped toward Watesa's army, planning to destroy, when she came face to face with a creature that looked similar to her.

"Not so fast," the creature said, spitting fire out of its mouth, before standing on its hind legs. Kimmy did the same, and soon she and Dagg were fighting.

As the children's mother's landed in Walby, they watched the scene in front of them, and couldn't understand why the children's guides were letting them fight.

What amazed them the most was that they knew none of their children had perfected their magic.

When Rain watched Kimmy fight Dagg, she let it go on for a little while, before she sighed. "I should jump in," she told her friend's seriously.

"Yeah, you could. But you know the rules. We're not here to help our children. We're not to use our powers for anything else, but to help our queen Firey escape."

"I know, but look at Kimmy, she's being overtaken by Dagg. All of us know that once our powers are spent, we won't be strong enough to go against Watesa." Rain looked at her friends, and watched them nod their heads.

"So be it then. Do what you will," Windy said.

"I agree. We can't let Kimmy fall, and Dagg is doing a good job to make it happen," Tornado, Dave's mom blurted.

"But if you look at the whole situation, all of our children are using their magic. Look at Manning. He's big as a mountain, and I'm afraid the way he's positioned, he's going to squeeze Firey," Raven's mom Wings said.

When they saw exactly what she was talking about, all the women looked at each other.

"Maybe not all of us need to use our powers because I'm going to fly around Manning, and see if I can talk to Firey. She'll know what to do," Wings told them.

"Excellent idea," Tornado agreed. "And Rain, you need to talk to Kimmy, she'll know what to do."

"I shall try then."

As Wings closed her eyes, she concentrated on her wings, and making her talons magical. As she chanted, she felt the flutter, and before she knew it, she had taken flight, high above the battlefield.

When she looked down, she saw the perfect way to land inside Manning's mountain.

As she circled, she hoped Manning would feel the goodness of her powers because it wouldn't take much for him to squeeze her.

She landed gracefully on one of the ledges, and summoned Firey to turn around, and look at her.

Once she did, Wings smiled at her queen. "What should we do?" she asked Firey.

"You should stop Manning. I know he's but a child still learning the craft of his magic, but I'm frightful he'll end up squeezing me to death. His walls are coming dangerously close and I'm powerless against him."

"We know Queen. So tell us what to do."

"You're all here then?" Firey asked calmly.

"Yes, we are. We came as soon as we were summoned."

"Then this is what you shall do. First, speak with Manning. Tell him to stop moving his mountain. Second, have Tibbs throw his sleeping spell on as many of Watesa's army as he can. Third, gather up the good magic, form a circle around the mountain, linking hands, and chant." Firey looked at Wings. "I hope you realize my future is in your hands."

"I understand, my Queen." Wings bowed, looked at Firey one last time, and then took flight.

As she circled Manning, she landed next to his ear. "You must listen, Manning. I am Renee's mother. I've just spoken to our queen Firey, and she said you must hold still. If you continue to let this mountain grow, you'll squeeze the life right out of her."

"How do I do that?" Manning was alarmed.

"Be still within your heart, and you'll stop moving."

"Okay."

"But you must concentrate hard, Manning."

"I will."

As Wings watched him, she noticed the mountain stopped. "Good job. Now hold still. Soon you'll see the good power surrounding the outside of the mountain. Stay still, while we work our magic. If you can do that, you'll prove honorable enough to utilize what's been given to you."

"I understand," Manning told her concentrating.

"Now, I must go. Be still," Wings told him one last time, as she took flight back to her friends.

Once she landed, she looked at each of them. "Gather the good magic, and Rain you need to find Tibbs, he needs to cast a sleeping spell on all the bad magic of the land."

"I will find Tibbs and Tomkin. They will be stronger together, their spell twice as potent," Rain said.

"Good. The rest of us will gather the good magic, form a circle around the mountain, holding hands, while we chant."

"Do you think it'll work?" Windy asked.

"It has too, doesn't it?" Tornado asked, "We must save our queen, or the goodness of the land shall fall."

"Let's separate and do our jobs," Wings said, and then all of them were gone.

CHAPTER TWELVE

When Kimmy saw her mother floating around, she felt like crying. She was never so happy to see her.

She continued to fight Dagg, but anyone could see he was much more powerful then she was, and she knew she was badly beaten. Her body ached, and what she wanted right now was for someone to save her.

If she continued fighting against someone as powerful as Dagg seemed to be, she knew her short life would end.

She watched as he prepared to claw her again, but managed to duck out of the way.

When she counter attacked, he laughed at her. "You're no match for me, Karisma."

As soon as the words left his mouth, Kimmy knew what she needed to do.

As she concentrated, she felt herself change into a giant ball of fire. Then she bounced against Dagg, and heard him scream in pain.

She retracted, and then bounced against him a second time. Again, he screamed out, and when she looked at the damage, she realized she had burned him badly.

Squinting his eyes, he turned to face her. Kimmy noticed the hatred in them. "This isn't over Karisma. I'll return more powerful then I already am. Then I will find you, and you and I will once again go to battle over good and evil. Watch for me, Karisma, and expect me. When I come again, I'll destroy not only you, but your entire fleet of magic."

"I don't think so," Kimmy yelled, as she bounced against Dagg, more powerfully the third time.

"You shall suffer the worse pain when I return. Until then." He stared at her, turned, and limped away.

When she felt something falling on her, she looked up, realized it was raining, but only on her, then she heard her mother's voice. "You did well, Karisma. Now it's time to gather the good magic around the mountain. Help me gather our people. Once this is done, lead them to Manning's mountain, we must hold hands, and chant our magic."

"Okay, Mother," Karisma answered, then, bounced away.

As Kimmy found Dave, she told him what her mother had said, and he helped her tell the good magic of the land, what they needed to do.

Tibbs and Tomkin had thrown their sleeping spell on all the bad magic, and soon all were on the ground sound asleep.

Then they were all gathered around Manning's mountain, waiting for someone to start the chant.

When they heard Kimmy's mother start it, they at once knew what to say, as they all joined in, everyone concentrated, and spoke together to free the queen.

"Oh great powers, of this hour, grant freedom for our good queen. Take the madness, bring us gladness, and free the goodness of our queen. Firey, Firey is the queen, in the land of Panora we will sing. Bring the enemy to understand, that they can't win against our land. Free our people of this evil curse, return us to our given birth. If you shall side, goodness will ring true, we ask the powerful most high to do. Grant our wish, that we walk free, to continue on the mission that was meant to be. So, shall we, stand by your side, and hold our heads with Panora pride. Please we beg, blend all your magic, so we may win, and escape the tragic. Our queen we need to guide the way, please restore the peace, we need each day. We've much young magic, in those we teach, we can't win the war, with this unfair breech. Don't let it continue, we ask of the most high, free our queen, wave your hand, and let us fly."

Once they were finished, they repeated their chant until they saw the sky open, lightening speared to the land, shocking all the bad magic, and eventually a calm settled over the land.

When they heard the bubble holding Firey captive burst, a rush of water splashed over the side of the mountain, and they all cheered, as Firey stood on top Manning's mountain.

She smiled down on all of them. "Very well done. Now my people of Panora, let's go back to the place of resting. There's much to talk about, and more to plan." Then she looked at Kimmy, Bobby, Shelby, Renee, Dave, and patted Manning's mountain.

As soon as she touched it, Manning felt himself shrink, and before he knew it, he was normal again, and Firey was floating. "Now my children with the young magic, your training will resume at the house of resting, for now. There's much to do, and we must hurry from this evil land, before Watesa arrives. She is on her way. Now, hurry my good people." Firey waved her hand, and one by one, they all disappeared, then, reappeared outside Firey's house.

"Wow, how'd she do that?" Dave asked.

"Magic." Kimmy smiled at him, and he noticed she was bleeding on several parts of her body.

"Come on, Kimmy. You need to get cleaned up." Bobby threw his arm around her, and led her into the house, as the others followed.

As soon as Kimmy saw her mother, she ran over to her, and threw herself in her mother's arms.

Rain pulled Kimmy out of her embrace, touched every wound on her child's body, and they healed instantly. Then she smiled at her daughter. "You did well, my child. But you've still much to learn."

Kimmy nodded, and stared at her mother with tears in her eyes. "Do not cry, my child. All is well in the land of Panora."

"But will you leave again?" Kimmy asked.

"I'll be here a few days. We've much to discuss, and you've much too learn. Come now, Firey needs all of us." Rain put her arm gently around Kimmy's shoulder, and led her into the colorful room.

Once they entered Kimmy noticed all her friends were sitting next to their mother's, staring in the fire, in the center of the room.

As Rain led Kimmy to the empty chair, they both sat, and waited in silence.

Kimmy let her eyes stray to the fire, which was burning orange, and found she couldn't pull her gaze from it.

"Now good people of Panora, what happened today, were a calling of the most high. Our magic is suffering because our numbers are few. The evil of the land in Walby have grown in numbers, and thus their magic is more powerful than ours. For now, the magic of the people from the planet earth, have been brought here, to rejuvenate, if you will, and to restore your powerful magic." Firey's eyes swept the room, and she noticed now the only one's not staring at the fire, we're the six new children. "You all must focus, and learn all there is to know. Your training with the elders of Panora, and all the land of goodness, shall be intense. We've very little time to get our world perfect, and during this time, we must perfect, and nurture our magic. Our grandmother's, as you earthly people call them, will visit us in our dreams to teach us of our heritage. At the end of this long road, all the good people of Panora will have grown richer by the knowledge of the elders, whom have decided to bless us with their power. Let none of us falter and we shall succeed."

When Firey stopped, she looked at all of them. "Any questions?"

When Rain held her hand up, they watched Firey nod. "How

long shall we stay, Queen?"

"For as long as it takes. And, I might add that if your children grow dependant of your shelter, and don't take their responsibility seriously and learn their magic, then I'll be sorry to say that I'll be given no choice but to send all of you back to the planet earth. On the other hand, if the children keep their distance, work hard with their guides from sun up till sundown, you'll be permitted to stay. Those are the rules set forth by the higher powers."

Kimmy raised her hand.

"Karisma?" Firey asked.

"At the end of our training, like the end of our day, are we allowed to spend time with our mother's then?"

"I'm sorry, Karisma. It states in the stars that they too, will be in higher training, and that each good person in Panora must learn the magic that is their heritage, without interruptions from their children. Now, let's stare into the fire, and listen to what the highest queen of Panora has to say, shall we?" When they all turned their attention to the fire, Kimmy noticed the color had changed from orange to blue.

As she stared, she saw her grandmother Culver's face in the fire. "My children, the secrets have finally been revealed. My given name is Weather, my earth name was, Heather. I sit on the most-high throne of power in the land of Panora." She smiled through the fire at Kimmy, and the other five children, Bobby, Shelby, Manning, Dave and Renee.

"Now children, listen carefully. The only people you are to trust are your guides. Work hard so at the end of the day you may visit with each other, but not with anyone else. You shall take your meals together, sleep together, but train separately. At no time, are you to use your magic without the permission of your guides. Only if Firey requires you to use it, then you shall do so. If you follow orders, work hard; the land of Panora shall be yours. Someday my children, you'll let go of your own children, to come to the land of Panora, as your mother's did. They too, will learn the magic bestowed upon them through their birth. Then, when the time is right, you too shall join them here in the good land, and their teaching will begin. Now it's late, my magic is spent, and you're all tired. It's time to relax, and get ready for tomorrow. It will be a hard day for most. Word has it; Watesa is gathering more of her army to invade the land of Panora. Kimmy, Dagg is restless, and waiting to come for you. Use your talents and your magic wisely. You'll need it." Then they all watched Grandmother Culver disappear.

Firey clapped her hands. "I'm so joyful that we're all here. Now first thing in the morning, we'll gather right here in this room, and talk about what we shall do. Until then..." They watched Firey blow smoke toward the six children, and soon they were sleeping.

Firey looked at the elders of the land. "Come, we've much to talk about," Firey said, leading them outside, where they gathered around the second fire.

As soon as they settled, Windy spoke, "will our children be alright?" she asked worried.

Firey laughed. "It's funny how all you earthly mothers always ask that question. Why I remember when each of you was young, your mother's gather around this very fire, and asked the same question. So, I shall tell you what I've told them. Your children will be as good as their upbringing. If they listen, obey, and work very hard, they shall do well. If they stray, and become defiant, the enemy will capture them, zap their magic, and they will fall forever to the evil side of the land in Walby. Now, if you're confident that you've taught them well in the ways of their manners and their abilities to follow orders each one shall be fine. If you've faltered in any way, well you each know the outcome. Now let's listen to the spirits of the land for they've much to say."

"Elder's of the land of Panora, we've gathered your strength for magic is needed to save your given land. Through the strength of all of you, with the help of your young children, we'll once again enter battle. It will be at this time, goodness will be tested. As the evil land of Walby grows stronger, I ask all the elders of our land to look upon their upbringing, hold onto the words your mother's once spoke to you so long ago. These are the words your children must hear, so lay the whisper of each one of your voices upon their young ears, and they too, will begin to understand what is needed. If none speak of the past, mistakes will go on forever. It is here and it is now, that your young children with the pure magic must hear the words of wisdom the land of Panora lives by. It is through your words, our children will understand what is happening. Now, mind you, the children will think it to be unfair, unjust if you will that we took them out of their childhood in order for them to learn the ways of their magic. Be strong, and do not allow your children to grow selfish in what they want. Give them what they need, and they shall make each of you proud. Go forth with the convictions your mother's had, and your powers shall increase, until you too, will be considered the most high. It is when we teach our own, that the full powers bestowed upon us are set free. Now you all shall plan with Firey. I shall depart, only to meet with you again tomorrow night. Take the magic to bed with you, and let the seeds of your heritage grow," the spirit voice faded, and Firey stood.

"Do any of the elders have any questions?"

"Only one." Rain looked at her.

"Then speak, Rain," Firey said.

"When our children learn the truth, and once the war is finished, will they be allowed back to earth?"

"We'll see what happens. If in fact they are granted permission to inhibit the planet earth once again, then they shall be expected not to use their magic down there."

"And if they do?" Tornado asked.

"Then it will bring destruction slowly to their planet."

"But will it harm our children?" Manning's mom looked worried.

"It could Hurricane, but you already knew that answer. You've all been taught about the powers of Panora. On the planet earth, if your children go against the rules of Panora and use their magic, it will indeed break through the fields around the nuclear bombs, and could indeed start worldly mass destruction. So I suggest you teach them well, with the time you're allowed to spend with them. If you listen, and if your children take to heart the words you speak, all shall be well. If not..." Firey stopped talking, looked at each of them, nodded her head, and was gone.

Rain looked at her friends. "Do you think the children will listen?"

"Did we?" Bobby's mother Windy asked.

"I think most of us did," Rain answered, and they heard Dave's mother Tornado clear her throat.

"Oh, right." Rain laughed. "I forgot you breeched the barrier. Remember when Tornado tried to go back to earth?" she asked.

"How could we forget?" Windy answered.

"Yeah, I thought we were all going to die, that day. When you breeched the barrier this whole world shook all of us to the core. Thank goodness, you stopped when you did, or we would not be here today, teaching our children of our heritage," Hurricane said.

As they looked over at Violet, Shelby's mom, they all saw the sadness in her eyes. "Why are you so still tonight, Volcano?"

"What'd you mean?" She stared at her hands.

"You've not asked any questions. What's wrong?" Rain asked gently.

"I'm frightened of what will happen with our stubborn children. We all know they are not like any of us. They're all different, and think its okay to make their own decisions, and speak their mind about everything." She twisted her hands nervously.

"This may be true," Rain said. "But we were not as innocent as your leading us to believe. We too were defiant, and we still came out of this world okay."

"Yeah, but we listened to our mother's, but our children are different than we were. I have a feeling it'll be nothing but trouble. I can feel it."

"Come now," Windy said as she stood. "We need to believe in our children." She smiled. "Tomorrow will be a brighter day, with more positive thinking. Now we must rest. Shall we?"

"Yes, I guess," Shelby's mother said.

"Listen, we can't change what's going to happen," Rain said, "the only things we can do for our children are teach them the difference between the right ways and wrong ways of the land of Panora. Other than that, we can't make them do anything else."

"Yes, we can. If they get out of hand, you know as well as I do, we can use our very own magic to stop them," Windy answered.

"Yes, so we can, but then it weakens us for the war ahead," Hurricane said.

"Then let's teach our children well, convince them to listen, and ground them until their twenty on earth if they don't." Rain laughed, and her friends joined in as she led them all to their separate place of resting, outside Firey's house, and up into the trees surrounding the land.

CHAPTER THIRTEEN

When Kimmy woke up the following morning, she left the colorful room, and walked outside.

She stood still for a moment enjoying the silence.

Everything looked beautiful to her, and so green. It was as if overnight someone had taken a crayon, and colored the land brilliantly.

"So, you felt me summons you?" Kimmy heard the deep voice ask.

She spun around, and saw Dagg standing there.

"What? Can't find your tongue? That's different," Dagg said.

"What're you doing here?" Kimmy challenged.

"I told you, I would come back. I told you it's not over yet. So here I am. What a shame it'll be when your magical family wakes up and finds you gone." Dagg circled her, as Kimmy tried to think.

"Dagg, do you think you're going to get away with whatever you're planning on doing?"

"I know I will."

"But you'll be caught. After all, you couldn't hold our Queen, what makes you so sure that you can hold me?"

Dagg laughed, and drooled. "You silly human, I guess the good magic as you call it, and your queen, has failed to tell you what happens when an earthling's captured before they learn how to properly use their magic."

"Oh don't fool yourself, we've talked about it." Kimmy lied.

"If you talked about it, why are you out here? Did you miss the part about how no earthling shall wander outside the protected walls of the queen? Or are you just stupid?"

"I wanted some air, and didn't see the harm in it. Besides I wasn't expecting you to be here."

"Well surprise. I am. Now you're coming with me. I'm taking you to Watesa, and she's going to decide what to do with you."

When Kimmy reached for her ring, she realized it was gone, and no longer on her finger.

Dagg laughed. "Looking for this?" He held up her ring. "Oh, too bad, I took it off the second you stepped outside the safety of the walls. Now it's mine. You're powerless without it." He laughed, as he swept her up, and flew away.

When Firey looked in the colorful room, she noticed immediately, Kimmy wasn't there.

She turned, and went outside. When she found it empty, she reached for the locket around her neck, opened it, and sprinkled green glitter.

Before she knew it, all the good magic of the land was gathered before her.

As she took in their sleepy faces she realized with a heavy heart that Kimmy was gone.

"I've gathered all of you because something bad has happened." She waited a beat to let what she told them sink in, before she spoke.

"What happened?" Rain asked as she sighed.

"Karisma's missing," Firey answered.

"What'd you mean missing?" Rain sounded panicked.

"Just what I said Rain, she's gone."

"Where did she go?" Rain blurted.

"I don't know."

"But how could she be missing?" Bobby asked upset.

"Listen, gather close so I can tell you what I think happened."

When the magic of the good land gathered closer to Firey, she took a moment to look at each of them. "I don't know where Karisma is. Now, I shall make a fire in the pit, and look there for the answers."

As she flung her fingers towards the pit, a fire ignited, and Firey stared at the yellow flames licking the air.

When she nodded, she looked at her people. "Watesa has her."

"What?" Shelby was alarmed. "What'd you mean Watesa has her? How did that happen?"

Firey glanced toward the fire. "She was taken early this morning." Firey looked miserable. "Apparently, she wandered out here without guidance."

"So?" Bobby shrugged. "What does that mean? We've wandered before, but nothing like this has happened."

"True." Firey nodded her head absently. "But you wandered when you were mere mortals of the world. You had nothing to offer anyone. Not true now."

"Do you want to explain that?" Dave snapped.

"I'll try. Please sit on the ground and focus on becoming one with the land."

Once everyone was seated, Firey waited a beat, before she again looked each of them in the eye. She read the conflicting emotions, and knew that it wouldn't be easy trying to explain what happened.

"Right now, Karisma's gone. We can't save her yet either. If anyone tries they'll be met with suffering."

"Why?" Renee asked quietly.

"Because Raven, Karisma's powerless, and so are all of you."

"We are not," Manning argued. "We did a fine job helping you escape."

"Yes, you did, Mountain, but this is different," Firey answered.

"How?" Bobby asked.

"It's different because Karisma holds the highest power of all of us."

"What? I don't understand," Dave snapped. "So why don't you start talking. Maybe then we'll have a clearer picture of what you're talking about."

"Okay. I shall try." Firey turned, and stared into the flames of the fire once again, before she looked at them. "Children, you must understand Karisma's been captured. Now this time she's not in the dungeon where Watesa kept you last time. This time Watesa is quartering Karisma in the castle."

"What do you mean she's quartering her?" Shelby demanded.

"Quarters mean she shares Watesa's dwelling. That's where they've taken her."

"So let me get this straight. She's actually being held against her will in Watesa's house?" Bobby asked agitated.

"Yes," Firey answered.

"So let's go get her," Dave said, "why are we sitting around talking about it?"

"It's not that easy," Firey answered.

"Sure it is," Renee offered. "We just have to think about our magical power, think about a plan of action, and before nightfall, we'll have Karisma back here with us."

"Yeah," the others instantly agreed.

"Children, part of the problem was none of you understand what your powers mean, leaving you clueless to what's going on here."

"No we're not!" Shelby yelled. "You act like we don't understand anything, but we do. We're not stupid, and I feel like the way you talk to us implies that."

"Not at all. Now hush, so I can tell you what I mean."

When they fell quiet, Firey cleared her throat, "Karisma's grandmother is the highest power of the land, and Watesa knows this.

This is a hindrance in two ways. First, it makes it harder to teach all of you humans about your magic. Second, it makes it very difficult to rescue Karisma."

"Difficult how?" Bobby demanded clearly upset.

Karisma's mother Rain stepped forward. "Listen to me children."

When they swung their eyes to stare at her, she nodded gently. "All of you are very intelligent humans when you want to be. Now, you need to listen, before Karisma gets hurt. Understand?"

As she watched the children, she knew they were clearly shaken by what had happened.

"Now, let's see if I can't explain this whole thing. Karisma's grandmother Culver has the highest power of the land, which is why Watesa has taken her. She knows she holds the key to all the magic here on these lands. Karisma's powers are so great that once trained in her ways of magic, she could battle the evil part of the land, and win victory single handedly, without any of us. But unfortunately, right now, she's helpless."

"Why doesn't grandmother Culver help her then?" Dave asked.

"Because she can't. Look, it works like this. Karisma was brought here with the rest of you to train. She was given one part of her magic, which was the sapphire ring. Firey instructed her never to take the ring off her finger, which Karisma never did. But because she stepped outside the safety of the house, they've captured her, and they've also taken her ring. She's now powerless, and only a mere human."

"How did they get the ring?" Renee asked.

"The dark land's power is much stronger then Karisma's."

"Yeah, but our power's are stronger than theirs right?" Renee asked.

"Not right now. Because they took Karisma their power is stronger," Rain answered.

"That doesn't make any sense." Bobby looked confused as he glared at her.

"I know you're upset Bobby, but right now they only thing we can do is prepare."

"So how do we do that?" Dave asked. "I really wish someone would start talking about what we're going do, because I want to bring Karisma back, and everything you've told us is useless. Now let's get down to business."

Kimmy stared at Watesa defiantly. "Why am I here?"

Watesa stared at her with her one purple eye. "Because you're worth more than the rest."

What'd you mean?" Kimmy tilted her chin, and glared at Watesa who laughed.

"Kimmy, or should I call you Karisma? I'm in the highest power now because of you."

"Yeah, whatever. Anything you say means nothing."

"It should mean something. You'd be foolish not to listen." Watesa snapped her tentacle. "You anger me."

"So? Do I look like I care?" Kimmy asked.

"No, that's what's going to get you in trouble." Watesa laughed again.

"I think that's what's going to get you in trouble," Kimmy shot the words at her.

"Human, you're way out of line. I'm the one with the power, not you. Now, a wise human would tell me everything they know."

"What'd you talking about?" Kimmy snapped.

"I'm going to ask you a series of questions. When I do, you're going to give me the answers." Watesa stared at her.

"And if I don't?" Kimmy asked crossing her arms over her chest.

"If you don't. I'll feed you to Dagg."

When Kimmy laughed, Watesa snapped her tentacle. "Do you dare laugh at me?" she raised her voice, causing the room they were in to shake.

"Yes, I'm sorry, I do." Kimmy laughed harder. "You think you're so sure of yourself, but you're nothing. The good magic of the land is more powerful than you could ever dream of having. If you think I'll answer anything, and betray my people, you're mistaken."

"Oh, you're going to answer my questions, or Dagg will have you for lunch." Watesa closed her eye for a moment, and before Kimmy realized it, she was shackled to the wall.

"Now, are you going to do things my way?" Watesa asked glaring at Kimmy.

"What'd you want to know?" Kimmy snapped trying to pull her arms out of the restraints.

"First, tell me the powers of your grandmother."

"No."

"What did you say?" Watesa sounded shocked.

"I told you no. I'm not telling you anything."

"So you're refusing to save your own life to protect the others?" Watesa was stunned.

"Yeah, I guess so. Look, you ugly thing, I don't care what you do to me, I'll never reveal the secrets of our heritage to you."

"Even if it means, you die?"

"Yeah, even if it means I die," Kimmy answered.

"Why would you give up your life for them?"

"Because I'd save our world from you."

Watesa snickered. "Obviously, they've failed once again to tell you of your powers. You see, I'm not the only enemy. You're good world has many."

"Then why wasn't I aware of it?" Kimmy challenged.

When Watesa stared at her, Kimmy looked away. "Because you're a human, and Firey must've thought you weren't ready to hear it all. I'm telling you, I'm the kindest evil of the land. Other enemies are approaching fast, and once they get to this side of the land, they won't be nice. They won't have conversations with any of your people. They will seek, and destroy. That's what they've been trained to do."

"Haven't you been trained to do the same?" Kimmy blurted. "If you expect me to believe anything you're telling me, then you're just as stupid as the rest. I don't trust you, or anything you tell me."

"But you must. The evil in the land is approaching. Once they arrive, they'll capture Firey, and your mother. Then…"

"You're just saying that so I'll talk." Kimmy looked at her.

"No, I'm not." Watesa snapped her tentacle again, and Kimmy saw the darkness of the people traveling over the land toward Panora.

"What?" Kimmy shrugged. "Don't think I believe what you're showing me either. It's only another illusion of yours."

"You silly human, what I'm showing you is the darkest power. They hold all the bad magic and they'll be here by tomorrow night."

"Yeah right. If they're the darkest magic, then what are you?"

"I'm not as dark as they are."

"Whatever. If it's bothering you that much that they're coming, release me, so that I may get back to Panora, and warn the others."

"You fool. I'd never release you. It's because you're my prisoner that neither good nor the bad magic of the land can touch me," Watesa spat the words at her. "I'd be absolutely out of my thinking zone to release you."

"So, let me get this straight. As long as I'm here the dark magic can't touch you?"

"That's right, and neither can the good. I can't be over thrown, and no harm shall come to me, as long as you're here."

"Are you sure about that?"

"I'm positive, you silly human. Why do you think I captured you? Your problem is you've never listened when people have spoken to you. When Firey tried to make you understand she was wasting her time. You always thought you could do what you were told not to. Karisma you believe you're invincible. Well, you're not, especially right now."

"Why not? Face it. What you just told me, is not only do you need me to protect you, but as long as you hold me captive my powers are of no use, right?"

"That's right." Watesa smiled, reveling yellowed fangs.

"So what Dagg said about eating me was all a lie. A ruse to scare me." Kimmy laughed. "He's not very bright is he?"

"He'll fight you again, and he shall win."

"We'll see. So, if I'm so powerful give me back my ring."

"What?"

"You heard me. If I'm here, what harm will it bring, if I put my ring back on?"

"Sorry, you can't be allowed to do that."

"Why not?" Kimmy demanded.

"Because you fool, the moment your finger touches the ring, all your good magic comes back. The only saving grace is you're not trained in all the magic."

"So, what's the big deal? Just give me the ring?"

"No."

"Well, it doesn't matter. I'm here because the people of the good land wanted me here. Now, I don't know about you, but I'd say if they can take me from earth, and bring me to the land of Panora, then they can take me from Walby. Wouldn't you agree?"

"Is your mother on this side too? In Panora?" Watesa asked.

"Why?"

"Because I know the darkest magic will capture her. Without you, she's weaker in her own magic. If they reach her, she'll be forced to travel back with them." Watesa nodded toward the travelers once again.

Kimmy shrugged. "My mother will be fine, and I know you're only trying to scare me. Now, I need to rest. I've had a long day already." Kimmy closed her eyes.

"What? Just like that. You've ended our conversation just like that?"

"Yeah, that's right. When you've got something worth saying, wake me up. Until then, this conversation's over." Kimmy kept her eyes closed, and finally heard a shuffling noise, and the snap of Watesa tentacle, and finally Kimmy knew she was alone.

CHAPTER FOURTEEN

When Firey walked over to Bobby, she saw the sadness in his eyes and knew she needed to comfort him. "I know this is hard on you. But you must stay strong and focused on what needs to be done. If you don't, Kimmy will be in more danger then she's already in."

"I figured that. What other danger's coming?" Bobby asked.

"How do you know there's other danger?"

"I can feel it like a heavy blanket."

"Meaning?"

"You know, it feels like a heavy blanket is lying across my chest, and I can barely breathe! That's how I feel."

"Boulder, you need to release that feeling. Put it to rest. If we all do exactly what we've discussed your Karisma will be fine."

"And if someone sways?" Bobby's eyes glittered dangerously.

"Then we lose her forever."

"Can I talk to my mom for a few minutes?" Bobby asked.

"I'm sorry, it's not allowed. Not even for you. I know your heart is troubled, and Kimmy is your friend, but I can't allow another breach to occur. If I allow you to speak with your mother, another portal will open, and magic that is more powerful will spill through into our land. I can't, and won't allow it to happen, again."

"But what's going to happen when the other evil power arrives?" Bobby wanted to know.

"A great war will take place. But without Kimmy you know what'll happen."

"Yeah," Bobby sighed. "I wish I would've heard her wake up this morning because I could've stopped her."

Firey nodded. "Kimmy's strong willed, much like her mother. But this time she should have heeded the warning of what she had been told. But she turned a deaf ear on the whole situation, causing grief for all of us."

"I don't think she did it on purpose." Bobby defended her.

"I never said she did." Firey smiled. "The only thing I'm saying is that if she would've considered the consequences before she decided to wander, we'd all be better off then where we are now."

"Well, that's how Kimmy is. But let me tell you something. When things happen, I'd rather have Kimmy in my corner than anyone else. She's someone that everyone can rely on."

"I know," Firey sighed. "Now I must go. Train well, Boulder."

As Bobby stared, he watched Firey melt, and then she was gone.

As Shelby watched her mother, she had an overwhelming desire to walk over to her, but knew she couldn't.

To breach the barrier, would unlock unwanted danger, and Shelby wasn't going to let it happen.

"Come now, let's get started shall we?" Tekio asked her.

"Yes, let's get started," Shelby answered, trying to focus.

———※———

As Renee thought about what happened to Kimmy, she wanted to cry. She knew how scared Kimmy would be.

As she stared at her trainers, she wondered how they could be smiling at a time like this.

That alone made it impossible to concentrate. Finally, Renee blurted, "What's your problem? Can't you see I'm too upset to learn anything new right now?"

"We know you are, Raven," Flam told her sadly. "But you must get with it. We're on a time schedule here. Now enough with the pouting that you human's love to do. We've much bigger things to do. Now are you ready?"

"No," Renee pouted again. "I feel like I'm going to cry over what's happened to Kimmy. Wouldn't any of you feel the same?"

"Of course we would. But the difference is, we would take the energy we're wasting on pouting, and thinking, and put it to good use," Crowey told her. "Now, when you're ready to be serious about what your job is, you let us know." He folded his wings across his chest staring at her.

"Fine, you're right, and I'm sorry. I'm ready when you are."

"Good, that's a girl. Now let's get started," Flam said smiling.

Dave looked at his guides, Tomkin and Zambo, and then he shook his head. "Sorry guys I'm not in the mood to train."

"What?" Tomkin tapped his foot, impatiently. "What'd you mean?"

"Just what I said. I'm worried about Kimmy, and the only thing everyone wants to do is practice. I need time to figure out how to help her escape."

"But you'll know if you learn your magic," Zambo said.

"I already know how to do my magic," Dave snapped at them. "Watch."

As his trainers stared, they watched him turn into a dagger, and then he began floating.

"That's good. That's real good. Now let's get serious, Dagger. You need to pay attention. Half the problem is that tongue of yours. You don't know when to keep it still. Now change back. You're not allowed to use magic unless we say you can," Zambo said.

Dave blinked hard and was once again standing before them. "Why'd it hurt so much that time?" he asked rubbing his arms.

"Because you changed into a dagger without our permission," Zambo answered.

Dave shrugged. "So what?"

"So what? It's not allowed," Tomkin scolded him.

"Says who?" Dave questioned.

"Says the laws of Panora."

Dave waved his hand. "I don't care about the laws. When are you going to realize the only thing I care about is saving, Kimmy."

"We got that." Zambo took a step forward. "What we don't get is why you don't stop your mouth from running, and open your ears to listen."

"Because I don't have too, and why is everyone always commenting on my mouth? Look, I want Kimmy to come back here, so I'll do whatever it takes. But I'm telling you, we need to hurry. Firey said there's not much time."

"Then stop sidestepping us," Tomkin said.

"What does sidestepping mean?" Dave asked confused.

"Are you not listening to us? What you've just told us a moment ago, is exactly what we've been telling you? As far as your mouth goes, it's always running, so stop it, Dagger."

Dave threw his hands in the air. "Let's get down to business. I'm tired, and the sooner we get this over with, the faster Kimmy will return. I'm ready when you are."

As Manning sat with his trainers, Tibbs, Grubbs, and Zambler, he watched.

They were showing him more ways to use his magic, and he found the whole thing extremely cool.

"I want to try it now," he blurted, sounding rushed.

"Not yet," Zambler said.

"Why not?"

"Because you're not ready," Grubb's answered.

"Yes, I am. I'll bet you I can do it just as good as you can, if not better." He glared at the three of them.

"What's wrong with you human children?" Tibbs asked.

"What'd you mean?"

"You know what I mean, Mountain. You're all impatient, and want everything right now."

Manning shrugged. "So?"

"So? It doesn't happen like that. It's takes time to develop your magic, and you've got to know when to use it, and when not to use it."

"Yeah, so I've been told." Manning looked at them. "Listen, this whole thing needs to move quickly, I'm worried about Kimmy, and I need to go get her. She's not strong right now. She's been stripped of her powers, and now she's human again."

"We know," Zambler snapped. "But you not listening isn't helping."

"What'd you mean? I'm listening."

"No you're not!" Grubbs yelled. "If you were listening you'd know what to do, but you're not listening, and you're certainly driving me out of my comfort zone. I never raise my voice. Not like this. But do you hear me screaming?"

"I think the whole land of Panora hears you," Manning said, laughing.

"That's it. I'm finished. When you're serious, come find us. You had better think about what you're doing, Mountain. You're not just messing with your life, but you're messing with Karisma's as well."

"Okay." Manning looked at the ground, then back at his trainers. "I'm ready to listen. Teach me my magic."

When Kimmy opened her eyes, she saw a guy standing in front of her. "Who are you?" Kimmy asked.

"My name is Flipple."

"What?" Kimmy sounded confused.

"My name is Flipple," the guy repeated.

"What do you want?" Kimmy snapped, "And why are you watching me sleep?"

"Because I think you're human."

"Oh aren't you smart?" Kimmy laughed snidely. "Let me guess, you work for Watesa, right?"

"That's right. I do."

"So what'd you want?"

"I want you to trust me enough to talk to me."

Kimmy giggled. "No thanks. It's not happening."

"Why?" Flipple looked hurt, with his short dark hair, dark eyes, and short stature.

"Because I don't trust anyone in the land of Walby."

"I'm not from Walby," he said.

"Yeah, right. Whatever."

"I'm not. I'm from the land of Vanduesa."

"Whatever, I've never heard of that land before now."

"Well, that's where I'm from," Flipple said.

"Good for you. Now, why don't you go back?"

"Go back where?" Flipple shook his head. "I'm clearly lost. Do all you humans use such funny language?"

"Yeah, I'm afraid so."

"Well, I find it most disturbing." Flipple stared at her with his dark eyes.

"Why are you staring at me like that?"

"Because I've not seen many humans."

"So?" Kimmy snapped. "This isn't a freak show. So stop it."

"What's a freak show?" Flipple asked.

"I'm not talking to you anymore. Now, I'm going to close my eyes, and when I open them, I'm going to hope you're not standing there anymore."

When she heard Flipple laugh, she glared at him. "What's so funny?"

"You are. Just because you don't want me here, doesn't mean I'm going away."

"Why not. Run along. You know be gone, disappear, do something."

"I can't. Watesa sent me to keep an eye on you."

"Well, tell her I'm fine, and go find someone else to stare at, okay?"

"I can't."

"Yes, you can," Kimmy heard another deep voice join their conversation.

When she turned her head, she saw a tall guy, with dark hair, and the most startling blue eyes, smiling at her.

"Oh great, who are you?" she asked.

"The name is Petrello."

"What?" Kimmy smirked. "Whatever, do me a favor and go away."

"I can't, and besides I've seen you on Earth before."

"You're lying because I've never seen you before now."

"That's because one of my magic powers, gives me the ability to change my appearance. I'm telling you I'm Petrello."

"I've heard everything now." Kimmy rolled her eyes. "Besides, what kind of a name is Petrello?"

"A good one." He looked first at her, then at Flipple. "You can go. I'm here to take over."

"But Watesa told me not to leave, until she told me personally that I could."

"I'm telling you to go. She sent me." Petrello looked at Flipple.

"Well, if you say so. I just don't want Watesa upset with me. Are you sure she sent you?"

"Oh, yeah."

"Are you sure it's okay if I leave?"

"Of course. Come on, if it wasn't, why would I tell you that?"

"To get me in trouble," Flipple said.

"Yeah, but I wouldn't do that."

"How do I know?"

"You don't. But if I were you, I'd take off while I had the chance. Who knows how long you'll be stuck with the human the next time."

Flipple looked at him. "If you say so."

"I say so, now go."

As Flipple walked out of the room, Petrello looked at Kimmy. "Are you ready to get out of those chains?"

"Oh my gosh, yes," she answered him.

"Good. Now give me a moment to help you."

Kimmy watched him close his eyes, and then she felt her hands being freed.

She rubbed her wrists, then, smiled. "Thanks."

"You're welcome. Now you and I need to talk."

CHAPTER FIFTEEN

As Kimmy stared at Petrello, she smiled. "How come everyone here has such weird names?"

"Weird names? I'm sorry, what does that mean?" he asked innocently.

"It means funny names."

"Funny how?" Petrello rolled his eyes. "You human's are funny. I don't understand what you mean, but just forget it."

"So why do you think human's are funny? Aren't you humanized?"

"No," Petrello answered.

"Okay. I thought maybe you were." Kimmy stared at him a moment, but when he said nothing; she put her hands on her hips. "Why did you free me?"

"It's a long story."

"Yeah, and I've got time," Kimmy answered. "Unless you're here to take me back to the land of Panora?"

"No, I'm sorry. I'm not powerful enough to make it happen."
"Then why are you here?" Kimmy asked sounding disappointed.

"Actually my mother sent me."

"Who's your mother?"

"Her earth name is Stacey. Her given name is Sparkle."

"Does my mother know her?" Kimmy asked.

"Yes. As a matter of fact the two of them use to be good friends, until the truth was revealed about my heritage."

"You lost me again."

"Okay, back on earth the two of them were friends, before I was born."

"So what happened?" Kimmy asked.

"After your mother and my mother got into a fight, she request-ed permission to permanently live in the land of Panora." Petrello looked at her.

"What was the fight over?"

"I'm getting to that," Petrello sounded impatient. "Like I said, after the fight my mother requested permission to live in the land of Panora."

"You can do that?" Kimmy was shocked.

"Yes," Petrello told her.

"So, go on."

"Well, that's why I not humanized, as you call it."

"But this whole thing is confusing." Kimmy looked at him.

"Why is it confusing?" Petrello asked.

"Because my mother's so nice to her friends, I can't imagine her driving your mother back here forever."

"Well she did," his voice was harsh.

"Are you sure?"

"Yes, I'm sure. If I wasn't, I wouldn't tell you that."

"Okay, so my mom forced the two of you to come back here for-ever. Why?" Kimmy dropped the question on him, and then waited for the answer.

She watched Petrello squirm in his seat.

Finally, he looked at her. "Because my mother was having a baby from both parts of the land," Petrello said.

"What?"

"Yeah, that's right. I've got parents on both sides. My father's from Walby, my mother's from Panora."

"Then why was she allowed to come back? Isn't there a different land for that?" Kimmy asked.

When Petrello shook his head, he pulled his eyes away from her. "My father was killed, and that's the only reason it was allowed."

"So Firey granted your mother permission to live on the land in Panora?"

"Yeah."

"And after all that you decided to what? Be like your daddy?" Her voice was condemning.

"No."

"Then why are you here?"

"What'd you mean?"

"You know what I mean. What're you doing in the kingdom of Walby?"

"At first I worked for Watesa."

"Traitor," Kimmy spit the words at him.

"What?"

"You heard me. You're nothing more than a traitor. A guy like you has no loyalty."

"You wrong about that."

"Am I?" Kimmy stared at him, and watched as he shifted his body again.

"Yes, you're wrong. As a matter of fact, if I'm such a traitor, why am I here talking to you?"

"Because you were bored. Wanted something to do, and thought it would be fun to taunt me," Kimmy said.

"That's not true. If that's what I wanted, I'd have gone somewhere else, besides this horrible place."

"Yeah right."

"Yeah, right. Look, are you going to let me finish?"

"Sure, go ahead. I've got nothing else to do, obviously."

"Okay, as I was saying, I came to Walby to find you. My mother sent me, and since I'm part of both worlds, I'm allowed access to both."

"Oh I get it. You mean since you show no loyalty to either side, because that would require you to make some sort of a decision, you've decided to play both ends of the land against the middle, right?"

"That's not funny."

"I'm not laughing, Petrello."

"Anyway, you should consider yourself lucky that I'm able to travel. At least you've got someone to talk too."

"Who says I want to talk?" Kimmy was looking at him upset.

"I just thought since you were taken, I could come here, and find out what to do."

Kimmy threw her hand over her heart. "My hero. You're such a man that you couldn't figure out a better excuse for being in the kingdom of Walby, and you want me to believe your story?"

"I don't care if you believe it or not."

"I know. You're going to say it's the truth, right?" Kimmy stared coldly at him.

"Yeah, something like that."

"Well, Pet boy, I'm not buying into your story, so don't expect me to tell you anything."

He glared at her. "Don't call me that. Look, I just want to know what you wanted me to do."

"For starters, you could go away. I don't talk to indecisive people. Especially, since you come from both sides of the land."

"I'm not what you think I am."

"Yes, you are."

"No, I'm really not. If you would be quiet long enough, maybe you'd hear the truth of my words."

"I doubt it. Now go." Kimmy swung her eyes to the door.

"If I walk out the door like you're suggesting, then I'll have to put you in chains again."

Kimmy eyed them, and then looked at Petrello.

"Okay fine, you can stay, only if you help me figure out how to get out of here."

"I don't know if I'm strong enough to do that by myself."

"Hello, what'd I look like to you?"

"A human with no powers." He finally smiled.

"Yeah, I am. So what? You're not going to help me?" Kimmy eyed him.

"I never said that. I only said, I don't think my powers are strong enough."

"If you believe that, then you'll be right, and I'll be stuck a prisoner forever. Can't we at least try?"

"I guess." He looked at her.

"Face it, if you try to help me, you could end up changing my mind about the crumb I really think you are."

"Thanks."

"You're welcome. So are you going to help?"

"Not yet. I need to know a few things first."

"Are you kidding me? What on earth would you need to know that we haven't already talked about?"

"I need to know that if I try to do this, you'll help me convince Firey that I'm more good magic, than bad."

"I don't know how I can convince her of that."

"Oh my gosh, quickly. Watesa is coming." Petrello closed his eyes, and before Kimmy knew it, the chains were wrapped around her again, just as the door burst open.

"Watesa, how nice," Petrello addressed her.

"Petrello, what're you doing here?"

"I came to give Flipple a break."

Watesa floated over to Kimmy, stared at her, and then laughed.

"I find it funny the highest power in the land of Panora, now resides with me."

Petrello smiled. "Only you could pull something like this, and manage to get away with it." He smiled at Watesa.

"I know. It's because of who I am. I've got the highest powers in the kingdom of Walby."

"I know."

"You also know how I don't like traitors."

"Yes, I know." Petrello looked at her.

"Good. I take it you're not one?"

"No way. My daddy taught me better than that." Petrello glanced quickly at Kimmy.

"Your daddy was a fine man. It was a shame that he was killed."

"Thank you."

Watesa nodded, and then directed her attention back to Kimmy. She snapped her tentacle, and Kimmy saw the land of Panora appear on the wall next to her.

"Take a good, long look. Do you see how hard everyone's working on perfecting their magic?" she snapped.

"Yes," Kimmy answered.

"Well, they're not going to be able too. Do you want to know why?"

"Sure," Kimmy answered.

"Because their highest power's on this side of the land. Without you, none of them are strong enough to rescue you."

"That's not true. Firey's our queen, and she'll know what to do."

"Karisma, you just don't understand." Watesa shook her head. "Firey use to be strong, until you entered the portal and arrived in Panora. Once that happened, it weakened Firey and all the others."

"How come it didn't weaken you?" Kimmy demanded.

Watesa laughed. "Oh it did, until you were captured. I was almost without power, but once we had you, I was magically recharged. Now, I stand before you, with all my beauty and I'll never let you go."

"They'll never let me stay," Kimmy said.

"They're powerless against me!" Watesa screamed, snapping her tentacle, and the land of Panora disappeared.

"I guess time will tell, huh?" Kimmy smirked.

"Why are human's so disobedient?"

"I guess it's how we're raised." Kimmy giggled.

"Enough!" Watesa yelled, "One more word, and it'll be your last. Do you understand?" Her purple eye glittered dangerously.

Kimmy nodded.

"Very well." She swung her eye to stare at Petrello. "You shall stay with her through the night. If anything happens, notify me immediately."

"How?" Petrello asked.

"Get word to me. You know I'm unable to monitor Karisma, unless I stand next to her. My magic is slowly returning. By morning, I should be fully restored."

Petrello nodded. "Consider it done."

"Good. Now I'm going to rest." Watesa floated to the door, turned one last time to stare at Kimmy, then she slammed the door.

＊＊＊

Firey looked at Rain as they gathered in the colorful room.

"Do you think it'll work?" Rain asked her.

"I'd say it has too. If this plan doesn't work, then Kimmy will be gone forever."

Rain shook her head. "I don't think I'd be able to handle that."

"I know. Let's not dwell on what the future holds, until we know for sure what it is, okay?"

"Okay," Rain agreed.

"Now there's something else I must tell you. Which is why I summoned you alone," Firey said.

"Go ahead. I knew something was wrong. Usually you summons all of us together."

"I know." Firey floated over to Rain. "What I'm going to tell you will evoke feelings you long ago forgot about."

"What is it?" Rain asked.

"It's something delicate."

"Please just tell me." Rain pleaded.

"Well, do you remember Stacey?"

"Yes." Rain stared at the floor. "Her given name is Sparkle."

"That's right. She's here in the land of Panora."

"I know. You granted her permission to live here, when all the other lands forbid it."

"That's right, I did."

"Why?" Rain accused.

"Why what?"

"Why did you allow it?" Rain asked.

"I allowed it because it was the correct thing to do."

"Why?"

"Because she's from here," Firey answered. "What happened between her and her husband was of no one's concern. Sparkle was young, and her heart led her where she shouldn't have gone."

"Exactly, this is why she should've gone to live in the kingdom of Walby. Not on the wholesome land of Panora."

"That's nonsense. She was part of this land as well."

"Until she turned into a traitor," Rain shouted.

"It's the past. Rain you need to let it go."

"I've tried, but you know how I feel about it."

"Yes, over the years, you've made it quite obvious how you feel."

"Good. Anyway, what about her?"

"She came to help us."

Rain laughed. "You can't be serious? What'd you mean she came to help us? She stepped over the boundaries of the land, and you and I both know it's against the rules to do that. Now, you want to let her help us? Is that what you're saying?"

"Yes, but there's more."

Rain glared at Firey. "Go on." She encouraged her queen.

"Sparkle has a son."

"A what?"

"A son."

"Okay." Rain shrugged. "What does that have to do with what we're talking about?" Rain's voice was chilly.

"It has everything to do with it. You see her son's name is Petrello. He was born in the land of Panora."

"So?"

"So, I wanted you to know as we speak, he's with Kimmy in the kingdom of Walby right now."

"What?"

"That's right," Firey said.

"Why did you allow it?" Rain asked bitterly.

"Because he's the only one who's allowed to travel to both sides of the land and you know that."

"So?"

"What'd you mean so?" Firey asked.

"So, why did you allow him to be with Kimmy?"

"I allowed it because I'm the queen. I don't need your permission to make decisions."

"Okay." Rain shrugged. "So what's he trying to do?"

"He's gone to Kimmy to find out how we can help her escape."

Rain laughed coldly. "You think a traitor such as Petrello will help her? You think he'll go against Watesa?"

When Firey didn't answer, Rain turned. She saw Sparkle standing in the door.

"I don't remember inviting you here," Rain said harshly.

"I wish you still weren't mad. You and I were so close when we were young."

Rain held her hand up. "Please, let's not go back in the past, to what use to be."

Sparkle walked in the room. "I just want you to know that Petrello is a good boy. He offered to go because he can without drawing suspicion."

"So?" Rain shrugged her shoulders.

"So, now I guess we wait until he comes back here in the morning."

"Is he staying with Kimmy all night?" Rain was shocked.

"Yes," Sparkle answered.

"Why?"

"So she's not alone. He told me he didn't want to leave her in the kingdom of Walby."

Rain walked toward the window, and stared over the land, before she turned back to address Firey and Sparkle. "So what's the plan?" she asked.

"Everyone knows what the plan is. Now it's time to execute it," Firey answered.

"Is everyone ready?" Sparkle asked.

"Not yet." Firey stopped her. "The two of you really need to set aside your differences, so it doesn't run interference with what we must do." She looked at the two women. "Now I'm leaving the two of you to do just that. Do not come out and join the rest of us, until you're both united. Is that clear?" she asked.

When both women nodded, Firey turned, and left them.

CHAPTER SIXTEEN

As Bobby watched his friends, he felt an impending feeling of doom settle in his chest.

He looked at his trainers and he realized Juniper was staring at him.

"What's wrong?" Bobby asked.

"Something's not sitting right with you." Juniper was matter of fact.

"What do you mean?"

"I mean, I see the worry in your eyes. You need to focus, and stop worrying about Karisma. She'll be fine, eventually."

"How do you know?" Bobby snapped. "You're not the one in Walby. Kimmy's helpless right now, and I'd rather be with her, then stuck here."

"If you were with her, it would only mean the two of you would be powerless, instead of just her."

Bobby looked at the ground. "If she's so powerful then why is it, she's has nothing now?"

Juniper stared before he answered. "It goes like this. Your powers are you own, as long as you never lose the gift the Firey gave you. For instance, if you lost your medallion or it was taken from you that would be it. You'll instantly become human again."

"But I don't understand what jewelry has to do with anything."

"It's not for me to explain. As you move along with everything that's happening, you'll come to understand all of it. It'll be then your full understanding will come into play."

"So if I'm powerful right now, and the rest of you are as well, why can't we go rescue Kimmy?"

"We shall, when Firey says. Not a moment before, either. She's the queen, and we must listen to her," Juniper scolded.

"Whatever. Then teach me quickly, so I can go find her." Bobby glared at Juniper.

"First, you must be willing to focus."

"I am. Now let's get started."

As Rain and Sparkle joined the other mother's everyone waited with baited breath.

Rain looked at all of them, nodded her head, and the circle was formed. As they all held hands, Rain noticed that Sparkle's fingers were cold, and she smiled.

When they were young, her fingers always stayed cold, and Rain knew it was a sure a sign that Sparkle was nervous.

"Are you ready?" Rain asked them.

When they all nodded, she began the chant. "Oh great powers up on high, save our Karisma, don't let her die."

Rain heard the others join in, and soon their voices carried on the wind, throughout the land of Panora.

"We are the mother's whose powers are great, make the good magic without haste. Free our Karisma, from the dark queen, let her come back to Panora unseen. We ask almighty highest one, to do the favor, as shall be done. Our Kimmy, Karisma, needs our magic, so she can be spared the tragic. Let no other stand in the way deliver us Karisma on this very special day."

As the women repeated the chant, they felt the electric charge pass between their hands, and knew it was working.

When Rain tipped her head to look toward the sky, she knew the others were doing the same.

Then all the women saw Grandmother Culver high above sitting peacefully on the clouds.

"My children," she addressed the land of Panora loudly. "Soon, the Great War will begin, and it is of utmost important that all of you stand united." Grandmother Culver pointed her old, twisted finger toward all of them. "Let none of you come undone. Let no man, woman, or child, forget why we're all gathered. You've all passed through the portals by choice, whether you believe that or not. Look to your own hearts for the answers to why you're here," she paused a moment, before she continued. "Now, let's talk about Karisma, shall we?"

"Yes," the people of the land in Panora simultaneously agreed.

"Very well. She's powerless for a spell. Soon, she'll discover the way to evoke her magic, minus her ring."

"Why does she get to do that, and we can't?" Shelby demanded.

"Child." Grandmother Culver stared at her. "You mustn't fret. Instead, you must understand the powers of command. Karisma sits higher than any of you. Her powers are amongst the highest, as her given birth right. Soon my children all will be revealed. Stay focused on your own magic, for the time is drawing near. Never wander outside the safety of Firey's dwelling. To do so will result in capture. We've enough to worry about right now." She looked at each of them again, and they all felt the gentle kiss she laid upon their cheeks. "Now you've got more magic. Go forth my children, and claim your heritage. Walk soft, carry your magic as your shield, and rescue Karisma. Watesa is becoming stronger as days pass because she holds our highest power captive. Now, in three hours, it shall come to pass, and it'll be at that time that the magic in your hearts will fully come alive. Be brave, train well, and most importantly, listen to those who are older, and wiser."

As the people of Panora stared, they watched grandmother Culver, slowly fade into the clouds, until she slowly disappeared.

Then Firey turned, and smiled at all of them. "Let's gather around and prepare."

As Kimmy stared at Petrello, he felt uncomfortable. "Will you stop looking at me with those eyes of your?" he snapped.

"What? Why? I'm only watching what you're doing."

"Yeah, I understand that. But you're making me nervous."

"I don't see how," Kimmy said.

"Because you are, and I have to remember the spell to release you."

"Well, could you hurry? If you haven't noticed. I'm still in the chains, and any second now, I'm afraid someone else will come to relieve you."

"No, you heard Watesa. I'm stuck with you until morning."

"Then what traitor, huh? Once you no longer have to be stuck with me, what're you going to do? Sneak off to perform the dark magic your daddy taught you?"

"I don't have to listen to this, you know. I could put a silent spell on you, if you keep calling me a traitor."

"You wouldn't dare," Kimmy challenged.

"Yes, I would. If it would keep you quiet long enough for me to remember, I would."

"Yeah, but you heard what Watesa told you. I'm the highest power of the land. Do you really want to do something like that to me?"

"Yes."

"Why?"

"Because to tell you the truth, you're irritating me."

"Yeah, well, you're irritating me too, but that doesn't mean that I'd cast a spell on you."

"Because right now you can't."

"I could try," Kimmy said.

"Yeah, but you'd only be wasting energy that you need to have to help escape."

"What about you wasting energy to cast a spell so that my mouth stays quiet. The same rules apply to you."

Petrello smiled at her. "Yeah, but it would be so worth it. You ask more questions than anyone I know."

"So what? Is there something wrong with that?"

"Yes. I already told you. Now be still." Petrello closed his eyes, and Kimmy could tell he was concentrating.

When he opened them, she noticed his blue eyes were sparkling. When he touched the chains that had her trapped, she felt them give, and soon she was rubbing her wrists again.

"Thanks. Now what?"

"Now we sneak through the dwelling onto the land."

"And if we're caught?" Kimmy looked frightened.

"Then the queen will punish us. Now more than ever you've got to keep that mouth of yours closed. Not a sound should escape your lips. Do you think you can do it?" he asked her.

"I can try." Kimmy shrugged.

"It's important to make it happen. So instead of trying, do it," he ordered.

"Fine. Are you ready then?"

"Yes."

"Oh, wait one more thing before you open the door."

"What is it?" Petrello was impatient.

"Can't you just think of some other spell where you can make us disappear, then reappear in the land of Panora."

"You're unbelievable. If I could do that, believe me I would've already. Now come on. We've got no time for nonsense."

"Do you think if I tried my magic it would work?" Kimmy asked quickly.

"What did you have in mind?"

"I don't know. So far I've only been able to change into a horse, a dinosaur, and a fireball."

"So, continue."

When Kimmy stopped, Petrello saw the serious expression cross her face, and then she smiled, when she felt the slight brush of something across her face. She lifted her hand; touched her cheek, and then she heard the whisper.

"Be true to your magic, Karisma. Close your eyes and visualize. The land of Panora, awaits."

Kimmy kept her eyes closed, and when she opened them, she looked at Petrello. "I think I know the perfect spell."

"That quick?" he asked.

"Yes." She smiled. "But you've got to hold my hand."

"How do you know?" he asked suspiciously.

"Because I know it's what you've got to do."

"Okay, fine." He put his hand in hers, and she squeezed it softly.

Then he heard her chant, and soon they were floating. When they reached the door to the room they were in, Kimmy and Petrello passed right through it, continued down the hall, through the twists and turns of the dwelling, and were soon outside.

"How did you do that?" Petrello asked.

"Be quiet. I don't want anyone to hear us," she snapped.

"Funny, it's usually me telling you that." He smiled, and Kimmy smiled back. "Not this time."

As they floated, Kimmy became confused, and for a moment, she didn't know the way back to Panora.

"Kimmy, you turned the wrong way," Petrello said.

"How do you know?"

"Because I was raised in both lands and I know the direction of each. Now you must turn around and head back."

"Fine." Kimmy spun in a circle so hard Petrello felt his stomach tumble.

"That wasn't nice, Kimmy."

"Who said anything about being nice?" she answered.

"I should've known better," Petrello said.

As they continued to fly, suddenly something crashed into the two of them. For a moment, they went flying through the air, and finally slammed into a tree.

Kimmy let Petrello go, and knew she was tumbling quickly to the ground.

"Ah, now I've got you." Kixmox was standing before her.

"No you don't," Kimmy said, as she stood.

"Yes, I do."

"What happened?" Petrello asked, staring at Kixmox.

"I'll tell you what happened," Kixmox answered. "Kimmy tried to kidnap you, and I stopped it. Why, if it hadn't been for me, you'd have ended up in the sordid land of Panora."

"Is that where she was taking me?" Petrello asked playing along with Kixmox.

"Precisely," Kixmox answered.

"What do you want?" Kimmy demanded.

"I want you for a late night snack, but I don't think Watesa would be happy about that. So for now, I want you to come with me back to the dwelling."

"No way. I'm not going." Kimmy told him defiantly.

"Yes, you are. You're powerless remember?"

"Excuse me." Kimmy put her hands on her hips. "Did you not just see me flying through the air?"

"Oh I saw you, and I'd call it fluttering, more than flying," Kixmox growled.

"Well, I don't recall asking you, anyway," Kimmy shouted.

"Now come along. Watesa wants you," Kixmox said.

"I'm not going anywhere with you," Kimmy argued.

"Yes, you are." Kixmox growled again.

"No, I'm really not."

Kimmy reached over, grabbed Petrello's hand, and closed her eyes.

Before she knew it, she felt her feet leave the ground, and then heard the snapping of teeth below her.

As she looked down, she saw Kixmox jumping high, and snapping at her feet.

Then she turned, and she and Petrello headed in the direction of Panora.

"How did he sneak up on us like that?" Kimmy demanded.

"I don't know. You'd do well to remember you're in the land of magic, where anything is possible."

"I know that," Kimmy snapped. "But if I've got all these powers, why didn't I see it before it happened?"

"I don't know. They probably threw up there invisible shield, so they could approach undetected."

"Oh, you just have an answer for everything, don't you?" Kimmy glared at him.

"You asked. Gosh, what do you want from me?"

"I want you to use your magic to help me. That's what I want. I also want you to tell me what magic you can perform."

"No way. I'm not allowed to tell you. Besides, you're the highest power of the land. You should be able to tell me the ways of my magic. I shouldn't have to tell you."

"Well right now my magic radar is broken. So tell me."

"No."

"Okay, if you don't want to help, you leave me no choice."

"What'd you mean by that?"

"What I mean is you leave me no choice, but to let go of your hand." Kimmy was serious.

"You wouldn't dare do that to me."

"Oh wouldn't I? How confident are you?" She smiled snidely at him.

"I'm confident enough to know that if you let me go, you'd have a lot of explaining to do to your mother."

"Yeah, but you told me she doesn't like your mother anyway. So..."

"So word has it, they're standing on a united front now."

"Oh really?" she asked sarcastically.

"Yes, really. I wouldn't lie to you about something like that."

"I think you would."

"No I wouldn't." He shook his head, then, stared at her.

"How do you know?" Kimmy asked impatiently.

"I felt the words from Panora being whispered in my ear. Did you not hear it?"

"No."

"Well, they are standing united, and maybe you didn't hear it because you talk too much." Petrello laughed loudly.

"I don't think you're funny."

"I do." He snickered.

"Fine. I'm letting your hand go on the count of three. If all you want to do is laugh at me that's great, but you'll do it from the ground, and I promise you, I'll be the last one laughing."

"How do you figure?" he asked her.

"Because once I let go of your hand, and you fall to the ground, I'll laugh harder at you because you'll be trapped in the land of Walby, forever. I'll learn everything I've got to learn about my magic, and I will cast a spell that makes it impossible for you to cross the lands like you've been doing."

"Fine, if I tell you I'm sorry, will you let me continue to travel with you?"

"I might. I could think about it. But you need to stop being so cruel. I don't like it."

"You're just use to Bobby," he teased.

She shrugged. "Maybe. So, knock it off. If you upset me one

more time, I'll let your hand go without telling you."

Petrello fell quiet, and both continued flying across the land.

Several minutes later, both felt the force of something slamming into them again, and knew they were falling to the ground rapidly.

After that, they remembered nothing.

CHAPTER SEVENTEEN

When they felt the tremor move over the land in Panora, everything stopped.

Firey looked up, then, stared at the ground, as the whole land shook.

Finally, she stared at everyone. "Come gather close, there is news to tell."

"What news?" Rain asked.

"There's news of Kimmy and Petrello."

Rain threw her hand in the air. "Good heavens please let my child be safe."

"Rain, come now," Firey gently told her.

As they gathered around Firey, she waited until the ground stopped shaking.

Once the tremors stopped, she looked at each one. "The news is bleak. It speaks of a different capture. It appears that spies of Watesa are holding Kimmy and Petrello. Close to the border of Panora. X-Eyes, and Crumby have cast a spell upon them," Firey informed them.

"But how?" Rain asked.

"Yeah, how?" Sparkle wanted to know.

"From what I'm gathering, Kimmy and Petrello escaped from

Watesa's dwelling, right by the border, where they were captured. Now, they're trapped between Panora and Walby. It's not good. At this moment, they're deciding what's going to be done with them."

"What'd you mean?" Rain was panicked.

"Just what I said." Firey looked at her.

"Can't we go there?" Sparkle asked, but already knew the answer.

Firey looked at her sadly. "You already know the answer to that."

"Hold on a minute," Bobby blurted. "First of all who are you?" Bobby asked staring at Sparkle. "And who's Petrello?"

When all eyes turned to Sparkle, she looked at the ground. "My name's Sparkle and Petrello's my son," she answered.

"What's he doing with Kimmy?" Bobby asked.

"He went to the land of Walby to try to rescue her. Or, at least to make sure she was okay. Then he was either going to bring her back here, or carry the news of her well being back to Panora."

"Why?" Bobby demanded.

"Why what?" Firey asked.

"Why did you send him? I mean all day we've done nothing but train, and I think we're all strong enough to go to the kingdom of Walby. Now I say, enough is enough." He swung his eyes, and stared at his friends. "Are you with me on this?" he demanded.

"Yes," they answered.

"Then let's go." Bobby tried to walk away with his friends, but as they turned, they realized a group of people surrounded them.

"We can't allow you passage to leave." Bobby's mother Windy told the children.

"I don't care, Mom. You know how I feel about Kimmy. It's taken everything in me to be separated from her today. I'm going to rescue her, and I don't care what you or anyone says."

"Then we shall use our magic to keep all you children here and we shall win," Firey said.

"Why would you try to stop us?" Bobby demanded. "You didn't stop Petrello."

"Because it's not safe," Windy answered.

"Ever since we got here, it hasn't been safe." Bobby eyes glittered.

"That's true, but right now, it even more unsettled," Firey offered.

"So." Bobby shrugged.

"So it won't be allowed," Firey was firm.

"What if we try to leave anyway?" Bobby asked.

"Then, like we said, we'd stop you," Firey answered again.

"You know what, I no longer care. I'm going anyway." Bobby turned to look at his friends, who nodded.

When lightening zigzagged out of the sky, it hit the ground in front of Bobby, and snapped, as blue sparks shot out towards him. Then all eyes, turned upward.

Perched high on a dark, storm cloud sat grandmother Culver. She immediately pointed her finger at Bobby, then at each child. "This is the last time I'll tell any of you this. Listen to your elders. They're wise, and know the rules of Panora. If you defy them again, by arguing, I'll see to it, that you're immediately transported back to earth as your punishment. It'll be on earth, when you're all alone that you'll want to come back to the land of Panora to find out what's going on. Now, I had better not be disturbed one more time. Is that perfectly clear to you, Bobby?"

"Yes. But I never told them to bother you." He nodded toward the elders.

Grandmother Culver laughed. "You don't have too. I hear everything that goes on, and let me say, I'm not thrilled. You earth children have a lot to learn." Grandmother Culver looked at each of them. "I suggest you start listening. You've been disobedient since you've gotten here and it had better change. In the land of Panora, children are raised to respect their parents and learn from them. You'd be wise to remember that if you hope to survive here. If you continue doing what you're doing well…" She stopped.

"What?" Bobby whispered.

"You shall die in the land of Panora, and there will be nothing we can do to stop it. This isn't recess at school. So, wise up, and take this mission seriously. If I so much as hear the echoes of argument from any of your lips again, and if your bitter, disrespectful words force me to show myself again, when I'm trying to recharge and rest for the Great War, that'll be it. Your time on the land of Panora will be finished, and you'll immediately go back to earth, as quickly as you shall blink your eyes," her voice was direct. "Now I've things to do."

All of them watched as she flew to another cloud, as graceful as a bird, and disappeared.

When Kimmy woke up, she looked around, and realized that she was in a tree. Petrello was lying next to her, and she noticed he had a small gash to the side of his head.

"Petrello, can you hear me?" she whispered.

"Yes," he whispered back.

"Where are we?"

"We've been captured again by two of Watesa's spies. Their names are X-Eyes, and Crumby."

"Can we escape?"

"Not yet. Don't try anything until we've got time. They're coming. Pretend you're sleeping."

Kimmy closed her eyes, heard a shuffling of something draw near to where she was, then it stopped. "So this child holds the highest power of both the lands?" X-Eyes asked.

"That's what they say. I find it strange that something that looks like that could be so powerful don't you?" Crumby asked.

"Yes, she's weird looking, and it's almost hard to cast my eyes upon her." X-Eyes stared down at Kimmy.

"I guess you don't have to be beautiful to hold power," Crumby said.

"I'd say so, because this creature certainly is not," X-Eyes agreed.

"So what shall we do with them?" Crumby looked at X-Eyes.

"We shall wait one night, until Watesa grows strong within her power to travel. As soon as this creature breeched the portal, all magic in every land weakened."

"I agree. Why it took all my strength to stop them, and I still feel the spell draining me." Crumby looked at Petrello. "What about him. Doesn't he work for Watesa?"

"Yes. The creature must've captured him. Now, we should move him to a more comfortable spot of resting." X-Eyes was serious.

Petrello stretched, and looked at the spies.

"So you're awake. That's good news." Crumby fluttered his wings, and landed on Petrello's arm.

"Yes. My head is torturing me," Petrello said.

"From the fall," X-Eyes was matter of fact.

"Yeah," Petrello agreed, as Kimmy continued to lie with her eyes closed.

"So what do you know of the creature?" Crumby asked.

"Very little." Petrello lied.

"Is it true she holds the power over both lands?"

"Yes."

"Is she powerful?"

"Yes," Petrello answered.

"How so?" Crumby asked.

"Powerful enough to chant her spells through her sleep, and turn any of you into bait for other creatures," Petrello answered.

"Do you think she's chanting right now?'" X-Eyes asked.

"Yeah. It's what she does."

"How do we stop her?" Crumby asked upset.

"You can't." Petrello shrugged his shoulders.

"So should we move her to the dungeon?' X-Eyes asked.

"No. She's okay right where she is for now. If she tries anything, then we shall move her. But if she wants to escape, she'll do so, whether she's lying here or in the dungeon." Petrello was serious.

"She's an ugly creature, kind of looks like you, Petrello." Crumby laughed.

"Thanks."

"No problem. You've both got those human features about you. It's quite disturbing if you ask me. Personally, I don't know how you can stand it. Day in and out you look, human." Crumby looked up at Petrello from his arm.

"You think a fly like yourself is good looking?" Petrello snapped.

"I'm not a fly. I'm a handsome insect," he said.

"Yeah, right."

"I am," Crumby argued.

"Enough, Crumby. We both know we're better looking than they are, so drop the conversation. We've got more important things to talk of," X-Eyes said.

"Like what could possibly be more important than my good looks?" Crumby asked, puffing out his chest.

"Well, the high powered witch that's lying there for one thing. As ugly as she is, she's still powerful." X-Eyes reminded him.

"True," Crumby agreed.

"So Petrello you think it's safe to leave her right here, you say?" X-Eyes stared at him.

"Yeah, she'll be fine. We hit pretty hard when we landed. Look at her, she's out cold."

"True." X-Eyes flew over, landed on Kimmy's nose, and waited. "Yeah, she's out cold. Her stump never even flinched when I landed on it."

"It's not a stump," Petrello corrected him. "It's called a nose."

"Whatever." X-Eyes said, "stump, nose, it's still disgusting, anyway you look at it."

"Yeah, true." Crumby flew over to where X-Eyes were and buzzed around Kimmy's head.

"Look you two, why don't we leave her sleep. I don't know about you, but the last thing I want is the highest powerful witch of the lands to wake up."

X-Eyes flew off Kimmy's nose, and then landed on Petrello's arm, and Crumby buzzed nervously in front of Petrello's face.

"Will Firey and her army come to get her?" Crumby asked nervously.

"I don't think they'll cross the border. You must remember that if Watesa is weak so are the others."

"So what'd you think is going to happen?" X-Eyes asked.

"I'm not sure." Petrello shrugged. "I guess we wait to see what she does." Petrello nodded toward Kimmy. "I mean if she chants about destroying both of you, then we'll be in trouble."

"What about you?" Crumby asked annoyed. "You didn't mention anything about her destroying you."

"You're right I didn't. I'm bigger then both of you and it would be harder to diminish me."

As Kimmy laid there listening to Petrello, she immediately started chanting the first thing that popped in her mind. She didn't know whether the chant would work or not, but she knew Petrello was telling her to do something.

When she heard the screech of something, then the silence, she felt Petrello grab her arm. "Good job. You apparently did something and both X-Eyes and Crumby vanished. Now let's go. Time is important, and we must reach the land of Panora."

As Kimmy stood, she smiled at Petrello. "I did it."

"Yeah, you did. The problem is not knowing where they went."

"I think they're long gone. I asked that they be removed from the land of Walby, never to return."

"I don't believe you're strong enough to make that happen, yet. Come on. Concentrate so we can fly. I feel Watesa moving over the land. We haven't much time."

"Wait a second. I thought the flies said she'll wait one more night to restore her power."

"Don't believe them. They're mere flies, which are nothing more than Watesa's spies. Now we must hurry and travel fast."

As Petrello and Kimmy held hands, Kimmy closed her eyes, chanted, and then felt their feet lift off the tree.

Soon they were flying, until Vixbit landed on Petrello.

"I'll save you Petrello!" Vixbit yelled. Then he flew onto Kimmy's nose. "Listen here, you release him and no one gets hurt." Vixbit stared at Kimmy. "Land in that tree over there. The queen's coming. Your capture can't be avoided. Watesa is stronger then you."

"I don't think so." Kimmy reached up with her free hand, then, swatted her nose, and Vixbit went spiraling out of control toward the ground.

"Keep flying, Kimmy," Petrello encouraged. "I feel Watesa approaching fast."

———————

As Bobby listened, he felt defeated. He knew they were leaving soon to cross the border in Walby, but he wanted to leave hours ago.

"Now everyone knows what's expected?" Firey asked.

"Yes," the people answered at once.

"Can I ask a question?" Bobby blurted, stopping everyone.

"Go ahead," Firey encouraged.

"What magic powers does Petrello have?"

"Many, one of which is the ability to start fires. His given name is Petrello, meaning petroleum. That's one of his strongest powers."

"What else can he do?" he demanded.

Firey smiled, and felt the jealousy coming from Bobby's spirit, toward Petrello being with Kimmy.

"He knows a few more good tricks." Firey winked. "But then again, so do you, Boulder."

When Bobby nodded, he felt better. At least he did something much cooler then Petrello. He could turn himself into rock, or anything he wanted.

After his lessons in magic that day, Bobby knew he was magically stronger then Petrello, and couldn't wait to show Kimmy all he had learned.

"Let's move out my good people of Panora," Firey said, and they all started traveling.

CHAPTER EIGHTEEN

As Watesa flew over the land, she felt her powers weaken. She stopped briefly in a tree to rest and let her eye scan the area. She snapped her tentacle against the thick tree branch and watched the land of Panora appear.

She watched Firey's armies approaching, took out her sword rubbed it three times and Kixmox appeared.

"Firey's armies are approaching. Get word to the armies of Walby. When you're finished doing that, throw up the invisible wall around the land, and I shall do the same."

"Then why use my power?" Kixmox growled. "You can do the same as me?"

"Fool, don't argue with me. I'm weaker right now because that wretched witch is here. Now go. Do what I say, and I let you live." Watesa snapped her tentacle, and Panora disappeared along with Kixmox.

As she concentrated, she felt a sliver of magic escape her tentacle toward the border, and hoped her shield would be strong enough to prevent Firey's army from crossing over into the land of Walby.

When she tried to take off from her resting spot, she couldn't. So, she laid her body down for a quick rest, knowing she had once again used all her magic.

Firey felt the bad magic moving over the land, and finally as she floated, she raised her hand.

When everyone came to a halt, she looked at them sadly. "Watesa threw her shield around the land of Walby."

"So break it down," Shelby said.

"I can't. Watesa also cast a spell to weaken all of us."

That's crazy. I still feel strong," Dave shouted.

"For now, you do, and only because you're still young. In time, you'll feel the power of your magic draining."

"I say, we keep moving," Bobby told them harshly. "Remember the purpose here. Kimmy's trapped on the other side of the land and we must save her."

Rain stepped forth. "All here me now," her voice became loud and strong, and echoed over the land of Panora. "Our magic is depleting, and soon we'll have the need to rest. Those of you, who feel drained, show your sign of hands."

When Bobby spun around, he couldn't believe more than half the people had raised their hands.

"You've got to be joking. Can't you people reach deep, and pull your magic to the surface?"

"That's enough," Juniper, one of Bobby's trainers said.

"Quite enough," Onebuyo his other trainer echoed.

"So now what, huh?" Bobby asked spinning around. "Do you think you're not brave enough to continue?"

"Bravery has nothing to do with it," Firey answered sadly.

"That's it Bobby Martin. If you so much as utter one more word of disrespect, you'll be grounded forever once we return to earth," Windy his mother reprimanded. "We all know how much you want to save Kimmy, but we must do what's good for the whole of the people, and not just what you want to do."

Bobby fell quiet.

"Very well. Let's rest right where we stand, for a spell. When we awake, we'll all be stronger for it," Firey told the people, and Bobby noted how weak her voice sounded.

"Will you be okay?" Bobby asked loudly.

"Yes, my child," Firey whispered. "I just need to recharge."

As the group settled on the land, Dave and Manning walked over to Bobby, and when Renee and Shelby saw them, they too walked over, and settled on the ground a little distance away from the others.

"So do we rest?" Dave asked them.

"I think we should. I don't know what's going on, but Firey is weak," Renee spoke softly.

"Very weak," Shelby agreed.

"I say we wait until they fall asleep. Then the five of us should leave and rescue Kimmy. Face it, we're younger, and we've obviously got more energy than they do." Manning nodded towards the others. "Besides, I don't like knowing Kimmy is traveling through the land of Walby with a complete stranger."

"He may be a stranger to us, Manning, but not to the land of Panora," Renee answered gently.

"Yeah, well, none of us know who he is, so I agree with Manning. As soon as they're sleeping, I say we sneak away, find Kimmy, and come back. By then, maybe they'll be awake, and we'll be heroes," Dave said.

"I don't want to be a hero." Shelby shrugged. "I just want to know Kimmy's still alive. I mean can you believe it? She is the highest power in either land. That's crazy. I wonder how she got so much power."

"She was born into it," Manning answered. "That's what I get out of the whole thing. I mean you all saw the power of grandmother Culver. Now come on, Kimmy's part of that bloodline. It'll be cool when we return to earth knowing magic. Just think about how many girls we can cast a spell on to like us." He laughed. "Just joking. But I'd love to cast a spell on my teachers and have one year without homework, and still get straight A's."

"Yeah, that would be cool," Bobby said.

"Come on, cheer up, Bobby," Shelby told him. "Soon, we'll be out of here, and going to get Kimmy. Look at the bright side it won't be long until we're with our friend again."

"Yeah, I know. I just want her here now," Bobby told them sadly.

"Man, I think that's who you're going to marry some day." Dave laughed, and the rest joined in.

"Maybe. I guess we won't know until it happens though." Bobby was matter of fact.

"Oh I think it'll happen." Renee smiled. "The two of you wouldn't know what to do without the other."

"Yeah, for real. It wouldn't surprise me to hear Kimmy tell me how much she missed you too, Bobby." Shelby teased.

Finally, he smiled. "I just want her back with us. I hope you get that. I just feel like a part of me is missing."

"We know," Renee said, "just hang on a little while longer. Soon, we'll be able to leave."

When Bobby nodded, the others turned to watch the people of Panora scattered over the land.

When they saw them start to lie down, they knew that soon they would leave the protection of their queen once more to save Kimmy.

When Petrello looked at Kimmy, he smiled. "You're doing well with your magic."

"Thanks."

"Yep. But I think you should know, where not leaving the land of Walby tonight."

"What? Why? Are you going to hold me here? Are you a traitor like I thought? Tell me right now," she demanded as they flew over the land.

"I'll tell you, gosh. No, I'm not a traitor, but a shield has been cast across the lands, which means we won't be allowed to leave."

"I don't understand. Who cast a spell?"

"Watesa. She used the rest of her magic, along with Kixmox's."

"So we're trapped?"

"Yeah, at least for the night."

"No way." Kimmy shook her head. "I'll just chant a spell, and hope that you and I will be allowed to pass through."

"You can't. You're not as strong as the queen, yet," Petrello said.

"Then I'll call out to my grandmother for help." Kimmy was determined to find a way out of the land of Walby.

"She won't answer."

"How come you always think you know everything?" Kimmy snapped at him.

"Because I've been raised here, and I know how it works, especially in time of the Great War."

"How could you know, you're not that old?"

"I'm older then you are."

"I know how old you are. Sixteen, right?"

"I told you I was sixteen, but I lied about it. I'm really eighteen."

"So you're an adult, and four years older than I am. You couldn't have seen that much in your short time here."

"I've seen enough to know what's going to happen. Listen, if we fly into the shield, we'll die."

"What? How do you know?" Kimmy was nervous.

"Because I do. Once a spell is cast, and someone tries to break the barrier of it, but isn't strong enough, the magic of the spell drains the energy right out of the opposing person."

"So if we cast a spell on the land of Panora, and someone tried to breech the barrier, they would die."

"Yes. Now you're learning."

"So what'd we do now?"

"We'll find somewhere to hide, until I know it's safe to try the shield."

"Okay, where?"

"Can you see up there where the two lands come together?" Petrello asked.

"Yeah, I never noticed the difference between the lands before," Kimmy said. "Everything in Panora is alive with color, and everything in Walby is stripped barren."

"I know."

"Yeah, but that shocks me. Why hadn't I noticed?"

"Because when you were still human with little or no magic, your eyes allowed you to see things as you normally would. Once your magic becomes stronger, you'll start to see things how they really are."

"That's amazing. If you ask me, the last time I was in Walby, it looked the same as Panora. The only difference was the colors in Walby hurt my eyes, but the colors in Panora didn't. It's really weird," Kimmy sighed.

"What's wrong?" Petrello asked.

"I want to be back in Panora. All my friends are there, including Bobby, and he's the best there is, and I know he misses me."

"Yeah, but we can't rush what's happening without bringing danger upon us. If we do things in an orderly way, then it'll be much safer."

"Yeah, but still."

"Land over there." Petrello pointed to a huge tree, with thick bark.

As Kimmy landed, she looked around. "Won't somebody see us? We're out in the open."

"No. Not as long as we sit here, and don't move around. Most of the land is sleeping, on both sides. They're gearing up to restore their magic."

"For the Great War?" Kimmy asked.

"Not yet. They're restoring their magic in Walby to keep you here. In Panora, they're restoring their magic to rescue you."

"What can I do to help Panora?"

"Rest. That's the only thing you can do."

"I'll try." Kimmy studied the land. "What's that?" she asked Petrello.

"What?"

"Over there." Kimmy nodded. "What is that?"

"It looks like someone's caught in the shield."

Kimmy stood.

"What're you doing?" Petrello asked.

"Going over there. If it's someone from Panora, we can't just sit here, and do nothing."

"Yeah, but we don't know who it is. What if we get down there, and find out its people from Walby? We'll be captured for sure."

"Well, fine. I'll go without you, traitor."

"Fine." Petrello stood.

"Don't feel like you've got to come with me. I don't need you to protect me," Kimmy was snide.

"I know that," Petrello snapped.

"Then, sit down," Kimmy ordered.

"No. If you're going, so am I."

"Fine, but don't get in my way, and don't tell me what to do once we get there."

"Okay, I won't." Petrello eyed her.

As Kimmy took his hand, they flew close to the shield, and she watched both in horror and fascination as her friends broke the shield.

"I thought you said no one could pass through the shield?"

"I didn't think anyone could."

"Yeah, right." Kimmy purposely landed hard, jarring Petrello.

Then she ran over, hugged Shelby, then Renee, kissed Dave on the cheek, and smiled, as she grabbed Manning's hand.

When she spun around, she saw Bobby standing there, and she ran to him, and leapt into his arms, laughing.

"You're all crazy, but I'm so glad you are. I've missed all of you so much." When Kimmy pulled back, she noticed something different in Bobby's eyes, which had never been there before. So, she looked away, and slowly he put her down.

"What's the big idea?" Kimmy asked them. "I've heard that people can die if they passed through the shield."

"Yeah, well, we've heard the same thing," Bobby said, holding her hand, smiling.

"So how did you do it?" Kimmy asked.

"We held hands and the shield sucked us through it."

"Oh that's great," they all heard Petrello tell them.

"What's wrong?" Kimmy asked.

"If the shield sucked them through, it did it for a reason." Petrello stared at them.

"What's the reason?" Kimmy asked.

"It sucked them through to weaken their magic. Now no one is allowed to pass, from either land for two days, two nights."

"Who are you, and how do you know?" Bobby glared at him.

"I'm Petrello, and I've lived on both sides of the land, so I know the rules governing each side."

"I don't remember anyone asking for your opinion." Bobby eyed him.

"Yeah, well no one did. I just thought it would be helpful to know." Petrello glared right back.

"It is helpful," Renee said, holding out her hand. "I'm Renee and this is Shelby." She nodded. "That's Dave, and Manning, and oh yeah, Bobby."

"I knew that was Bobby. Kimmy's talked about him a lot." Petrello rolled his eyes, while the two girls giggled, and the guys watched him.

"So, now what?" Dave asked Petrello.

"We go back to the tree that we were in, before Kimmy spotted you, and we rest. We'll need all our magic in the coming days. Being stuck here won't be fun, but if you listen, we should be alright."

"Who said you're the boss?" Dave asked harshly.

"No one. I never said I was either. I just thought I'd be helpful, and let you know what it would be like on this side of the land."

"Yeah, well we already know," Dave said, "we've been captured once already by Watesa, and managed to escape."

"Then you got real lucky," Petrello answered. "Now let's go. People in Walby are waking up, and we don't want to get caught." He looked at Kimmy. "If everyone holds hands, you should be able to fly us back to the tree we were in."

Kimmy nodded, as all them joined hands, and flew through the land of Walby.

CHAPTER NINETEEN

When the people of Panora began waking up, Firey noticed right away the children were gone.

She immediately woke the people of the land, and gathered them.

"The five children are gone." She closed her eyes. "They're in the land of Walby, and thank goodness most of the children have reached the age of fourteen. But I wish I could've continued their training. It is at this time, the children, well most of them, will come into their powers. All of us know the rules of Panora. Once a person comes into power, they are to use their given names from the land of Panora. Earth names are to be left on earth. Sadly, none of the children know the rules of their powers, so if they continue to call one another by their earth names, their powers will not fully activate. This means all the powers bestowed upon them, will not work, until they realize this secret. "

"So how do we let the children know this?" Rain asked.

"We don't. I hope that Petrello will tell them, but even that's stretching it. Petrello is used to the rules of Panora only. He was raised here, and only knows that the children in Panora come into their full power at the age of eighteen. To my knowledge he doesn't know the rules governing children raised on earth, and that their full powers come at the age of fourteen." Firey heard the collective sighs of the people, then, she opened her eyes.

"So hold on." Rain raised her hand. "What can we do to let the children know?"

"There's nothing that we can do."

None of the people said anything.

"Because the children allowed the shield to suck them through to the land of Walby, they're now in great peril. I had hoped to convey to each of them, to listen, and not stray from the good of Panora, but once again, none of them listened, or took heed in my warning. At least not the five who remained, after Karisma was taken from us. As far as I'm concerned, she didn't listen either. She wandered outside the safe walls of my dwelling, and was kidnapped. It's because of this; we shall not pass through to the dark land, for two days, two nights. Only on the third day will we be allowed to travel. Then, it shall be bleak. From this point on, I'll be unable to know whether the children are okay, or if they've been captured. We all know the children were our purest magic on the land. Now, Watesa will surly tap into it, and begin stealing their magic."

"How's that possible that Watesa can take their magic?" Tornado asked.

"It's possible because the children disobeyed all rules set forth in Panora. They trespassed through the shield Watesa had around Walby. Once the children entered, they gave up their protection of Panora, and now they shall sacrifice their magic. Watesa will steal it."

As she stared at the good people, she noted the worry in their eyes. "On the other hand, all of us know how mouthy and stubborn the six of them are, and surely the children will give up nothing without a fight. Now, the only thing left to do is wait."

"Do you think the five children found Karisma?" Rain asked.

"I'm not sure. I'm not allowed to see because of the shield, and as all of you know with Karisma on the other side of the land, my powers have weakened."

"Do you think Petrello is still with all of them?" Sparkle asked.

"I'm not sure. The best we can hope for is Petrello and Karisma are still together, and the other five are strong enough to stay together. If any of the children break away from the other, they're going to be instantly overpowered by the magic in Walby."

"Then what will happen?" Windy, Bobby's mother asked.

"We'll know immediately at first signs of trouble, because Panora will tremble, then shake."

"What about the children's magic in Walby? Are they trained enough, and strong enough to use it?" Tornado, Dave's mother asked.

"We shall see, but even if they are, they'll be no match for Watesa. Especially since Karisma is trapped in the kingdom of Walby."

"I have a question," Hurricane, Manning's mother blurted.

"Go ahead."

"What if all of us charge the shield around Walby? Can we make it through?"

"You already know the answer to that Hurricane. Of course we'd make it, but at what cost?" She stared at Hurricane for a moment, before she continued, "as long as Karisma remains captive on Watesa's land, she's entitled to drain her of her magic. That is the law of the land."

When all fell quiet, Firey smiled, to ease the worry. "Now, please rest. There's no point traveling all the way back to my dwelling. So we shall pass the time right here, until passage into the kingdom of Walby is restored."

When the children landed in the tree, all of them sat quietly as Kimmy put her head on Bobby's shoulder. "Thank you for coming to save me," she whispered. "Even though I feel awful that everyone's stuck here for two more nights."

"I don't feel awful. When I was on the good land of Panora, it was driving me crazy knowing you were stuck over here. I don't care what happens now. I know that if we're together, we'll be okay," he whispered.

"I hope you're right."

"Right or not, I made a choice, and that's it."

Kimmy smiled at him.

"So tell me about Petrello," Bobby whispered not wanting the others to hear.

"Well, I called him a traitor at first because he has parents on both side of the land."

"How can that be? I thought there were rules against it." Bobby was surprised.

"There are, but I guess his dad was killed, so Firey granted permission for Petrello and his mom, Sparkle to live in Panora."

"I don't like it. How do we know that he's not a spy for Watesa? If you think about it, he could be magically leading her right to where we are."

"I know I've thought about that. But so far, she hasn't caught us."

"How long have the two of you been together?" Bobby asked.

"Long enough to get caught by Watesa, if that was the plan."

Bobby nodded. "It'll take some getting use too, having him around I mean."

"I know. I felt the same way."

"Do you trust him, Kimmy?"

"I'm not sure that I'd tell him my deepest secrets, but I think I do. I don't know. Right now, I'm just trying to figure out exactly what he wants."

"Yeah?"

"Yeah, and I just found out that he's eighteen." She shrugged.

"He doesn't look like it. He looks the same age as all of us." Bobby glanced over to Petrello.

"I thought the same thing," Kimmy agreed.

"Well, I guess between the six of us, we'll figure it out soon enough."

"Yeah, if Renee doesn't figure it out for the rest of us, first." Kimmy nodded toward her, and both of them noticed how close Petrello and Renee were sitting to one another.

Bobby shrugged. "I totally trust Renee to know what to say, and what not to."

"Me too," Kimmy sighed.

When all of them heard the roar of the lion over the land, they immediately stood.

Petrello looked at them. "Sit down. By standing you're letting Kixmox know where you are," he scolded.

Kimmy sat, and the rest of them hurried over to Kimmy and Bobby, and quickly sat, when they heard the roar of the lion coming closer.

"Do you think he'll find us?" Shelby asked concerned.

"He could. Now, listen carefully," Petrello told them. "All of you hold the jewelry Firey gave you. Remember your magic, but don't use it, unless I tell you too."

"I don't trust you," Dave blurted.

"It's not about trust. It's about survival!" Petrello shouted.

"Just do it, Dave," Kimmy instructed.

As she watched all her friends holding onto their jewelry, she realized she no longer had hers, so she closed her eyes, and listened to the roar of the lion coming closer to where they were.

"Remember Vixbit, X-Eyes and Crumby." Petrello whispered.

"Who are they?" Shelby asked.

"Spies of Watesa's," Kimmy answered.

"Are they magic?" Shelby asked.

"Everyone and everything between these two lands hold magic," Petrello said.

"Great. What kind of creature's are they?" Renee asked.

"They resemble flies," Kimmy whispered.

"Oh that's peachy," Manning said, "talk about one of the most annoying insects."

"Hold your tongue. Some thing's coming. Be ready." Petrello sounded worried.

When they fell quiet, Kimmy felt the tap on her nose first. She wiggled it, and felt the sting.

Soon she collapsed sideways onto Bobby.

"What happened?" Bobby demanded, staring at Petrello.

"They've cast a spell of sleep to take her," he said.

"Well, I've got news for them. They're never going to get her as long as I'm here." Bobby's voice was full of conviction.

"Yeah, I agree," Dave echoed.

"There will be nothing either of you can do." Petrello looked at Kimmy. "There's something I can do, but Bobby you'll have to switch places with me quick."

"No way." Bobby shook his head.

"What'd you mean, no way?" Petrello asked him.

"You heard me. Now sit down."

"I need to be next to Kimmy so that I can travel with her when they lift her body."

"What?" Bobby asked shocked, "When who lifts her body?"

"Watesa's army. They've come to take her prisoner again. Since I'm the only one amongst us with the power and privilege to travel with her, so I need to go."

"No way. If they take her, they take me," Bobby voice was raised.

"Will you be quiet and listen," Petrello snapped. "If you allow them to take Kimmy without me, then you can kiss her good bye right now. If you think you're strong enough to fight the powers that are coming, you're mistaken. They're here to take all of us, but they won't keep us together. I guarantee you we'll be separated. But, if Kimmy's on me, and they think I work for this side of the land, I've more of a chance to help her, then any of you." Petrello stared at each of them.

"Let him, Bobby," Renee said.

"Yeah, I agree," Shelby offered. "Kimmy's been okay all this time, so I say let Petrello go. It's our only choice."

"No, it's not," Dave blurted. "It's funny how you two girls all of a sudden trust some complete stranger. Well, if you ask me. I say we all go together, then escape, and free Kimmy."

"It doesn't work like that." Petrello shook his head. "All you human's do is argue, when you should be listening. If you choose for me not to travel with her, then you may as well say good bye to the highest power of the land."

"How do we know we can trust you?" Dave asked.

"Because so far nothing has happened to her." Petrello nodded at Kimmy. "That should be proof enough."

When none of them said anything, Petrello stared at each of them. "I've got one more question for each of you."

"What?" Bobby glared at him.

"Why do all of you insist on calling each other by your earth names? Surely, you've been told your given names in the land of Panora."

"So?" Dave shrugged. "What's your point?"

"My point is usually once humans arrive in the land of Panora, all earth names are left behind. Didn't Firey explain that to any of you?" he asked.

"No," Renee answered.

"But that's ridiculous. It's the rule of Panora. So each of you tell me your given names because as long as you're here, that's what I'm calling you. Your earth names, from this point on become obsolete, as far as I'm concerned." He watched them, as he waited.

"My given name is Raven," Renee said.

Petrello nodded.

"My given name is Sunburst," Shelby said.

"Mine is Dagger," Dave blurted clearly perturbed.

"I'm Mountain," Manning offered.

"I'm Boulder." Bobby glared at him.

"And her?" Petrello nodded towards Kimmy who was still asleep.

"Her name is Karisma," Bobby answered.

"Very good. From now on I'm calling you by the name you were given in Panora. If you're smart, all of you will use those names while you're here."

"You're not the boss." Dave glared at him.

"You're right, I'm not. I'm advising you what to do, Dagger. Now you make the choice whether or not to listen. Apparently, you never do anyway, so why would this be different? Now, the armies of Watesa are near. I'm traveling with Karisma."

They all watched Petrello, then Bobby. When Petrello walked over, he tipped Kimmy toward him, and he held her tight.

The rest of them watched in amazement as the two disappeared.

"Great, where did they go?" Bobby was clearly upset, and before the rest of them could answer, each one of them popped, like a bubble, and vanished.

———— ⬥ ————

Watesa's army was gathered, and they were holding all five of the children.

"Good job." Watesa laughed.

"We thought you'd be pleased," X-Eyes told her.

"Oh, I certainly am. Is Karisma in the dwelling?" she asked.

"Yes," Vixbit answered.

"Is she guarded?"

"Yes."

"By whom?" she demanded.

"Flipple," Vixbit told her.

"And Petrello?"

"He's out cold with Karisma."

"Very good," Watesa was pleased.

"What will you have us do with them?" Kixmox growled, at the other five children they were holding captive.

"Take them and chain them separately in the dungeons."

"So let me get this straight. You want each of these unruly children separated?" Crumby asked. "Then chained alone, within the confinement of the cells they're put in?"

"Yes, that's right, you imbecile. Why must you act so stupid?" Watesa yelled.

"I'm not trying to be stupid," Crumby said, flying around crazily.

"Well, you are." Watesa snatched him up in her tentacle, and squeezed. "You're on my last tentacle, so it's time for you to get it together, quit flying around, and get to work. Do you understand?"

"Surely," Crumby gasped.

"Good." Watesa let him go, and watched as he struggled to fly, then she laughed.

"Be gone all of you. Take the children to their separate dungeons, and make sure this time they don't escape. If they do, and I find out who was guarding them, you shall perish." She stared at her army with her purple eye. "Now go." She snapped her tentacle, and they all disappeared.

As Karisma slowly came too, she was afraid to open her eyes. She felt weak, and knew she had been captured again.

"Did you see her move?" she heard the familiar voice of Flipple ask whoever else was in the room.

"Yes," she heard the voice of Crumby. "Should I sting her again?"

"Not yet. Let's see how she behaves first. If she tries anything, then do it," Flipple said.

"Don't you think she's ugly?" Crumby asked.

"Not really," Flipple answered. "I believe the humans think she's beautiful."

"Well, we're not human, are we? I think she's about as ugly as anything I've ever seen. You can tell she belongs in Panora. Everyone in that land is retched looking."

"Well, now that you mention it, not everyone is as good looking as we are," Flipple commented.

"Don't I know it? Look at her stump. It sticks out of her orb, and they use it to sniff, I've heard. Could you imagine having something like that right in the middle of your orb?"

"No, I couldn't imagine. The orb as we call it is referred to by the giants as their heads. Their stumps are referred to as their nose." He tilted his head, and stared at Karisma. "But you're right," Flipple said, still staring at Karisma. "Her stump does stick way out of her orb."

"And the funny thing is I'm tiny enough to use her stump as a slide. Wanna see?" Crumby asked excited.

"No, not yet." Flipple shook his head.

"Yeah, then they have those funny, white straight teeth. Where do you think they get those from?" Crumby asked.

"The snow. I heard it snows on earth."

"But how does it make their teeth white?" Crumby asked.

"They put it on their twigs, or fingers, whatever they're called, and rub their teeth with it."

"Oh. Their weirder then I thought." Crumby told Flipple. "So what about the things they use to get around. Where do they come from?" Crumby asked.

"Well, the giant people refer to those as legs."

"Their tree trunks too me." Crumby laughed.

"What are those other things sticking out from their trunks?"Crumby asked.

"The giants refer to them as feet," Flipple told him.

"How come you're so smart?"

"I listen." Flipple was serious.

"Well, if you ask me, feet are funny. They remind me of leaves on the trees, except their weirder, bigger, and stick out further." Crumby laughed, then, crazily started buzzing in front of Karisma's face. When he turned, he zigzagged over to Flipple, and buzzed in front of his face. "Wake her."

"I think she's already awake," Flipple said.

"Are you awake, you ugly child?"

When Karisma didn't move, he asked again, and when she didn't answer, Crumby landed on Flipple, yawned, stretched, then both of them felt the dust fall in their eyes, and soon both Flipple and Crumby were asleep.

CHAPTER TWENTY

When Petrello knew Flipple and Crumby were fast asleep, he cracked open his eye, performed another magic spell, and Karisma's chains fell quietly away from her body.

He went to her, and knew she was very weak. "Karisma, can you hear me?" Petrello whispered close to her ear.

He saw her head nod slightly.

"Do you think you're strong enough to travel?" he asked.

"I don't think I am. I'm so weak, and I don't know why."

"I'll tell you the reason, it's because Watesa is draining your magic, and she's becoming more powerful than ever."

He watched Karisma nod again, and knew just talking was taking too much out of her.

"Quickly, put your arm around my neck. If you stay much longer, you shall die."

When she didn't respond, he threw her arm around his shoulder, and held her tightly to him. Then he closed his eyes, chanted, and soon Petrello knew they were floating invisibly right outside the dungeon doors.

Petrello knew that was where the others were. As he carried Karisma, he stopped when he heard the voices rising out of the dungeon.

"Stop it," he heard X-Eyes tell someone.

"We don't have to stop, you fly," Sunburst said harshly.

"Yes, you do. If you don't stop what you're doing, all of you are going to suffer."

"What're you going to do? Land on my arm, and irritate me?" Sunburst snapped. "Or better yet, are you going to fly in my face, like your friend?"

"What friend?" X-Eyes sounded confused.

"What did you call him? Crummy or something?" She laughed.

"His name is Crumby."

"Whatever. I'll tell you what, why don't you release me, then land on the floor, so I can step on you."

"Very funny. You're going to regret being nasty with me when I tell the queen."

"Oh, now I'm scared," Sunburst was sarcastic.

"You should be she'll torture you."

"Bring it."

"What does, bring it mean?"

"It means run to your queen if you're not man enough to fight your own battles."

"I'm man enough."

"Then why do you hide behind your queen, huh?"

"I don't hide. I'm right here. Personally, I think all you humans are weird, and you don't know when to keep quiet!" he snapped at her.

"Well, I don't care what you think. I'm not here to please you. If you haven't noticed, we're on opposing teams. I'm from Panora, and you're from the doggie poop."

"What does that mean?"

"It means you eat poop, because you're a fly, and that's what you do, and it's disgusting, and you want me to stop being loud, when you're nothing more than an irritating poop eater?"

"Yeah, that's right. If you don't stop, I'll throw a spell on you to silence your mouth. Now this is the last warning you're getting."

When Sunburst fell quiet, she heard X-Eyes laugh. "Finally no words come out of your mouth."

"That's right, but let me tell you something, when Firey gets here to rescue us, you'll wish you we're nice to me."

"No I won't. I'm following orders, and that's part of my job," X-Eyes told her.

"Yeah, well follow the scent of the poop because all of us are strong in our powers, and if I were you, I'd leave while I had the chance."

"Well, I'm not going too."

Okay." Sunburst closed her eyes, and tried to transform into a fireball, but nothing happened.

"Don't try to cast a spell. You'd have to touch your jewelry for that, and you can't reach it," X-Eyes said, "besides, Watesa is feeding off your magic right now, and soon you'll weaken, until you can stand no more. Then I shall chuckle."

"You go right ahead and laugh. But when the good powers of magic take over the kingdom of Walby, we'll be the last one's laughing. I promise you."

"I hope you don't believe that because if you do, I'll have to laugh harder than I thought. Your people as you call them will never be allowed to enter Walby. Did you forget we hold, Karisma the highest power of the lands? Well, I hate to break it to you, but as long as she remains on this side of the land, she'll be drained of her magic, and Watesa will win the war. Once she's done with Karisma, she'll hunt Firey down, and steal her magic, and there will be nothing you can do about it."

Sunburst fell quiet, and yawned.

"See, she's slowly draining your powers from you."

"Who?" Shelby asked.

"Watesa. She's hard at work draining all of you."

"How do you know?" Sunburst demanded.

"Because I can feel the magic in the air, and you're tired."

When Sunburst closed her eyes, she instantly fell asleep.

"Petrello can you hear me?" Petrello saw the white light dancing close to him.

"Camille?"

"Yes, it's me."

"Yes, I can hear you."

"Good. Now don't try anything yet."

"How did you sneak through?"

"Pixie angels and fairies have their ways of flying unnoticed."

When Petrello stared at the white light dancing, he waited.

"The instructions are you are not strong enough to do this on your own."

"Then what shall I do?" Petrello asked as he sighed.

"You shall, wait."

"I can't. Watesa's draining all of them of their power. Now you must help me save them."

"Petrello you must listen to me. There is danger coming to the land of Panora, and then it will reach here, in the kingdom of Walby. We don't have much time to prepare."

"Who's coming?" Petrello asked.

"The dark magic from the land of Elvi."

"How long do we have to prepare?" Petrello asked.

"Approximately ten days."

"Then they'll arrive on what land?"

"Excuse me?" Camille asked.

"Which land are they coming to first?" Petrello asked.

"The land of Panora. It's weaker because Karisma was captured and brought here, so the dark magic will go to Panora, and they'll try to capture Firey, then they'll travel here to the kingdom of Walby to confront the queen. By then, she'll have grown stronger in her power because she holds Karisma."

"What shall we do?" Petrello asked.

"We shall wait for a spell, until my magic takes hold of that irritating fly." Camille danced crazily in front of him making him dizzy.

"Camille, why are you nervous?"

"Because we've a lot to do," Camille said.

"I know, so just tell me what to do."

"One minute," Camille paused, "okay, now we can enter the dungeon, release the children, and get them as close to the border as we can."

"We'll be captured again. We both know that."

"No we don't. This time I'm here with you, and we're stronger together. Plus, the good people in the land of Vanduesa are approaching fast. They're coming to help our queen."

"Flipple is from there, and now he's Watesa's spy."

"I know, but just because Flipple turned on his land, doesn't mean the people of Vanduesa are bad. Just the opposite. They'll help us in the land of Panora fight the Great War."

"Okay," Petrello sighed deeply. "Let's go release the children, and get close to the border like you've said. I hope this time, we're not caught."

"I told you, Petrello I'm here now, and things are about to change."

"How?"

"Because Redilla and Zuella are on their way too. Together we'll have more powers to save the children, and restore Karisma's powers."

"When are they arriving?" Petrello asked.

"Anytime now," Camille answered.

When he saw the dancing yellow and red lights in front of him, he smiled. "Redilla, Zuella, you made it."

"Barely, but we did. We had to fly really low to enter the land undetected," Redilla told him.

"But you both did it." Petrello smiled at the yellow light.

"Yes, we did," Zuella told him excitedly. "Now come, we've work to do."

"Wait," Petrello blurted.

"What?" Camille asked.

"Does Firey know you're all here?" Petrello asked.

When Camille cleared her throat, she said nothing.

"That's what I thought," Petrello said.

"Remember Petrello, do not let Karisma go. No matter what happens, you guard her tightly," Zuella whispered.

"I will, you don't have to worry about that."

"You're a good, what do they call them on earth? Oh yeah, teenager." Redilla laughed. "Not that it means anything to you because you're not from there, but…"

"Thanks." Petrello smiled.

As they followed Zuella, they descended into the dungeon to rescue the children.

Firey's eyes snapped open, and she stared at the sky, until the vision in her head showed itself clearly in the clouds.

The dark people from Elvi rode black horses toward the land of Panora.

As she stared, she received the message that she had ten days to prepare for the invasion.

She knew once the dark people from Elvi were finished with Panora; they would travel to the land of Walby. Their mission was to take the magic she had, and then go after Watesa's. After that was complete, they would capture Karisma.

As she silently summoned the good people of Panora to awaken, she watched the vision in the clouds dissipate.

Then Firey stood, and floated to the center of the circle where the good people of Panora had gathered.

"The darkest people of Elvi will arrive in ten days." She was bleak. "Two days, two nights, we are held in the land of Panora, from the breech that occurred. We must suffer two nights, two days fully to rectify the situation. Yesterday, when the children left, doesn't count. The day must start fresh, such as today. So this is day one. Now please sit, there's much too tell.

As Firey lifted her face she stared once again at the clouds, and a slight smile touched her lips. "The good land of Vanduesa will be here, hence ten days."

"But if Elvi and Vanduesa arrive on the same day, it'll be impossible to prepare for the Great War," Rain said.

"Ah, you're correct. However, I must discuss what each land has planned. Elvi, as you are all aware, will travel without rest. Vanduesa will take the time necessary to recharge their magic."

"Will Elvi take Karisma?" Rain interrupted.

"Let me finish." Firey held up her hand, as she continued to stare at the clouds. "Elvi has a partner picked for Karisma. The two will spend four years training their magic together, before the reunion takes place on Karisma's eighteenth birthday." Firey let her eyes travel over her people, before she once again trained her eye toward the sky. "Her chosen partner is Valtron." Firey heard Rain's sudden intake of breath, but continued to stare at the sky. "We all know who Valtron is. He's king of Elvi. He has chosen to marry Karisma."

When no one spoke, she swung her eyes to Rain, and noted the tears on her cheeks, but said nothing, then looked one last time at the clouds. "Valtron's magic is dark, and the culmination between him and Karisma will be unstoppable. Their children will be more powerful then we can imagine," Firey was matter of fact.

As she finally tore her gaze away from the clouds, she stared at the good people. "We mustn't let it happen," her voice was a mixture of anger and determination.

"There's little we can do to stop it," Hurricane blurted.

"Ah, you may be right, but to do nothing will end in disaster."

"We must get to Karisma," Rain said, "I'm traveling closer to the border, so I can see the invisible wall."

Firey smiled gently. "So we may continue traveling, as Rain has suggested, be prepared to go shortly."

As Redilla, Zuella, Petrello and Camille stood before the five children in the dungeon Petrello closed his eyes, and cast the spell for the magnetic bond between himself and Karisma, to free his hands and arms.

He then shifted her on his back, and concentrated.

"Let's turn the children into bees, so they'll be able to escape the chains, and fly with us toward the border," Camille ordered.

"Very well," Zuella agreed.

"Good idea." Redilla danced nervously, and Petrello nodded.

As the group went from one cell to the next, chanting, slowly the children turned into bees, and flew over to them.

None of them spoke, as they silently flew up the stairs of the dungeon, to the bright outdoors.

When all of them saw Watesa, Kixmox, Vixbit, Dagg, Rozello, Flipple, and Crumby gathered in the courtyard, none of them stopped.

They knew time was of the essence, and continued flying toward the border.

Watesa glared angrily at her army. "Imbeciles are what you are. I can't believe Karisma got away again!" she screamed, and then snapped her tentacle in the air. "I should've known none of you were smart enough for the task of guarding her. Not only did you stupid creatures let her escape, but also Petrello is gone again as well. We all know his loyalty is to the kingdom of Walby. Now as I look at my army, I laugh with disdain." She swung her purple eye, snapped her tentacle, and all of them screamed out in pain.

"Next time there's a breech, the pain I'll inflict upon you will be worse than anything you've ever felt." She held a tentacle high, then, stared at her army. "Where is X-Eyes?" she screamed again.

"Guarding the five children in the dungeon," Crumby told her visibly swallowing hard.

Watesa nodded. "Let's go," she said, as they went to the dungeon.

As Watesa stopped before the doors, she sniffed the air, then, spun around. "All of you had better hope nothing is amiss down in the dungeon. You're all complete imbeciles for leaving X-Eyes alone with those entirely unruly human's. Now let's go."

When the good people of Panora heard the high-pitched scream echo over the land, all eyes swung to Firey.

She raised her hand, touched her fingers to her thumb, and formed a zero. Within seconds, Firey stood in the center of the circle, lifted her eyes to the clouds, and heard the clap of thunder, then, grandmother Culver appeared.

Immediately, the good people saw how pale grandmother Culver was, and how her eyes weren't as bright as they usually were.

As she lifted her old, twisted finger, she pointed at them. When she spoke, her voice wasn't as loud as it normally was.

"My good people of Panora, I regret to inform you that I'm weaker than usual, so if I fade in and out during this session, please be patient and standby." Her vision faded, then, reappeared. "My magic is in need of restoration. Since Karisma's capture in the land of Walby, it's been extremely hard to recharge." Her vision faded again, the reappeared. "There's news that the dark people of Elvi are approaching, and all high powers are becoming depleted. I've cast a spell to slow down the army of Elvi, and now we wait to see if it took hold or not," her voice became softer. "I need the good people of Panora, and the good people of Vanduesa to recharge as quickly as possible for the coming days will require all our magic to fight Watesa, and take Karisma back to the land of Panora. As I speak, I hear more news that Karisma's weak."

"How weak?" Rain yelled interrupting.

"Weak enough Rain, not to be able to use her magic. So weak she can't stand." Grandmother Culver shook her head.

"Is it because of Watesa?" Rain demanded, as Sparkle put her hand on her arm for comfort.

"You know it is, Rain. Watesa will drain our Karisma until there's nothing left."

"Will she die?" Rain's voice cracked with emotion.

"You know the rules and boundaries in the land of Panora," Firey answered.

As Grandmother Culver stared, she nodded. "Yes, Karisma stands the chance of dying, if Watesa isn't stopped."

"Will my Karisma be gone forever?" Rain was crying.

"Her spirit on the land of Panora will exist no more."

"Then what'll happen?" Rain begged.

"Then Karisma will be transported back to earth. Never again will she be allowed in the land of Panora." Grandmother Culver faded again, and as Rain and the others stared, they knew her powers had depleted.

"Now what're we suppose to do?" Rain asked Firey panicked.

"Wait until grandmother Culver recharges. Until then, there's nothing we can do," Firey answered.

Rain felt her tears dripping off her face, and absently wiped them away. Then she looked at Firey. "There's not enough time to wait."

"You must," Firey insisted.

Rain stared at her. "My queen you wait. I'm leaving for Walby." Rain was determined as she looked at Firey.

"If you pass over you'll be stripped of your magical powers Rain, and you know it," Firey raised her voice as she spoke.

"Then, so be it. To do nothing will make me less of a mother."

"She's right," Sparkle agreed.

"Yeah she is," Hurricane blurted.

"I could fly all of us closer to the border of Walby," Wings told them.

"Very well." Rain nodded.

"Do you realize the mistake all of you are making?" Firey demanded.

"Make no mistake about it," Tornado blurted. "Karisma is about to die, and all our children are in Walby."

"But if any of you cross over the lands without grandmother Culver's permission, you'll lose the protection of Panora, and all of you could die."

"We know," Windy volunteered.

"We're willing to take our chances," Volcano told Firey seriously.

"And what happens to our land in Panora if you refuse to listen?" Firey questioned.

"You've much magic left here with you. Besides, you don't need us Firey. Usually we live on earth, and you've gotten along just fine," Rain informed her.

"So you're honestly going to force me to stop you? You're going to force me to use my magic on you?" Firey challenged.

"No," Rain told her sadly. "We want you to simply forget our magic, and look at us as mother's whose children need our help."

When Firey said nothing, Rain turned. "We leave in one hour. Go prepare."

CHAPTER TWENTY-ONE

As Petrello, Redilla, Zuella, and Camille landed by the border, they stared at the colorful lights shimmering through the invisible shield, then, Camille told the six children to wait by the tree. Once the children were sitting down, she gestured for Petrello, Redilla, and Zuella to join her closer to the boarder.

"They've strengthened it," Camille said.

"By how much?" Redilla asked.

"Well from what I can see, it's now strong enough to burn those who pass through it." Camille continued to stare.

"So now it's really dangerous," Zuella offered.

"Very dangerous," Camille answered.

"So what'd we do now?" Petrello asked concerned.

"All our concern lies with Karisma right now, and our powers need to stay strong." Camille danced crazily before the shield trying to find a weak spot. Then she turned, and stared at them. "The shield is much too powerful. If we pass through, it'll not only burn us, it'll take all our magic before we reach the land of Panora."

"Okay, so what's the problem?" Petrello asked.

"The problem is we're carrying six children, and they too shall be burned, then, stripped of their powers. Even if we did do it, and break through the barrier with minimal damage, we'd have no way to help the children because our magic would be gone. We'd need three days of resting before our magic would be allowed to become half way full. On top of that, we'd need ten more days to fully recharge," Camille said.

"So?" Petrello didn't understand the problem.

"So if the armies from Walby cross over, or the armies from Elvi arrive early, we'll be powerless against them," Camille sighed. "So now we've got major decisions to make."

"Okay, so let's hide somewhere off the path, and talk it through." Zuella was logical.

Camille looked quickly around. "Follow me. I found the perfect place."

She flew, and the rest followed her.

Where are they?" Watesa screamed again at all of them. "Where's X-Eyes?"

"Over here," X-Eyes answered weakly.

"Get up you fool!" Watesa yelled again, then, snapped her tentacle, and her army screamed in pain. "I should end it now for all of you."

"It would deplete your magic," Crumby said.

"I don't care. All of you are useless."

"Yeah, but without us, you'll be in peril," Kixmox said.

"I shall live peacefully without any of you fools. I give you a simple order, and yet none of you can follow it through." She glared at X-Eyes. "How hard was it to watch over the five disobedient children?"

"I was watching them. I just don't know what happened."

"I tell you what happen, you disgusting fly. They've escaped! They're gone, and I find you sleeping on the job."

"I wasn't sleeping. Someone cast a spell."

"How do you know that?" Watesa questioned.

"Because the sleep that gathered in my eye was green." He

showed her, and she knew he was telling the truth.

"Then we've traitors in Walby. Someone got through the barriers. Search the land, and don't come back until they're found!" she screamed, snapped her tentacle, and everyone disappeared.

As Wings landed close to the border of Walby, all the women noticed the shield was shimmering in brilliant colors.

"Oh that's not good." Rain held up her hand.

"No, it's not," Hurricane agreed.

"What's with all the colors?" Volcano asked.

"The colors show the sign of strength, you know that." Windy smiled.

"Yeah, and by the looks of all the colors, it's really strong. A sure sign that Karisma is trapped on the other side, right along with the rest," Tornado informed them.

"So, what's the plan then?" Sparkle asked staring at the shield.

Rain sighed, "I don't have one yet. Face it, if we pass through, our powers will be gone by the time we get to the other side."

"Then Watesa will have all the control she wants." Windy looked at them.

"Yeah, she'll have a lot of good magic combined with the bad, and then she'll be unstoppable."

"So what'd you want to do?" Volcano asked.

"I'm not sure," Rain answered.

"Me either," Volcano echoed.

"Personally, I say we wait, and keep an eye on the border. Who knows, maybe we'll catch a glimpse of something. But if we just carelessly enter the shield, it will weaken everything, and we'll be useless," Windy said.

"You're right," Rain sighed again. "I'm just so angry that I allowed this to happen. I should've spoken to Karisma about the danger of wandering off."

"Do you think it really would've made a difference?" Windy asked.

"Yeah. All the children are stubborn," Volcano said.

"It's our fault again," Hurricane blurted. "We've allowed them to be."

"True," Windy agreed. "But I thought all of us did a good job making them mind us, until now."

"Well we were the same way." Wings twisted her feathers. "I remember how each of us did the same things. The only difference was we were never captured for very long."

"That's because we were further in our training, before we ever tried anything like this." Rain reminded them.

"Well, that's not the point. Right now, we need to figure out what to do," Sparkle said.

When they heard the clap of thunder, rumble across the sky, all the women looked up.

Perched high on a cloud was grandmother Culver. "Rain, you mustn't cross over. None of you should, and shame on you for even trying to break the rules of Panora, especially, as old as all of you are now."

"But what about Karisma?" Rain asked.

"I'll tell you a story." Grandmother Culver smiled beautifully at them. "Once upon a time, seven beautiful girls came to the land of Panora to learn magic. They had about them the quickest tongues in the land. Why, everyone who knew them knew their tongues were as sharp as their minds, and as strong as their magic. One at a time, each of these beautiful girls, tried something outside the realm of Panora, throwing all caution to the wind. Because they thought at the tender ages of fourteen, they just knew everything. Including how the entire world functioned. No adult could tell any of those beauties anything. Those seven girls, with their stubborn streak, simply knew it all. Why, back in the day, I remember having to save them more than once and surprisingly they never learned, or listened to what any of the elders had to say. So, as fate would have it, they survived, amazingly, then went on to find their husbands, and eventually married. Now they all have wonderful children, just like they were, and the seven beautiful girls now stand before me, not knowing what to do to save their children, much like we did, when each of you did it to us. However, this is different. This is the time for the Great War, and now your children are trapped on the other side of the land, in Walby, where the darker magic lives, and none of you are powerful enough to break through the powerful shield around the land. But if you search your heart, you'll find the answer there. Maybe you won't be able to rescue them today, maybe not even tomorrow. But remember the children made a choice, and to test their courage and their loyalty, we must wait to see what happens."

"I can't wait," Rain blurted. "Karisma is the highest power of the lands, and she's my daughter. How can I wait?"

"Much like every mother had to do. Children do not come without challenges. We must let them learn from their mistakes, so as not to repeat them in the future. Now if Karisma is as smart as her mother, and I'm sure she is, then she'll figure it out, as will the rest." She stared at all of them with her laughing blue eyes. "Now rest, for there is much to do." Grandmother Culver held her hand out, and blew the dust towards them, and before any of them knew what happened, they were fast asleep.

As Petrello stared at Camille, Redilla, and Zuella, he waited.

"Here's what we will do," Camille announced. "I'll ask the children, if they want to cross through the shield."

"But what about Karisma? I think she's weaker than the rest because Watesa took a lot of her magic," Petrello said.

"True," Zuella agreed. "But she has the blood of the Culver's running thick and deep through her veins."

"Which means?" Petrello asked.

"Which means, she's stronger than the rest of us," Redilla whispered.

"Yes, but if Watesa is draining her magic, she won't be soon."

"Not true." Camille danced crazily. "You see, as long as Karisma isn't within Watesa's dwelling, there's only so much magic she can steal. Besides, now it's different."

"Different how?" Petrello asked confused. "You've lost me."

"It's different because we're here, and since we're strong enough in our magic, we can protect her from Watesa."

"So can I protect her too?" Petrello asked.

"No, sorry. You're one of the good-looking creatures from Panora. Don't get me wrong, I think Redilla, Zuella, and me are pretty too, just in a pixie angle and fairy kind of way."

"So let me get this straight. Just because I look like the humans, I'm not allowed to protect her?"

"It's not that you're not allowed it's that you can't protect her like we can. You're ordinary really. We pixie angles hold the special magic."

"I have magic too," Petrello argued.

"We know that. Look, I don't make the rules of Panora. I only live by them well enough to know what they are," Camille answered.

"So you're more powerful then I am?" Petrello was shocked.

"Not more powerful over all, just when it comes to Karisma," Redilla answered him.

"Look, you can still protect the others, just not Karisma," Zuella said.

"I'm still confused." Petrello looked at them.

"Okay, let me explain it again," Camille sighed deeply as if irritated. "Never mind."

"No really, I must," Camille insisted.

"Go ahead." Petrello listened.

"Okay, we're the pixie angles, and the fairy with one of the highest and purest powers in the land of Panora. Not to mention we're Karisma's trainers."

"Yeah?" Petrello shrugged. "So?"

"We're her guides, silly," Zuella said.

"I know, I heard you, so?"

"So we've got the special powers to protect her."

"Whatever. Wake her up then." Petrello rolled his eyes at them.

"Petrello, I shall wake her once I clarify what I mean." Camille looked at him. "You're very powerful because you were raised on the land in Panora. The human children were raised on Earth and aren't as powerful, yet. They've only just learned some of their magic, but not all. That's why you're allowed to protect the other five children, but not Karisma."

Petrello stared at Camille. "So I can't protect Karisma because she's more powerful than I am because…"

Camille interrupted him, "Because of the Culver's bloodline running, strong and pure through her veins."

When he nodded, Camille knew he had finally gotten it. Then Petrello looked at her. "Wake her."

"Okay, if I must." Camille danced over to Karisma, blew the dust, which sparkled, and danced toward her face, and is if on cue, Karisma's eyes opened.

Then Camille blew a different color dust towards the other five children, and soon they joined them.

"Where am I?" Karisma asked.

"In Walby," Petrello answered, "how are you feeling?"

"Weak," Karisma said.

Camille flew over toward her. "Stick out your tongue."

Karisma did, and Camille laid a speck of orange dust on it, and soon she stood. "Thank you, Camille. I feel much stronger, now. What're you doing here anyway?"

"We came to rescue you from Watesa." Camille pointed at her. "You made an awful decision, when you wandered outside the safety of Firey's dwelling."

"I realize that now."

"I hope you do," Camille reprimanded. "Now everyone in Panora is worried sick. Including your mother."

"Can you bring me back there?" Karisma looked hopeful.

"Sorry. We've got to wait. The shield around the land is much too powerful."

"Why?" Karisma asked.

"I'm sorry child, why what?" Camille shook her head, as if lost.

"Why can't we go back to Panora?"

"Because the shield is much too powerful. To cross through would bring great danger to all of us."

"What danger?" Boulder asked quietly.

"The shield will burn us, if we pass through it. Then, it would steal our magic before we reached the other side, and when we arrived in Panora, we'd have no magic to heal our burns." Camille answered.

"Ouch," Raven said aloud.

"Exactly," Redilla agreed.

"So are we struck here then?" Karisma asked looking around.

"I'm afraid so, at least for three more days," Camille answered.

"Three more days?" Sunburst pouted.

"Yes, now let's talk about how we're going to survive, shall we?" Zuella asked.

"Do we have a chance to survive on the land of Walby for three days?" Boulder asked.

"Yes, but only if you children listen. Now let's talk about what needs to be done," Camille said.

CHAPTER TWENTY-TWO

As Flipple and Crumby circled the land, Crumby started laughing, so Flipple shot him a look. "What's so funny?"

"You are," Crumby said.

"Why do you say that?" Flipple stared at him.

"Because you keep scratching your behind."

"Yeah, well that's because when Watesa struck out at all of us she managed to hit me right on my butt." Flipple rubbed it again, as Crumby laughed harder. "It's no laughing matter. My butt feels like its being stung a thousand times over by bees."

"Oh, that must hurt. Too bad I don't know what it feels like." Crumby laughed again.

"If you don't stop laughing at me, I'll swat you so hard your entire fly body will spin out of control."

"I doubt it."

"Why didn't Watesa's sting affect you?" Flipple demanded.

"I'm too small. She thinks it does, and I pretend it does, but she always manages to miss. So me, X-eyes, and Vixbit, always escape her wrath."

"Yeah, but not every time," Flipple sounded annoyed.

"You're clearly right about that. When she picks us up, and squeezes us with her tentacle it smarts," Crumby told him.

"I'll bet it does. I'd hate to be as small as you," Flipple said, as they continued flying, searching the land for the intruders, and the missing children.

"Well, I'd hate to be as big as you, or as ugly as those humans. I still can't get over how repulsive they are. Every time I look at them, I want to hurl."

"You're funny."

"What, it's true. They look like trees that have come to life." Crumby laughed, and then watched Flipple scratch his butt again. "You need to stop." Crumby smiled. "If you continue scratching like that, I'm afraid your butt's going to simply fall off, then, what'll you do?"

Flipple smiled. "I don't think it will, but I'll try to stop."

Crumby looked at the ground. "Did you see that burst of color coming from the ground below?" he asked Flipple excitedly.

"Where?" Flipple asked.

"Over there." Crumby pointed a wing.

"Yeah, what is it?" Flipple asked.

"I'm not sure, but we need to go check it out. If we don't, Watesa will be coming for us again, and I'd hate for her to sting your butt again."

"Me too." Flipple absently rubbed it again, causing Crumby to laugh. "Now let's go, Crumby. If trouble's brewing we need to know what tell our queen."

"I'll follow you." Crumby smiled, waited for Flipple to take the lead, and then he followed.

"Do you think anyone saw that?" Firey asked the good people of her land.

"I think everyone saw it, Firey," Zambler answered.

"Yeah, I agree. The whole sky light up in brilliancy." Tomkin smiled.

"Yeah, but do you think the children saw it?" Firey asked.

"Hard to say. We're not even sure they exist anymore, and if they do, well then we don't know if Watesa still has them or if they were set free." Tomkin looked sad for a moment.

"I know." Firey held her hand in the air, and everyone watched as she shot another fireball right out of her fingertips. The blue streaks left behind once the fireball was released turned orange and sizzled for a second.

"Doesn't that hurt your fingers?" Flam asked.

"No. When I first learned the trick, years and years ago, it did. Not anymore though." Firey smiled gently.

"You look tired," Zambler commented.

"I am," Firey said, "even though I rested earlier, there's so much going on, who can really rest all the way?"

"Yeah, I know what you mean." Tomkin jumped up. "I've got a tremendous feeling that the children are okay." Tomkin smiled hugely at Firey.

"I hope you're right, Tomkin," she told him gently.

"Oh I think he is," Onebuyo offered.

"Well, now if only we knew what their mother's were up too. Come my good people, let's go find out."

When Rain yawned, and tried to open her eyes, she found it difficult. The sun was blazing brightly in the sky, so she squinted, managed to see the blanket she had fallen asleep on, and finally sat up angry that she had been resting.

As she looked around, she saw all her friends were resting as well. "I hope you feel better," Rain said, "because now that we're all awake, the time has come to plan what we're doing."

When they heard the explosion, followed by the brilliant colors, they smiled.

"Firey is trying to find out whose okay in the land of Walby," Rain stated.

"Well, you should signal her back, and let her know that we are," Windy answered.

"I think she knows that," Rain said.

"How do you know?" Volcano asked, as another fireball exploded in the sky filling it with more colors.

"We're still in Panora. Besides, all she has to do is look in her ball of wax. She'll see us there," Rain answered. "Remember? That's how grandmother Culver used to track us, when we snuck away."

"Those were the days," Sparkle said, "I remember how much fun we had, and doing things we shouldn't have been doing. Great Grandmother Culver was so angry about it, that she made our mother's punish us, every time we misbehaved."

"Yeah, but look at us now. We're better because of it," Wings answered.

"Yeah, we really are," Volcano agreed.

"Now if we could only pass the lesson on to our children, and get them to listen, they would see all we've learned. I mean maybe we did sneak away a lot, and we turned a deaf ear on what our guides told us, but we never caused as much trouble as our children, and the stunts they've pulled." Tornado shook her head.

"Yes, we did." Sparkle's eyes were twinkling.

"How do you figure?" Rain asked.

"Because Rain, we were constantly exploring. Even when our guides told us not too, and grandmother Culver forbid us too, we did it anyway. Maybe we'd wait a week or two in between, but we did things, much like the children are doing," Windy told her.

"Yeah, well, why couldn't our children have listened better?" Rain smiled.

"Because they took after us," Tornado answered.

"Sadly you're right. So now I think that all of us should gather, and talk about what we're going to do," Rain looked at her friends.

When they formed a circle, Rain stood in the middle. As she lifted her arms toward the sky, all of them noticed the clouds parted, and silver dust fell, much as rain showers would have.

As the silver dust fell on them, each was restored, and felt stronger then they had only moments before.

As Rain turned to address them, her hair was covered in silver glitter. "Now it's time."

"Should we signal back?" Redilla asked when the sky lit up in brilliant colors.

"We can't," Camille answered.

"Why?" Karisma asked. "What is that anyway?"

"It's Firey's way to find out if any of us are alright," Zuella said.

"So why don't we signal back?" Sunburst asked.

"It'll give away our location." Camille stared at them.

"So what? If it does, we'll fight," Dagger blurted.

"We're weaker in Walby," Camille said.

"That may be true, but we're stronger together," Manning offered.

"Not by much." Camille looked at him. "We're not strong enough to start a fight in the land of Walby, without our queen, or not knowing if our magic will last long enough to prevail. Common sense tells me to continue hiding, until the strength of the shield weakens."

"Yeah, but who are you to make those decisions?" Dagger asked clearly annoyed.

Camille flew angrily around all of them. "When are you children going to understand that pixie angels and fairies hold some of the highest powers in Panora?"

"Maybe never," Dagger snapped looking seriously at her.

"Why is that?" Camille flew over to Dagger, waiting for his reply.

"Because if you were such high power, like you claim to be, we wouldn't be trapped listening to your explanation. We'd have already engaged in battle."

"That's not the point. Whether I'm powerful or not, I know the rules of the land, and I adhere by them." Camille flew crazily in a circle.

"Whatever, it only proves one thing to me." Dagger shrugged.

"What does it prove, smarty pants?" Camille asked snidely.

"It proves that you're not stronger in your magic than we are. If you were, we wouldn't be here," Dagger raised his voice.

"Yes, you would, and you are because of the laws and rules set in place."

"Yeah, obviously, which proves my point, now go talk to Petrello. None of us believe you anymore," Dagger snapped at her.

"You know what your problem is?" Petrello asked Dagger.

"Yeah, my problem is that I want to take my chances passing through the shield with my friends and none of you are brave enough to do it. So instead, you hold us in this tiny cave, and make us wait until of you say it's okay for us to leave and try the shield."

"Yeah, that's right, and what they've told you is the truth. If you cross, it'll bring nothing but heartache all the way around. So why do it?" Petrello stared at him, almost as if daring him to say or do something he wouldn't like.

"If it were up to me, I'd take my friend's, we'd take our chances, and get out of the land of Walby. If all you pixie angels and fairies were as strong in your magic as you claim, why are we waiting like sitting ducks to be found?" Dagger glared.

"What're sitting ducks?" Redilla asked.

"Never mind, gosh its way too hard to tell any of you anything. You understand nothing."

"They understand the ways of the lands." Petrello stood, and then stared Dagger in the eye.

"Listen," Karisma finally blurted. "All of you need to stop it. Arguing back and forth is a waste of energy. I know we're all tired, and we want to leave, but we can't. Right now, we just have to try to understand that." She looked at everyone.

"Finally a child with common sense," Zuella offered.

"We've all got common sense and brains too. We can make our own decisions," Dagger yelled.

"That's enough!" Karisma shouted, "Now we all know what's expected of us, and I guess we wait. The pixie angels and Camille lived here all their lives. They know how it works, and Petrello believes them."

"Since when does what he think matter?" Boulder asked.

"Since he's from the land on both sides," Karisma answered.

"Yeah, but have you forgotten he's a traitor?" Boulder blurted, and realized too late what he had done.

For a moment, no one uttered a word. They all stared at Karisma and Petrello then swung their eyes to look at Boulder.

"Did you tell Boulder that I'm a traitor?" Petrello looked at Karisma hurt.

"Yes, I told him I thought you were at first." Karisma tilted her chin defensively.

"Leave it to a girl to open her mouth about things she clueless about." Petrello glared at her.

"Listen, children. If you continue making all this noise by arguing, Watesa will find us," Camille scolded. "Then all this will be for nothing."

When all the children looked at her, none of them spoke.

They all heard the crunching sound at the same time, and as Camille looked at them, they knew someone had found them.

As Firey gathered her good people around her ball of wax, she stepped back as if someone had slapped her. She looked around, then, threw her hand in the air.

"What it is?" Tomkin asked alarmed.

"I can't see the children. The shield is preventing me from being able too."

"Can't you throw a spell to overpower what Watesa has done?" Onebuyo asked.

"No," the word rang with finality.

"Why?" Tomkin asked bewildered.

"Because Karisma is still on the land in Walby and the magic's too powerful, even for someone like me," Firey answered.

"Can grandmother Culver do it?" Zambler asked.

"No," Firey answered without hesitation.

"Why?" Zambler asked.

"Because she can't become involved yet."

"Then when can she help?" Onebuyo asked Firey.

"She can become involved with casting magic, only when the Great War begins. Until then, we're on our own." Firey stared at the empty ball of wax, as if mesmerized by it.

"So now what'll we do?" Tomkin jumped up and down in front of her.

When Firey took a moment to answer, all the good people on the land, waited.

Then she lifted her face toward the sky, and all the people noticed the tears on her cheeks, but said nothing.

Finally, Firey looked at all of them, and let her eyes stray around the crowd of people, before she addressed them. "We shall begin traveling, right now. We must reach the border quickly."

"Why? What's the rush?" Zambler asked.

"I've just received word that the dark magic from Elvi is growing more powerful the further they travel over the land. Now we must reach the border."

"Why?" Tomkin tapped his curly shoe on the ground, clearly annoyed.

"So when the dark magic arrives, we'll be able to stop them, or at least detain them from entering the land of Panora."

"Are we strong enough to hold them?" Onebuyo asked.

"I guess we shall see, won't we?" she answered.

CHAPTER TWENTY-THREE

As Rain stared at the shimmering lights, she watched the shield surrounding the land of Walby part. She rubbed her eyes, looked again, and then stared at her friends. "Look at the shield." She nodded towards it.

"Oh my gosh. Watesa parted it. She's wants us to enter," Windy said.

"Yes, she does," Rain agreed. "But we're not strong enough to enter, and she knows it. She's using the shield to get us to enter, then, she shall destroy us." Rain looked at her friends. "It's time to disappear from sight."

Her friends gathered close, and they all held hands, as Rain cast the spell. Soon the only thing left was smoke.

As they floated invisibly far above the land, they all watched the border.

"If the shield is parted, someone may come on the land of Panora, unwanted," Rain said, "if they do, we shall stop them."

"So you're telling us to use our magic?" Volcano asked shocked. "Yes."

"But I thought we weren't allowed too, until Firey told us?" Hurricane questioned.

"We're not. But we've got a decision to make. If someone enters the land of Panora, and we do nothing, the danger it will bring shall be devastating."

"Then we use our magic," Wings stated.

"Yes, we do," Sparkle agreed.

"Do you think it'll get us in more trouble with grandmother Culver?" Tornado asked.

"Since when do you care?' Rain smiled. "You've always done everything you're not supposed too."

"True," Tornado agreed.

"Are we all in then?" Rain asked.

"Yeah," they all agreed, and continued watching.

As Watesa watched the land of Walby from up in the tree, she intently trained her eye on the shield.

She wanted Rain and all her friends to wander through it. Once they did, she would end it for all of them.

She snapped her tentacle and saw the land of Panora. The border on the other side of the shield was empty, but she knew only minutes before someone had been there.

She felt the heat radiating through the shield, then, spilling onto her land.

She pulled out her sword, rubbed it twice, and Vixbit appeared. "Fly to the border go to the other side into the land of Panora, then, report back to me."

"Why do I have to go alone?" Vixbit complained.

"Because you imbecile, you're my spy."

"But can't Kixmox come with me?"

"No. He's much too big. The people in Panora will spot him easier. Now be gone you irritating fly." Watesa snapped her tentacle, hit Vixbit, and then he disappeared.

As she trained her eye back to the land of Panora, she watched the good people of the land traveling.

Then she closed her eyes, and chanted.

As Dagg stood just outside the entrance to the cave, he knew something weird was in it. He could smell it. He wrinkled his nose, and sniffed again.

Finally, he walked closer to the entrance. He knew it was hard to sneak up on the people from Panora.

It was hard to sneak up on anyone. The ground shook with each step he took.

As he blocked the entrance, he reached in, and swiped his claws through the cave.

When he felt nothing, he lowered his massive body, and peeked in.

"Come out of there, right now!" he yelled into the cave. "I can see you in there, and I'm warning you to come out, surrender, and I'll tell Watesa to be nice to all of you."

When several minutes passed, Dagg realized the people from Panora weren't coming out.

So, he opened his mouth, released a giant fireball, and waited.

"Oh my gosh." Karisma stood. "Don't even tell me it's that irritating dinosaur. What was his name again?"

"Dagg," Camille informed her.

"Yeah, that's it." Karisma nodded.

"Well, it is. Surely he knows we're here." Redilla flew around nervously.

"Yeah, so?" Karisma shrugged.

"Can you hear him?" Zuella asked.

"How can we not hear him?" Dagger volunteered. "He's loud, big, and irritating."

"But very powerful," Redilla answered.

"Yeah, and so are we." Boulder stood, looked at the entrance of the cave, and took a step forward.

"Don't be foolish," Petrello ordered Boulder. "If you get too close, Dagg will either claw you, or set you on fire."

Boulder looked at Camille who nodded. "Petrello's right, he will."

Boulder stopped walking, and saw Dagg's massive claw swipe through the cave. He stepped back with the others just in time to avoid the fireball.

"Hurry children, gather around, and put your backs against the wall of the cave," Camille ordered.

Once the children were lined up, Dagg shot another fireball, and all of them could feel the heat from it upon their faces.

"Don't move. Don't breathe too hard either," Camille snapped.

When another fireball lit the cave, all of them held their breath, and no one moved.

"I know you're in there. I can smell you, and now I'm telling Watesa. She'll come here, take Karisma, and the rest of you shall perish." They heard Dagg's deep laugh echo through the cave.

Then the ground began to shake, and Camille flew in front of the children, urging them to keep quiet.

Even when the ground stopped shaking, and they could no longer hear his footsteps, Camille signaled not to say a word.

When they watched Camille fly to the entrance, she landed just inside, peeked her tiny head around the corner, and flew back over to them.

"He's gone, and now we must leave. He'll bring Watesa back here."

"But where should we go?" Petrello asked.

"Well, I don't know," Camille snapped at him. "But we can't stay here. Now cast your spell for invisibility, and we'll do the same," Camille said, nodding at Redilla and Zuella, and soon they left the cave, undetected to the naked eye.

As Dagg raced over the land, he tripped, and heard laughter. As he lifted his head, he saw Crumby and Flipple. "Help me up," Dagg ordered.

"Like I can lift a dinosaur." Crumby continued to laugh.

"What's so funny?" Dagg growled.

"The way your butt's high in the air. Why if Watesa could see you now, she sting you." He chuckled.

"Yeah, until I told her that you two imbeciles set a trap, and I got caught," he said, pushing his massive body in an upright position.

"Well, we we're trying to prevent the children from getting through," Flipple told Dagg.

"Yeah, well you should've done it better."

"Oh, I forgot you're the dinosaur who knows it all." Crumby smirked.

"That's right I am." Dagg glared at him.

"No, you're not," Crumby protested. "You know nothing. You're ugly too."

"Says who?" Dagg challenged.

"Says me," Crumby answered, buzzing irritatingly in Dagg's face.

"I don't care what you think. I should just eat you for a snack."

"Yeah, try it. I'll make your belly hurt so bad, you'll wish you would've never touched me," Crumby said bravely.

"My stomach's too big for you to irritate it."

"Try me," Crumby challenge.

"Enough," Flipple yelled. "Did you find out anything, Dagg?"

"Oh, I found out plenty." Dagg nodded.

"Like?" Flipple asked irritated.

"They're in the cave up there." Dagg nodded. "Now out of the way, I need to tell Watesa what's going on."

"Should we come with you?" Flipple asked.

"Yeah, good idea." Crumby laughed. "Maybe she could sting

your butt again Flipple, and I can laugh even harder then I already am."

"What'd you mean?" Dagg looked confused.

"Never remind," Flipple answered.

"So should we come with you?" Flipple asked again.

"No, stay here. If you see them leave the cave, stop them," he ordered.

"Yes, sir." Crumby saluted Dagg.

"I'm serious, Crumby. If you let them escape, Watesa will sting more the Fipple's butt."

"Yeah, she will," Flipple agreed.

"Fine, then we wait. But hurry up, Dagg. You take forever."

"It's because I'm larger then you." He looked with disdain at Crumby.

"You could say that again. If I didn't know better I'd tell you to work out or something." Crumby laughed. "But as for your face, I'm sorry there's nothing we can do for that." He laughed harder.

"I ought to eat you, just because I can." Dagg snapped his jaws towards Crumby.

"You missed." Crumby laughed harder.

"Because I meant to. The next time, I won't."

"Excuse me, don't you have to run to Watesa like a good dinosaur, and tell her you found something?" Crumby asked flying erratically in front of Dagg's face.

"Yeah, I do. Just remember what I said," Dagg glared in his direction.

"Oh, I will, I certainly will, and Dagg cover your butt. I heard Watesa likes to sting them, and judging by the size of yours, I'd say it's big enough to keep her busy for weeks." Crumby was still laughing, as Dagg roared loudly at him, then, lumbered away.

Flipple looked at Crumby. "You really should be nicer to Dagg."

"Why?" Crumby asked.

"Because he's bigger than you are. Believe me he'll hurt you whether you believe it or not."

"Well, he'll have to catch me first." Crumby landed on Flipple shoulder.

"He will. If he wants you, he'll catch you," Flipple sounded convinced.

"Well, let's not worry about it right now. Let's get over to the cave and see what's going on, shall we?" Crumby asked.

"I guess, but be quiet. We don't want them to know we're there."

"I won't, gosh. You can trust me. I don't want to ruin it."

"Good, because if you do, I'm telling Watesa exactly what happened."

"I got it, I got it. Now let's go."

As Camille circled the area, she saw Dagg lumbering toward Watesa's dwelling, and then she saw Flipple and Crumby approaching the cave.

"Do you see them?" Zuella whispered.

"Yes." Camille smiled. "It's a shame that we're not there."

"I agree. But you know Dagg has gone to tell the queen," Redilla informed them.

"Yes, it appears." Camille nodded.

"I say we challenge that dinosaur to a fight, before he reaches the dwelling," Karisma said.

"We can't. We're not strong enough." Camille looked at her.

"Well, now what're we going to do?" Karisma asked.

"We're going to do what Firey would want us to do," Camille answered.

"What's that?"

"Hide."

As Firey pulled out her ball of wax, she stared. She could see nothing, but knew the shield around the land of Walby had parted, and all the women were gone.

She stopped, and all the good people of Panora stopped as well.

"What it is?" Tomkin asked impatiently.

"I don't see Rain, or any of them," Firey told the group. "What I do see is that the shield has parted, and I hope none of the women passed over."

"Do you think they would?" Zambler asked.

"I don't know it's hard to say. I know each of them we're worried about their children, so I simply don't know," Firey sounded defeated.

"Let's not fret." Tomkin jumped up and down. "We must continue on our way, so if they're in trouble, we can help."

"You're right," Firey said, glancing one more time in her ball of wax, before she put it back in her pocket, and the group began to travel once again.

Onebuyo stopped next to Firey. "How much longer till we arrive at the border?"

"Not long."

"Do you think we'll find the women?"

"I hope so. I'm also hoping they didn't fall for the trick Watesa's playing on them with parting the shield."

"They're very smart women, especially Sparkle," Onebuyo said," They won't do it."

"I wish I was as sure as you are." Firey smiled.

"Well, I'm confident, and you should be too. You've trained them well, and they'll know not to pass through."

"You're right. I did teach them almost everything they know about the land. But I can't help but remember what they were like when they were younger."

"We've all been like that." Onebuyo was serious. "The difference is we're the elders of the land now. They won't go against the rules and laws of Panora."

"I hope you're right."

"I am. I know you've trained them well, and that's what you need to remember."

"I will. Thank you."

"You're welcome." He smiled, and went to join Zambler, as they continued to travel quickly over the land.

CHAPTER TWENTY-FOUR

As Valtron the king of the dark land of Elvi raced over the land on his black horse, he finally raised his hand.

His army stopped, and waited for him to speak. "Karisma is the one I'm seeking. She'll become my wife eventually. First, we shall take four years to get to know one another, and then we shall have the most power in all the lands combined. We shall rule, and let no creature stand in the way. If anyone tries, they'll meet the wrath of our ultimate power and die," he snarled, as he looked at his army with his red eyes. His gray hair was long enough to touch the collar of his shirt, and his fingers were old, wrinkled, and crooked.

"Valtron, you must warp into a different looking creature before we arrive," Quiznot his spy told him.

"I know that you fool. You dare to interrupt me, when I'm speaking?" he screamed loudly.

"No King. I heard you pause with your words first, then I spoke." Quiznot watched him, trembling.

When the king merely swatted him, he flew away.

"So we shall continue to ride, until I say we rest," the king said.

"But Valtron, you've heard there's trouble in Panora. If we continue riding we'll weaken our powers," Mumu his guard informed him.

"I realize this. I also realize I'm in charge. Anything I say we do. If I wanted your opinion, I'd have asked you to open your mouth. Your job is to guard me. Nothing more, nothing less." Valtron stared at his guard.

When Valtron watched Mumu nod, Valtron lowered his hand, and the army from the land of Elvi continued to ride.

As Chesquat stopped, all his people halted. His eyes darted over the land and then they came to rest on his people from the land of Vanduesa.

When he sighed loudly, the people knew whatever had stopped him wasn't good.

"Valtron is riding closer to the land of Panora."

"We already knew that," Quian his spy said.

"Yes, you did. But he's more powerful than before."

"How's that possible?" Leano his guard asked.

"I'm not sure." Chesquat looked somber. "The vision of how it's happening is not clear to me at the moment."

"Do you think Valtron's tapped into someone else's powers?" Mophellia his pixie angel asked him, as she flew in circles in front of her king.

"It's possible. But like I said, the cause of his power is unknown right now."

"I don't understand why. You're powerful enough to see the hidden causes behind things. So why can't you see it?" Joqueal his dinosaur asked loudly.

"There's a spell cast upon him. The spell itself is called, no looking through the magic glass."

"Who is responsible for the spell?" Tryamo the fly asked the king.

"I just told you, I don't know. I can't see anything about him. I can only feel his movements. He's grown restless, and news from the land of Panora speaks of Valtron taking Karisma as his mate."

He heard the collective sighs of his people.

"She's only but a child," Mophellia, the pixie angel blurted.

"Yes, this is true. However if this is who he's chosen, he shall get her."

"What can we do to stop him?' Leano his guard asked.

Chesquat held his hand high. "Open your ears my good people from the land of Vanduesa and listen. Only then will you understand what I am saying to you. It's a waste of time for me to repeat things I've said only a moment before. Now, I'll say this one more time, before we shall continue with our journey to Panora. Valtron is becoming stronger because of some unseen power. He intends to ride to the land of Panora in search of Karisma. It'll be at that time, he'll try to kidnap Firey, steal her powers, before he ventures to the land of Walby. He will seek out Watesa, steal her powers, and destroy her. If he succeeds, and captures Karisma, he will then become the king of the entire lands and all the cities of this world, as we know it. We must do everything we can to prevent it. So while we travel, keep your magic to a minimal, so that when we arrive in Panora, we shall be fairly strong." His eyes scanned the faces of his people, watched them nod, then Chesquat lowered his hand, and the good people from Vanduesa continued to travel.

Karisma stood in the tree watching the land of Walby. She knew for the moment, she was safe because she was still invisible to the naked eye.

As Boulder watched her, he knew she was troubled. "What's wrong, Karisma?" He walked over to stand beside her.

"I don't know," she told him glancing quickly at him, and then, back over the land.

"Yes, you do, and you have to tell me."

"Okay, fine. But you're going to think I've lost it completely," Karisma said, as she again looked at him.

"No I won't. I just want you to tell me what's going on."

"I keep hearing a voice talking to me."

"What? What kind of voice?"

"I'm not sure. It's a voice I've never heard before, and it sounds older."

"I don't understand." Boulder looked at her with concern.

"Me either. But you asked what's wrong and I told you. Now I don't know what to do."

"There's not much you can do, besides tell Redilla or Zuella."

Karisma smiled at him. "That's a good idea, thank you." She stepped forward.

"Are you going to tell them now?" Boulder looked surprised.

"Yes. It's been going on for a while, and the voice is making my head ache. The sooner I know what's happening, the better I'll feel."

"Do you want me to come with you?" Boulder asked.

"No. I think I'll be fine. Thanks though." Karisma smiled at him.

"You're welcome."

As Karisma walked over to her guides, she cleared her throat, then looked at them. "I must tell you something, and I need your help."

"What is it, Karisma?" Redilla asked concerned.

"I keep hearing a voice inside my head," Karisma told them honestly.

Redilla immediately threw her hand over her tiny mouth. "Whose voice is it?"

"I don't know. It's one that I've never heard before."

"What's it saying?" Zuella asked not liking the sound of it.

"It's saying that he's coming for me, and that I should make it easy on him, and surrender when he arrives."

"You're completely sure that's what the voice is saying?" Redilla flew around her head.

"Yes."

"What else?"

"Well…"

"Come on Karisma tell us," Zuella said, "we can't help you sort it out, if you don't tell us everything."

"Okay fine. The voice told me, he'd kidnap Firey, steal her powers, and then destroy Watesa. He said that he and I will rule the land, and have children so powerful no creature would be able to stop us."

"What else?" Redilla asked with urgency.

"The voice said that we'd court for four years, then marry. He says he's traveling here to the land of Panora, and will arrive four days from now."

"Four days, you say?" Zuella asked.

"Yes, four days. Who is it?"

"His name is…" Redilla paused. "Can I speak with you in private Zuella?"

"Certainly." Zuella and Redilla looked at Karisma. "You wait right here, we'll be back in a second. We first must speak with Camille."

As Karisma stood waiting, again the voice started talking, and this time Karisma paid very close attention. She knew something was wrong, and she wanted to know who the man was, and what he wanted.

Boulder went over to his friends. "Something's going on with Karisma."

"Like what?" Sunburst asked.

"She told me some man is talking to her." Boulder shrugged.

"Who's the man?" Raven asked.

"She doesn't know. She said she's never heard the voice before.

"So how's he talking to her? Is he here or something?" Mountain asked looking over toward where Karisma was standing.

"I guess she keeps hearing his voice inside her head."

"What?" Dagger stood. "That's not cool. Who is it?"

"I just told you, she doesn't know." Boulder looked at them. "She went to tell Redilla and Zuella."

Petrello looked at them. "I'll bet I know who it is."

"But of course you do," Sunburst was sarcastic.

"Whatever. I won't tell you then." Petrello stared ahead.

"Well since you opened your mouth, you better tell us," Dagger snapped clearly perturbed that Petrello jumped in their conversation.

"I think it's Valtron," his voice was nonchalant.

"Who's Valtron?" Raven asked.

"Yeah, who is he?" Dagger stared at him.

"He's…"

"Petrello, could you please join us?" Redilla shouted cutting him off.

"Yeah, just one second."

"No. Right now," Redilla ordered.

"Sorry." He walked over to the pixie angels.

"Great. They're obviously hiding something from us." Sunburst folded her arms across her chest, and then looked over to where Redilla, Zuella Camille, and Petrello were standing.

"Yeah, who is Valtron?" Dagger asked.

"Who knows, but I don't like it," Mountain answered.

"I don't know about any of you, but the name Valtron is a strong one, don't you think?" Raven asked looking at her friends.

"Yeah, so?" Sunburst answered.

"Yeah, what's your point?" Dagger asked.

"Well, maybe he's more dark magic or something," Raven offered.

"Oh that's great," Boulder blurted. "Could we please have another guy after Karisma?"

"Calm down." Dagger looked at him. "We don't know anything yet."

"True," Sunburst agreed. "You know what? It doesn't surprise me that Karisma has all these guys after her, she's so pretty."

"Yeah, I know." Boulder glared at her.

"What? All I'm saying is even at school, guys like her, but she never pays attention to it."

"And?" Boulder was clearly upset.

"And, what? That's it. I'm only saying that Karisma is beautiful, so it doesn't surprise me that the guys in this world think so too." Sunburst looked at the ground realizing she had hurt Boulder's feelings. "I'm sorry. That wasn't cool."

"No it wasn't, even though you're right. I'd be a fool to think other guys don't see the same things in her that I do."

"Okay, you two. Get over it. We've got other things to do right now, besides throw words around. Hurting each other isn't cool. So let's just forget this whole conversation." Dagger looked at Boulder, then Sunburst.

"Yeah, you're right," Boulder sighed.

"I know. Now let's go talk to Karisma, and try to find out what's happening in her head." Dagger led them over to her.

When Karisma smiled at her friends, Sunburst and Raven hugged her. "What's wrong?" Raven asked rubbing her back.

"I don't know. Someone keeps talking to me." Karisma looked around again, as if expecting someone to sneak up on them.

"What're they saying?" Mountain asked.

"That they're coming to the land of Panora first, then Walby. They keep telling me over and over to surrender to them the second they arrive." Karisma sounded worried.

"Who is it?" Dagger asked concerned.

"I don't know," Karisma sighed deeply.

"Well, then I guess we don't leave each other for anything," Boulder said.

When she smiled, Boulder took her hand.

"Yeah, I agree. We don't know what's going on, but we'll help protect you, Karisma," Raven said.

"I appreciate it, I really do. But something tells me whoever's talking is really powerful. I believe once they arrive that's going to be it. I'll be taken prisoner, and never see any of you again."

"We won't let them take you," Dagger said.

"Yeah, I know you won't on purpose. But I've got a feeling it won't matter when he reaches me. He's coming here to steal magic, and to get me," Karisma's voice choked with emotion. "The scary thing is I don't even know where he's from, or who he is."

"Well, I say let's go over and interrupt the meeting Redilla, Petrello, Camille, and Zuella are having," Dagger said, staring in the direction they were in. "I mean I think we're entitled to know what's happening, especially since it involves you, Karisma."

"You're right," Karisma answered.

"I know. Now if it concerned anyone else outside our group, I wouldn't care. But this is too close to ignore. Besides, we need to know how to protect you, so let's go."

As they walked over to Redilla, Camille, Petrello and Zuella, they all realized they could see them, but not hear them.

As they continued to walk closer, Dagger fell back, landed on his butt, and then shook his head. "There's something around them."

"What'd you mean?" Boulder asked.

"Just what I said." He stood, with the help of Mountain's hand. "Walk closer to them, with your arms out. You'll see what I mean." He nodded.

Boulder walked with his arms out, and soon ran into the invisible wall. "I see what you mean." He turned around, and looked at his friends. "It's a shield of some sort."

"Yeah, it is. Nice of them to let us know." Dagger was clearly upset. "Now what?"

"I don't know. They look preoccupied." Raven stared at Redilla,

Petrello, Camille, and Zuella standing closely together.

"Yeah they do. I don't even think they saw what happened to Dagger," Sunburst said.

"I don't either, so this must be really bad," Karisma blurted.

Boulder put his arm around her, then, hugged her. "It'll be okay. As long as the six of us stick together, nothing's going to happen."

"I wish I believed you." Karisma tried to smile. "But I don't. I know whoever's talking to me, is powerful enough for the four of them to shield themselves away, so they can talk privately without any of us hearing the conversation."

"Okay, so at least we know what we're up against then," Raven offered. "It'll be easier to prepare. Now if this person is as powerful as we think, we must stay on high alert. That means we rest in shifts, and Karisma isn't allowed to go anywhere, without one of us."

"That's easier said than done." Karisma looked at her friends with tears in her eyes. "I mean if this was something happening on earth that would be different."

"What'd you mean?" Boulder asked.

"I mean there's no magic on earth. Not like this anyway. So it ups the odds that whoever's talking to me, is going to get me."

"No they're not." Boulder kissed her temple.

"Yes, Boulder, they are. Now, I think we should try to figure out who it is, and maybe then we can figure out how to stop him."

"So how are we going to do that?" Mountain asked.

"I think we should start by trying to contact grandmother Culver. If that doesn't work, then we contact our mother's or Firey. Someone's got to have the answers."

"And if no one does?" Sunburst asked, and saw the look Boulder gave her. "What Boulder?"

"I can't believe you said that," he sounded upset.

"What? I'm only telling everyone the sooner we realize we're trapped, the better. If we could contact them, don't you think that

Redilla, Zuella, Camille, and Petrello would have already?"

"You're right. But I haven't tried, and according to them, I'm the highest power of the land," Karisma said.

"True. So I guess you're right." Sunburst smiled trying to make Karisma feel better. "I don't know what I was thinking."

"You were thinking about everything, and you're right. I don't know that I'll get anywhere when I try this, but I've got to do something. That man's voice is slowly driving me insane."

"Is he still talking? I mean doesn't he stop for breaks?" Raven asked curiously.

"No, he doesn't, his voice just keeps repeating itself over and over, as if it trying to put me in a trance or something." Karisma bit her thumb nervously.

"Well, then, I think we should try it," Boulder encouraged her.

"Yeah, I agree." Dave nodded.

"Then we'll start right now." Karisma looked at them. "Now gather around, and form a circle. I don't know if this is the way to set it up or not, but so far, all of us have seen Firey gather all the good people of Panora this way, in a full circle."

"I think you're right, Karisma," Raven agreed.

As the six of them formed a circle, Karisma heard the voice inside her head grow stronger, as if it were trying to drown out her request from the higher powers.

When she looked at all of them, her eyes were filled with worry. "We must hurry. I think whoever's talking to me, knows what we're about to do."

"How do you figure?" Dagger asked.

"Because his voice is getting louder, even as we speak."

"Okay, then let's start," Sunburst said.

When the six of them held hands, they felt the electric current run through their fingers, and then they felt their bodies begin to float, and soon they disappeared.

CHAPTER TWENTY-FIVE

Redilla, Camille, Zuella, and Petrello were talking about what was happening to Karisma, when they felt the wind pick up, and viciously slap them in the face.

"What's going on?" Petrello asked.

"It's Valtron," Camille answered.

"What'd you mean?"

"Just what I said. He's upset about something, and I think maybe he is listening to what we're talking about."

"How can he do that?" Petrello asked.

"He's the king of Elvi. He has many different powers, and if he's not stopped, he's sure to gain even more," Zuella answered.

"So I say we stop talking, and tell the rest what we're going to do." Petrello turned, but didn't see the six of them anywhere. "Where did they go?" he yelled over the wind.

"Oh no." Camille flew through the shield searching the trees, as the rest followed. "I think he took them."

"Valtron? You think Valtron took them?" Petrello looked at Camille alarmed.

"Yes," she said, loud enough so he would hear her over the sound of the wind.

"How could he have done that?" Petrello glared at the pixie angels. "Huh? I knew we should've included them in our meeting. I just knew it. Now I've let Karisma and my mother down."

"You did no such thing," Zuella reprimanded him.

"Yes, I did. I should've insisted they be involved. Then maybe this wouldn't have happened."

"Well it did. Now let's stop arguing, and feeling guilty, and figure out what to do," Camille said, as she tried to fly in place over the rush of the wind that was whipping through the trees.

"Fine, let's talk, and this plan better be good. The six of them don't trust me as it is. Now they really won't trust me."

"Then if that's the case, they'll trust none of us. We were all here when they disappeared," Camille said, "now stop it, and let's get to work".

As the seven women flew just on the other side of the border, Rain looked first at the ground, then at her friends. "We've got an intruder." She nodded toward the ground.

"What is that?" Volcano asked pointing at the little creature flying over the land of Panora.

"That is Watesa's spy. I think he goes by the name of Vixbit," Rain informed them.

"Well, what should we do?" Hurricane asked.

"I say we scare the little varmint, until he goes back to his side of the land." Wings was serious.

"I say we interrogate him, find out if the children are okay, then give him a good swat, and send him back." Sparkle smiled.

"I'd say that's a good idea," Rain agreed.

"So we're going to capture Vixbit?" Windy asked.

"Yes." Rain nodded.

"Are all of you ready then?" Tornado asked.

"Yeah. Let's do it. I want to know our children are okay, and where they're keeping them." Rain flew off toward Vixbit.

As Vixbit landed on a bush, he stared around the land of

Panora, but saw nothing.

He secretly admired the colors, which sprayed over the land in brilliancy.

Then he raised his huge eyes toward the sky. When he still saw nothing, he decided to fly around to get a closer look.

Before he knew what happened, he was stuck in something sticky. Then he heard the laughter.

"Vixbit, I'd say you're on the wrong side of the border," Rain addressed him. "Now if you want to make it out of Panora, you're going to answer some questions."

"Never," Vixbit yelled.

"Are you sure you don't want to answer the questions?" Hurricane asked, spinning her fingers quickly above him, and they all watched Vixbit sail around and around in a circle.

"Stop it," Vixbit yelled.

"Are you going to cooperate?" Rain asked impatiently.

"No, and all of you know the reason. Besides, if you don't free me, Watesa will come."

I doubt it, but even if she did, so what?" Volcano said, "Are you going to talk now, or are you afraid that Watesa's going to cast a spell on you?"

"Listen, if Watesa finds out what's going on, she'll come for all of us. Then she'll sting us, and that hurts so badly," Vixbit whined.

"Oh, no. Don't go there with me. You're way too small to get stung," Windy said.

When Vixbit looked at them, he rolled his eyes. "Fine, what'd you want to know?"

Just then, the wind picked up around them, and the women instantly held hands, as they watched Vixbit spin quickly again in the web.

"What's going on now?" Vixbit yelled.

"Valtron," Rain shouted without thinking.

"What'd you mean Valtron?" Sparkle sounded alarmed.

"Just what I said," Rain yelled over the wind. "He's cast a spell over both the lands and is coming for Karisma," her voice rose hysterically.

"Then we'd better do something," Tornado yelled.

"There's nothing we can do." Rain closed her eyes, as she braced with the others against the ravishing winds.

When Firey felt the wind lifting her hair, it stole her breath as she raised her hand.

She knew the only power strong enough to do that was Valtron's, from the land of Elvi. "Brace yourself," she yelled to the good people of Panora, trying to fight against the wind, and felt powerless to protect them.

Suddenly she realized how weak she had become since Karisma's capture, and knew Valtron was coming to the land of Panora, then, he would continue on to Walby, in search of Karisma.

As the wind viciously slapped her face, she felt the tears sting her eyes, so she closed them, and waited.

Watesa felt the wind shake the tree she was in, and for the first time, in a long time she felt frightened.

She knew the only one capable of slipping through the protective shield, she had cast around the kingdom of Walby was Valtron.

She knew without a doubt, he had cast a spell, and created the wind.

As she struggled to see with her one eye, she found it impossible to do so. The wind sharply slapped at her from all angles, and it took everything in her to keep hold of the branches of the tree with her tentacles.

The message he sent rang over the wind loud and clear. He was warning both lands that he was coming for Karisma to take her as his mate. After four years had passed, they would be married.

The news was grim, and as Watesa finally gave up trying to keep her eye opened, she closed it, and let the wind continue to batter her body.

When Dagg stumbled toward Watesa's dwelling, it amazed him how strong the wind was. As he turned around, he was startled to see Flipple and Crumby following.

"I thought I told both of you to watch the cave," he yelled over the roar of the wind.

"You did," Flipple yelled back, "but we decided to follow you, once we discovered the cave was empty."

"Empty," Dagg yelled louder, "what do you mean empty?"

"Just what Flipple said, it was empty," Crumby yelled.

"Well it looks like Watesa dwelling is empty too," Dagg roared. "What's with the wind?"

"I don't know, but it can't be good," Flipple continued to yell, "the people from the land of Vanduesa said there's only one person of this world who can create such a wind storm throughout the lands."

"Who's that?" Dagg yelled.

"Valtron, the king of Elvi."

Dagg threw his head back, tried to laugh, but the strong wind cut it off.

"You don't believe that, do you?" he yelled.

"Yes, I do. With everything that's going on between the lands, it wouldn't surprise me if he's not on his way."

"Why would he be?" Dagg asked.

"Because both sides are weakened because Karisma is here. So it's the perfect time," Flipple answered.

When the three of them heard the message carried on the wind, they all closed their eyes, and waited.

As grandmother Culver watched all her people struggle with the wrath of Valtron, she sat back, sighed deeply, and knew it was against the rules for her to intervene.

If she did, she would instantly be stripped of her powers for disobeying the law set forth on the lands.

As she turned her eye from the clouds, she saw the black horses barreling over the land toward Panora.

She watched as Valtron's red eyes glowed, and his long gray hair blew behind him in the wind, with a smirk on his old face.

Tipping her head, she looked up, and waited for the answers to come. In her heart, she knew there was nothing she could do to prevent what was happening.

She also knew that Valtron was coming first to the good land of Panora, and then he would travel to the kingdom of Walby to search for Karisma.

As she waited, grandmother Culver listened as best she could over the roar of the wind.

She hoped before too long, great grandmother Culver would appear, and tell her what to do to stop the destruction moving over the lands.

Chesquat stopped, as he noticed the wind picking up. Then he held up his hand. "Get ready. Valtron has cast his strongest spell over all the lands."

"How do you know?" Leano asked, yelling over the howling of the wind.

"Because I can taste the pepper in the air, and it leaves a bitter taste in one's mouth, much like Valtron does." Chesquat was serious as his eyes scanned the land.

The huge gush of wind rushed up out of nowhere, knocking all of them from their horses.

Then Chesquat heard the sound of laughter, and knew Valtron's spirit had traveled with the spell he cast.

When Chesquat heard the message from Valtron being carried over the wind, all of them closed their eyes, as their horses whinnied, and instantly Chesquat feared the worse for Karisma. He knew Valtron had come to take her as his mate, but he also knew no one would be able to stop him.

He turned his face into the wind challenging Valtron, and when he felt the slap on his face, he immediately looked away.

Chesquat knew the coming of the Great War would be hard won. Victory over Valtron wouldn't be easy, but deep down Chesquat knew they would be fighting for more than their powers; they would be fighting to take Karisma away from Valtron, and the land of Elvi. Then they'd have to bring her back to the rightful land of Panora where she belonged.

As Kixmox slammed against the side of the cave, he growled in the wind.

Never had he felt power, such as now. The wind had literally picked him up, slamming him into the side of the cave.

Kixmox was helpless, and knew if the wind didn't die down soon, he would be seriously hurt.

As the wind mixed with the land and dirt in Walby; it stung Kixmox's eyes, and finally he gave up the fight.

He closed his eyes and heard the male voice, which carried over the wind, and knew this was just the beginning of what lied ahead.

As the six children continued to travel high above the land, Karisma noticed right away how strong the wind became, and then she heard the voice again.

"I'm coming closer to the land of Walby, and then you shall be mine." She heard the dark laughter, which chilled her.

Karisma quickly glanced over at her friends and she knew by their expressions, they heard the voice as well.

"Don't let go of one another," Karisma yelled over the noise of the wind.

"We won't," Boulder yelled back. "Because if that guy thinks he's going anywhere with you, he's got another thing coming."

"Yeah, I totally second that," Dagger yelled.

"Count me in for three," Mountain yelled.

"Listen, I've been thinking," Raven screamed. "Do we still have the jewels?"

"Oh my gosh, maybe," Sunburst yelled back answering Raven.

"Then maybe we need to use them to find Dagg," Raven's voice was loud.

"For what?" Karisma asked.

"To get your ring back," Raven screamed.

"It's worth a try," Boulder yelled, agreeing with her.

"Yeah, but is it worth it? I mean if we still have our jewels maybe we should use them to get out of here," Dagger shouted.

"Excellent idea, but I still think we need to find Dagg first," Sunburst agreed.

"Yeah, we need to find Dagg first," Mountain, shouted. "Then find the way out of here."

"Why find Dagg?" Dave was confused.

"Because Karisma is the highest power, but she needs her ring and Dagg has it. If we find him and steal the ring back, it'll strengthen all our powers, and protect her more from Valtron."

"I think you're all geniuses," Karisma yelled, "but how are we going to find Dagg and steal the ring without letting go of each other?"

"I guess whatever hand we use to dig the jewel out of our pocket, the person next to us will have to hang onto our leg. Then our one hand will be free to hold the jewel, and we'll still stay connected. Then once all of us have our jewels, we'll lock arms, freeing our hands. You know what I mean?" Mountain asked.

"Yes, so instead of holding hands, we'll be holding legs," Sunburst yelled.

"Exactly, until we all have our jewels, then we'll lock arms. Since Karisma is the most powerful, she goes first," Dagger yelled. "Give me your leg Karisma."

Karisma lifted her leg, and then Dagger grabbed it letting her hand go.

When Karisma pulled her jewel out, she was thankful she hadn't lost it. The green jewel shimmered in her hand as she chanted.

The position she was in, made her want to laugh for a moment. With her one leg being held by Dagger, her hand being held by Boulder, they flew through the raged wind surrounding them.

Finally, all of them had managed to get to their jewels, then they all locked arms with the person next to them.

When they were finished, each of them looked at the other, then, Karisma nodded.

The six of them, with their jewels in hand, started to chant.

Valtron raced over the land. His black horse ran at such a speed it merely looked as if it were flying.

Then Valtron abruptly grabbed his horse by its reins, pulled, and then held his hand up. "They've figured it out."

"Figured what out, King?" Quiznot asked.

"They've taken their jewels into their hands, and they're going to get Karisma's ring!" Valtron shouted.

"So what does it mean?" Zealot his pixie angel asked.

"It means you idiot, that she'll gain back a lot of power once she has it." Valtron pierced all of them with his red eyes.

"Okay, so we go find Karisma, and steal her before she gets the ring back," Rummety his dinosaur told him.

"Good idea," Tresknot the fly congratulated him.

"Move in a circle," Valtron told his people.

As his people formed a circle, they watched the fire fly out of his finger tips hit the ground, and then Valtron stared into it.

"I see she's a smart one." He smiled slightly. "But she needs to be stopped. I think I know what they're going to do, and we must hurry." He pulled his eyes from the fire. "If any of you let her slip through any portals, I will end it for you. Do you understand?" Valtron stared at each of them, and watched them nod. "Very good, now let's ride."

When Valtron blew his breath toward the fire, it instantly went out, then he kicked his horse, and he and his army took off over the land.

"Oh my gosh, I think he's closer," Karisma told her friends, grateful the wind had died down.

"How do you know?" Dagger asked.

"Because I can feel him," Karisma answered.

"Look there's Dagg," Sunburst shouted.

"Let me handle it," Karisma told her friends.

In one sweeping motion, Karisma closed her eyes, and her friends watched her chant.

"How are we going to do this without letting go of each other?" Sunburst asked.

Karisma opened her eyes. "Watch."

When all of them felt themselves zooming to the ground, they couldn't believe it.

"Dagg's going to see us." Boulder was alarmed.

"Not if my spell worked the right way, he won't," Karisma said with her eyes closed.

When they swung down close enough to Dagg, the ring he had, suddenly lifted into the air, floated over to Karisma, and everyone watched as it slid down her finger, without anyone's help.

"That was cool." Mountain laughed.

"Yeah, I'd give anything to see that again." Dagger looked pleased. "How did you do that?"

"Magic." Karisma smiled. "Now let's get out of here, Valtron's coming quickly. Now close your eyes."

As they did, Karisma started chanting, and soon her circle of friends, were flying quickly over the kingdom of Walby.

CHAPTER TWENTY-SIX

Rain looked over at her friends, as they flew over the land of Panora, and then she heard the deep voice of Valtron shatter the peace. "Ladies, I'm coming to your good land. Once I arrive, I'll steal all your magic, because I can. Then I shall find Firey do the same thing to her, then, well, you know what comes next, don't you Rain?" His laughter shook the land of Panora.

"You think you're powerful enough to challenge all of us?" Rain shouted. "I hope you still have that confidence once you arrive here. I know that Karisma is gaining in strength. So how will you fight all of us?"

"Oh, but as Karisma is gaining in strength, so am I. Did you forget who I am?" Valtron's voice was bitter, and as it spilled over the land, each woman tasted the pepper in their mouth from the air.

"Think what you will. If you make this personal, Valtron, I shall combat you to the end," Rain snapped.

When Valtron laughed again, all of them noticed the pungent odor. "I'm closer then you think, Rain, and more powerful then you'll ever know. Once I arrive, I'll take Karisma, bring her to the land of Elvi, and she shall forever rein the lands with me."

"Ha. If you believe that, then you're sadly mistaken. My Karisma has more strength in a strand of hair, then, all your magic combined."

"We shall see, won't we?" His dark laughter rang over the land of Panora, again. "Until then Rain, watch your land, you just never know who's going to breech the border."

When Rain hesitated, the land of Panora grew eerily silent, and all of them knew he had left.

"Where do you think he went?" Windy asked.

"I think he's gone to find Karisma," Rain's eyes were filled with sadness.

"None of that," Tornado scolded. "We must stay strong and determined for Karisma and the rest of the children. Remember they're all together, and when Valtron tries to take Karisma, none of the children will let it happen without a fight, especially Boulder."

"Yeah, you're right. All the children will band together to form a front. Hopefully it'll be strong enough to hold Valtron," Volcano said.

"It won't be. They're missing too many links," Wings answered.

"What links?" Sparkle asked.

"They're separated from Redilla, Camille, Zuella, and Petrello," Wings answered.

"How do you know?" Rain choked on the question.

"Because I can see them vaguely."

"What? Why didn't you tell us?" Rain demanded.

"Because the visions just popped in my head, but unfortunately I'm not strong enough to show it to the rest of you."

"So where are the children?" Rain asked quickly.

"In the land of Walby still," Wings answered.

"What're they doing?" Rain asked alarmed.

Wings smiled. "They're flying over the land. All the children have their arms locked because they're holding the jewels from earth."

"They're what?" Rain asked incredulously.

"They're holding the jewels Karisma and Boulder brought here from earth, and their smart enough to know that to form a strong alliance, they must be intertwined with each other. So they've linked arms." A soft, proud smile touched each of the woman's lips.

"Do you think they'll be strong enough?" Volcano asked.

"Hard to say. Valtron is the strongest of the lands right now," Rain said.

"No grandmother Culver is," Tornado answered.

"True, but she's not allowed to intervene." Rain reminded them. "If she was, Valtron wouldn't even be here."

"Yeah, that's also true," Volcano sighed.

"Listen, can you see Petrello?" Sparkle asked Wings.

"Not yet, the only things I see are the six children, and even with that it's full of static."

"Could you try to focus on him, please? I just want to make sure he's okay," Sparkle pleaded.

"I shall try," Wings told her, and they all noticed the serious expression come over her face.

"Do you see him yet?" Sparkle was impatient.

"Not yet," Wings answered.

"Let's give it a moment, shall we?" Windy said.

As the women continued to fly, they were all paying such close attention to Wings, that none of them saw the trap that Valtron had set.

Grandmother Culver watched the children sailing over the kingdom of Walby, and knew what they were going to do.

She stomped on the cloud, clearly irritated, and wished she could stop them, before they did what they planned on doing.

As she turned her eyes to the golden door, she silently called on her great grandmother Culver for the answers, as she had been doing since this whole mess started.

But unfortunately, the golden door remained closed.

"If you could give me a moment of your time, great grandmother

Culver, I'd be so thankful to you."

When the gentle breeze lifted grandmother Culver's hair, she smiled, and watched as the door opened.

Her great grandmother, Thelma Culver, walked over to join her on the fluffy, white cloud, and grandmother Culver felt peaceful in her presence.

"My child," Thelma Culver, whispered. "Trouble is brewing in all the lands. This is but a turbulent time, with lots of peril. The children you seek help for, are beyond both of us. They're the future of Panora. They must figure this out without our help. Unfortunately, the children weren't educated quickly enough before their many captures. Now I can't help any of you, until the children learn the truth of their heritage. It is only when Karisma asks me to help that I shall be allowed too. You know the rules and law governing the land of Panora and I shall not break them."

Grandmother Culver looked at her. "Karisma is asking me for help, but I know I can't help her."

"That's correct." Thelma Culver smiled at her.

"But I must. I'm afraid of what shall happen if Valtron is allowed to capture her."

"We mustn't change what's meant to be. To alter the future, shall destroy the past. You know that." Thelma Culver placed her hand on grandmother Culver's head.

"Now I bring you peace my child to let what may come, happen. It is truly out of our powerful realm that Karisma is not familiar with the chain of command. If I so much as lift a finger to help her, the higher powers of the land of Panora will come down, and rein fury upon us all. We must trust the children are smart enough and wise enough to do what's right."

"But they aren't. They're as stubborn as their mother's were."

Great grandmother, Thelma Culver smiled. "We've all been stubborn. It's part of our heritage and who we are. Never underestimate the power of children. They're smarter then we give them credit for, and more powerful then we think. Take a moment to look at the world through the eyes of the children, and you'll find the answers there."

"Yes, I know this to be true. But what if they accidentally slip through a portal?" Grandmother Culver twisted her fragile, old hands nervously.

"Much like you did?"

"Yes."

"Then they shall learn even more about the world they're from. Now I must go, the elderly powers are calling me back." Great grandmother Thelma smiled peacefully at grandmother Culver. "Worry never changes the outcome. It only makes you worry more. Trust in the children to make the right choices and that's all we can do." Great grandmother, Thelma walked through the open golden door, as grandmother Culver watched, and soon she was gone.

As she turned her sadden eyes back toward the children flying over the land of Walby, grandmother Culver felt the vibration flow quickly through her body, and knew what the children were planning to do. Then she turned her eyes away from them, and screamed through the clouds in agitation because she couldn't help.

"Now does everyone understand what we're going to do?" Karisma asked her friends.

When she saw them nod, they closed their eyes, and soon they felt like they were falling.

"They've left." Valtron stopped his horse abruptly, then, swung around to glare at his people.

"What'd you mean they left?" Remmety the dinosaur asked.

"Just what I said," Valtron was upset.

"But where did they go?" Tresknot the fly asked.

"I'm uncertain." Valtron stared at nothing.

"Well, you're the powerful one. You should know where they

went," Zealot the pixie angel said, flying crazily in front of his face.

"I know that, but there's been some sort of spell cast, and now Karisma's whereabouts are no longer clear."

"Aw, that's a shame," Quiznot his spy told Valtron seriously.

Then Valtron smiled. "I've got the perfect solution to remedy the problem." He looked at his people. "If I can't have Karisma, then the next best things are her mother, Rain, and her queen, Firey. Now let's ride." Valtron demanded, as once again their horses flew over the land.

As Dagg reached for the ring, he stopped, turned, and glared at Flipple and Crumby.

"Where's my ring?" Dagg growled at the two of them.

"What ring?" Crumby asked.

"Don't play stupid with me. You know what I'm talking about," Dagg growled.

"No really, I don't. What ring?" Crumby asked again.

"Yeah, I don't know what you're talking about either," Flipple said to Dagg.

"Both of you know what I'm talking about. The ring I took from Karisma is gone."

Crumby laughed. "She's must've stole it back when you weren't looking."

"It's not funny." Dagg snapped his jaws toward Crumby.

"Yes it is." Crumby held his stomach, and laughed harder. "It's hilarious if you think about it. Here, a human tree sneaks up on you, steals her own ring back from you, a dinosaur of all things, and now you want us to tell you where the ring is. Obviously, she snuck in here, with her pearly snow white teeth, and leafy feet, and stole her ring back."

"It's not funny, and if you don't stop laughing, I'm going to swat you so hard, you're never going to stop spinning," Dagg roared again.

"Look, Dagg's right, Crumby. It's not funny that Karisma took the ring back. It was probably powerful and laced with magic, which would only help strengthen our side of the land. Now if she took it back, the land of Panora will win the Great War."

"So what?" Crumby snapped at him. "I don't care who wins, as long as I survive, and I will. Flies have a way of surviving anything."

"I wouldn't be so sure about that, Crumby," Flipple said. "Besides, we've got other things to talk about. Like the wind that blew us around earlier."

"What about it?" Crumby asked bored.

"Well, I'll tell you. If Valtron is the one responsible for the wind, then we're all in trouble, and I'm not just referring to the kingdom of Walby, but the land of Panora and Vanduesa too."

"How do you figure?" Crumby wanted to know. "After all the kingdom of Walby is the land of the dark magic, just like the land of Elvi is."

"That's true. But Valtron isn't nice. He doesn't care whom he has to destroy to get what he wants. He'll do it, and if it means he destroys us in the process, then so be it."

"I don't believe you. You mean to tell me, this Valtron will end our world because he doesn't want to share the power with another dark magic?"

"That's exactly what I'm saying. I should know I was raised in Vanduesa. I know the rules the laws and the people well enough to know how it all works." Flipple was serious.

"So what? I don't think you know everything, especially when it comes to things like this. Now I think the three of us should find Watesa, and ask her what's going on."

"If we could find Watesa, don't you think we would've already?" Dagg asked annoyed.

"I don't know. You're pretty stupid for a dinosaur." Crumby laughed.

Dagg was annoyed. "You're irritating."

"Yeah, well at least I'm not a huge, ugly beast like you," Crumby said.

"Listen, both of you stop. Now, let's talk about what we're going to do. We can't seem to find our queen, and that makes me think something happened to her when Valtron cast the wind spell upon the land," Flipple sounded alarmed.

"So what? Maybe he did take her. Now at least all her people in the kingdom of Walby can decide who gets to rule the land. Personally, I think it should be me." Crumby puffed out his chest.

"I'd never vote for you, fly," Dagg growled again.

"So what? Everyone else would."

When the three of them heard the clap of thunder, they stopped talking, and lifted their eyes toward the sky. "What was that?" Dagg asked.

"It was the meeting of the two lands," Flipple answered.

"How do you know?" Crumby asked.

"Because thunder only rumbles that loud, when war in the clouds is about to start."

Yeah, right." Crumby laughed, until he heard the clap ring loudly over the kingdom of Walby again.

"Come on, we need somewhere safe to hide." Flipple urged as he led the other two down the path that led to the woods.

CHAPTER TWENTY-SEVEN

Rain realized too late that they were trapped. All her friends looked at her helplessly.

"What're we going to do now? You know it's only a matter of time before Valtron gets here," Volcano said.

"Yeah, we know," Windy, answered.

"I can't believe Valtron did this to us." Tornado was furious.

"I can, and I should've expected it," Rain sighed.

"How could you, it's not like you knew what he was going to do. We thought for sure he was going after Karisma," Sparkle whispered.

As Rain stared through the glass on the square box they were trapped in, she was amazed, that they continued to float. "You all know that he was going after Karisma, but apparently something went wrong with his plan."

"Yeah, I should say." Volcano laughed. "The kids obviously made something go wrong with Valtron's plan."

"Yeah," Rain sighed, then, looked at her friends. "Any spells we cast will bounce off the glass, and backfire on us." Rain shook her head, as she stared at the land of Panora. "I wish grandmother Culver, or Firey would intervene. I'm sure they know we've been captured."

"Do you think Karisma knows?" Wings asked hopeful.

"I doubt it. She's still but a child, young in her magic," Rain answered.

"Yeah, but she keeps shocking us all the time with the things she does," Windy volunteered, trying to cheer Rain.

"Yes, but even this is too much for her, I'd imagine." Rain turned, looked at her friends, and tried to smile.

Sparkle looked at Wings. "Have you been able to pick up anything on where Petrello is?"

"No. I'm sorry. Everything is static." Wings looked at her with compassion.

"It's okay, and not your fault," Sparkle said, "anyway, I'm up for suggestions, so does anyone have any?" Sparkle asked all of them.

"None. I'm fresh out." Wings shrugged.

"Me too," Volcano sighed.

"Well, let's not give up," Hurricane said.

"Okay, so what should we do?" Rain looked at her.

"For one, let's not forget who we are. For two, let's use the time we have to create a plan that will get us out of here," Hurricane offered.

"Okay," Rain agreed. "Let's form a circle."

Firey stopped the good people of Panora, and then looked at each of them sadly.

"I carry news that Rain, Windy, Volcano, Hurricane, Tornado, Wings, and Sparkle have been captured by Valtron."

"That's unheard of," Zambler yelled. "Where are they?"

"The news speaks that they're still in the land of Panora toward the clouds," Firey said.

"Let's go get them," Tomkin shouted.

"We can't. The news I'm receiving speaks of a glass square so thick, any magic cast upon it shall indeed backfire."

"That's ridiculous. It's time for a meeting," Zambo looked at everyone.

"I agree," Flam blurted.

"Me too." Wrenny nodded.

"We haven't time," Firey said. "The news is that Valtron will be here on the land of Panora, soon," her words hung in the air with finality.

"We can't give up. What're you suggesting?" Zambler stared at her.

"I'm suggesting my good people in the land of Panora that you all leave me here. Go find a hiding place, and wait until he is finished."

"No way. I'm not leaving you," Zambo said.

"Me either." Zambler walked over to stand beside her."

"Well, I'm certainly not leaving my queen. How could you even suggest such a thing?" Tomkin jumped up then down.

"I agree that's just not the correct thing to do," Tibbs agreed.

"Yes it is, because my friend's Valtron wants me and Rain. When he arrives any resistance will be met with force."

"I don't care. If that's how it's going to be, then he shall fight against all of us," Zambler shouted, and Firey knew he meant what he said.

"I'm sorry I can't let you do that." When she raised her hand, she was too quick for the good people of Panora, and soon they all vanished, leaving Firey standing alone.

Camille, Redilla, Petrello and Zuella all stared into the clear tree bark floating in front of them. To them the floating bark reminded them of a giant transparent, hollow log, encased in glass. Inside the log, floating in front of them, they watched Rain, Windy, Volcano, Tornado, Hurricane, Wings, and Sparkle.

"They've been captured. Valtron's on his way to get them," Camille said.

As they continued to stare, a leaf appeared next to the tree bark. The leaf was bluish in color, and trapped inside the leaf was Firey, wrapped in a windstorm of some sort.

"He's going to take all of them?" Zuella asked shocked.

"It appears that way," Camille whispered.

"But we must do something." Petrello was clearly upset.

"I think we should, but what? We're not strong enough to stand up to Valtron," Camille said.

"So, what, we don't even try?" Petrello asked.

"I never said that," Camille answered.

"Yeah, she's only trying to think the whole thing through. I don't know what we're going to do now. Firey is our queen, and Rain is the mother of Karisma," Redilla stated.

"Oh my goodness, Redilla. That's it. I'll bet Valtron can't catch Karisma, that's why he's going after them," Camille said.

"I think you're right. But we don't know that for sure," Petrello stated.

"Yes, we do. If Karisma was captured we'd see three pieces of nature, but we've only seen two."

"Are you sure about that?" Petrello asked.

"Positive. That's one of the ways we can check on one another, and you know that," Zuella said.

"True, but what if he's blocked Karisma from showing herself. It's been known to happen."

All of them stared at Petrello for a moment, and then Camille shook her head. "It's not possible. Karisma could still let us know something. Her powers are greater than Valtron's, and if he's captured her, she would let us know," Camille sounded convinced.

"Well, if he doesn't have her and the other five, then where are they?" Petrello demanded.

"We don't know," Camille answered. "But at least Valtron hasn't captured them. Now come on, let's see if we can find them."

"Good idea," Petrello said through clenched teeth.

"What is it now?" Camille asked him.

"I just keep thinking had we involved all of them the first time, they'd all be here with us right now."

"Nonsense. You don't know that anymore then we do," Camille scolded him.

"Yes, I do, and even if they weren't right here, at least if they'd been invited when the four of us talked, we would've seen what happened. Now here we are clueless."

"You need to focus, Petrello. We all know how important all of them are, but there's no sense in crying over fallen leaves because it's getting us absolutely nowhere," Camille smiled.

"Yeah, so you've said more than once," Petrello's voice was snippy. "So pixie angels and fairy what's the plan?"

"Come, Petrello, we shall tell you." Camille looked briefly at him, nodded at Redilla and Zuella, and they all took flight.

As Firey waited for Valtron, she knew she had made the correct decision when she made the good people of Panora disappear.

Then, she let Rain, and all the others know that she'd been captured.

Now at least she knew Valtron would never find the good people of Panora. Rain and her friends, yes. He had already trapped them because they had been separated from Firey when it all happened.

The same would be true for Camille, Redilla, Zuella, and Petrello. If all of them had been with her when she cast her final spell, she would have nothing to worry about, but unfortunately, none of them were, and now they were on their own.

The spell of invisibility and protection she had cast over the good people in Panora, had weakened her though, and now she knew there was nothing left to do but wait for the dark king of Elvi to arrive.

Watesa couldn't believe she had been trapped for so long. It had taken forever for her to finally get free.

As she stared at the tree, which somehow had tangled around her, she suddenly shifted her purple eye toward the sky, and knew it was only a matter of time before Valtron arrived.

When she heard the clap of thunder, it made her jump, but she knew what it meant.

There was only one thing that could make the thunder roll deeply; it meant a war in the clouds was starting. Now Watesa knew the outcome wouldn't be good.

If a war was brewing between the higher powers of the world, she knew she was insignificant against it.

As the thunder rolled again, Watesa started walking toward her dwelling.

When Karisma landed, she shook her head, looked around, and saw a leaf dancing in front of her, along with a tree bark, which reminded her of a hollow log.

In the see through tree bark, she saw her mother, Windy, Hurricane, Volcano, Wings, Tornado, and Sparkle trapped in the thick glass box, which was floating in the air.

In the bluish leaf, she saw Firey trapped in a vicious windstorm. Her blond hair was flying around her helpless face, and Karisma saw the tears, which soaked Firey's cheeks.

The message she received was Valtron had captured them. She abruptly looked at her friends with misery in her eyes.

"Do you see all of them?" Karisma asked not sure what she was feeling. A part of her felt helpless against what she was seeing, another part felt fury.

"Yeah, we see them," Boulder sighed.

"Yeah, and now what'd we do?" Dagger asked shrugging his shoulders.

"What I want to know is where we are," Raven blurted.

"Yeah, I want to know the same thing," Sunburst agreed.

As the six of them looked around, the realized they were back in the abandoned building and Boulder was the first one to speak, "No way, how did we end up back here?"

"Where?" Sunburst asked.

"Oh my gosh, I can't believe it. Now what're we going to do?" Karisma asked hysterically.

"Where are we?" Raven wanted to know, as she looked around.

"Yeah, what is this place?" Mountain asked, as he looked around the building.

"I'll tell you where we are," Boulder offered. "We're in the abandoned warehouse in Plymouth that started this whole mess."

"You mean we're back on earth?" Dagger was shocked.

"Yeah, I think so." Boulder nodded.

"But how is that possible?" Karisma asked, walking toward the door.

As Boulder followed, he pushed the door back, and all of them realized they had been teleported back to earth somehow.

When Karisma turned around, she ran back over to the leaf, which was still floating, along with the tree bark, then she rubbed the green jewel she had in her hand, and asked her mother, and Firey to help her return to the land of Panora.

When nothing happened, she looked at her friends, and then walked over to the corner where she and Boulder had originally found the treasure chest.

She saw it nestled, as it had been, when they first found it under the floor boards.

"Help me unbury the treasure," she sounded rushed, as she began throwing the wood off it.

"What're we going to do?" Sunburst asked. "Did you see our mother's, they're trapped by Valtron, and here we are safe and sound back on earth. I don't think so. Somehow we have to figure out a way to return."

"I know," Karisma said.

"But how are we going to do that? If the portals are closed, we'll never make it back," Mountain said.

"First, let's get the treasure unburied," Karisma told them still tossing the wood off the chest. "Then, we'll see what we can come up with. Maybe there is another jewel that will help transport us back to the land of Panora."

"And if there isn't?" Dagger asked softly.

"Then I'd say everyone back there is in a world of trouble. Especially if I'm one of the highest powers of the land." Karisma looked sternly at them. "Now help me."

As the six of them uncovered the chest, Karisma looked at Boulder, then he lifted the lid, and all of them stepped back.

"Where did all the jewels go?" Karisma asked frantically.

"I don't know," Boulder answered, "maybe someone else found out about them, and took them."

"No, no, that's not what I want to hear." Karisma shook her head, and stared into the chest before she knelt down, and ran her hands along the bottom of it. She wanted to find a trapped door, or something to lead them back to Panora.

When her search revealed it was nothing more than a waste of time, she lifted her eyes to her friends. "We need to figure this out quickly. I'm afraid if we don't get back there quickly, something bad is going to happen."

"I agree." Raven told her. "Now you need to stand up, the color of the leaf just changed. The tree bark just became a different color."

As Karisma stood, she walked over, and looked at the people she loved. The tree bark was slowly closing, and turning black.

The leaf was evaporating, and turning red. "Do something," she shouted.

"What should we do?" Boulder asked, watching what was happening.

"I don't care, think of something," Karisma demanded.

"Okay, what would you like us to do?" Mountain asked frustrated.

"I don't care. Look at them, they're disappearing, and I don't like the colors, and the fact that we're not going to be able to see them. I like it even less that we're all here back on earth, and not in the land of Panora, or Walby for that matter. Now, I feel totally lost, almost as if earth is foreign to me now."

"Karisma, you need to settle down," Boulder said, "getting all upset, and letting your mind spin around all that's going on, is going to distract you. If you're distracted, all of us will be too."

Karisma looked at him. "You're right. But right now, I need all of you to think for me."

"Yeah, we got that," Dagger said, "but right now, in light of our circumstances, we should go back to your house Karisma, and try to figure out what we're going to do. Besides, I think once all of us get there, we should eat, then take showers, and try to decide how to get back."

"I can't believe you're thinking of a shower and food right now, Dagger." Sunburst was angry. "Here people that we love need our help, and that's all you can think about?"

"I don't think he meant it like that," Mountain interrupted. "I just think that Dagger meant if we had full stomachs, with real food, instead of the leaves and berries we've been living on, along with nice showers, it would help clear our heads. Then we could sit down, and logically plan what we're going to do."

"I don't know how any of that is going to help," Raven said softly. "In my opinion, all of that is just going to take up a lot of time that we don't have. Besides, I'd much rather stay in the swing of things. If we take all the time you're both suggesting I'd for one would feel really guilty. I mean think about it. People we love need us, but yet both of you want to eat, and shower. It so typical, and selfish."

All of them looked at Raven surprised she said what she did. Usually Raven was the nicest one out of all of them.

"Look, I didn't mean it to sound selfish. I was just trying to calm Karisma down. I thought if we had somewhere to go, what could it hurt if we ate, to keep our strength up, and everyone of us needs a shower, but never mind. I think I'll just stand here with my mouth shut, and not offer my opinion anymore." Dagger looked hurt which was unusual for him.

"We know you're only trying to help," Karisma blurted feeling bad. "But let's form a circle, holding our jewels, and chant about going back to Panora. If it doesn't work, then I think we should go back to my house, as Dagger said. Then we'll eat, and shower, then try to figure out a different way to get back and help the others."

"Okay." Boulder agreed as he held his hands out.

As the others gathered around, they formed a circle, linked arms, closed their eyes, and chanted.

When nothing happened, they tried it again.

Again, when they opened their eyes, they were still standing in the warehouse.

"Maybe we're doing it wrong," Sunburst said.

"Wrong?" Karisma lifted her brow. "This is the way we've done it since we learned our magic."

"Yeah, but maybe it only works this way on the land of Panora, and Walby. Maybe we've got to do it differently here on earth." Raven was serious.

"Well how did you and Boulder do it, when you came here in the first place?" Dagger asked.

Karisma looked at Boulder.

"Well, we looked in the chest, picked up a couple jewels, saw different things like the knights, and the little men with the curly shoes, then Karisma picked up the green jewel, and everything became blurry, and before we knew it, we were in the land of Walby. Or wherever it was we ended up." Boulder shrugged.

"Okay, so why did you pick the green jewel, Karisma?" Mountain asked.

For a moment Karisma felt embarrassed, and then felt her cheeks turn pink. "I picked the green jewel because it reminded me of Boulder's eyes." She stated looking at her friends for their reaction.

When none of them said anything, Karisma was surprised. She knew before all this happened, had she said something like she just did; it would've been met with the usual teasing they were all capable of doing.

"Okay," Raven spoke, looking at all of them. "Maybe you should put the green jewel back in the chest, and you and Boulder should do what you did before."

"I don't think it'll work," Karisma answered.

"Why not?" Dagger asked.

"Because the rest of the jewels are gone. In order to recreate what we did, all the jewels would have to still be in the chest, but they're not. I'm afraid if I let go of the green stone, that it will disappear, and then what?"

"Then we'd be in more trouble then we already are," Mountain answered.

"Exactly. Which is why I won't chance it," Karisma answered.

"So what's left then?" Raven asked.

"There's nothing left. I guess now we'll go to my house and do what Dagger suggested. Maybe once we've eaten and showered our minds won't feel so foggy," Karisma said.

"Then let's go." Boulder walked back over to the door and pointed.

When the others looked, they realized that the black tree bark and the red leaf were gone. In their place, they saw an orange path.

Karisma ran over to it. "Do you think we should take the path?" She looked at Boulder.

"No, personally I think it's a trick."

"Who would do that?" Karisma asked.

"Valtron. I wouldn't trust it just yet. Now let's go. I want to stick to our plan. Besides, if we jump on the path, it might lead us directly to him, and even the land of Elvi." Boulder stared at the orange path, thinking.

"You're right." Karisma looked at Boulder.

"I know. If you think about it, we know everyone we love is trapped. I'll bet you this orange path is Valtron's way of getting us back to the land of Walby. He wants you, Karisma, and I believe he would stop at nothing to get you."

"You're right." Karisma nodded.

"Yeah, and I agree with both of you." Dagger looked first at the orange path, then at his friends. "It wouldn't surprise me if Valtron's set a trap for all of us. It makes sense. You're the one he's after Karisma. Now that we're back here, he's powerless. Unless he can come here, and that I seriously doubt."

"Why do you doubt it?" Karisma wanted to know.

"Because if he could, he would already be here. Valtron doesn't strike me as being patient. He strikes me as someone who stops at nothing to get what he wants, and he doesn't care who he hurts in the process."

"You mean he's like you were, before we ended up in Panora?" Sunburst stated, and realized too late she had said it a loud. "I'm so sorry. I didn't mean it."

"Yes you did, and you're right. He's like I use to be before this whole thing started. Now, I'm different. I know what words can do to someone, and I've tried to change. Unfortunately, Valtron doesn't care. He wants Karisma and that's it."

Karisma linked arms with him, and smiled. "I'm proud of you Dagger." She kissed his cheek. "Now let's go."

"Wait." Sunburst walked over, kissed Dagger's cheek, and then squeezed his hand. "I'm with Karisma. You've done a good job."

"Thanks." Dagger smiled.

Then Raven walked over, smiled, and kissed his lips, shocking everyone, as she blushed. "You're the best, and you always have been."

He smiled shyly at her. "Thanks Raven, I think the same thing about you."

As they left the warehouse, Valtron slammed his pixie angel in the head, and glared. "They figured it out. They're too smart for their own good. Now it's time for the second plan, and by the time, I'm done, they're going to wish they had jumped on the orange path, I just offered. Now it's too late. They've made their choice. Let's get ready," he growled at his army, as he walked away to prepare.

CHAPTER TWENTY-EIGHT

Rain looked at her friends, heard the whisper in her ear, and then nervously twisted her hands in front of her.

"What is it?" Sparkle asked concerned.

"It's Karisma. I've just gotten word that Valtron has her."

"What?" Volcano asked devastated.

"Yeah, I guess she was captured in the land of Walby." Rain felt the tear hit her cheek, then she turned slammed her hand against the glass, and screamed.

"Are you sure that's what you heard?' Windy asked, as she walked over and put her arm around Rain's shoulder.

"Yes. I know what I heard, and the message was loud and clear."

"What did they say?" Hurricane asked.

"That Valtron took Karisma along with all the children, and that they're heading to the land of Elvi." Rain stared out the thick glass, then back at her friends.

"I wish there was something we could do," Tornado mumbled.

"Yeah, me too. I guess the only thing left to do, is try to cast our last spell," Rain said.

"But you know if we do that, once we get to the land of Elvi, we'll be powerless to help the children," Wings answered.

"You're right," Rain sighed, "I'm just so angry over how

things turned out."

"We all are. Had we known what was going to happen to our children, we would've never granted permission to grandmother Culver to take them here, and teach them of their heritage." Tornado looked out over the land. "Wait a minute." She moved closer to the glass to get a better look. "I don't think we're in Panora anymore."

As the rest of them gathered around the thick, clear glass, Rain threw her hand over her mouth. "Where are we?" she mumbled the question.

"It looks like we're now in the land of Elvi." Sparkle rubbed Rain's back. "I'd know this land anywhere. It's where they took my husband Trod, when they killed him."

"Oh my gosh, you we're there?" Rain asked shocked by what Sparkle just told her.

"Yes, they made me watch."

"That's awful. I'm sorry," Windy offered.

"Thanks, and yes it was awful. But I don't want to think about it right now. What I do want to think about is how to get out of here. This land is covered in wickedly, bad magic. Look down there; see all the fires, and how strong the wind is blowing? They call this the land of Elvi, and I can see why. This land has virtually no color, besides the color of the fire. Everything else is black and white. To live here would drive me insane."

"Me too. I mean if you look at it, there's nothing comforting about it. They're fires everywhere, and where there is none the land is barren, stripped of all color, much like the land of Walby," Rain commented.

"Yeah, but it's worse here because of all the fires," Hurricane said.

When they saw Rain lift her hand, they all fell quiet, watched her concentrate, then she slowly lowered her hand. "Firey is being brought here too, and as soon as Watesa is found, she'll be joining us."

"So he's taking everyone?" Volcano asked confused.

"Yes, I guess so."

"But what would he want Watesa for?" Tornado asked looking confused.

"To strip her of her magic," Rain answered.

"But why. Doesn't he have enough dark magic?" Windy asked.

"Apparently, he wants it all at least that's what they're telling me." Rain looked at them. "All of you realize what this means right?"

One at a time, all the women nodded, before Sparkle broke the silence.

"I would love to be strong enough to put Valtron out of his misery," her voice was full of contempt.

"All of us would, Sparkle. Unfortunately, because of what happened with Karisma, and her being as stubborn as she is, she made a choice to wander, and not obey the rules and laws set forth in Panora, and now sadly we're all going to pay dearly for it," Rain said. "I'm sorry my daughter caused all this to happen to us."

"Don't be ridiculous. If Karisma wouldn't have done it, one of the other ones surely would have." Tornado smiled.

"Yeah, but still, my Karisma has never been one to live by the rules." Rain smiled.

"Yeah, and neither do the rest of the children," Hurricane offered. "Face it, it's always been what one does, they all do, and they don't worry about being in trouble, until five minutes before they come home."

"I envy all of you," Sparkle said, "all your children had one another growing up, and I wish Petrello would've had that same opportunity."

"Well, we do too," Tornado said, "but unfortunately because of the situation, he couldn't be allowed to have it. But that's the past, and the future is looming fast ahead. Now ladies let's get our mind back to the land of Elvi. We're trapped on the darkest land in this world, and I for one want to know what we plan on doing about it."

"There's nothing we can do, until Valtron decides it's time for our glass square box to land. Until then, I guess we continue to float helplessly around this grim, dark forsaken land, and hope for the best," Rain said.

"Yeah, but at least when we land we'll be able to gather more information then we have now, and hopefully somehow, we'll be able to locate the others," Hurricane answered.

"Yes, hopefully, but we all know Valtron isn't nice, wherever he's hidden the children, will be in a place difficult to find. If he's even brought them here," Sparkle said.

"Oh he has. If the message Rain received is accurate, Valtron brought them here, to watch us squirm," Windy was adamant when she said it.

"You're right. He'll want to see us squirm."

"And we will, which I'm sure will give him great joy," Wings said.

When Sparkle sighed, they looked at her, noted the sadness in her eyes, the worry lines around her mouth. "I wish I knew where Petrello was."

"We do too, Sparkle," Rain said. "I don't know what's worse, knowing that your child was captured by the darkest magic in the land, or not knowing anything at all. Although at this point, I'd think I'd be thankful that he hasn't been captured with the rest."

"Maybe he has been, and we don't know it yet." Sparkle looked out over the grim land of Elvi.

"That could be, but I'm pretty sure I would've seen him with the rest," Wings answered.

As Sparkle nodded, Rain felt compassion for her. She knew it was difficult either way. Even though she knew where Karisma and the other five children were, it didn't make it any easier, then not knowing at all.

Rain turned, stared over the grim, bleak land of Elvi, and wondered if Petrello was all right, how the other six children were doing, and then she wondered if any of them would survive all the dark peril, which lay ahead.

As the six children walked down the street to Karisma's house, she stopped in front of it, stared at her friends, then back at her house.

Now her house looked strange to her, and so did everything else on earth.

When she turned once again to glance at her friends, she looked worried.

"What is it?" Boulder asked her.

"I wonder if my dad's home, or if he's at work." Karisma laughed, but it sounded forced. "I don't even know what day it is."

"None of us do, so I guess there's only one way to find out," Raven said.

As the six of them walked up to the door, Karisma found the spare key, unlocked the front door, and all of them went in.

The house was quiet, and as Karisma walked through it, they all noticed the dining room. The chairs were toppled over, and burnt, white candles littered the table.

She looked at her friends, but none of them spoke as she continued inspecting the house. She noticed her parent's bedroom door was partially opened.

As she walked down the hall towards it, she peeked in the room, and saw her dad encased in a block of ice on the bed. The room was deathly cold, and as Karisma rubbed her arms, she went over to the bed, and stared at her dad through the ice. For a moment she felt like crying, but she knew right now she had to be strong. "Do you think he's alive?" she whispered.

"Yes, at least I do," Dagger answered.

"Why do you think he's in ice?" Karisma dragged her eyes away from her dad to look at her friends.

"I don't know." Boulder shook his head.

"Me either," Sunburst said.

"Yeah, this is really weird," Mountain stated.

"I know," Karisma whispered still rubbing her arms. "Do you think we should do something?"

"No," Raven shook her head.

"Why?" Karisma was startled.

"Because I wouldn't do anything until we know what's going on. Now let's go back down to the kitchen, get some food, and since they're three bathrooms, let's start the showers, then we'll all feel better, and after that we'll talk about what to do," Sunburst said.

"Sounds like a good idea," Dagger agreed. "Now while everyone goes to the kitchen, I'm jumping in the shower. I feel nasty. It's been days since I've had an earthly shower, and then I'll eat."

"Yeah, I call second bathroom," Sunburst blurted.

"And I'll take the last," Mountain said.

"Okay, while you're all in the shower, I'll go find something for all of us to eat." Karisma turned, walked out of the room, down to the kitchen, and then started making food.

"Do you think we'll get back?" Boulder asked as he helped her with the sandwiches.

"I hope so. I can't stand even being here. I know bad things are happening in Panora, and here I sit, on earth getting ready to stuff myself with food, and then take a nice long shower. Talk about feeling guilty."

"Well don't," Raven scolded gently. "We've all been through a lot, and obviously, someone wanted us back on earth. The funny thing is I haven't figured out whom yet."

"I don't know that we'll ever know," Karisma sighed.

"Oh I think we will, which is why even on earth we have to be careful." Boulder was serious.

"You don't think those people and creatures will come here, do you?" Karisma looked at Boulder.

"They could. I wouldn't put anything past them."

"Me either," Raven agreed.

When the three finished making sandwiches, they took a shower, and less than an hour later, all of them felt better.

"Now what?" Karisma asked from the sofa where she was sitting.

"Now we need to figure out how to get back," Raven answered.

"Yeah I know. What's bothering me is the dining room. I mean there are burnt, white candles on the table, and all the chairs are tipped over. What'd you think it means?" Karisma looked at each of them.

Boulder shrugged. "It could mean anything. What we need to do is find out if your mom wrote anything down about the land of Panora. If she did that would be helpful."

"Yeah right. Like she would," Dagger blurted.

"Yeah for real. I don't think she would because what if my dad found it?"

"True, but we don't know if he knows about Panora or not," Sunburst offered.

"Yeah, but still, if he was a part of that world, I would think he would've arrived like my mom did." Karisma nodded as if agreeing with herself.

"Not necessarily," Raven said. "I mean we all know our mother's are in Panora, but none of our father's." She stood, and then paced the living room, before she snapped her fingers, and looked at them. "I think we should go to Boulder's house. It right around the block."

"For what?" Boulder asked.

"To see where your dad is. If he's encased in ice, then we know our mother's more than likely left them that way, when they ventured to the land of Panora."

"But why would they do that to them?" Karisma asked.

"Who knows? That's what we'll find out eventually. Now let's go." Raven started walking over to the door.

"She's got a point with what she said. At least if Boulder's dad is the same way, we'll know it's somehow connected to what's going on." Dagger stood.

As the others agreed, they walked the short distance to Boulder's house, and when they entered, Boulder went directly to his parent's room. Lying on the bed encased in ice was his father.

"See. I told you." Raven smiled.

"Yeah you did. Now what does it mean?" Boulder asked.

"I don't know this whole thing is too strange for me to figure out," Karisma moaned.

"Well, let's get back to your house, Karisma, and try to figure it out," Mountain said, as he led the way.

———— ◈ ————

When Firey was led to the land of Elvi, she closed her eyes against the pallor of it. She knew what Valtron was capable of doing, and she was helpless to stop it.

As she was dropped suddenly, it jarred her entire body. Then she heard the dark, sinister laughter. "So we meet again," Valtron's voice boomed loudly in the darkness of the room.

"Yes, Valtron, we do," Firey answered. "Now why don't you tell me why I'm here?"

Valtron laughed again. "No. Why don't you tell me where Karisma is?"

"I don't know," Firey sighed.

"You're lying to me. You know where she is."

"No I really don't."

"Well then perhaps I shall tell you where she's at."

Firey waited in the darkness for him to speak.

"She's back on that dreadful planet she came from. Now I want to know who put her there," Valtron yelled.

"I don't know," Firey answered, as a slight smile touched the corner of her mouth. She was secretly pleased that Karisma had slipped back through a portal, and wasn't in this dreadful land.

"Well, I see your not cooperating. So, I'll have my guard take you to your quarters. You'll forgive me if I don't feed you first." He laughed. "Oh, and you'll forgive me if the accommodations arc less then what your comfortable with."

Firey stood still, and didn't answer.

"Do you want to say anything to make me change my mind, before I decide your fate?" he asked her snidely.

"No," Firey answered.

"Very well, have it your way." Then he called Mumu his guard. "Take her to her quarter when that is done; bring me the rest of them so that I can decide what's going to be done to them."

"Very well, my King." Mumu bowed then lifted his fingers, and Firey felt her feet leave the ground, as Mumu took her to her quarters.

As Rain and the others waited, they felt the chill slide over their bodies, and each one shuttered.

"He's coming," Rain whispered.

"How do you know?" Hurricane asked.

"Because I can feel him, and so can you," Rain answered.

When they heard the snap of glass, they felt the entire box, lift, and then fall hard to the floor.

"Sorry. I really must teach my men how to land better." Valtron laughed, as his red eyes glowed with hatred.

When none of the women said anything, he glared at them. "Which of you is responsible for Karisma going back to earth?" he blurted, paced, and then threw a fireball at them, which melted the box they had been kept in.

When none of the women answered, he repeated the question. Still no one answered.

"I can see you're all as cooperative as your queen. It's a shame really. The only thing I'm asking is who is responsible that's all."

When all of them stared at him, they watched him change into a handsome, young man. His scraggly gray hair, turned black and curly, and touched his shoulders. His once red eyes were suddenly startling blue. "Well apparently none of you ladies are going to tell me what I want to know about Karisma. So I guess I'll just go to earth, and find out what happened for myself." He laughed. "What? Don't you ladies like the way I look?" Valtron asked. "Well that's a shame then. I'm sure once I find Karisma, she'll appreciate it. After all, she's young, beautiful, and soon she and I will start our courtship. Then once four years pass, we shall be married. We will rule the world, as it should be ruled. Then our children will take over, and everything I've ever wanted shall be mine."

"She'll never let it happen!" Rain shouted at him, "You make me sick!"

"Finally, someone's spoken?" Valtron laughed again. "What's wrong Mom? Don't want to see your little girl married off? What, I'm not good enough for her?"

"No," Rain told him harshly.

"Well, I don't really care what you think." Valtron laughed. "Now I'd love to stay and chat, but I really must go. Thanks for the magic, by the way."

"What're you talking about?" Sparkle finally asked.

"Oh Sparkle. Is it really you? Why I haven't seen you since your husband was killed." He laughed. "Such a shame, but to answer your question, I'm talking about how I managed to steal all your powers, and none of you even realized it. Thanks for not using that one last spell before you entered the land of Elvi. It gave me even more power. I'm sorry ladies, you really didn't think I'd let you enter with your magic, did you?" He stared at them. "Well if you did, you've underestimated me. I've stripped all of you from your power, and I took everything your queen had too."

All of them remained silent because none of them knew what to do. If what he was saying was true, they were all powerless against him.

"Well, I shall leave now. Wish me luck on my journey. Tell me is Earth as beautiful as the land of Elvi? Or is it as dreadful as the colorful Panora?" He laughed again. "Well since none of you feel like talking, I've got something to do." Valtron lifted his hand, and the women watched him disappear.

When they felt their feet leave the floor, they floated roughly to the dungeon, where they were separated, and when the big, steel bars slammed closed, the women knew they were in serious trouble.

CHAPTER TWENTY-NINE

Before Valtron left the land of Elvi, he had one more stop to make. This one was to Watesa.

As he stood before her, he laughed. "You're useless, and I'm glad you're not in power anymore. Thank you so much for your magic. Now, I've got things to do." He stared at her. "If you'll excuse me, I'll have my guard show you to your quarters."

As Watesa stared, she was hoping one of the imbeciles from the land of Walby would be brave enough to come here and rescue her.

Before she was captured, she used her last bit of magic to let her people know what happened.

When she felt her body leave the floor, she floated roughly to her quarters. It was a tiny room, with a big, steel door.

As the door slammed, she knew her world was finished, and she knew that it was only a matter of time, before Valtron made all of them into his workers.

When she looked at the walls of her room, she realized it was only big enough for her to sit. If she tried to move, she wouldn't be able too.

Finally, she felt a tickle in her eye, and she closed it, and fell fast asleep.

As Rain and the rest of the women sat in the dungeon, none of them spoke.

They were all lost in their own thoughts of what Valtron had told them.

As Rain stood, she paced, and wondered if Karisma was back on earth. If she was, Rain hoped she would still be careful.

Right now, there was nothing Rain could do to help warn her daughter. Despite the fact that Karisma was stubborn, she knew her daughter would be no match for the mighty Valtron. Not now that he had stolen all their magic, plus the magic of the queens.

As she thought about her daughter, she knew how Karisma was. She was definitely street smart, and after her time spent in Panora, Rain hoped that she had become worldly smart, as well.

The worst part about the whole thing was Rain knew that Karisma and all the children were on their own.

She ran a hand through her hair, when she realized that if Karisma were on earth, maybe her magic would fail her.

As she sat down on the floor, she felt the tingle in her eyes, and knew a spell had been cast over all of them, and soon she was sleeping.

As Camille flew over the land of Walby, she halted, when she received the message.

"There's news from grandmother Culver," Camille said.

"I didn't think she was allowed to do that since we're trapped in the land of Walby," Petrello blurted, as they all stopped.

"She isn't, as long as all is well." Camille looked at him.

"What happened?" Petrello asked, as his heart leaped in his chest.

"The news is very bad," Camille answered, listening.

"What is it?" Petrello demanded.

Camille held up her hand to silence him, and Petrello watched the grim expression on her face.

As he looked at Redilla and Zuella, he noted the worry in their eyes as well.

Finally, Camille looked at them. "The news coming in speaks of many captures."

"Who's been captured?' Petrello cut her off.

"If you'll be hushed for longer than one second, I'll tell you." Camille glared at him. "Now quit interrupting."

Petrello nodded, and then waited.

"As I was saying the news is bad. The land of Elvi has captured Firey."

"When?" Zuella asked.

"I'm not finished yet," Camille said sternly.

"Sorry," Zuella fell quiet.

"Valtron has also captured Rain, Hurricane, Windy, Tornado, Volcano, Sparkle, and Wings. He's also captured Watesa."

"Where are they, and what can we do?" Petrello asked impatiently.

"They are being held on the dark land of Elvi."

"What about Karisma, and the rest of them?" Petrello asked.

"It is said that the children were transported through a portal back to the planet earth." Camille looked at them.

"That's good news at least." Petrello smiled.

"No, Petrello, it isn't. You see, grandmother Culver just informed me that Valtron also knows the whereabouts of Karisma and the other children. He's now on his way to earth."

"What?" Petrello looked at her upset. "What do you mean? How can he be allowed to enter Earth? I thought it was against the rules and laws governing all the lands."

"It is." Camille looked at him. "But Valtron is much too powerful now to be stopped. He's stolen everyone's magic, including more dark magic from Watesa. Now I'm sorry to report, he's unstoppable."

"No he's not." Petrello glared at her. "I can't believe you said that. The good people of the land in Panora still have the four of us, and there's got to be something we can do."

"Petrello there is nothing. Why even grandmother Culver just told me that."

"I don't care. If there's a way to get back to earth, then I demanding one of you to tell me how to do it," Petrello's voice was full of emotion.

"You won't be allowed to slip through the portal. Valtron's too powerful, and he's made sure no one gets in or out," Camille said sadly.

"Fine, then we travel to the land of Elvi, and fight there."

"We can't Petrello. The land is much too powerful." Camille looked at him. "We're all just as upset as you, but there's nothing we can do, but wait for the outcome."

"That's not fair. I refuse to wait, and do nothing. If that's what the three of you chose to do, then so be it."

"Listen Petrello, you must understand the power of magic," Redilla said.

"Yeah, I do. I also know Chesquat is traveling with the good people of Vanduesa. When will they arrive?"

Camille looked at the ground, then back at him. "They won't be. They too have been captured."

"Oh great, just great," Petrello shoved his hands in his pockets.

"Petrello, you must do as we say and continue to wait this out with us," Camille instructed him.

When the four of them heard the clap of thunder, they turned their eye toward the sky.

"The war in the clouds will take place within three weeks," Zuella said.

"How do you know?" Petrello asked.

"Because that's the news I just received."

"Who will the war involve?" Petrello asked.

"The Culvers and the Elvinights."

"But such a war has never taken place in all the years I've lived here, so why now?" Petrello asked.

"To regain power back over the lands," Zuella informed him.

"So what do we do right now?" Petrello was so mad, and impatient that he couldn't stand it a second longer.

"I've already told you, we wait for news, and instructions." Camille was agitated with him.

"No." Petrello lifted his hand, and before any of them could stop him, he was gone.

As Karisma heard the knock on the front door, she paused.

"Who do you think it is?" Boulder asked cautiously.

"I don't know," Karisma answered.

"Well I think we should answer it," Mountain said, walking over to it. He looked out the peephole. "It's Elise."

"Really?" Karisma asked excitedly.

"Yeah, really." Mountain smiled.

"Should we let her in for a minute?" Sunburst asked.

"No," Dagger answered.

"Why not?" Raven asked surprised. Elise was another one of their good friends.

"Do you really want her involved with what's going on?" Dagger stared at all of them.

"No, but what harm will it do to say hi." Karisma shrugged.

"A lot. She's going to want to come in. Then she's gonna want the latest gossip, and then she'll ask all of us where we've been, and what're we gonna say?"

"Just open the door," Karisma told him.

"No," Dagger said.

"Fine." Karisma breezed by him, pulled the door open, then smiled at her friend.

Elise was pretty. Her light brown skin, and shoulder length, black, silky hair, made her green eyes sparkle. "Thank goodness you're finally home. I've been worried you know." She hugged Karisma.

"Hi," she greeted the rest of her friends, and as she hugged them she noticed the worry in their eyes and the sadness on their face. "Is this a bad time?"

"No, don't be silly. There's never a bad time when it comes to seeing a friend." Karisma grabbed her hand, and then led her to the living room.

As Elise sat down, she felt uncomfortable. "Look, if I'm imposing I could come back later."

"No you're not imposing. But we do have a lot of things to get done," Dagger blurted.

"Yeah, we do," Mountain agreed.

"Do you want me to leave?" Elise asked.

"Well, it's not that we want you to leave, it's just that we're in the middle of something, and we really need to take care of it," Dagger's voice was rushed, as he stared at Elise then his friends.

"Well, okay." Elise stood.

"Nonsense, sit back down," Sunburst said, "so how are you, Elise?"

As Elise stood, she watched all her friends looking at each other, and knew she had barged in on something important. She had never had the bond the six of them shared, and a part of her envied it. "Look, obviously you're all busy. How about if I leave, and come back later?"

"No. I want you to stay," Karisma said, "I want your opinion on something."

"Okay." Elise hesitated. "What?"

"Well, what I'm going to tell you is top secret. You can't tell anyone." Karisma looked at her seriously.

"I won't," Elise said, still feeling uncomfortable because they were all behaving strange.

"Good. Now, sit down. This could take a while."

As Karisma stared at her friends, they knew she was going to tell Elise everything that had happened and let her.

When she was finally finished, they all watched Elise. First, she squirmed, then, she stared at them. "Oh my goodness, I can't believe what you've told me, and I don't know what to do to help."

"Actually, Elise, I told you everything because I wanted an outsider's opinion that I trusted."

"Okay." Elise twisted her hands. "What'd you what me to say?"

"Well for starters you could tell us what we should do." Karisma smiled.

"Yeah, that would be good because right now all of us are confused, and maybe you could help us figure it out," Sunburst said.

Elise stood. "First of all, I would search your mother's things, and find out if she kept a diary or anything talking about the land you mentioned."

"Panora?" Raven asked.

Elise shrugged. "Yeah, I guess."

"Look Elise, we all know how this sounds, but you've got to believe what we've told you," Mountain stated.

"I do, but it's not what I was expecting. Look, if I told all of you a story like the one Kimmy just told me, well, you'd all think I was losing it." She tried to smile, but couldn't pull it off. "Besides, if you ask me, it's all a little scary. I mean you're talking about magic and a completely different world then the one we live in. So, I'm sorry if I seem a little nervous. Like I said, I wasn't expecting what Kimmy just told me."

"We understand. But anyway, on to what you were saying," Mountain urged her to stay on track.

"Well, like I said, I think we should search your mother's room, and look for anything she might have written on the land you've been too." Elise smiled at Karisma.

"Okay." Raven nodded for her to continue.

"Then, I'd pay attention to everything happing around here while you're all on earth. I wouldn't go anywhere or do anything. I mean you don't know what that dark lord is capable of doing."

"True." Karisma smiled. "Oh, by the way, he's not a lord, he's a king. Do you think he might come here?" Karisma asked all of them.

"He could. If he planned to steal everyone's magic as you told me, then I say there's a good possibility that he'll try. You did tell me that he wants you, right, Kimmy?" Elise asked.

"Yes." She smiled.

"What?" Elise asked.

"I'm sorry I'm use to my given name on the land of Panora now."

"What?" Elsie asked confused.

"Yeah, we've all been given names from the land of Panora," Dagger said.

Elise held her hand up. "Okay, then tell me what they are."

"Mine's Karisma."

"They call me Boulder." Bobby smiled.

"Dagger." Dave tipped his head, and watched her smile.

"I'm Mountain," Manning sounded older then he was.

"My given name is Sunburst. Isn't that a pretty name?" She giggled.

Elise nodded.

"Mine's Raven."

"Okay, I'll try to remember, but I'm not guaranteeing it. Now let's go see what kind of notes your mother kept in her room," Elise said. When they all stood, they followed Karisma up the stairs toward the bedroom, in search of answers.

CHAPTER THIRTY

Petrello landed on earth, but he didn't know how he managed to get there, and had no idea where he was.

As he looked around, he read a strange sign, and thought it said, "Taco Bell", whatever that meant.

He looked around, and noticed many people standing in a line at a counter, and then he noticed how everyone in line was going up to the counter to talk to the person on the other side, and Petrello realized the whole situation was too busy for him.

When he saw other people sitting around funny looking things, he realized they were eating strange looking food.

Finally, he walked up to a group of kids. "Excuse me, could you tell me the location I'm at?" he asked.

One of the kids smirked. "Yeah, you're at Taco Bell."

"What's Taco Bell?" Petrello asked.

"You're playing with us right?" One of the kids laughed.

"What does playing with you mean?" Petrello was completely lost.

"Listen, weirdo, why don't you go bother someone else, before we tell the manager," another kid said.

"What's a manager? Is that like a king or queen?"

"Oh my gosh, I've heard everything now." One of the kids glared at him. "Go away."

Petrello shook his head, saw the doors leading out of the Taco Bell, and left.

As he started walking, he pictured Karisma in his head, held out his hand, and watched her photo slide out of his fingertips.

Then he turned around, marched back into Taco Bell, and found the group of kids again.

"Has anyone seen her?" Petrello asked holding up the picture of Karisma.

"Hey, I know her," someone from another table blurted.

"You do?" Petrello walked over to him.

"Yeah, I do."

"Do you know where I may find her?"

"Who are you?" the teenager asked.

"A friend." Petrello was glad he had paid attention when the human children talked.

"If you're a friend, I shouldn't have to tell you where to find her." The teenager eyed him critically.

"That's true. But I'm a newer friend of hers, and I was wondering if you could tell me where she's lives."

"What? No way, weirdo. Get lost."

"I'm already lost," Petrello said, making him laugh.

"Whatever. I'm not going to tell you where she is." The teenager eyed him, before he stood.

As Petrello watched him leave Taco Bell, he followed, cast a spell on the guy outside in the parking lot, and turned him into a toad, picked him up and stared at him. "Tell me where Karisma is, and I'll change you back into the rude human you are."

"Who are you?" the toad croaked.

"I told you a friend."

"Do you have a name?" the toad asked.

"Petrello."

"What?"

Petrello picked up the toad, and shook it hard. "You heard me. My name's Petrello. Now either you take me to where Karisma lives, or I'll toss you into traffic."

"Her name's Kimmy."

"Fine, whatever you say. Are you going to take me to her house?" he asked holding his arm out toward the rushing traffic.

"Yeah, just don't drop me."

"I won't. Now tell me which way to go."

When Petrello finally reached Karisma's house, he put the toad in his pocket, and passed through the front door.

When he didn't see anything, he floated up the steps, and heard the familiar voices coming out of one of the strange rooms. He floated over, and smiled. "I'm so glad I found all of you," Petrello blurted.

"Oh my gosh, thank goodness you're here." Karisma ran to him, and gave him a hug.

"I am too," Petrello said, pulling the toad out of his pocket. "What should I do with it?"

"With what? That toad?" Dagger asked.

"Well, he was a human, until he wouldn't tell me how to find you, Karisma. Then I had no choice but to turn him into a toad."

When they all laughed it felt good. "Well who is it and where did you find them?" Karisma asked.

"I found him in some place called, "Taco Bell," and for the life of me I can honestly say that was the strangest place I've ever seen."

Everyone laughed again, and then Karisma looked at Petrello. "Yeah, but that doesn't tell me who the toad is."

Petrello shrugged. "Some guy who was in Taco Bell who claimed he knew you, Karisma."

"I don't understand how he would know that you were looking for me?"

"Because I printed a picture of you, like this," Petrello concentrated and held out his hand as everyone watched a picture of Karisma shoot out of his fingertips. Petrello grabbed the picture and handed it to Karisma. "I showed your picture to a group of teenagers at Taco Bell and none of them knew you, but..." He jiggled the toad in his hand, "He did so I asked him where you lived and he told me to get lost. So I followed him outside when he left, and I asked him again where I could find you and he refused to tell me, so I turned him into a toad and held him out in oncoming traffic until he finally gave in and led me here."

"Oh, no, Petrello, how am I going to explain that to the toad?"

"What'd you mean?"

"What she means is what is she supposed to tell the toad? People on earth don't perform magic like that, unless you're a magician. So she wants to know how to explain to the toad what happened," Boulder said.

"She won't have to. I'll clear his memory of this and he won't remember anything."

"Well in that case, just take him outside and release him," Karisma said.

When he stared at her, she shrugged." What?"

"Are you all going to come with me?"

"Yeah, sure," Karisma answered.

"I'll go." Dagger looked at them. "Keep searching."

As he walked out of the room with Petrello, none of them saw the black shadow, which landed right outside the window, watching them.

When they heard the laughter fill the room, all of them stopped, looked around, and when they saw nothing, they continued their search.

As Valtron watched them, he smiled, and knew in just a little while he would confront them. First, he had something else to do.

Karisma continued to search, and she felt a cold chill flow

through her, so she spun around, looked at the window, but again saw nothing.

"What's wrong?" Boulder asked, as he noticed the worry around her eyes.

"Nothing except I feel like we're being watched." Karisma stared at the window.

"Do you think something's wrong?" Boulder asked.

"Yeah, do you think someone followed us back from Walby?" Sunburst asked.

"I don't know. I wish I knew more about my magic. If I did, I'd know for sure if someone followed us." Karisma looked nervous.

"Well if they did, we'll know soon enough." Mountain looked at the window. "I've got a feeling that whoever's making you feel this way, won't remain in the shadows long."

"You're right. So, for now I think all of us need to stay alert. I don't want any surprises," Karisma said.

———⸭《◉》⸭———

After Petrello changed the toad back into a person, the guy took off running down the street, and Petrello and Dagger laughed.

Then Petrello looked around outside, and his eyes stopped on the tree by the side of house.

"What is it?" Dagger asked him.

"We've got company." Petrello floated to the door.

"What'd you mean, we've got company?" Dagger asked.

"Just what I said. Someone else besides me, slipped through the portal."

"Who?" Dagger asked as the two of them climbed the stairs.

"I don't know yet. The vision isn't clear."

"How can that be?" Dagger asked. "I mean you've had magic for a long time, and were properly trained how to use it, so why can't you see who it is?" Dagger stopped Petrello right outside the door and waited for him to answer.

"Look, Dagger, I need to tell everyone at once what I think is going on, and who is here from the other side."

When Dagger nodded, they entered the room, and Petrello knew right away that Karisma already sensed the present.

"We need to talk," Petrello said.

"Okay." Karisma stopped searching, and then lifted her eyes to his. The others did the same.

"Gather close," Petrello said.

Once they were gathered, Petrello walked out to the hall and the others followed.

"I think someone from the other side managed to get through the portal. I think they're here."

"Who is it?" Karisma asked, nervously.

"I don't know yet. I told Dagger that I can feel whoever it is, but I can't see them."

"Why not?" Sunburst asked. "Aren't you one of the powerful ones from both sides of the land?"

"Yes, but that doesn't mean I can see who's here. The only thing I can do is tell you what I think."

"I agree with you, Petrello. I know someone's here. I felt it when I was in the bedroom," Karisma said, confirming what he was saying.

"Okay, so explain why you can't see who it is," Dagger demanded from Petrello.

"I believe I can't see them because they're more powerful then I am," his words struck a chord of fear in all of them.

"What'd you mean?" Karisma felt alarmed.

"Just what I said." Petrello nodded toward the bedroom. "Whoever is here is right outside the window. I believe they're in the tree."

"I feel it too," Karisma answered. "When we were searching the bedroom I felt a cold chill."

"Wait a second," Raven stopped them. "If you're not powerful enough to see who is lurking outside, then why can't Karisma see them? She's supposed to hold the highest powers of the land."

"Yeah, Raven, you're right. Unfortunately, though, all of you kept sneaking off, instead of properly training," Petrello said.

"So can't you teach her what she needs to know?" Boulder asked.

"No," his word hung in the air.

"Why?" Sunburst stomped her foot, then glared at him. "I don't understand."

"I can't teach her because I'm not her guide or her king."

"Okay, so how do we prepare?" Karisma asked.

"I'm not sure. I guess the best way is to keep searching the room, and hopefully you'll find something useful." Petrello lowered his head.

"Excuse me. I'm a little scared right now. I mean hello? I don't know what's going on, but if someone followed all of you from the other side, and now they're here, what's going to stop them from trying something on me? I don't have any magic," Elise sounded alarmed.

"Nothing." Petrello looked at her.

"Wrong answer, Buddy." Elise looked at all of them. "What happens if they take me?"

"Then we find you, and bring you back," Dagger answered.

"Yeah, right, okay. You mean like you did with your Mothers?"

"Ouch," Dagger answered.

"Look Elise, if you want to leave, we'll walk you home." Karisma offered feeling sorry for her.

"Not a good idea," Petrello stated. "She's been seen with us already. If we walk her home, and leave her alone, it won't stop whoever is here from taking her. I'm sorry, Elise, but you'll have to stay with us so we can try to protect you."

"Stay with you?" she asked surprised. "For how long?'

"Until we know it's safe to let you leave," Petrello answered.

"So how long will it take? A night, a week, a month, what?" She was now hysterical, and wished she would've never stopped by Karisma's house.

"For as long as it takes." Petrello was serious.

"What? Oh my gosh, I can't believe this." Elise stomped her foot, much the same way Sunburst always did, and Petrello wondered if that was a trait with human females.

"Well believe it. You're staying until this is over." Petrello's eyes pierced hers.

"Fine." She threw her hands in the air. "Then we better keep searching, and come up with a plan, and all of you had better protect me. Oh my goodness, I just want to go home. I'm scared because I don't know what's going on, and I'm not afraid to admit it either." She twisted her hands, and then looked at her friends.

"It's okay to be scared. We've all been there." Karisma smiled. "Now let's get back to our search."

As they reentered the room, Petrello's eyes rested on the bed. "Is that your father, Karisma?" He nodded toward the ice Karisma's dad was encased in.

"Yes."

"Typical," Petrello commented.

"What'd you mean, typical?" Karisma looked at him.

"What I mean is it's typical for human's to use the "frozen in time" spell, on their spouses, when they must leave earth."

"What does that mean?" Boulder wanted to know.

"The spell frozen in time means that when your father wakes up, it'll still be the exact same day it was when the spell was cast, and he went to sleep."

"I'm confused," Raven said.

"Me too," Elise agreed.

"You see, when Karisma's father wakes up, everything will be the same as it was before he had the spell cast upon him. He'll never realize that Karisma or her mother ever left. That's why the spell is called, "frozen in time." Petrello suddenly snapped his fingers. "Karisma, you need to cast a spell right now to talk to your father."

"What? How?"

"Concentrate on his thoughts and teleport your mind to join his. If it works, then ask your father if your mother has a journal, and where she keeps it. If anyone knows, he should. Now this is what we need to do. Gather in a circle, and link hands, but first we need to light a white candle." Petrello looked around the room.

"There's some in the dining room. I'll go get them," Karisma offered.

"I'll go with you," Boulder said.

After the candle was lit, Petrello and the others formed a circle, linked hands, then Karisma focused on her dad. When she felt the vibration, she knew the spell had worked, and asked her father the first question. "Does Mom keep a journal?"

"Yes," he answered.

"Where does she keep it?" Karisma asked smiling at her father.

"She tucks it between the mattresses on the bed." Her father smiled handsomely.

"Between the mattresses?" Karisma was a little surprised.

"Yeah that's right. Your mother is smart." Her father laughed.

"Thanks, Dad. Oh, wait a second, you do mean the mattress on yours and mom's bed right?"

"Yeah, that's what I mean. At least that's where she used to keep them. If you don't find them there, try the attic."

"Dad, you said them. Does mom have more than one diary?"

"Yes, Kimmy, she has several." He smiled again. "Your mother wrote every night."

"Thanks, Dad." Karisma kissed his cheek, then pulled her mind away from her dad's, opened her eyes, and looked at her friends.

"My mom keeps her diaries between the mattresses on the bed."

They surrounded the bed, lifted the mattress, and saw several journals, and a glittering, purple jewel.

Karisma reached over, and picked it up. When she felt another vibration rush through her body, she gasped. "Quickly grab all the journals, and link arms. Something's happening."

Immediately the journals were collected, and soon each of them were holding one, including Karisma.

Then they linked arms, and soon all of them felt the vibration shake them.

When they saw their Mother's trapped in the dungeon in Elvi, Karisma realized all of them were sleeping, and knew a spell had been cast upon them.

Then the picture of their mother's disappeared, and they saw their queen Firey. She was suspended over one of the many fires on the land of Elvi.

When they heard the laughter, it was followed by a deep, unfriendly voice.

"Karisma, I've been waiting for you," Valtron's voice filled the room, sounding pleased. "Unfortunately, you're too quick for me, and now time's been delayed. It was never supposed to end like this. So let's just refer to what just happened as a temporary pause," he whispered. "Now, the war shall not come to pass yet. There's more to do because you unruly, rude humans are too smart. You've found the purple stone, and now everything..." Valtron's voice faded fast, but was replaced by the familiar sound of grandmother Culver.

"Listen children, what that menace was trying to say is that Karisma managed to pause time in our world. In your hand, my child, you hold one of the fourteen jewels that were once part of Culver's Treasure. Because you found the first jewel, everything, as we know it is paused in time. Including what's going on with everyone trapped in the land of Elvi. Now all of you must travel forth, and find the thirteen others."

"Excuse me, grandmother, I'm confused," Karisma whispered. "What do you mean everything paused?"

"Just what I said, my child. Now I need all of you to pay close attention to what I'm about to tell you."

"But wait. I'm still confused," Karisma blurted, "and I don't understand what you mean about pausing time."

"Listen, Karisma, you found the purple jewel, and now time as we know it, has paused. Always remember, as long as you hold tightly to the purple jewel, time shall continue to be still."

"What does that mean? Does it mean that everything turns back to the way it use to be?" Karisma desperately wanted it too.

"No child. It means the journey for Culver's Treasure has just begun," her grandmother sighed.

"Now here's the final diary that your mother gave to you when this whole thing started." Grandmother Culver handed Karisma the book. "You see when your mother gave you the diary everything happened so fast after that, you left the diary at Firey's dwelling. Now my children, on your new journey take time to read the journals." She smiled. "Right now the journey begins. It's up to all of you to go forth and find the rest of the missing jewels. Children you need thirteen jewels to complete the circle of Culver's Treasure, and only then will all the secrets of your life be revealed. Remember when this comes to pass the Great War of the lands will ensue."

"I think I know what you're saying, but I thought we were supposed to be training for the Great War," Karisma asked, rubbing her arms.

"Oh, you were, until all of you stopped listening, and did whatever appealed to you. When that happened, it changed everything…

but you've done well, Karisma, Boulder, Dagger, Raven, Sunburst, and Mountain." Grandmother Culver smiled, again. "As far as Elise is concerned, she is yet another link needed on this journey. Petrello is too. Now all the pieces are where they should be. Now go forth on your journey."

"So I don't get to go home?" Elise sounded upset.

"No, my child. But you do need to know that your given name in the land of Panora is Excite. Your Mother's earth name is Natalie her given name is Nature. Excite, you were born in the town of Elcro, and now I give you your earrings."

Everyone watched as the earrings materialized out of nowhere, and appeared right in front of Elise. The earrings were big, and displayed the four seasons of nature, plus the many faces of emotion.

"Put them in your ears, my child. Wear them proudly, listen loudly. Do not let others lead you astray, you'll do well as you journey on your way."

"I can't believe I'm not going home," she whined. Then felt the earrings on her ears.

"Believe it. You're needed here," grandmother Culver told her a bit sternly.

"Then why was I left on earth? Why didn't I leave with the others?" she asked.

"Because all pieces of the universe come together when it's time, and not a moment before."

When all the children fell quiet, grandmother Culver smiled. "Now on with the rest of the legend, are you ready?" Grandmother Culver watched the children nod. "Very well, then I shall continue, together the eight of you shall continue on your journey, finding the jewels of Culver's Treasure, but remember along the way to write the chapters to fill your very own journals, for someday your children will need them to find their own heritage, and it is up to all of you to lead them correctly. Now I bid you so long, until our paths cross again."

"Wait," Karisma shouted sounding panicked. "Will we ever see any of you again?" Karisma's eyes were filled with tears.

"Only after the first five jewels are found, then yes, you shall. The adventures all of you write along the way should simply be called, the unspoken secrets of the missing jewels. Now go forth, and stand united at all times, and reclaim your heritage. Until we meet again, remember who you are, what you've learned, and how much you've grown. All the good people in the land of Panora are proud of each of you. May the queen of the land and all the higher powers of Panora guide you, as you take flight on your own search for the treasure, which shall connect all the worlds together through the jewels you shall discover. Remember Karisma, you're the highest power, and the survival of Panora, and the ones you love, largely rests on how successful your journey is. Now be gone, and may you never forget the legend of Culver's Treasure." When grandmother Culver's voice began to fade, Karisma and her friends felt the tears of sadness on their faces.

When each felt the sudden vibration, it was much stronger than anything they had ever felt, and when each of them felt their feet leave the floor, they each floated to the opened window. The white candle blew out, and all eight of them were shot through the sky, like yellow shooting stars, in search of the next jewel, the next chapter, the next world, which they hoped would bring them that much closer to learning the truth about who they really were, and perhaps somewhere out there, they would find the answers to all the questions they had, not only about their lives, but also about all the unspoken secrets.

CPSIA information can be obtained at www.ICGtesting.com
Printed in the USA
LVOW040224011211

257307LV00001B/199/P